Feb. 14, 1984

For lovely Patricia
My latest new best
friend — Love,
George

PROCESS OF ELIMINATION

Also by George Baxt

The Neon Graveyard
Burning Sappho
The Affair at Royalties
"I!" Said the Demon
Topsy and Evil
A Parade of Cockeyed Creatures
Swing Low, Sweet Harriet
A Queer Kind of Death

PROCESS OF ELIMINATION

A NOVEL BY
GEORGE BAXT

St. Martin's Press
New York

PROCESS OF ELIMINATION. Copyright © 1984 by George Baxt. All rights reserved. Printed in the United States of America. No part of this book may be used or reproduced in any manner whatsoever without written permission except in the case of brief quotations embodied in critical articles or reviews. For information, address St. Martin's Press, 175 Fifth Avenue, New York, N.Y. 10010.

Library of Congress Cataloging in Publication Data

Baxt, George.
   Process of elimination.

   I. Title.
PS3552.A8478P7   1984   813'.54   83-17767
ISBN 0-312-64777-8

First Edition

10 9 8 7 6 5 4 3 2 1

This book is for

*Frances Baxt
Susan and Ronald Goldstein
Barbara and Richard Kam*

PROCESS OF ELIMINATION

Prologue

I loathe funerals. There are no surprises. Until very recently I hadn't been to one in years. Not since Andrew went over the cliff. Loathed Andrew. I didn't loathe the twins, but still, they had to die. And now I suppose some of the others will have to go too. And that moronic oaf I stupidly thought I could trust. Oh well, that's life. Murder is really so easy. The twins were a bit messy, but with hindsight, easy. The others were easy too. They'll never find out about the others. They haven't even guessed. I was far too clever. Is it really all these years since I . . . oh the hell with it. It's a waste of time dwelling on past triumphs. There's the future to look forward to. Such a serendipitous group they are. My brothers. My sisters. My victims, by process of elimination. And nobody will ever know it's me. I'm the least likely suspect. I'm distraught. I'm crying so bitterly. Good performance. Mustn't overdo it. Ah, now, that's better. Now I'm in control. I'm always in control.

1

Bella Wallace was never one to squander an entrance. As she swept into Tomaldo's, she paused dramatically at the top of the small staircase that separated the bar from the dining room of the restaurant. In that brief moment, she was the cynosure of all eyes at the bar. The bartender whispered to a tourist that this was indeed the celebrated television personality, Bella Wallace, and that she frequently lunched at Tomaldo's because it was convenient to the studio from which her monthly interview show was televised. The restaurant was freshly minted chic, a new jewel in the diadem of the upper West Side of Manhattan. It had elbowed its way onto Columbus Avenue between a tired saloon and a fast food pizza parlor, both of which were doomed to be gobbled up by Tomaldo's in its hunger for expansion. Tomaldo himself, a sleek Italian in his mid-thirties, hurried from his desk at the foot of the stairs to greet the great lady personally. "Miss Wallace, how lovely to see you again and how lovely you look! My wife wouldn't dare wear apricot."

"Neither would I usually," said Bella with the trace of a lisp her vast audience of women found so endearing, "but today I feel aggressive. Has my guest arrived yet?"

"Miss Graymoor is waiting at your table." He led the way to the table, which was situated at the far end of the dining room. The crafty Tomaldo knew that celebrities, while feigning a desire for anonymity, wallowed in the attention they felt they justly deserved. Queen Elizabeth entering Westminster Abbey would be no match for Bella Wallace crossing the dining room.

At the table, Laura Graymoor watched the procession with amusement. Dear God, she thought, the pig's wearing apricot. It makes her look like an overripe casaba. She sipped her aperitif, shoved a cigarette into her jeweled holder, ignited the lighter and blew a smoke ring clear across an adjoining table. She regretted not having brought the laundry; she could have polished off that chore in the time it was taking Bella to cross the room.

"Darling Laura, do forgive me for being so late," said Bella in an unnatural falsetto that might have curdled cream, "but a last minute emergency arose on this week's show. I've lost Paul Newman."

"To what?"

"So I was on the phone lining up a replacement, and guess who I got?" Laura shrugged. "Your husband."

"Harvey? My Harvey on your program? Whatever for?"

"I've never interviewed a claims adjuster before. I thought it was a good opportunity to present my audience with someone new, you know, fresh, not just another tired sex symbol."

"Harvey *is* sexy sometimes." That really wasn't fair, thought Laura; Harvey is sexy always, although not always with Laura. "Harvey this week, the rest of the family next month, you're really doing the Graymoors in depth."

"Why not? Yours is a very fascinating family." She suddenly remembered Tomaldo was still hovering over them. Bella ordered an aperitif for herself, she and Laura agreeing they'd decide what to eat after the aperitif had arrived. After Tomaldo left, Bella leaned forward conspiratorially. "Any new leads on the murders?"

The murders.

Lydia and Annette Graymoor, two of the ten orphans adopted by Helga and Andrew Graymoor over the past forty years, had been found brutally slain in the Soho loft they'd shared for the past two years. The crime, which had occurred over a month ago, had made headlines for about four days. Both victims had been bludgeoned to death with a miniature knight on a horse sculpted by Annette. To cover his genuine grief Harvey had suggested the culprit might have been an art critic. He had found Annette vastly third-rate, though she seemed to sell well. The other victim, Lydia, had been a creative dancer, and Harvey had charitably refrained from suggesting she'd been done in by a choreographer. Harvey had found her talents fifth-rate, but Lydia had always been in demand with small, brave dance groups who went touring in cities Laura insisted missionaries hadn't even heard of.

"No new leads, the poor darlings," Laura said to Bella. "There was no sign of forced entry to the loft, so it was apparently someone known to both or either one of them. But to be battered beyond recognition. I mean poor Harvey had to identify the bodies and he insists he made a wild guess as to which was which. We were never very close to the girls. I mean they were the last two of the ten to be adopted, and by that time Harvey and I were entering our teens and discovering the mystery of the island and each other."

"The mystery of the island," echoed Bella in a sepulchral voice. "Graymoor Island. Graymoor Mansion. Why hasn't anyone else ever thought of doing a show about the Graymoors?"

"They have, but old Andrew always discouraged it. But now that the old bastard's dead, it's all signals go with Helga."

"You don't really mean to call your adoptive father an old bastard." A waiter had brought her aperitif and Bella wondered aloud why Tomaldo had lost interest in her. The waiter reassured her Tomaldo would reappear to take their orders personally.

"Andrew Graymoor was an absolute monster."

"But he adopted ten children!"

"It wasn't his idea. He went along with it to keep Helga

happy. Helga wanted to have children, but she couldn't. And she wasn't about to spend the rest of her life alone in a vast, forbidding mansion on an isolated island off the coast of Connecticut. Being married to a dour Scotsman was one thing, but living the life of a dour Scot was another."

"Why in the world did she ever marry him?"

Laura favored her hostess with a look of wide-eyed astonishment. "He was gorgeous and gorgeously rich, and she was a poor underpaid stenographer in his office. She never dreamt she would one day become a millionaire in her own right." Laura grimaced. "Those deadly awful romances she grinds out like sausages. Have you ever read any of them?"

Bella leaned forward again. "I *dote* on them." Laura suppressed a shudder. *"Love's Lingering Lust, Love's Lonely Longing* and, my favorite of favorites, *Love's Lewd Lies."*

"You *are* serious." Laura was staring at her with the sort of compassion she usually reserved for a retarded child.

"They are my secret vice. That's why I can't wait to get my hands on Helga Graymoor." Tomaldo returned as promised, and they ordered their salads. In the wake of his second departure, Bella rummaged in her oversized purse and found a tape recorder. She favored Laura with a lavish wink. "You don't mind if we do a little research before the food arrives?"

"You warned me this would be a working lunch." Laura almost added, taking up time that I can ill afford to spare. I've got a showing of my spring line in a few days and a Laura Graymoor fashion show even brings the competition in from Paris and Rome. But instead she lit another cigarette and leaned backward with her arms folded.

"Let's start with Graymoor Island. How far back does it date?"

"The island itself? God knows. Maybe it sprang up during the Ice Age. It's much like so many of those isolated islands that dot the coastline of New England. I know it fell into Graymoor hands before the start of the Civil War. Now let me think. Yes. Got it. It was old Evan Graymoor, the robber baron, who bought the island." Bella was all concentration. Her eyes were hooded, and she nodded her head slowly as she absorbed this information along with the tape recorder. Now Laura could understand why the woman was such a successful interviewer. "When he bought it, some of the mansion was built, but not as we know it today. You see, it turned out the place was honeycombed with subterranean cellars and hidden passageways—"

"Oh, wow, what a story."

"—and cells with chains imbedded in the walls and there's even an underground river that leads into the Atlantic."

"Who built all that?" Bella sounded like a street gamine set free to forage in a sweet shop.

"It seems one of the previous owners was a notorious smuggler and slave trader. Down below was where he kept his contraband goods and his poor contraband slaves. Ironically, old Evan Graymoor was an abolitionist. Graymoor Island was a central safe house for runaway slaves making their passage to Canada. You know, those hidden passageways have never been mapped. Old Andrew used to warn us kids that people have mysteriously disappeared down there, never to be heard from again, but of course we pooh-poohed those stories until Robert got lost and it took five search parties three days to find him."

"Which one is Robert?"

"I loathe Robert."

"Ah, yes, but which one is he?"

The salads arrived, but Bella made no move to switch off the recorder. When Bella promised a working luncheon, she meant business. "Bella, I have to explain something. To my knowledge, the ten of us never knew where we sprang from. I mean there was a very dodgy period there when Harvey and I realized we were very much in love and wanted to marry. You see, I suddenly got this horrible thought that perhaps we actually *were* brother and sister but Helga assured us that wasn't the case, although I thought I detected a very wicked gleam in old Andrew's eye at the time. How that man hated us."

"You really believe he hated you? You really believe that?"

"My dear Bella, please stop feigning innocence. Andrew Graymoor *despised* children. The more of us Helga adopted, the less time he spent on the island."

"No matter how much he loved Helga?"

"You should have seen the way he behaved once her books started catching on. He used to order cartons of them just so he could stand in the middle of one of the drawing rooms and tear them to shreds page by page. I think he sort of liked me, though. He once took me down into the subterranean passages and actually brought me back. He was showing me the wine cellars. There are lots of wine cellars."

"Let's get back to Robert."

Laura pushed her salad aside. "Let's take them in order. The first to be adopted was Martha. Martha is now forty and a spinster and she lives on Graymoor with Helga. She's her companion. She's her nurse. She's her favorite. She's trapped."

Bella commented wickedly, "Perhaps she'll inherit everything."

"I'll get to that later," commented Laura somewhat mysteriously. "After Martha came Robert. He's an investment counselor. His company controls and administrates the trust willed all of us by Andrew."

"If he left you that well off he couldn't have hated you that much!"

"I didn't say he left us well off. He left us a trust. Be patient, Bella, you're going to hear it all before we finish coffee. As I said, I loathe and distrust Robert. Among his other faults he led Martha to believe that someday he'd marry her. She's still waiting to be led to the altar. Poor dear."

"Robert is still single?"

"Still single. As the third of the lineup, I give you Victor, who is a lawyer. I used to like him when I was a child. He didn't try to play 'Doctor' with me the way Robert and Harvey did."

Bella said warmly, "But you married Harvey."

"Good old Harvey. Back to Victor. He's been involved, that we know of, in a number of shady deals that have kept him just a few inches this side of the law. On the few occasions when it seemed John Law was finally going to close in, it was Helga and Robert and their connections to the rescue. Victor and Robert were always as thick as thieves, no pun intended."

"Victor never married?"

"Oh, yes. The beautiful, frail, fragile Greta. She took an overdose of sleeping pills a few years ago. For Helga's sake, we agreed it was accidental. There were no children. Now we come to Arnold."

"You sound as though you enjoy Arnold."

"Oh, our Arnold is a hoot." Laura's eyes sparkled as she explained Arnold. "Our Arnold earns his living by preying on wealthy women who adore being his victims."

"For want of a better word, you mean he's a gigolo?"

"He's a whore, but very good at it. You see his name in all the society columns. He seems to be everybody's favorite extra man, and of course being Helga Graymoor's son doesn't hurt a bit. I had drinks with him the other night. The poor darling admits he's getting a bit long in the tooth and his days as a professional escort are numbered. Why he's even thinking of marrying again."

"How many wives has he had?"

Laura stared at the ceiling as though expecting to find the number of Arnold's ex-wives stenciled there. Laura enumerated a steel heiress, a faded movie star, a Hungarian maneater who put the Gabors to shame, ". . . and that little mouse of a chocolate heiress who is still in that very private sanatorium in Texas. Arnold gave her a very hard time. He detested chocolate. I think that's Arnold to date. Which brings us to Natalie."

"Natalie Graymoor? You mean that woman who plays at that piano bar over on East Fifty-eighth Street?"

"That's poor old Natalie. Frustrated opera singer and sex symbol. Widowed three times, God help her, and barely thirty. Harvey thinks she poisoned the three of them, but I think she sang them to death. Ever hear Natalie sing? It's like swine-feeding time in Ohio. It was vicious Andrew who kept encouraging her. He told her she had a voice that belonged to the world. He never clarified which world he had in mind, but surely he meant the nether. So that takes care of Natalie. Not running out of tape, are you?" Bella adjusted the recorder and, after ordering coffee, Laura continued. "After Natalie came Lydia and Annette. They were twins."

"That wasn't mentioned in the newspapers when they were murdered."

"They didn't look alike, but Helga says they're twins. Which brings us to Nicholas, since there's little to add to the tragic saga of Lydia and Annette. Nicholas is my pet. I simply adore Nicholas. Unfortunately, Nicholas is a loser. He's a clerk at Bloomingdale's. But, oh, how beautiful he is. He should have been a professional model. But poor dear Nicholas just hasn't got what it takes to be anything. Nicholas, you see, is a fourteen-carat idiot. Not a brain to call his own. He is married to the equally mindless Marjorie, she of odd manners and bad intentions. Marjorie is the last of a dying breed. She is a manicurist. One so totally inept that you consign your fingers to her at the risk of being nicknamed 'Stumpy.' Yet somehow, she floats from beauty parlor to beauty parlor and from manicurist's tray to manicurist's tray staring vacantly ahead at everything except the finger she's supposed to be beautifying. We are not quite sure if the union of Nicholas and Marjorie was one of the Almighty's little jokes, but they've been wedded something like two years now. I sure hope they sleep together because they sure as hell don't talk to each other because they sure as hell have nothing to say to each other. You see, Marjorie is hoping that Nicholas will one

day inherit a lot of money and perhaps one day Nicholas will."
"You've skipped yourself and Harvey."
"Oh, we're between Victor and Arnold. First came Harvey, the claims adjuster who earns a very good living and deserves his very wicked reputation. He's the bane of many major corporations, especially when he's adjusting a claim against them."
"Is he a good husband?" Bella was famous for sudden shafts like this one.
"If you mean is he a good provider, it doesn't matter because I make plenty on my own."
"I mean is he a *good* husband?"
Laura smiled and poured herself a fresh cup of coffee. "I seem to recall he was great in bed."
"You're so honest."
"I'm today's woman. What's to hide? Everybody knows he plays around. The only one who denies it is Harvey."
"And do you have your little affairs on the side too?"
"May as well. There isn't all that much that's interesting on television." Laura sipped her coffee. "But I'll tell you this much, ours is very much an until-death-do-us-part proposition. No matter who else is involved, we're very much in love with each other."
"Now Laura," said Bella in a voice that dismissed all their preceding conversation as being secondary in importance, "you made a very mysterious allusion to this trust left by Andrew Graymoor to all you children."
"And Helga."
"And Helga. Now what form does this trust take?"
"Andrew created a tontine."
"A *what?*"
"A tontine. A tontine is an insurance policy whose benefits can be collected only by a single survivor. Dear old Andrew left this tontine in trust to Helga and us ten children."
Bella sat straight up. "But only *one* of you can collect?"

"That's right."

"He tied up this entire fortune into this one tontine?"

"Except for the house and the island. That belongs outright to Helga. But everything else, all those vast millions of dollars, are tied up in the tontine."

"My God. If you hope to collect, you have to outlive all the others!"

"That's right. And Lydia and Annette have already been murdered. That leaves nine more to go."

Bella stared into her cup of coffee. Laura wondered if it had acquired the mystic faculties of a crystal ball. Bella raised her head and then cocked it to one side like a quizzical pigeon. "Laura, I'll bet you've been thinking what I'm beginning to think."

"The murderer is one of the nine survivors."

"You're reading my mind."

"Just the small print."

"Your husband agrees with you?"

"It's the first thing we've agreed on in months." She was staring past Bella, across the dining room to the head of the stairs. "And speak of the devil, here's Harvey now."

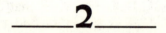

A woman once commented that Harvey Graymoor conducted himself like an open invitation. Even men liked him. As he stood at the head of the stairs hunting for anyone who resembled his wife, he was aware of the interest he was creating in an assortment of patrons in the restaurant. As a child battling for position against nine siblings, Harvey most times commandeered the spotlight, by fair means or foul. Here was a child who saw to it that his hunger for attention was fed, until he met his match in Laura. Rather than fight her, he joined her, and so they were married. He heard Tomaldo's unctuous "May I help you?"

"I'm looking for my wife," said Harvey in his resonant matinee-idol voice. "She's lunching with Bella Wallace."

"Of course. Please follow me. I did not know you were expected."

"I'm not. I'm a surprise." He walked well behind Tomaldo, suspecting the restaurateur might leave an oil slick in his wake. Bella leaned back in her chair, watching Harvey approach with the look of a chubby suburban matron who had just selected dessert. Laura seemed amused. As a matter of fact, thought Harvey, Laura always seems amused when she sees me, as though surprised to find I'm still around.

"Hello, darling," said Laura huskily, "what a nice surprise."

Harvey said to Tomaldo, "See. Even she knows I'm a surprise." Laura introduced Harvey to Bella as Tomaldo departed. Harvey borrowed a chair from the next table and joined the women. A waiter appeared and Harvey ordered coffee. "I hope I'm not interrupting. Laura said this was going to be a working lunch."

Bella hoped she was being her most bewitching. If Harvey Graymoor played around, she was eager to join his team. "I've just been hearing about the tontine. What a terrible thing to do to all of you!"

"All minus two," corrected Harvey. To Laura he said, "Marjorie phoned me this morning."

Laura reminded Bella, "Nicholas's wife." She wiggled an index finger. "The manicurist." To Harvey she said, "I didn't know she could dial."

"She remembered something concerning Lydia and Annette." While Laura arched her eyebrows, Harvey said to Bella, "All this is off the record, of course."

"Of course," agreed Bella.

Harvey continued. "It seems she had lunch with Lydia the

day before the twins were murdered. Lydia told Marjorie that she and Annette had been approached by some smooth character who offered to buy up their future legacy for a fraction of its supposed value."

"Marjorie must be kidding," said Laura.

"Oh, no. This same character approached Nicholas yesterday." He reached for his wallet and took out a slip of paper. "Nathan Manx, that's the joker's name."

Bella said, "I thought legacy buyers only existed in England."

Laura's eyes widened. "Then you've heard about this sort of thing?"

"Oh, yes," said Bella with her usual authority, whether she knew what she was talking about or not. "One of the news programs did a segment on it a couple of years back. These people mostly seek out young members of the aristocracy who are in line to succeed to some form of inheritance and while waiting are usually hard up. So they offer a deal to pay them something in return for their deeding over the inheritance. All perfectly legal and aboveboard."

"Isn't that quite a gamble to take when the inheritance might turn out to be a mere fraction of what was expected?" asked Harvey.

"It seems they do their investigating pretty thoroughly before entering a transaction. As I recall, few of these people lose much on the deals they make. In fact, they keep coming out ahead quite smartly."

"Question," interjected Laura. "I thought the contents of a will were privileged information."

Bella shrugged. "All of you know about the tontine."

"That's because Andrew told us. We know it exists because it's administrated by Robert's investment firm. And from what we can gather, it just keeps growing and growing and just the thought of it makes me ill. Now I wonder how this Mr. . . ."

"Manx, Nathan Manx," said Harvey.
"Now how do you suppose Mr. Manx heard about the tontine?" Laura was lighting another cigarette.
"I wish you wouldn't," said Harvey.
"You wish I wouldn't what?"
"I wish you wouldn't smoke so much."
Laura blew a smoke ring and then favored Bella with a winsome smile. "See, he still cares." She patted Harvey's cheek.
"You're such a dear to be concerned. But let's get back to Mr. Manx." The waiter finally brought Harvey's coffee.
Harvey's eyes on the waiter were lethal. "I ordered this coffee months ago."
"Sorry, sir," said the waiter as he poured. "One of our machines is broken." He beat a hasty retreat.
"About Mr. Manx," Laura prompted Harvey.
"Yesterday evening Mr. Manx called on Nicholas."
"Aha," murmured Laura. "Same proposition?"
"Same proposition. Which is what reminded Marjorie of the offer made to Lydia and Annette. So since she's always considered me the smartest one of the bunch, she got in touch with me immediately."
"Does she know if the girls offered to accept Manx's proposition?"
"The girls turned him down. In fact, Lydia was so upset she was all for telling Helga what was afoot." Harvey was furiously waving away the smoke from Laura's cigarette. Laura got the message and stubbed out the offender in the ashtray. "I suppose if either Lydia or Annette had discussed it with Helga, the old lady would have let us know."
Bella's eyes narrowed. "I sense something terribly sinister about all this. Harvey, I think you should track down this Nathan Manx and demand an explanation."
"The explanation is simple enough. One of us is working with Manx."
"Oh, dear," said Laura dejectedly. Harvey patted her

hand. "It's awful to think we might have a murderer in our midst. Because if we do, Harvey, darling, you and I are projected victims."

"I know, dear," said Harvey airily, "which is why from now on I wish you'd exert a bit more time looking over your shoulder suspiciously."

Bella was drumming on the table with her fingers. "I think you should tell all this to the police."

"I will," said Harvey, "as soon as I have my meeting with Nathan Manx." He winked at Laura. "Glad I remembered where you said you'd be lunching. I wanted you to know who I was seeing, in case I'm found murdered."

Bella noticed the expression of concern on Laura's face and found it touching. "Please don't be found murdered," said Laura. "I've gotten terribly used to you." Harvey rewarded her with a kiss. "I'll phone you later, darling." To Bella he said, "Nice to meet you at last."

"You're going to be seeing more of me," said Bella, and Harvey wasn't sure if he found the prospect inviting. After Harvey left, Bella said to Laura, "To think that something like Harvey Graymoor could evolve from that old cliché, childhood sweetheart. You know, your Graymoor story is getting a little bigger than I planned. I mean what I had in mind when I first contacted you was the story of Helga Graymoor, the fantastic authoress of scores of gothic romances and the ten youngsters she adopted and how they grew. This, I said to myself, will be quite a piece of cake. But now the cake's got some fresh icing, and the icing's a very rich red. Blood red. The color of murder. Now," she said with resolution, "I'm going to wait on this story, Laura, but I want you to promise me it remains my exclusive. I want to wait and see what your husband's investigation leads to."

"It can only lead to what all of Harvey's investigations lead to. No good. I have to get back to my showroom. I've got a bevy of high-priced fashion models waiting to be fitted."

"Of course, you've got a new collection coming up." She signaled a waiter for the bill. "When is it?"

"Day after tomorrow at three. Can you come?"

"I'd love to." She looked down dejectedly at her apricot creation. "I'm beginning to feel awfully dowdy in this expensive piece of kitsch I'm wearing."

"Oh, not at all," said Laura with an impish grin. "I think it's positively you."

Martha Graymoor felt like a Brontë heroine as she stood at the edge of the cliff staring at the angry waves breaking against the cruel rocks below. A Brontë heroine's hair would have been blowing wildly in the wind, her skirts billowing as though possessed by unknown demons, her eyes searching the horizon anxiously for a Heathcliff or a Rochester depending on which Brontë heroine she chose to be. But Martha's head was covered by a sensible woolen cloche, and her body was encased in a heavy leather coat. Her skirts couldn't billow because she was wearing blue jeans, and her feet were shod with heavy boots. To a casual observer, Martha would look about as appetizing as Tugboat Annie sailing into the eye of a hurricane. Seagulls circled and squawked overhead, while the heavy gray clouds threatened a storm.

"Robert!" she cried, but only the seagulls responded. Her eyes welled with tears as she picked her way down from the cliff, back to Graymoor Mansion. She paused to rest on a rock that jutted out from the escarpment, staring at the vast prominence below her that had been her home for almost forty years. Was I ever pretty, she wondered, was I ever truly sought after? When she was a child, she remembered, Helga and Andrew had entertained frequently. There had been specially chartered boats to ferry the guests from the mainland, and if the weather grew inclement, there was more than enough room for visitors to spend the night. But children are admired out of politeness, not passion. Later, when Martha was entering her teens and already in love with Robert, two years her junior, there were fewer and fewer parties, just as there was less and less love between Helga and Andrew. And now, she thought with sad resignation, the parade has passed me by and it is too late to be either pretty or truly sought after. Still, there is always Robert and as long as there is Robert, there is always hope. She felt the first drops of rain and began to hurry.

Helga Graymoor sat at her sturdy oak desk in the second floor salon, known now as it had been for the past three decades as Helga's writing room. She held a pencil in her arthritic fingers, completing her daily entry in her diary. A fresh thought assailed her, and she released the pencil, letting it drop lightly across the small ledger. She sat back in the antique Queen Anne chair and stared across the room through the windows, watching Martha make her way down the cliff, scurrying against the imminent storm.

"My poor Martha," she murmured softly, "my poor darling Martha. Always hurrying, but never a destination." With a painful effort, she got up from the chair and crossed to the fireplace. She thought of ringing for a servant to stoke the fire, but then remembered the servants no longer lived in. They came over by boat in the morning and returned by boat in the late afternoon. Winston, the handyman, saw to his chores while, Rebecca, their cook and housekeeper, prepared their meals and left the dinner in the warming oven. Only the cleaning woman sang. This was Juanita, who uncomplainingly looked after the small section of Graymoor Mansion shared by Helga and Martha and then equally uncomplainingly opened the other wings of the house to accommodate any number of visitors. Helga was very generous each Christmas. Helga raised her head and stared at a portrait of her late husband, Andrew Graymoor, painted fifty years earlier when the sight of him could stir her to sexual excesses. "Oh, Andrew," she whispered mournfully, "why were you such a disappointment?"

"Perhaps you expected too much of him." She hadn't heard Martha enter, yet she wasn't startled by her voice. Martha always spoke softly, melodiously, almost apologetically. Martha came to the fireplace and began to prod the ashes with a poker. Then she fed it some kindling and logs, and the flames licking their undersides seemed sensual and erotic.

"Andrew was born in the wrong century," said Helga as she crossed to the windows. "He should have been a buccaneer or a general in some glamorous war."

"There's nothing glamorous about war, Mother."

"Oh yes there was, when it was fought for the Warner Brothers. Were you up on the cliff again?"

"Yes."

"I suppose there's no point in repeatedly warning you how dangerous that is?"

"I can look after myself."

"But, sweetie, if you're not here, who will look after me?"

Martha went to the desk and began straightening Helga's things. "Are you thinking of starting a new novel? It's been three years since your last one."

"I'd love to start a new one, but this blasted arthritis is so agonizing."

"You could dictate to me," offered Martha eagerly. "I could transcribe it for you. I could brush up on my typing. Oh, let's do, Mother. It would be so nice to share a project!"

Helga went to Martha and threw her arms around her. "To share a project. My poor Martha. My poor darling Martha."

"Oh, not that again," said Martha impatiently. "'My poor Martha. My poor darling Martha. Tied to her mother. No man of her own. No children. A spinster.'"

"You mimic me mercilessly," said Helga with a haughty sniff.

"Well, I'm so tired of the litany," said Martha. "For God's

sake, had I chosen to, I could have left here years ago."

"And done what? You're trained for nothing but companionship. And waiting around for Robert. . . ."

"The hell with Robert!" stormed Martha.

"Now she says it," said Helga blandly.

"Annette and Lydia pleaded with me to come live with them."

"And if you had? You'd be dead too. You'd be dead the way they're dead. My poor darlings, my poor untalented darlings. Oh, why, why, why is death so impertinent?" She was sitting at the desk again. "I wonder if the police are still doing something about them. Do you suppose they've given up, marked them 'unsolved'? How awful to think of Lydia and Annette being marked 'unsolved.'"

"That leaves two fewer," said Martha with a sudden freshness. "Two fewer. The curse of the tontine. A good title for a penny dreadful."

"Oh, Andrew, you wicked Andrew, to perpetrate such a horror. He got that from his Scottish ancestors. Tontines originated in Scotland, you know. I wonder if the Macbeths had one."

Outside, the storm broke with a ferocity that caused the mansion to tremble. Thunder crashed about overhead, and a crackle of lightning caused a momentary flash of incandescent beauty in the room. Martha stood at the window with her arms folded, drinking in the beauty of the raging storm. "You know what I think?" cried Martha. "I think the murderer is one of us." A crash of thunder underlined her statement. "And you know what else I think, Mother? I think you're harboring the very same suspicion." She crossed slowly to Helga, who sat stiffly in the chair, staring into the fireplace. "Who do you think it is, Mother? Certainly not you or me. We were both here on the island. We're each other's alibi. But the others, which of the others? Who was it Father said had homicidal tendencies as a child? I'm right, aren't I?

Didn't I once hear him yelling that one of us was a young killer?"

"I don't remember." Helga's voice was a faint, ghostly whisper.

"Try, Mother, try. It was when your toy poodle disappeared...."

"Esmaralda," sobbed Helga.

"Esmaralda, of course. We all went looking for her and Laura found her strangled in one of the wine cellars. I remember Father scolding her for going down into the cellars alone, and Laura laughing. Laura was always the defiant one, afraid of nothing. Do you suppose she knew where Esmaralda was because she put her there?"

"Now you're being ridiculous!" exploded Helga.

"Perhaps it was Nicholas. Esmaralda was always frightening him into tears by nipping at his ankles. You caught him kicking her once."

"I kicked Nicholas." She shifted restlessly in her chair. "Nicholas couldn't plot a murder or anything else. His head is a rich repository of stupidity."

"Victor? Didn't he cause his lovely Greta to die indirectly?"

"Her death was an accident—You must stop provoking me!"

"Arnold? Natalie? Beloved Harvey?"

Helga held Martha with her eyes. "Or Robert?" In the distance they heard a fresh rumble of thunder, a monster gaining momentum, preparing to explode around them with molecular ferocity. The electricity began to flicker.

When the thunder finally detonated, Helga's hand flew to her throat. "I've had enough of this talk about murder," said Helga in a voice underlined by threat. "Let's talk about other things. Yes, I have been thinking about a new book, and why shouldn't you help me? It would help occupy our time here and the Lord knows we have plenty of time that could use occupying. And you know what? I have a perfectly marvelous title." She sat back imperiously. Martha waited. Helga pronounced each word as though she were polishing a precious jewel. *"Love's Lascivious Lips."* This was punctuated by a well-timed clap of thunder.

Harvey stood in the middle of the block on West Forty-second Street staring up at the building that housed the office of Nathan Manx. The entrance was situated between a porn movie house and a once-famous legitimate theater that was now featuring a triple bill of Kung Fu thrillers. Staring about him at the wreckage of humanity—winos, junkies, pushers, muggers, and teenage runaways with eyes already too old for their young faces—Harvey felt like a swimmer in the middle of a deadly tide of slimy mud. He wished he wasn't so well dressed. Entering the sleazy lobby, he was assailed by a stench of stale urine and cheap wine. He studied the tatty directory and found that H. Manx occupied Room 601. He crossed the lobby to a bank of two elevators. He pressed a button for service, and after what seemed like two years, an elevator finally surfaced. As he entered the cage, he wished he was armed. A knife, a gun, an eggbeater, anything. Harvey was frightened.

The elevator's ascent was slow and tortuous. Harvey was positive Everest could have been scaled in less time. When it stopped finally, the door slid back slowly and Harvey found himself alone in a hallway that was dank and unappetizing. He found Room 601 at the end of the corridor. Nathan Manx's name, now peeling with age, was neatly lettered on the door under the number 601. There was no clue as to the nature of Manx's profession. Was this a suitable habitat for a man offering to buy up legacies? Certainly not, thought Harvey, and if I had any sense, I'd get the hell out of here. On the other hand, he thought, having come this far, and having told Laura I was coming here, I might just as well knock on the door.

He knocked and waited. Then he knocked again. He'd spoken to Manx earlier that day. They'd agreed to the appointment. Manx had sounded anxious and greedy. Manx should, therefore, be waiting anxiously and greedily in his office. Harvey tried the doorknob. It gave easily. He entered the office slowly, advancing just a few steps over the threshhold. He saw a desk, a swivel chair behind it, and behind that, a window that afforded a splendid view of an adjoining brick wall. On the desk was a lamp that was brightly lighted, as well as a telephone, a desk pad, and an old-fashioned inkwell. There were two straight-back wooden chairs facing the wall. On his right, Harvey saw a door slightly ajar and figured that it led to a bathroom.

"Manx?" Harvey's voice seemed unnaturally weak. "Nathan Manx?" He advanced a bit further into the room, shutting the door behind him. He crossed to the bathroom door and looked in. What he saw envelopped him in a robe of nausea. A man he assumed to be Nathan Manx was seated on the throne fully dressed, his legs stiffly pointed toward the office, his hands hanging loosely by his side like salamis on hooks in a delicatessen, his head hanging and slightly canted over the bathroom's basin. Manx's throat had been cut and the small room was a nasty symphony of gore. Fortunately, Manx's jacket was hanging on a hook behind the door, sparing Harvey's having to touch the body. Harvey found a wallet in an inside jacket pocket and examined it thoroughly. Yes, this had been Manx.

Harvey found credit cards, driver's license, pictures of a chubby lady with two chubby daughters under ten years of age, and an assortment of business cards that included invitations from several masseuses and a variety of singles bars that Harvey was positive had to be both sordid and salacious and possibly worth investigating. There was thirty-six dollars in cash and a neatly folded sheet of paper. He unfolded the sheet and read a list of names that he recognized as the heirs to Andrew Graymoor's tontine. There were lines neatly drawn through the names of Annette and Lydia Graymoor. Next to Nicholas's name there was a question mark and there was another question mark next to his own name. Harvey exhaled softly, put the paper into his own jacket pocket, and replaced Manx's wallet.

Harvey then crossed to the desk, but a careful search revealed nothing. Most of the drawers were empty. Nathan Manx was obviously a small-time operator who had gotten himself into a fatal situation. Harvey walked to the door to the hallway, opened it a crack and, when he was sure the coast was clear, left the office, shutting the door behind him. It seemed an eternity before he escaped into the street. He had to walk to Fifth Avenue before locating an unoccupied telephone booth, and phoned the police anonymously. Now feeling like a good citizen, Harvey strolled south along Fifth Avenue, heading for Laura's office and showroom on the fringe of the Garment Center.

He wondered how he could be whistling so jauntily when he was up to his neck in murder. Annette and Lydia, his adoptive sisters, had been murdered. Nathan Manx, who, he was positive, was connected to their killings, was now, hoped Harvey, in a better world lacking only his chubby wife and children. And Harvey was now quite certain that one of his adoptive relatives was an obsessed, maniacal murderer. He could hardly wait to share this depressing news with Laura.

3

The Laura Graymoor label on a dress assured the buyer of style and sensibility. Women of all heights and widths and most ages could wear Laura's clothing. At the start of her career, she had come to the wise decision not to compete with the specialists both at home and abroad and as a result made a respected name for herself in the garment industry. Her workroom in a loft on West Thirty-sixth Street just off Fifth Avenue was a constant beehive of activity, and today, with just forty-eight hours to go before the unveiling of her spring line, Laura was wondering if she was too young to retire. Her assistants were raising hems, lowering necklines, and opening seams around hips. Table tops were ringed with stains left by containers of coffee, and Laura's receptionist was falling madly in love with Harvey. Amidst the relative calm of the reception room, Harvey had taken the trouble to admire the young lady's coiffure, which caused her dull eyes to sparkle briefly and her mottled skin to take on a pinkish hue that made her look like a fading watercolor. The girl was newly employed and had never seen Harvey before.

"Mrs. Graymoor said she didn't want to be disturbed by anybody, but if you say you're her husband. . ."

"Oh, I'm her husband, all right. I can tell you the location of a couple of provocative moles on her right hip. . . ."

The girl said hastily, "I'll page her."

Two minutes later, Harvey was kissing Laura in the privacy of her office. "It has to be urgent if you're dropping in on me like this," she said.

"I found Nathan Manx with his throat cut."

Laura exhaled and sat at her desk. Harvey reclined on a couch as he described in lurid detail how he had found the body. Then he waved the list he had taken from the dead man's wallet. Because he obviously had no intention of abandoning the couch, Laura left her chair, snatched the list, and scanned it rapidly. She stared down at Harvey.

"Harvey," she said in a voice that meant business, "I think you should call the police, admit you found the body, and demand protection for all of us."

"We won't get it. Too expensive." He sat up. "Don't look so distrait." He took the list from her and put it back in his pocket. "From the look of Manx's office and the seedy building in which it's located, I can fast guess his profession. He was probably a process server, part-time bag man, just this side of shady. When he was hired to be the go-between for whoever is behind the offers to pre-buy the legacy, he probably had no idea of the size of the prospective inheritance. It was probably Nicholas who spilled those beans. So Mr. Manx undoubtedly decided he deserved a better fee than he'd agreed upon and was now dangerous. So farewell Nathan Manx, leaving behind a chubby wife and two chubby daughters."

"Now how do you know that?" Harvey told her about the snapshot. "And what about the question mark next to Nicholas's name?"

"Just probably means Nick is thinking it over. What with, God only knows."

Laura sat on the desk. "This probably means the others were not yet approached. You weren't. I wasn't and, of all of us, Martha and Helga are the least accessible."

"They're also sitting targets."

"You've just sent a shiver up my spine. Harvey, don't play detective. I mean, I know you're pretty good at it when you set your mind to it, but this is different. Please go to the police."

Harvey left the couch and put his hands on Laura's shoulders. "Sweetheart, I think we should keep this in the family."

"Not funny."

"It wasn't meant to be. I'm being practical. Next week Helga celebrates her seventy-fifth birthday. That's the excuse for the family's yearly get-together on the island."

"Giving you the opportunity at dinner to announce quite archly, 'I suppose you're wondering why I've asked you all here.'"

"You're warm. But I'm going to make the murderer give himself away."

"It could be 'herself.'"

"Could be. I suppose Natalie might be a closet maniac. That voice of hers could be responsible for any number of aberrations."

"And me? What about me?"

"If it's you, I'll wring your neck." He kissed her lightly on the tip of her nose.

"You're abnormally affectionate today. Is it because you're truly concerned or because your girlfriend's left you?"

"*What* girlfriend?" He hoped he sounded appropriately appalled. "I haven't had a girlfriend in months. Besides, they mean nothing. They're like coleslaw on a corned beef sandwich. You're my first girl and my only girl. My God, we've known each other since we were toddlers. I know some who would be sickened by the thought."

"Harvey," said Laura wearily, "I've got to get back to work. Go someplace and adjust a claim."

"Don't you want to hear my plan? I worked it out while I was walking over here. You see, the important reason why going to the police is out of the question at the moment is because once we're all gathered on the island, we'll be out of their jurisdiction. Maybe jurisdictions cooperate."

"Well, then, let's alert the Connecticut police to the situation." She opened a silver box on the desk and took out a cigarette, which she lit with a desk lighter while Harvey frowned his silent disapproval. "Better still, alert Martha and Helga to watch out for any surprise visitor." She was deep in thought for a moment and then exclaimed, "Nicholas!"

"Yes?"

"The question mark after his name. On the list. That could mean he's a marked man! My God, supposing he's been murdered!"

"In Bloomingdale's? Nonsense. Now be quiet and listen. I think Helga and Martha are comparitively safe until the rest of us are disposed of." Laura shuddered. "Murdering *them* up front would really be giving the game away."

"But they're so vulnerable alone on the island."

"Which, to be perfectly cruel, is exactly why the murderer knows they'll keep."

"And us? Harvey, you and I. And Robert and Victor. We're all well off. Why would any one of us jump at the chance to pre-sell?"

"Now there's a chill up *my* spine. My dear, I'm quite positive we're marked for murder. Like Koko in *The Mikado*, this monster is skipping about singing 'I've got a little list' and it doesn't make sense. There's got to be more to it than wanting to buy us out." There was grudging admiration on his face as Laura, quite cool and composed, exhaled a perfect smoke ring.

"Then you'd better have a very clever plan, darling. And I mean *very* clever."

"I think I do."

"Isn't it wonderful. The entire family will be together again for my birthday celebration!" Helga was like a young girl again, her eyes alive with excitement and expectation. Martha thought at this moment the old woman was shedding years with her enthusiasm. The staff were gathered in the library, and Helga was happily issuing instructions. Rebecca promised to reach new heights of culinary artistry. Winston would double as butler, and Juanita would prepare the extra rooms and brighten them with fresh flowers brought over from the mainland. "Everything sounds wonderful," said Helga and then a memory caused her face to darken. Martha knew she was thinking of Lydia and Annette. She dismissed the staff, and after they left, she took Helga by the hand and led her to a chair. They sat next to each other and for a moment gazed in silence at the garden, now bare of leaves and flowers with the approach of winter. Even the punishment wreaked by the previous night's storm seemed minimal.

"I'd like to buy a new dress," said Martha, breaking the silence.

Helga turned to her with a warm smile. "Of course, dear. Come to think of it, I can't remember the last time I saw you in something frilly and feminine."

"I think I'll take the boat over this afternoon. Why don't you come with me? It'll do you good to get away from here for a change." Martha persisted, "We could have tea just the way we used to do years ago. We might even see a movie. Say you'll come with me."

"I would, except the sea was looking awfully rough this morning. You know I'm a rotten sailor. It would be just my luck to take a turn and fall overboard. Now you wouldn't like that, would you?"

"No," said Martha, speaking barely above a whisper. "I wouldn't like that at all."

Marjorie Graymoor said to her husband shortly after he arrived home from work, "Your fingernails are filthy." He had found her in the kitchen trying to remove a take-out pizza from a carton without spilling most of it on the table.

Nicholas waved the afternoon newspaper under her nose. "Look who's been murdered!" Marjorie slapped the newspaper away. "Take a look!" She looked and gasped. There was a photograph of Nathan Manx under a headline proclaiming a mysterious gangland slaying.

"Do you suppose he was with the Mafia?" she asked while licking her fingers.

"I can't imagine the Mafia wanting to buy out my inheritance."

"Why not? I hear they'll buy anything."

"Do you think I ought to go to the police?"

"What for?" She was artfully trying to quarter the pizza with a butter knife.

"To give evidence."

She stared at him with a look of ravishing perplexity. "What evidence?"

Nicholas sometimes wondered if there was anyone in the

world dumber than his wife. He never once offered himself up for consideration. "That Manx made me a proposition. Say, I wonder if he approached any of the others?"

"Well, we know he saw Annette and Lydia."

"I mean since then. My head hurts."

"It always does when you try to think. What do you want to drink with the pizza?"

"A beer. Well, I suppose we'll find out soon enough next weekend."

"What's next weekend?" When Nicholas told her about the planned celebration at the island she responded, "I don't have anything to wear."

"Sure you do. What about that pink thing that's maybe a shade too tight?"

"It's one of Laura's. She'll recognize it."

"She'll be flattered."

"Your family doesn't like me."

"Of course they like you." He pondered for a moment. "As a matter of fact, I don't think they give it much thought."

"I told Laura you had an offer from Mr. Manx."

Nicholas was in the process of removing his tie and jacket. "Why'd you tell her?"

Marjorie was wearing her little-girl-lost look. "Because she's smart. I also told her Annette and Lydia had the same offer. And you know something, that's kind of funny."

"What do you mean?"

"Well, Lydia and Annette were murdered right after Manx made the offer. Then Manx makes you the offer and now *he's* been killed. Nicky, you didn't kill him, did you?"

"Oh, now that's a fine thing to say."

"You didn't like him. I could tell you didn't like him. You said after he left he was a greaseball."

"I didn't like him and I didn't trust him. But, why should I sell? I'm the youngest. I'm bound to outlive all of them."

Marjorie's face brightened perceptibly. "Say, I never thought of that!"

"Sure you didn't. All you think about is which kind of pizza to bring home for dinner." He pondered briefly and then asked her, "Have you ever heard of anybody o.d.'ing on pizza?"

"I need a new dress."

"Oh, for crying out loud! Well, get it at Laura's. She's always said you can have a discount. And nothing too expensive. *Please.*"

He reread the brief article on Manx's slaying. Sleazy office in a sleazy building. Throat cut. Was Marjorie right? Was there a connection between the three murders? Manx had come to him just a few days ago. Annette and Lydia had been his adoptive sisters. They were all heirs to the blasted tontine. Nicholas was feeling very uncomfortable. His palms were sweating. He looked across the table at Marjorie who was munching thoughtfully on a mouthful of pizza. "Honey?" She looked up. "I'm going to phone Harvey."

Harvey was sitting opposite an old friend in a secluded booth in an Italian restaurant tucked away on a Greenwich Village side street. The old friend's name was Mickey Redfern, and he was so absorbed in listening to Harvey that his plate of spaghetti marinara was congealing. Mickey had a way of sitting half-hunched forward, his hands hidden under the table very gently clasped on his lap like an obedient schoolboy. Every so often he nodded his head as though to assure Harvey he was absorbing and understanding every word. Harvey spoke slowly and meticulously, occasionally interjecting, "What do you think?" to which the reply was invariably "Sounds good to me." Mickey was a muscular man in his late thirties with the face of a retired prizefighter, though he had never been a professional. He knew the CIA had a dossier on him thoroughly detailing his activities as a mercenary in Asia, Africa, and South America. He was positive they had nothing about the series of hit jobs he had executed over a decade ago when he considered himself still just a callow youth. For the past five years, as he had explained to Harvey, he had been "clean." He did private police work and was responsible for highly effective results for Harvey on a number of intricate claims adjustments. He loved cracking a phony insurance suit. He wallowed lavishly in dirty work but used physical violence only as a last resort because he had long ago recognized the killer in himself. A television producer wanted to pattern a series based on Mickey's exploits. Mickey was uninterested. His current girlfriend told everyone he was a pussycat.

Harvey had finished speaking and was sipping his dry martini, which now tasted wet. "What's uglier than a warm martini?" he asked with a grimace.

"Warm it works quicker." Harvey's comment on the martini reminded Mickey he had a dish of food in front of him. He pushed it aside with a brief grunt of disgust. He placed his hands on the table. His fingers were immaculately groomed. Marjorie Graymoor would have approved.

"What do you think, Mickey?"

"I think you got an interesting case on our hands."

Harvey liked the way he said "our hands." Mickey never procrastinated when a deal was offered. It was a quick "yes" or "no." He relied on his gut feeling. "The clan begins to gather when? Next Friday?"

"Next Friday."

"Assuming nobody else gets bumped off between now and then."

"I think it'll stay cool until then."

"Well, what I think I should do is a little fishing off the coast of Connecticut. Maybe there's flounder running."

"You can hire a boat in the village. East Gate."

"And when I want to spook around the island, where's the safest place to land without rousing the natives?"

On a paper napkin, Harvey drew an outline of the island, indicating the mansion, the cliffs, the actual Graymoor wharf where the mansion's boat was tied up, and then about half a mile beyond the cliffs on the other side of the island, he indicated a small cove. "I used to disappear here for hours when I wanted to be alone. With ten kids elbowing for space, it wasn't easy to find solitude. This is where I made love to Laura the first time. There's a cave here. In the summer it's hidden by gorse and underbrush, but now you'll be able to see it. Don't get too venturesome and go exploring. It's tricky. Laura and I, I think, are the only two people who know where it leads to. But there's a passage that eventually connects to the mansion. Also," he tapped another part of the map with his pen, "there's a cabin here. My father used to use it when he'd go bird watching or whatever it was he did when he wanted to get away from us, which was often. It's not used anymore. I had a look in on it last time I was on the island, which was this past Labor Day weekend. It's still in pretty good repair. There's a cot and it's got a bathroom."

"Don't worry about me. I've roughed it before." Harvey smiled. He knew everything about Mickey's 'roughing it.' "What do I do if by accident I run into either your sister or one of the hired help?"

"Just tell them you were out fishing and just pulled in for a look around. No need to warn you not to use the stove."

"Well chum," said Mickey affably, "what say we go someplace for something to eat?"

Nicholas dialed the number again. Still no reply. Now where could Harvey and Laura be this late? "Honey!" he yelled to Marjorie, who was in the bedroom putting up her hair. "Do you hear something on the fire escape?"

"Stop that, Nicky!" screeched Marjorie. "Stop making me nervous!"

But Nicholas was at the window bravely staring out at the fire escape. He saw only the resident pigeons. Fire escape. Walk-up. Poverty. I suppose a man could kill to get out of a situation like this.

* * *

Dombey's was a typical watering hole in the East Fifties frequented mostly by middle-aged businessmen and their somewhat younger prey. It boasted a fairly good menu, a bartender celebrated for his liberal drinks, and an extremely good pianist named Natalie Graymoor who seemed to have memorized the entire catalogue of Broadway show tunes. Unfortunately, every so often she chose to raise her voice in song, described by one denizen as a cross between the late Jeanette MacDonald and a rhinoceros in pain.

Laura was alone at the bar, sitting on a stool, elegant legs crossed, watching Natalie through the mirror behind the bartender. Natalie Graymoor. Three times widowed yet she still preferred her maiden name. Laura was glad she did. Laura couldn't remember any of the married names. Laura studied her adoptive sister as she tore through a second chorus of "Anyplace I Hang My Hat Is Home." She hadn't seen her in months, not since the previous Labor Day weekend at the island. Natalie's face looked puffy, and her hair could have used a fresh henna rinse. She's been letting herself go, thought Laura, the way some girls do when an affair has ended badly. She asked the bartender, "How much longer before Miss Graymoor takes a break?"

"She's not that bad."

Laura smiled. "She's not bad at all. In fact she's pretty good. And she's my sister."

"Oh, well now," said the bartender, "so have one on the house."

"Don't mind if I do. Sort of quiet here tonight."

"It's slackening off all over town. We always know how the other cribs are doing. It's the economy. Real rotten. Real awful rotten." He placed a fresh drink in front of Laura as Natalie played a coda, left the piano in the wake of a deafening silence, and joined Laura at the bar. She kissed Laura lightly on the cheek and sat on an adjoining stool.

"Welcome to the morgue," said Natalie in her sandpapered

coloratura. To the bartender she said, "Mix me a double anything." To Laura she said, "To what do I owe the pleasure?"

"Oh, Harvey is busy elsewhere and I've had a bitch of a day preparing for my showing on Friday, and by the way, why don't you come?" Natalie nodded and Laura continued. "Now why do you look like hell?"

"I thought you'd never notice. I'm getting over a bad one, that's all. Just as well. He was too expensive. Maybe I should have taken that other guy up on his offer."

"What other guy?" The bartender handed Natalie her drink.

"You know." Natalie took a swig. "He said you said you and Harvey would think about it."

Laura wondered if the blood was draining from her face. She felt giddy. "Think about what?"

"The tontine, selling off our potential for a fraction. Not too bad a fraction at that now that I look back on it."

"When was this?"

"Let me think. I think it was Sunday night. He came in just after I finished my first set. Now what the hell was his name?"

"Nathan Manx."

"That's it! Why are we playing cat and mouse? Why give me the impression you don't know what I'm talking about?"

"Just a little surprised, that's all. I never met Manx in my life." She was about to add that Harvey had, but caught herself. "I know he's seen Nicholas. And Nicholas told Marjorie he'd seen Lydia and Annette. But he never saw me. He lied."

"Probably to gain my confidence. I hate liars, don't you? Looking forward to next weekend? I can't think of a thing to buy Helga. Got any ideas? Perfume's useless. You buy her a book, she thinks you're trying to tell her something. Anyway, I'm so broke I can't see straight. You couldn't lend me fifty, could you?"

"Sure. No sweat." Laura found five ten-dollar bills in her handbag and discreetly clasped them into Natalie's hand.

"You're a dear. What do I do about this Manx?"

"You don't have to do anything."

"He said he'd be back over this coming weekend to see me."

"He won't be. He's dead." Natalie gasped. "It's in the late edition of today's afternoon rag. Have you told anybody else about his offer?"

"No. Not anybody. In the first place it sounded so nutty, and in the second place I've been caught up in my own problems, and in the third place with the way business is dropping around here, I'm worried the boss'll be dropping all excess baggage beginning with me."

"Don't worry. I won't let you starve."

Natalie was signaling the bartender. "Sweetheart, you got the late edition?" He reached under the bar for his newspaper and gave it to Natalie. She found the story about Manx's murder. "Now isn't that cute? Throat slit from ear to ear." She folded the paper and placed it on the bar. "That's why you're here tonight."

"Well, I thought it would be a good idea to check in on you. You were always my favorite sister."

"So you've been deep into this murder with Harvey. I suppose Marjorie phoned to ask your advice after Nicholas told her he'd been approached by Manx." Laura nodded. "And Marjorie told you about Lydia and Annette. And now they're dead and so's Manx." She rested an elbow on the bar and propped up her chin with the palm of the hand. "So you and Harvey think there's a connection."

"You always were one of the smart ones."

"And it's all tied to that lousy tontine."

"On the nose, sweetheart."

"So maybe there's a crackpot killer on the loose out to keep the tontine to himself."

"That's what it looks like."

"And we'll all be together on the island a week from now. Gee," she said, sitting up, crossing her arms and doing a fairly good impersonation of Katharine Hepburn's voice, "don't we Graymoors have all the luck, darling!"

4

Arnold Graymoor was walking purposefully along an eerily silent street in the East Fifties, muttering angrily under his breath, hands jammed into his overcoat pocket, not so much to protect them from the cold as to keep them from strangling someone. It was not yet midnight, yet here was he, Arnold Graymoor, suave, sophisticated, at one time more socially sought after than a prince of royal blood, a darling of the darlings, suffering a rejection from a woman who was damned lucky he had even deigned to escort her to dinner. And what's more, he growled to himself, she stiffed me with the bill. Me, a king among con men, treated like a supporting player in a bad movie. He reached his destination and entered Dombey's, slamming the door shut behind him.

"Take it easy, brother," warned the barman.

"Now how'd you know that's our brother?" asked Natalie cosily, toasty warm from her third double anything.

Laura flung out her arms with genuine delight, crying, "Darling Arnold, just the person I want to see!"

Still seething, Arnold removed his overcoat, flung it over the rear of a booth, kissed his sisters, and then leaned against the bar and ordered a Scotch on the rocks. "Would you believe I have just been given my walking papers by some fat old nothing from Hershey, Pennsylvania, and what's more she stuck me with the bill. Hershey, Pennsylvania, yet!" His eyes locked with Laura's, where he detected little sympathy. "I know what you're thinking. Serves me right."

"Serves you wrong," replied Laura airily. "As a feminist I disapprove of your cavalier attitude toward women. Now you're getting your comeuppance and I second the motion."

"You're drunk."

"Oh, no no no, darling. Only two sheets to the wind. The third is waiting in the wings. What I think, Arnold, is that you should take tonight's rejection as a serious omen of things to come. As I see it, your alternatives are limited. You can either marry a wealthy old lady and comfort yourself there's all that wealth to enjoy, or find a job." She watched Arnold lift his drink to his lips somewhat shakily. "Now your hands are trembling. Is it anger or palsy?"

"Do you know any wealthy old ladies who are single?" he asked.

"Only Helga." Natalie guffawed. Laura laughed, and then said, "You're coming up on forty, sweetie, and after that they tell me it's all downhill."

"And next weekend we pay homage to our beloved mother. I think just this once I'll skip it and wire her some roses."

"Oh, no, you don't!" cried Laura. "We're all going to be together on that island. Don't you try to weasel out of it."

Arnold eyed her with suspicion. "What's up?"

"What's up where?"

"What's up on the island?"

"Why are you always so suspicious of everything? You were that way even as a child. I remember you wouldn't eat your porridge without poking around in it for what seemed forever thinking you might find some foreign substance."

"I always did that after one of you tried to nauseate me with a dead beetle."

Natalie nodded her head up and down. "I remember that. Oh how you cried when you spooned up that beetle. Who played that filthy trick on you?"

"There *was* a little monster in our midst," said Laura in a strange voice, "wasn't there? I think Father had his suspicions, especially after little Esmaralda was found dead."

"Oh, little Esmaralda," wailed Natalie.

Arnold was reading the newspaper that Natalie had left on the bar.

Laura was speaking softly. "I remember Father's arguing with Helga in the writing room. He wanted to send one of us away and Helga told him he was acting like a fool. One of the few times, come to think of it, that I ever heard her raise her voice to him. She never did raise her voice much, did she, Natalie?"

Natalie screwed up her face, trying to conjure up a faded vision of Helga in a state of pique. "Not very often, come to think of it. She used to get angry with Robert sometimes. Remember?"

"Yes, Robert and those stupid practical jokes of his."

"She once got angry at Victor," remembered Natalie. "I think she caught him stealing money from her purse or something."

"I remember. It wasn't her purse. It was the housekeeping money. It was old Lottie who fingered him. What a marvelous day that was, and Victor ran away and hours later they finally found him in one of the caves. The one near the hidden cove. He didn't venture very far into it."

Natalie said drily, "He didn't have the guts to venture very far into anything. I think when he finally married Greta he thought he deserved a distinguished service medal."

"Poor Greta," sighed Laura. "She was too pretty to die."

Natalie had screwed up her face. "Wasn't it Robert who got lost for days or something?"

"Or something." Laura was staring at Arnold, who was re-reading the article on Manx's murder. "Did you know Nathan Manx?"

Startled, Arnold dropped the newspaper. "What do you mean?"

"Natalie's met him. So's Nicholas. And Marjorie says Annette and Lydia were approached by him shortly before they were murdered."

"I saw him yesterday," admitted Arnold.

"He was murdered yesterday."

"I know. I was almost caught by the police."

Startled, Natalie involuntarily grabbed Laura's hand. With her free hand, Laura signaled to her sister to remain calm while she spoke to Arnold. "You're not telling me you killed the man?"

"That's right. I'm not telling you I killed the man." His eyes widened as he emphasized, "I did not kill Nathan Manx. I had an appointment to see him. I was late. When I got there, he was already dead. Ugly sight. I hightailed it out of there and as I got out of the elevator in the lobby, the police were hurrying in. And since you obviously know what Manx had on his mind, I can tell you I was damned interested in his proposition. I mean I am not just dead broke, I am poverty-stricken."

"I just loaned Natalie fifty."

"Oh, did you? Hey, Nat, interested in going halfies?"

"No way, darling. Go scrounge up your own." She had relaxed her grip on Laura and decided to return to the piano. There weren't more than half a dozen patrons drinking at the tables, but Natalie was never sure when one of the club owners might turn up to check if she was giving value for money. She sometimes suspected the bartender spied for them. Seated at the piano, Natalie rubbed her fingers together, played a few chords for attention, and started a spirited rendition of "I'll Be Glad When You're Dead You Rascal You."

"Good old Natalie," said Arnold wryly. "Always a song for the right occasion. Where's Harvey tonight?"

"Dinner with a business associate." She looked at her watch and decided it would soon be time to call it a night.

"Don't go yet," said Arnold. He was staring into his drink morosely.

"Sweetie, I can let you have some money tomorrow. Come over to the showroom. We do the payroll on Fridays. I should go home because I've got a showing tomorrow afternoon."

Arnold's eyes lit up. "Lots of rich ladies!"

"Oh, for crying out loud, Arnold. There'll be mostly buyers. And buyers expect to have *their* tabs picked up. But come by anyway around three, there may be some stray pigeon for you to aim at. I wonder if Robert or Victor were contacted by Manx?"

"They're too rich to be interested."

"He didn't contact us, though he told Nicholas he had."

"What does Harvey think about all this?"

"Oh, he suspects dirty work at the crossroads. I can tell you what we've discussed because sooner or later you'll come to the same conclusion. Harvey thinks Manx's murder is in some way connected with those of the girls. He thinks one of us is out to kill the others and claim the tontine. Not interested in letting nature take its course."

"Isn't there something very dumb about that? I mean if all of us are being picked off one by one, who ever remains has got to be the murderer."

"That's right, but you have to have the evidence to prove it. And so far, the killer is being very shrewd. The cops are baffled by the murders of Annette and Lydia, and as for Manx," she shrugged, "it's too soon to tell, but I'll give you odds they've got no leads."

"And that's why it's imperative we all be out on the island for our cozy get-together?"

"I suppose."

Arnold laughed and chucked Laura gently under the chin. "The old movie bit. Get the suspects together under one roof and wait for the killer to make a slip. *If* he makes a slip. Haven't you told me too much? Supposing I'm the guilty party. Forewarned is forearmed."

"You're not smart enough to whip up this plot. I'm not being insulting, I'm being practical. You've always had the attention span of a five-year-old child. You could never concentrate on anything long enough even to find out if it was interesting. Now murder requires very heavy concentration unless it's unpremeditated. This scheme was very cleverly worked out. The only flaw so far was poor Mr. Manx, and that we suspect, is because he got a little greedy. And now the only other way I'll be convinced you're the murderer is if you don't show up next weekend."

"I'll be there. And I'll be at your place tomorrow."

"By the way, how much cash do you need?" Arnold mentioned a sum. Laura whistled. Natalie left the piano and rejoined them.

"I'm going home," she said while stifling a yawn. "I have contributed above and beyond the call of duty, besides which my genius is falling on deaf ears. Arnold, be a sweetheart and walk me home. Being mugged can be so lonely."

"You can walk us both home," said Laura, putting on her coat. She yelled to the bartender, "What's the tab?" While he totaled her bill, Laura slipped into her coat and said, "I think next weekend is shaping up as a lot of fun."

"What about Helga's money?" Natalie and Laura stared at Arnold. "Well, what about her?" he persisted. "Surely we're all in her will. Wouldn't it be less complicated to kill her and collect? Well, wouldn't it?"

"I suppose it would," said Laura, "but I'm hard put to guess what sort of provisions she's set up."

"Very romantic ones, I'm sure," suggested Natalie.

Laura said to Arnold, "She's a very shrewd lady, our mother. My guess is she's set up individual trusts. Tough and unbreakable."

"Are you guessing or do you know?" asked Arnold.

"I'm guessing. I'm not as close to her as Martha is."

"Isn't Victor her lawyer?" asked Natalie.

"I assume so." Laura handed the bartender some bills. "Keep the rest," she told him, and he saluted her smartly. She turned back to the others. "But that doesn't necessarily mean he drew up her will. In fact, since he would be one of the heirs, I'll bet she dealt with one of the locals in the village."

Arnold was leading the way to the street. "Of course, now

that Annette and Lydia are dead, their shares in Helga's estate will probably be divided among the rest of us."

Natalie shivered as Arnold opened the door to the street and a cold blast of air hit them. "God, but you're ghoulish, Arnold." Arnold bared his teeth in a cold grin. Laura wondered if indeed she had told him too much. She was anxious to get home to Harvey.

It was shortly after midnight, but Marjorie was already fast asleep. Nicholas was in the other room staring at the television. The sound was low and the video reception was poor. Night sounds made him uneasy, and his eyes went from the hallway door to the window leading to the fire escape to the ceiling where he could hear his neighbor shuffling about in his bedroom slippers. Nicholas crossed to the television set and shut it off. He went to the hall door and satisfied himself for the fifth time that it was securely locked. He crossed to the window that led out to the fire escape to make sure again the lock was in place. Then, gently, he peered through the blinds. There was no one on the fire escape, he saw with relief. He crossed to the bathroom. There he stared at himself in the mirror. As handsome as he was, Nicholas was not a vain man. What he was looking for was the fear he knew he'd find; he hated himself for being a coward. Staring at himself brought back a memory of his father.

"Go on, go on Nicholas, jump into the water."

"I'm afraid," said the small boy in a weak voice.

"Jump in, damn you!" shouted Andrew. "When you live on an island you have to learn how to swim!"

I still live on an island, thought Nicholas, and I still don't know how to swim. Without washing his face or brushing his teeth, Nicholas went to the bedroom and undressed. He got into bed. Marjorie lay on her back, breathing softy. Nicholas put his right arm under her and raised her gently. His left hand fondled her breast. Marjorie awakened, not too surprised to find herself the subject of a passionate overture. It didn't surprise her or bother her or excite her. She knew they'd both be fast asleep within ten minutes.

When Laura returned home, she found Harvey at the bar mixing himself a drink.

"One for me too, please. I've had quite a night." She removed her coat, flung it across the chair, went to Harvey, and on tiptoe kissed his cheek. "You reek of gin, garlic and. . ." she sniffed again, "veal piccata."

"Where the hell have you been this late? I've been home for over an hour and I don't mind telling you I was just about to call the police."

"To confess to finding Manx's body?"

"Don't try to be funny when I'm angry. Here's your drink." She took the glass and sank onto the couch.

"If you hadn't been in such a hurry to hightail it from the scene of the crime, you would have run into our Arnold."

"You're kidding."

"The two of you could have gone off arm in arm to investigate a porn parlor or something similarly sordid in the area."

"What the hell are you talking about?" He sat down next to her and Laura told him in detail of the previous hours with Natalie and Arnold.

"Do you think I told Arnold too much?"

"It doesn't matter. He's not a great one for absorbing."

"I sometimes think he's underestimated." Suddenly, her face was a study. "Harvey, I think we've always underestimated the others in this family." She had his attention. "Take Nicholas for starters. Just another pretty boy as far as we were concerned and the number one butt of Father's bullying. We make jokes about his stupidity and yet, is he really all that stupid? Maybe somewhere inside all that denseness there's a thin vein of genius waiting to be mined. Some fascinating crimes in the past have been masterminded by some seemingly submental specimens. Then there's Martha. Mousey Martha tied to Momma's apron strings. How do we know she's not skillfully playing Helga for her money? Has she really been hanging in there all these years waiting for Robert to reveal his dormant passion or is she after bigger game? How do we know she hasn't been having a secret affair with someone on the mainland?"

"Keep going, you have me fascinated."

"That's what you get when I'm left to a solitary dinner. I get to thinking too much and it's been a long time since I've given the family much thought. Tonight I studied Natalie. The only one to hit a three-bagger though all of them left her widowed. How can she live the way she lives? I mean sitting in that dingy room, playing that tinny piano, night after night, drinking, sitting at the bar between sets. I suppose she picks up something symbolizing transient passion every so often—"

"Just to keep her hand in."

"And she had to borrow some money from me tonight." Harvey swished his drink about and then took a healthy swig. "I don't see how she can go on much longer this way. She has to know her voice is a liability. And Arnold, poor old Arnold. He's yesterday's news. He's coming by the showroom tomorrow for a check."

"I didn't know you were going in for philanthropy."

Laura sighed and said, "I can't leave them hanging on the ropes. They're family. Arnold can see the end of the rope and then what?"

"That was some pretty shrewd thinking on his part about the possible contents of Helga's will."

"Exactly. At last we get a glimpse of some shrewd thinking from Arnold. Now if he could only apply that elsewhere, somewhere profitable."

"Maybe he is," suggested Harvey solemnly.

"And Lydia and Annette. We barely knew them. Each fighting to carve a little niche for herself with absolutely no encouragement. Did we really ignore the twins all that much?"

"We were busy finding out then why girls were different from boys."

"How'd your dinner go?" asked Laura in an abrupt switch of subject.

"Successfully. Mickey's enthusiastic." He told her about his conversations with Mickey Redfern. When he was finished, Laura went to the desk to check the telephone answering machine. "I've already taken off the messages."

"Anything important?" Laura was fearful of any last minute crisis concerning her showing the next day.

"Robert wants me to call him in the morning and Victor wants *you* to call him in the morning."

"Victor? Oh, of course. Probably needs some help in deciding on a gift for Helga. Which reminds me, what are we giving her?"

"Oh, please, don't ask me to make suggestions at this hour." He had come up behind her and enfolded her in his arms. "Let's go to bed and rekindle some old passion."

"If we're rekindling, it'll be old." He kissed the back of her neck. "I suppose there's no point in claiming I've got a headache."

"No point. We've got plenty of aspirin."

In her overcluttered and overfurnished studio apartment in a high rise just off Second Avenue, Natalie sat at a card table staring at the five ten-dollar bills given her by Laura. She had dealt them neatly and stared at them as though they were a pat hand in poker. She reached for the glass of neat gin she had poured for herself earlier and then slammed the glass down. "Sons of bitches," she murmured, "those three sons of bitches, dying on me like that." She leaned back in the chair, stifling tears. "What the hell have I got to live for?" she shouted. "I've got to lay my hands on that money!" She heard her neighbor banging on the wall for silence. She stood up, causing the chair to crash backward onto the floor. She took the glass and flung it violently against the wall. "Up you, buster!" she screamed. "Up you!"

Money. I need money. And there's a lot of it in this family and I mean to get some, like I mean *now*.

Arnold stood naked in front of the floor length mirror in his ornately naughty bathroom. He stared at his nude body, taking inventory. Physique still good, he decided, and his other asset remained formidable. He studied his face. Good, he decided. Perhaps a bit world weary but then it's the sort of characteristic that usually appeals to lonely women. He arched his eyebrows and narrowed his eyes. Ah, that's the look he favored. Danger. Women loved danger. Women.

I am suffering a severe shortage of women.

I am suffering a severe shortage of cash.

Both shortcomings have got to be remedied. What did Laura say, marry a rich woman or find a job? Well somewhere there's got to be a rich woman waiting to be courted and preyed upon, or perhaps acquired the way sportsmen win horses in a claiming race. Laura must be a rich woman. She's lovely and kind and generous (thank God) and still in love with her husband. But what if I can't find another woman susceptible to what that bitch tonight referred to as my "daintily dubious charms." Hershey, Pennsylvania, yet!

Then I have to get some money somehow. I can't go on borrowing indefinitely. The family has money. Damn that Manx, why did he have to die? I would have made the deal. The money could have taken me to Los Angeles where single rich women are more profuse and stupider. Now how do I get that money? By outliving the others? He smiled at himself in the mirror and whispered, "Perhaps."

5

Mona Norris, Victor Graymoor's private secretary, had attended Vassar College with the sole intention of winning a degree in rich husbands. Four years later, mission unaccomplished, having made peace with herself, the occasionally contented spinster thanked her lucky stars for that day Victor had selected her to be his private secretary. For the first few months, she successfully bluffed a knowledge of legal mumbo jumbo thanks to the kind assistance of another lady in the office who was marking time until she reached retirement age. Now Mona was Queen of the Mountain, keeper of the keys, ruler of the roost, the boss's right arm, good ear, and occasional lover.

"That's sexual harassment," her roommate had said to Mona when Mona confessed she and Victor were having a part-time affair.

"Oh, no, it isn't," said Mona with a wicked smile. "That's job insurance." Shortly after his wife Greta's suicide, Victor awarded Mona a lavish bonus and she moved into an apartment of her own. She knew she was just one of an assortment of Victor's divertissements, which was fine by her. It hadn't been fine by Greta, but Mona was smarter. She was also younger, more healthily attractive, and made no bones of her availability to the frequent bidder. Mona, who was a busy lady both in and out of bed, had a very busy Friday ahead of her and wished Victor would get off the phone and continue with the dictation.

Victor Graymoor was unsuccessfully battling middle age. His hair was dyed an unconvincing shoe polish brown and hung over his ears like tiny doormats. His clothes were just a shade this side of preppy, and he worked out at a nearby gymnasium at least three times a week. He referred to both men and women as "you guys" and was a recognized habitué at a number of discos. Although his law firm was considered a successful one, at least two of his four partners were waiting for the one false move that could be used to force him out. Victor was never very good at dealing with honest men. Victor also lived well beyond his means. Greta's life insurance had managed to cover three of his more outstanding debts, but Victor always needed more. Mona knew this, the partners knew this, and Victor knew they knew. It couldn't have bothered him less. Victor had been taught by his adoptive father to be a survivor, and he had every intention of surviving. He frowned at Mona as she stifled a yawn. Into the phone he said, "Well, thanks for taking the trouble, Laura. I didn't know you had a big day today. See you next week." He hung up and smiled his ocelot smile. "What's the matter, cutie? Up a little late last night?"

"You should know," said Mona in her most seductive drawl.

"Take a little extra time on your lunch hour and run me a little errand." Mona groaned inwardly. "There's a gourmet shop up at Madison and Sixtieth that imports French truffles. . ." Helga doted on imported delicacies. She didn't look forward so much to eating them as displaying their fancy packaging. "Are you listening to me?"

"Of course I am," said Mona.

"You looked like you were off on some distant planet."

"I was just wondering if you were planning on seeing me over the weekend."

"Do you have to know this minute?"

"I have a life of my own."

"I pay for it."

"You get value for money. I was thinking of flying down to Virginia to see my mother."

"Why don't you bring her up here?"

"No, thanks."

Victor spun the swivel chair a few degrees to the right and stared out the window. Mona tapped her pencil impatiently on her stenographic pad, and Victor frowned. It wasn't Mona who annoyed him, it was the conversation with Laura. She had told him about the previous evening with Natalie and Arnold and their financial predicaments. "I am not my brother's keeper," Victor had snapped, and Laura agreed with him that he wasn't and didn't have to be, but it would be generous just the same if there was some way to help either one of them in their predicament, especially Arnold. "At least Natalie can play the piano for something of a living," Laura reminded him, "but Arnold is a frozen asset. I mean all he can do is titillate older women, but there's a whole younger generation of men equally talented, younger, and probably better looking catching up on him." And then she added an afterthought she had practiced for fifteen minutes. "Isn't there any way to break into the tontine?"

Victor had told her pompously that it was impossible and this was not the time to discuss it. Laura had very cleverly avoided any mention of Nathan Manx or the murdered twins. She had baited Victor with Natalie and Arnold's predicaments, assuming that if he knew about Manx, he would have suggested the two take him up on his offer if he hadn't seen the previous day's newspaper item about Manx's murder. So Laura felt Victor didn't know of Manx's existence, or else was being shrewdly devious in sidestepping any mention of the man. Victor shook his head and sighed.

Mona broke into his reverie. "Is something the matter?"

"Do I look as though something's the matter?" he snapped as he positioned the chair in her direction.

"I just thought we ought to get on with the dictation. I've got a heavy work load on my desk and then there's your errand—"

"All right, all right!" He pressed his fingers against his temples and then said to Mona, "You're an only child, aren't you?"

"That's right."

"God, but you're lucky."

When Robert Graymoor's secretary, Edna Farmer, was asked to describe him, after no thought whatsoever she promptly said he looked like a cross between the late movie star, John Wayne, and any number of professional golfers. Edna had been with Robert for close to ten years, almost from the time he opened his office as an investment counselor. She neither worshiped him nor despised him, she just thought he was a fair employer. She suspected several clandestine dealings on his part to which she, as his confidential secretary, should have been privy, but on the other hand, she'd learned years ago to accept the fact that Robert was private and secretive. She knew he was an adopted son and had been brought up on Graymoor Island, and she knew about the tontine because their company administered it. She thought it was a vicious bequest and wished just once she'd been in a position to tell that to the late Andrew Graymoor, but the only possible recourse to accomplishing that would be by way of spirit message at a séance and Edna didn't go in for that sort of hocus-pocus.

On occasion, when prompted by an inquisitive friend or neighbor, Edna speculated on Robert's continuing bachelorhood, never attributing the condition to any form of perversion on Robert's part but to the old bromide, "I just guess he's not the marrying kind." Neither was Edna, who was now fifty something and long ago had stopped believing in miracles. But if there were any hope of a stray miracle wandering into her neighborhood, Edna would opt for the attentions of Harvey Graymoor. "Now *there's* a honey," Edna had told her newest best friend in the office, a gentlemanly file clerk. "He's married to his sister." When the file clerk blanched and seemed on the verge of the vapors, Edna explained that they were adoptive siblings and had different sets of parents. The file clerk still found it necessary to excuse himself and make tracks for the men's room, where he spent fifteen minutes applying a cold compress to his fevered brow.

Just hearing Harvey's voice on the phone, as she was now, gave Edna a tingle she usually reserved for her favorite television series hero. "I'll tell Robert you're on," she cooed into the phone. Robert took Harvey's call immediately.

"How goes it, old chap?" asked Robert jovially. Robert was an anglophile much given to using "old chap," "I say there," and the occasional "what ho." Laura swore she once heard him gasp in astonishment, "Od's bodkins."

"I got your message last night, but it was too late to call back. What's up?"

"I had a very strange phone call from Helga yesterday." Robert paused.

"What was strange about it?"

"I gathered that she was alone and Martha had taken the boat over to the mainland to buy a special dress for next weekend."

"That's hot news. I don't remember seeing Martha in a dress since her confirmation."

"She got on to the subject of the twins. Did I know if the police were still pursuing any leads?"

"Well, do you know?"

"I'm on top of it. The case is still very much alive. Detective Wylie keeps in touch with me."

"Norman Wylie?"

"You know him?"

"Oh, sure. He helped me on an insurance fraud about a year ago."

Robert said with a smile, "You get to know just about everybody."

"I don't know the mayor. Let's get back to Helga. What else besides the twins?"

"Remember the Esmaralda thing?"

"Who could forget Esmaralda? Laura finding the poor mutt dead in one of the wine cellars."

"Well, Helga wanted to know if I ever gave any thought to who might have killed the mongrel."

"She wasn't a mongrel, she was purebred. She was a good dog. I'm beginning to miss her all over again."

"Anyway, it was all very strange and I'm beginning to wonder if Helga's not getting senile."

"Did her questions make sense?"

"Well, sure they did."

"Then she's not senile."

"But all this brooding on the twins and a dead dog?"

Harvey changed the subject as he had planned to. "Is there any way of breaking the tontine?"

Robert was taken by surprise. He uttered a slight gasp, which didn't escape Harvey's ear, and then said, "Absolutely no way. What's the matter? You're not having any financial difficulties, are you?"

"No, no, I'm just dandy," Harvey assured him, and then recited his rehearsed litany on the sad financial situations of Arnold, Natalie, and Nicholas, carefully avoiding mentioning the late Nathan Manx. Harvey's peroration was so tear-stained, he thought surely the least Robert could respond with was "Well, let me see what I can do."

"It's unbreakable," said Robert in a voice that could cut steel, "and I hope none of them is considering anything foolish."

"Well," said Harvey with a touch of whimsy, "Laura thinks if Arnold can no longer sell his body to women, he might try selling it to science. As for Natalie and Nicholas, one can but hope for an unexpected upsurge in their fortunes. And as for Helga, let's wait until we get out there next weekend. I'm looking forward to that, are you?"

"Oh, sure. You know I am. I was even thinking of taking a few days off and getting up there a little earlier. I haven't spent much time with Helga and Martha lately."

"There was Labor Day."

"That seems ages ago."

"And didn't Martha pop into town on a surprise visit a couple of weeks ago?"

"Did she? I didn't know anything about that."

"I'm not sure she did. It's just that Laura caught a glimpse of her or someone who looked like her coming out of a restaurant on Lexington Avenue. But you know Laura, she might have been drunk."

"I've never seen Laura drunk."

"Oh, haven't you? It's a lot of fun. Anything else I can do for you?"

"No, no. I just wondered if perhaps Helga had phoned either of you with the same problem."

They said their good-byes and hung up. Harvey snorted. Helga phone us? Why us? It was Robert who was her pet.

And Robert was thinking, Arnold and Natalie and Nicholas. The three fools. Why don't they team up for a club act? He buzzed for Edna.

As Edna settled into her favorite chair, Robert said, "Edna, I'm going to try and get away next Wednesday, Thursday morning at the latest, so don't schedule any appointments."

"You have a meeting at the bank Wednesday morning."

"Oh yes, of course," said Robert, "I'll certainly keep that appointment. Now, anything urgent?"

"Oh, no. In fact, it's awfully quiet."

"Yes," said Robert, "I've noticed that myself."

Laura's show seemed to be going swimmingly. She herself compéred the presentation, describing each outfit smoothly and with a nice undertone of sex appeal and ear appeal to blend with the eye appeal. Harvey, seated in the back of the showroom, noticed with approval the number of buyers scribbing away on their pads. He also saw Arnold sitting in the front row looking like a giant mastiff poised to spring—at whom, Harvey was not too sure. A good half a dozen prospects for Arnold were scattered throughout the room. Harvey was feeling sorry for Arnold. What a way to live. Where had it begun? Certainly somewhere back in the dark ages of their childhood. But what had seeded this compulsion to live off rich women? Was it the wealthy wives who came to the island as guests back when guests were welcome? Or was it Arnold's inability to lock into any sort of a career? Harvey knew a lot of Arnolds. He'd met them in California and Florida, in the south of France, and in Tangier. He'd watched them operate in Acapulco, and they comprised a select coterie in New York. He wondered if they qualified for Medicare. Perhaps they needed an organization to look after them in their old age, something like the Ziegfeld Girls Club. Now Arnold was smiling, and Harvey thought, oh, good for old Arnold. He's scoring. He's smiling at someone at the other side of the room. Harvey's eyes were kleiglights as they swept the room in search of Arnold's conquest. He saw Marjorie, Nicholas's wife. Harvey's shoulders sagged. Poor Arnold. Harvey felt like rushing up to his adoptive brother with a pail of water and a sponge, wiping off his face as one does to a prizefighter between rounds. But Arnold looked terribly nonchalant and above it all as Laura introduced her *pièce de résistance,* her crowning glory, the item she was depending on to be her best seller, a three-piece garment that adapted cleverly for morning, afternoon, or evening wear. Laura was rewarded with a generous round of applause, and flushed and smiling, she found Harvey in the back of the room and lifted her hands above her head with fingers intertwined, the acknowledged champion.

Fifteen minutes later, buyers and guests were milling about the room sipping champagne and gorging on pretentious little sandwiches and a rich assortment of bite-size cakes. Laura managed to whisper to Harvey, "It's a smash," and then hurried away to find Marjorie. Marjorie had phoned her earlier and pleaded with her to help her select a dress for Helga's weekend. Laura saw that Arnold had snared the buyer from Dallas. Oh, good choice, boy, she thought to herself, just don't push it too hard. The lady eats men for breakfast.

"Laura!" Marjorie had found her.

"Hi, sweetie, enjoy the show?"

"The greatest, Laura. Just the greatest." She and Laura sideswiped cheeks. "I want them all. What do you think? What would suit me?"

"The last item is just your size."

"Oh, my God. Not that one. That's your biggest number. I can't afford *that!* "

"What's to afford? It's a sample that was made up especially for the show. I can't sell it. And it's perfect for the weekend." She grabbed Marjorie's wrist. "Come on and try it on before my dim-witted model decides she wants it."

Harvey watched Laura and Marjorie disappear backstage. He craned his neck and spotted Arnold and the buyer from Dallas. Arnold had his little date book in his hand and an expectant smile on his face. The lady seemed to be devouring Arnold with her eyes. And why not? Her head came to just a bit above Arnold's waistline. Langley, one of Laura's assistants, arrived at Harvey's side with a tray holding a Scotch on the rocks. "I've been looking all over for you," said Langley in a voice coated with whipped cream. "Laura said you'd perish without a Scotch and we can't have you perishing on the premises, can we?" Harvey took the Scotch gratefully and sipped it for texture.

"Perfect."

"Imported. How'd you like the show?"

"I thought it was terrific, but of course I'm prejudiced."

"So am I because I work here, but I honestly think it's her best yet. The orders are coming in like flying saucers. Why, she'll soon be supporting you!" he gaily gurgled as he wafted off.

"Where'd you get Scotch?" Arnold, looking pleased with himself, had appeared at his elbow.

"It was brought by a good fairy. Laura looks after her own. Want a sip?"

Arnold took the glass. "Want a gulp." He took a deep swig. "I've just made an assignation with a munchkin. God, I've sunk low. Seems she's a buyer from Dallas. When I suggested dinner tomorrow, she growled and bared her teeth. It took me a minute to realize she said 'yes.'"

"How do you get her to pick up the tab?"

"Oh, Mighty Mouse was way ahead of me. She made it clear she's on a heavy expense account so we go where she wants to go, and where she wants to go you pay the bill with gold bullion. She's staying at the Helmsley Palace. I hope Laura doesn't mind."

"Why should she mind unless the lady isn't buying?"

"Oh, she's buying all right. I told her I'm Laura's brother. She's buying the line and she's buying me, generous little sprite. And there's Laura with our Marjorie, and our Marjorie looks as though she's just won the sweepstakes."

Marjorie was saying to Laura as they made their way through the crowd to join Harvey and Arnold, "You're so wonderful to me!"

"I'll have it wrapped and waiting for you at the desk when you're ready to leave."

"And please tell Nicholas it was a gift. He was so frightened I'd spend too much, but I can't go to the island looking like a frump."

"Of course not. Don't worry, I'll take care of Nicky."

"And would you please tell him to stop being so frightened?"

Laura stared at her sister-in-law. "Is he that frightened?"

"He was up most of the night checking the hall door and the window that leads out to the fire escape. He's absolutely convinced someone in the family is out to kill you all off. And he can't stand the apartment any longer. And it's really such a sweet little apartment, I mean especially after where I grew up." Laura recalled some pathetic story of a mill town in upstate New York. She remembered Marjorie's astonishment at indoor plumbing. How had she and Nicholas ever found each other? "We were so lucky to find it, it's so cheap. So what if it is a walk-up? But he's impossible. He says it's unfair, there's so much wealth in the family and that stupid tontine. He thinks it should all be divided fairly and squarely, and I think that's communism."

Why you old-fashioned thing, thought Laura as they reached Harvey and Arnold, who were now sharing the Scotch. "There's lots more of that," said Laura. "The two of you are behaving like a couple of nomads who just found the oasis." She looked around the room. "Where's Langley?" Her voice grew louder. "Anybody see Langley?" She saw Langley and signaled him for more Scotch. "Langley is such a treasure. I found him at Gucci's being rude to a movie star. It was love at first slight, and I appropriated him right on the spot." Harvey kissed her.

"Congratulations. It's a big hit."

Laura beamed. "It's even bigger than I anticipated. Thanks, darling." She turned to Arnold and asked, "How'd you make out with Dallas?"

"Bingo."

"Oh good. Everybody's cup runneth over. And here comes Langley, and the clever boy's brought the bottle." She stared at Harvey as Langley refilled the glass. "Do you really intend to get stoned this early?"

"Not at all," said Harvey with the hauteur of a man about town. "I intend to have you take me to a very expensive dinner as befits a woman of your newly acquired means."

"It's a date." To Marjorie and Arnold she extended an invitation to join her and Harvey. Arnold had other plans, but Marjorie was eager to accept.

"I won't know for sure, though, until I see Nicholas later. I think it would do him good to get out more often. We're at home so much."

Poor little mouse, thought Laura, restraining an urge to throw her arms around her or else pat her affectionately on the head.

"Excuse us," said Harvey as he walked Laura out of their hearing distance, compensating Arnold with the glass of Scotch. "I had an interesting conversation with Robert."

"Me likewise with Victor." They exchanged information. Laura's face was a study. "The hell Helga's senile. That's a lot of nonsense. It's easy to figure out what's on her mind. She's been thinking hard about the murders of Annette and Lydia. And does it go as far back as the murder of a dog? I told you a long time ago there was one of us Andrew especially loathed and wanted sent away, but somehow Helga prevailed and the culprit stayed. In fact, I'm beginning to wonder . . ." She paused, and Harvey realized she was staring at Arnold, who was now bantering affably with Marjorie.

"Beginning to wonder what?" Harvey prodded.

Laura looked into Harvey's face. "I'm sure she knows nothing about Manx unless the man got to Martha and Martha told Helga about it. But I think if Manx *had* approached Martha, she would have told Robert, and you say he never mentioned the man's name."

"Not a mention. Although he might have been playing his information close to the vest. You know old Robert, old 'I say, old chap' Robert."

"What I think, Harvey, is that Helga is brooding about murder."

"So are you."

"I should have said something to you this morning." Laura's brows were furrowed, and her face had darkened. "But we seem to be forgetting how Andrew died. Supposedly while walking along the cliff in one of his dark moods, he lost his footing and fell over, plunging to his death on the rocks below." She stared at Harvey. "It was one of the birthday celebrations. We were all there. It was after lunch when we usually wander off on our own. I remember you were going to investigate the condition of the cabin. And I went off with my drawing pad to do some sketching. I can't remember what the others were up to."

"For crying out loud," said Harvey, "you're not suggesting old Andrew was *pushed*?"

"Old Andrew was as sure-footed as a mountain goat. It was a beautiful day that day. I remember it clearly. It was crisp, and the sky was cloudless. There was no wind. I sat in our alcove sketching without discomfort. Nobody bothered to examine the spot from where Andrew fell. We all assumed he just slipped and went over. Don't you see, Harvey? That's what's probably begun to prey on Helga's mind. She's been suspecting all along what I've just started suspecting." She paused and folded her arms around herself as though warding off a chill. "Andrew was murdered."

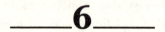

6

Bella Wallace had had every intention of attending Laura's showing, but something better had presented itself. His name was Norman Wylie, and he was considered a damned good detective. After her profitable luncheon with Laura, Bella had gone back to her office, and with her usual canny efficiency set into motion a private investigation into the Graymoor family. Within two days, she had acquired a dossier that would have put Watergate to shame. And now, on this sunny but cold Friday afternoon, she had acquired Detective Norman Wylie, the star of a downtown precinct celebrated on various occasions in television documentaries. Bella was pleased that Norman Wylie had agreed to an interview on her own turf, her lavishly decorated office.

Wylie was flattered that the internationally famous Bella Wallace had deigned to wave her wand in his direction and favor him with an audience. "I hate going above Fourteenth Street," Norman often commented. "It makes my nose bleed." But for Bella Wallace he'd swim through vodka with his mouth closed. Physically, Bella was Wylie's idea of paradise. So what if her hips were a shade too ample and her legs a bit stubby, albeit shapely; her chest was provocatively cantilevered and her rich, full-blooded lips were an invitation to the secrets of the sorcerers. He knew she was over forty, but forty was better than sixty and just about everybody knew that Norman didn't draw the line at anyone. If it looked good and was available, Norman staked his claim.

Bella couldn't believe her eyes when Wylie entered her office. She had expected bad language, bad breath, and a stomach punished by an excess of beer. Norman Wylie was a singularly pleasant surprise. He was not quite six feet tall, slender, certainly no more than thirty-four or thirty-five years of age, and spoke without a trace of accent. Although there were dark circles under his eyes, the face was handsome. The nose seemed to suggest it had once made contact with somebody's fist. She made a quick study of his left hand and was pleased that there was no wedding band. That didn't really prove anything, but it helped.

After Bella's secretary, Arabella Keats, served coffee, Bella got down to the business at hand. In less than fifteen minutes, she had filled the detective in on everything she thought pertinent to the story she planned to do on the Graymoors. When she got to the murders of Lydia and Annette, the overwhelmed Wylie relaxed. Now they were on his territory, but the tontine was news to him. Bella sensed there was some bristling going on under his seemingly cool exterior. When Bella suggested there was a possible link between the twins and the murder of Nathan Manx, Wylie almost screamed with frustration.

"I suppose Laura and Harvey Graymoor will have my head for this," said Bella as she refilled their coffee cups, "but I'm after a story and when I'm after a story, I mean run for the hills, the dikes have burst." She added with a sweet smile, *"Aprés moi le deluge,"* and he returned a smile to disguise the fact he hadn't a clue as to what she was talking about. His head was aching from too many mental notes. Whether Bella realized it or not, she had unplugged a faulty line of investigation. He heard Bella ask, "Did you know Nathan Manx?"

"Not personally. We don't get to know all the shady characters in town. But we get to know *of* them. How many others did you say were mixed up in this tontine thing?"

"Nine," replied Bella, who took five minutes to identify the remaining heirs. When she finished, Wylie's face was a study. He shifted in his chair and crossed his legs.

"I'm surprised Robert Graymoor didn't let me in on this. I mean the possible tie between the murdered twins and Manx." He cleared his throat and sipped some coffee. "We've been on the square with him, keeping in touch, letting him know the latest developments. He knows we need all the help we can get. Have you met him?"

"I've only met Laura and Harvey." She was wondering if it made some sense to visit Graymoor Island after all.

"Robert's a good Joe. He hangs in honest. But to keep this info from me. . ."

"Maybe he didn't know. I have a suspicion Manx was only contacting those heirs he suspected or knew were hard up."

"So with this tontine thing, there's only one who can collect, right?"

"Right."

"Boy. That sure could mean an expectation of a lot of corpses." He pondered for a moment, and then said softly, "Unless. . ."

Bella leaned forward eagerly. Here was a detective's mind

at work, and she wasn't often witness to this alien phenomenon. He was staring out the window behind Bella at a magnificent view of Lincoln Center. Bella decided it was time to prime his pump. His silence might continue indefinitely. "Unless what?" she asked.

"Unless there's the possibility of a conspiracy."

"You mean one says, 'I'll play dead until we dispose of the others and then after we collect we'll split the loot?'" He nodded. "I suppose it can be done."

"Anything can be done," said Wylie authoritatively, "but as to the degree of success . . . well, who knows?"

"Tell me about the twins. They didn't look like twins, I've been told."

"They certainly didn't look like twins when I last saw them." Bella suppressed a shudder. "They were bludgeoned beyond recognition. Laura Graymoor wasn't kidding when she said her husband had to guess as to which was which. Of course later we checked their fingerprints and dental work."

"They knew their assailant?"

"We think so. I mean no doors or windows were tampered with. Nothing was stolen and they hadn't been sexually assaulted."

"Do you suppose Nathan Manx might have killed them?"

"I've already run that through my private computer." He winked while he tapped his head with an index finger. "My guess is that murder wasn't Manx's type of action. What I know about Manx is this, he was a process server by profession, but for fun and profit he ran errands for some of the big boys up there on the other side of the fence. In other words, he was a bag man. What I'm giving you is just some of the flak I picked up from the boys uptown. I mean we don't cross over into each other's territories unless it's urgent. Of course now for me it's urgent and I'll have to dig a little deeper into Nathan Manx. Damn it. I suppose his office was stripped clean."

Bella didn't care how many bleeding bodies she left behind

when she was after a story. "Harvey Graymoor had an appointment to see Nathan Manx the day he was murdered."

Wylie stayed cool. It was nice information, but he didn't betray the fact. He knew Bella's reputation, that when she was hunting for information she was better than a French pig snuffling around for truffles. "Harvey Graymoor's a good man. I worked with him on some of his claims cases."

"Do you suppose he might have murdered Nathan Manx?" Her face was straighter than her assumption.

"Harvey Graymoor's no villain. He's a hero."

Bella was somewhat startled by Wylie's appraisal of Harvey Graymoor. "How can you be so sure?"

"What's the matter, Miss Wallace? All your years in the people business and you still can't tell the heroes from the villains?"

"Not these days. There's such a crossover. Everybody's got a touch of larceny in them. Some of the nicest people in the world have turned out to be murderers. I know a very famous lady who still insists Hitler was a pussycat."

"Harvey Graymoor doesn't have a killer's instinct. You see, when he identified the bodies, he got very sick. You can't play-act that. At least if he was acting, then he deserves an Oscar, because he was genuinely ill. Then he cried." That information surprised Bella. She would never have classified Harvey as the crying type. "Then he got angry and wondered how come I had called him to identify the bodies and not Robert, who I guess handles the family affairs. Well, the only reason I called Harvey was because when I went through Lydia Graymoor's address book, Harvey's was the only name I recognized and I always like to work with someone I'll feel comfortable with."

"I hope you're feeling comfortable with me."

"You? Why, Miss Wallace, you're a piece of cake."

"Well, just for that, you can start calling me Bella."

"Well, Bella, what else do you want to know from me?"

"When are we having dinner?"

* * *

When Harvey and Laura got back to their apartment, they celebrated the cocktail hour immediately. They called a cab and dispatched Marjorie home with her newly acquired dress, and after Laura clandestinely slipped Arnold a check, he hurried off to his doctor for a checkup and a vitamin shot. He had a suspicion the lady from Dallas was going to be a devil with a souped-up engine. Reclining on the sofa, drinks in hand, bowl of salted nuts on the coffee table in front of them, and shoes off, Laura and Harvey continued worrying the suspicion that old Andrew Graymoor had been pushed off the cliff and sent hurtling to his death.

"We were none of us angels," said Harvey, "but murdering Andrew. . ." He shook his head with disbelief.

"Remember what Helga used to say to us when we were kids?"

"Helga said a lot of things to us when we were kids."

"No, no, you know what I mean. When we'd been up to some sort of mischief and then were surprised that Helga knew all about it and could usually identify the culprit with some accuracy. I used to think she had an extra sense for that sort of thing." She was now sitting with her legs tucked under her, surveying the bowl of nuts as though it contained precious jewels.

Harvey snapped his fingers. "I remember! She used to say that the walls had whispered to her!"

"You got it!" Laura selected a nut and popped it into her mouth. "Helga's whispering walls!"

Harvey also chose a nut and then said, "I wonder what the walls have been telling her about Andrew's death?"

"And the twins," Laura added solemnly.

"Would Helga have known about Manx?"

"I don't know. I don't think so. Martha might have. I still think that was her I saw coming out of that shop on Lexington Avenue a couple of weeks ago. It was so damn crowded I couldn't get to her. Still, I might be wrong. You see, as I recall, the woman I thought might have been Martha was dressed with a certain amount of chic. Now as we both know, our Martha has no chic whatsoever. I mean if there was ever a hint of it, I never recognized it, because all I've ever seen her wear is jeans, outsized sweaters, and logging boots, and do you know something, I don't know if she's shapely. Do you know if she's shapely?"

"Have you forgotten we used to go swimming all summer long? Sure she's shapely, unless age has withered her and fortune staled her infinite variety."

"Man, when you mangle Shakespeare, you really mangle him." The phone rang, and Laura reached for the table behind her to answer it. It was Marjorie. She and Nicholas would be delighted to join them for dinner. Laura had almost forgotten proferring the invitation. They agreed to meet in a few hours time at a theatrical hangout in the West Forties, where the atmosphere was colorful and the servings generous, and the food sometimes edible.

After Laura replaced the phone in its cradle, Harvey groaned and then said, "A whole evening of those two. I mean dear God, when Nicholas last took an I.Q. test, he ended up owing them thirty-seven points."

"Just treat dinner like an investigation and then it'll be that much more pleasant."

As he selected another nut Harvey said, "Did I suspect I was marrying Pollyanna the glad girl?" Again the phone rang.

"Your turn," said Laura as she left the couch to refresh her drink.

Harvey was surprised to hear Norman Wylie identify himself. "Hi there, Norman." Harvey hoped he sounded affable. "What's the good word?" The word wasn't all that good. "How'd you like to come up for a drink and I'll explain everything. Still got the address? Fine. Fifteen minutes." He hung up the phone and then bombarded Laura's ears with a series of unpleasant expletives, all presumably descriptive of Bella Wallace. He held out his empty glass to Laura and requested in a tiny Oliver Twist voice, "More please." While Laura refilled his glass, he told her about Norman Wylie and Bella Wallace.

"It's just as well it's out in the open," said Laura, and repeated those words to Norman Wylie fifteen minutes later after he had settled into an easy chair with a tall Scotch and soda. Harvey gave Wylie every detail concerning his adventure with the dead Nathan Manx, concluding with his anonymous phone call to the police.

"Does that make me an accessory or something?" asked Harvey.

"Oh, that falls under all sorts of categories, Harvey," suggested Wylie as he surreptitiously studied Laura and awarded her a nine in the Norman Wylie Mental Chart of Feminine Assessments. "There's obstructing an investigation for openers."

"Have they found out anything about Manx?"

"There was nothing worthwhile in the office. You didn't give it a shaking down, did you?"

"I went through the desk drawers and found nothing."

"And what did you find in his wallet?"

"Now how do you know I went through his wallet?"

"You went through his wallet," said Wylie with assurance, "and I'll bet you found a list of names." Harvey almost dropped his drink. Laura was amused. She liked Norman Wylie. He had a wonderful way of inserting stilettos. "I know all about the tontine."

"Sure you do," said Harvey. "Bella Wallace and her big fat mouth."

"Harvey." Wylie spoke his name solemnly. "Harvey, the police pray for help from the Bella Wallaces of the world. They're better than professional informers. That's the whole point of interrogations. Question after question after tedious question until somebody finally makes a slip and we've dug ourselves one shiny little nugget. Sure I know what Bella's after."

"So it's Bella now, is it?"

Laura smiled again. Wylie was blushing and it was charming. "Why not?"

"Why not indeed. So what's Bella after besides you?"

"A good story."

"Oh, hot damn, I can see it now," Laura interjected as her hand moved in an arc projecting an imaginary headline. "'The Curse Of The Graymoors!'" She stretched her legs out, almost touching Wylie's, and it gave him a whisper of a thrill. "This is what comes of a simple projected story about Laura Graymoor, dress designer. Oh, well, what the hell, if there's a killer loose among us, three heads are better than one." She told Wylie about the forthcoming weekend on Graymoor Island.

Wylie fixed them both with a stern look. "You should leave playing detective to detectives."

Harvey told him about Mickey Redfern, summing him up with, "And Mickey is a very, very good man."

"So's the murderer," countered Wylie. "Of course, you know, we might be all wrong. Maybe there's no connection between Manx and the twins at all. Just a tragic coincidence."

"But we know better, don't we," said Harvey assuredly. "I suppose now you're going to call in all the others for questioning?"

"I've been getting an awful lot of very subtle flak from your brother Robert." Wylie assumed, whether adopted or not, that they all considered each other brothers and sisters, which, after asking them, Harvey assured Wylie they did.

"What is subtle flak?" asked Laura sweetly, wondering if she'd still have time for a soak in the bath before dinner.

"The usual. 'Any leads? Any suspicions?' You didn't notice me at the girls' funeral, did you?" He enjoyed their startled looks. "I came to the island on a fishing boat. I stood on a little hill just behind that very imposing mausoleum."

"It houses Andrew Graymoor. He was our adoptive father. We were surprised at the amount of people who hired boats to come to the island for the services. We didn't know the twins knew so many people."

"They probably didn't," said Wylie. "I suspect they were mostly curiosity seekers."

"The reporters and photographers were a bore," commented Laura. "I looked a mess in the morning paper. Fine publicity for a smart dress designer."

Harvey interrupted her. "What conclusions did you reach on that little hill just behind the imposing mausoleum?"

"I wasn't looking for conclusions." The little laugh he uttered Laura also found charming. She was beginning to regret her fresh promise to herself after the previous night's marvelous hour of love to remain faithful to Harvey forever, although in truth, Laura found it difficult to sublet her emotions. "It was just a police hound's instinct that attracted me to the island. It was my day off. I sometimes take little excursions on my day off. And it gave me a chance to see the famous Helga Graymoor in person. I had a girlfriend who used to dote on those romances of hers." He shook his head from side to side. "How anybody can read that crap? Oops, sorry."

"No offense taken," said Laura lightly. "Helga would be the first to agree with you. So if you weren't looking for conclusions, what did you find?"

"I found a family portrait I didn't expect to find. I mean I knew Harvey and Robert on sight, but the rest of you were a sort of surprise. It was pretty easy to guess who was family."

"What's the trick?" asked Laura. "We were the only ones seated."

"Nobody cried."

"I think by then we were all cried out," said Laura.

Harvey added, "You know I did mine when I was called in to identify the bodies."

Wylie shifted in his chair. "I'm always surprised and a little sad when women don't cry."

"Well, some of us girls are made of sterner stuff," said

Laura forcibly. "I only cry in the movies, mostly at the credits. Also, Mr. Wylie—"

"Norman."

"Thank you, Norman. To continue, also, we weren't all that close to the twins. They were practically the last to be adopted, along with Nicholas. In fact, I sometimes get confused as to whether the girls preceded Nick or was it the other way around, not that it matters much. So you see, much as we liked the girls, and I for one did like the girls, we weren't terribly close to them."

"They were off on their own most of the time," said Harvey. "Sometimes they let Nicholas join them on their excursions. All of us loved exploring the island, although it could be dangerous." Harvey explained the topography of the island to Wylie, who was fascinated.

"Hidden caves. Secret tunnels. Slave cells. Underground river." Harvey smiled as he refilled Wylie's glass. "Now why didn't I have a childhood like that?"

Laura was wondering what kind of a childhood he had had when he said, "I was just another street-wise kid in Hell's Kitchen." Satisfied, Laura wondered if he had read her mind. She also wondered if Harvey was going to tell Wylie that Arnold had also been in Manx's office after his murder.

Harvey gave Wylie his fresh drink and then returned to Laura's side. "Somebody else found Manx's body after I did."

There's an awful lot of mind reading going on around here, thought Laura, and then listened as Harvey told Wylie about Arnold's incident in Manx's office.

"You Graymoors sure get around," was Wylie's only comment after Harvey was finished talking. "Tell me about Arnold." Harvey told him. "I suppose now you'll be telling me his kind isn't the murdering kind." Laura told him exactly that. Wylie exhaled a weak little whistle and then sat back. "I suppose if I do call as many in as possible for questioning, my knowledge of Manx's connection with the twins then queers your plot for next weekend."

"It makes it harder," said Harvey.

"I don't suppose I could con an invitation for the weekend?" asked Wylie.

"Robert knows you," reminded Harvey.

"Well," said Wylie, "I've got to give this some thought. I'll tell you this though, if there's another murder before you all leave town next Friday, then nobody's leaving town next Friday."

"Now that makes sense," said Laura. "In fact," she added airily, "I'd almost welcome another murder. Then we'd be *sure* the killer was one of us. Well, you both don't have to look at me as though I was a blithering idiot."

"That's not the way I'm looking at you," said Harvey. "It's just that you make a great deal of sense, and it's given me a very sinking depressed feeling in the pit of my stomach."

Wylie looked at his wristwatch and got to his feet. He placed his glass on an end table while speaking. "I've got to be going. In the future, Harvey, try trusting me. After all, we've worked together fine before, there's no reason why we can't keep to that level of trust. I mean here we are, both after the same thing. A killer. Let me tell you this, I don't envy you this weekend of yours coming up."

"We can't very well cancel it," said Laura. "It's a tradition. Even the year our father died. . ." As she said "our father died," she locked eyes with Harvey. They hadn't told Wylie of their suspicions concerning Andrew's fall from the cliff. Harvey told Wylie. Wylie emitted another weak whistle.

"I repeat, I don't envy you two this weekend of yours coming up. I hope this Mickey Redfern knows what he's about. I'll be in touch." They watched him open the door to the hall. After he closed it behind himself, Laura turned to Harvey.

"I'm frightened," she said. "I'm very, very frightened." He put his arms around her and hugged her tightly.

From her bedroom window, Helga could see Martha walking along the cliffs. She always walks along the cliffs. Does she suspect what I suspect, that Andrew was pushed to his death from the very edge of that cliff, possibly from the very spot where Martha is now standing looking out to the sea? Why don't my walls tell me? Why don't the walls whisper the answer? It's been so long since I've heard the walls whisper, or is it that I've really closed my ears to what they have to say? Why? Am I afraid of what I might hear? Why am I terribly afraid lately of what I might hear? Robert promised he would arrive a few days before the weekend begins. That will be nice. It will be nice for Martha too. She bought such a pretty dress yesterday. So unlike Martha. So feminine. So provocative. I had no idea Martha had sex appeal. I suppose neither did Martha.

Martha thought she saw a boat sailing into what Laura and Harvey used to think was their hidden cove. Martha wasn't too sure. Her eyes had been playing tricks on her of late. She'd been to her eye doctor in the village yesterday, but he had told her she was suffering from strain and given her drops to relax the eye muscles. Then she had bought a dress that hadn't been her first choice. The first choice had been simple, black, sober. But the woman who owned the shop, after seeing Martha's attractive figure in her slip, had gaily trilled, "Shall we throw caution to the wind and try on an eye-popper?" And that was the dress Martha purchased. Last night, modeling it for her mother, she had been pleased by Helga's compliment. The memory of the previous night brought a small smile to her lips. And then she realized she was leaning too far over the cliff.

She was losing her balance!

Helga had flung open her window screaming Martha's name. "Look out! Martha, look out!"

Martha fought to regain her footing. I mustn't go over . . . I mustn't. With a herculean effort, she flung herself backward. She fell against a lonely, stunted tree and sat on the ground breathing heavily. Then she turned toward the mansion and waved her hand for Helga to see that she was safe.

She saw Helga shut the window. And now, thought Martha, I shall never hear the last of this. Helga will always be reminding me how I almost fell off the cliff to my death, just like Andrew. And she'll be sure to tell Robert. Will Robert act concerned?

I wonder. I really wonder.

Martha got to her feet and drew her windbreaker tighter around herself. She headed back to the mansion, a grim look on her face. There was always a grim look on her face now when she thought about Robert.

As far as Mickey Redfern was concerned, Harvey Graymoor could always have a second career as a cartographer. The small launch he had chartered in East Gate was beautifully seaworthy. The waters separating the mainland and Graymoor Island had been calm and placid. He had been warned by David Castle (of Castle Boats, East Gate) that the waters could be tricky and deceptive. He alerted Mickey to hidden shoals and treacherous crosscurrents on the ocean side of the island. Castle's advice and Harvey's impeccably accurate though rough map brought Mickey within sight of the secret cove in less than an hour. As he slackened speed for the landing, he thought he saw someone standing on the cliffs in the distance. Using his binoculars, he saw a woman and assumed it was the spinster sister, Martha. She was looking in the other direction, and he hoped she hadn't caught sight of him as he steered the launch into the cove. If she came down to investigate, he had any number of stories prepared. He had no intention of spending too much time on the island today. He liked to do his preliminary investigations by steps. An hour today. A few days later, three or four hours. He was mainly interested in locating the cabin. As Harvey had promised, there was a makeshift but sturdy pier at which he could tie up. Stepping out of the boat, he stared into the mouth of the cave. It looked like the gaping mouth of some prehistoric monster. To his left, Mickey saw a path leading upward. He scaled it slowly. It brought him to the top of the cliffs, an area not too far from where Martha was standing. He saw her lose her balance.

Damn!

Mickey's reflexes were quick. He hurried to her rescue but then, miraculously it seemed to Mickey, he saw her propel herself backward and land on her back against a stunted tree. He heard no outcry of pain; she just seemed to sit there with what Mickey thought was a look of surprise at her survival. He had heard a screech when he thought Martha was going to fall forward and wasn't sure if it was a hysterical seagull or a hysterical Helga. If the screech had been human, he hoped it was for Martha's benefit and not because he had been spotted. Harvey had assured Mickey the island was often visited by boaters and Helga didn't mind as long as they didn't attempt to trespass in the vicinity of the mansion. He watched Martha making her way down the path to the mansion and then went looking for the cabin. Again, Harvey's directions were right on the nose. The secluded hut was exactly where Harvey had said he'd find it. Mickey waited behind a tree for a few cautious moments to make sure there was no surprise inhabitant, and then hurried down to the cabin. It was unlocked, as promised.

The interior of the cabin wasn't rude; it bordered on the slightly nasty. There was the cot and the cupboard as advertised, but there were also cobwebs and field mice and creatures in the rafters that sounded suspiciously like bats. The floor hadn't been swept in months, possibly years, and as to the windows, they were a decided minus on somebody's housekeeping score. But Mickey shrugged and investigated the cupboards. Living rough was second nature to him. Compared to some huts he had occupied in other countries during other wars, this cabin was palatial. He found linens and cutlery and chose a shelf where he would store the few groceries necessary for the weekend. He checked the potbelly stove just for the hell of it, knowing he'd never use it. Behind the cabin he found the outhouse. He opened the door carefully, expecting to find it occupied not by any human, but by some indignant animal that might have claimed squatter's rights. It was unoccupied and also rather nasty. He made a mental note to hit Harvey up for a hardship bonus.

Fifteen minutes later, Mickey was back in the launch heading out into the open sea. Now he knew he was being watched. He could sense the eyes some distance away boring into his back. He headed out to sea deliberately in case whoever was spying on him was using binoculars. They couldn't catch a glimpse of his face if he kept steadily eastward. Then, in fifteen minutes or so, he would make an arc to port side and head back to East Gate. He assumed the sentry was Martha.

When she got back to the mansion, Martha told Helga the island had been visited by a stranger. "What did he look like?" asked Helga.

"I couldn't tell. He was in a small launch leaving the hidden cove. His back was to me. I was pretty sure I'd seen him coming in so I walked in that direction to investigate."

"I wish you'd stay off the cliffs. I get sore throats yelling warnings out the window. Did you hear me yelling?"

"I heard you. You saw me waving back, didn't you?"

"Yes." Helga sounded sullen. "I wish I'd been at the window that day Andrew was. . ." She was about to say "pushed over," but instead, coughed a bit.

Martha was warming herself at the fireplace. Helga's writing room was Martha's favorite room in the house. It was decorated with wonderful seascapes and furnished with sturdy but graceful antiques. Helga's desk was large enough to serve six for dinner comfortably without touching knees. Helga needed lots of room when she composed. Pages were scattered all over the top of the desk, and only Helga knew which belonged where. She wrote in a confusing scrawl on yellow legal pads and then spent hours, sometimes days, trying to decipher what she had scribbled. Occasionally in despair, she altered the plots of her novel to accommodate miles of illegible sentences. Sometimes this was an improvement; rarely was it a detriment. Her faithful readers would never be able to tell the difference. Even Helga couldn't tell the difference. Helga was chewing the eraser of the pencil she held in her right hand while trying to reread the paragraph she had just composed.

"How's it coming?" asked Martha.

"I can't tell yet. The book hasn't taken over from me, and it's worrying. Usually my books take over by chapter three. But here I am at chapter four. . . ."

"Chapter four already? But you only started yesterday!"

"I know. I'm doing this one in a white heat. There's going to be lots of blood and gore in this one." *Love's Lascivious Lips*. Helga's lips looked more rapacious than lascivious when she said "blood" and "gore" with a relish that made Martha feel uncomfortable.

"Is this a thriller?"

"A *romantic* thriller," Helga corrected her. "I've always wanted to try one, and this plot just fell into place like *that*." She tried to snap her fingers for emphasis, but it was awkward while holding the pencil.

"When do you want me to start typing the manuscript?"

"Oh, not for weeks," said Helga swiftly. "Not until I've sorted out all these scribblings. I'm such a messy worker, but that's the only way I can work." Helga's mind could be easily as messy, thought Martha as Helga jumped to a non sequitur. "You mustn't investigate strangers. They can be dangerous. As a matter of fact, I've been wanting to talk to Winston about it." Martha hoped the handyman was handy in case Helga wished to grant him a sudden audience. "I think we should post 'Keep Off' warnings where they'd do the most good. Then I think you ought to see the chief of police in East Gate and advise him that since we are two women living alone on this isolated island, something should be done to keep an eye on us." Her face brightened with inspiration. "Perhaps a helicopter patrol."

Martha was at the sideboard pouring herself a sherry. "Isn't that a rather tall and expensive order for so small a community?"

"Well, he should do something. We're heavily taxed here. And besides, I'm afraid." Martha crossed to Helga, carrying her glass, and patted the old lady gently on the shoulder. "Well, I am." She dabbed at her nose with a lace-trimmed handkerchief. "I mean we *are* isolated. Look at poor Lydia and Annette. Right in the heart of Manhattan! Oh, I do hope the New York police are doing something. Robert wouldn't lie, would he? He says they're hot on the trail of something or another, but there's so *much* crime in New York City, I should think all these investigations are just one large mass of confusion. Have we decided on the menus for next weekend?"

"Rebecca is running some up."

"She mustn't forget Robert will be here a few days earlier. He doesn't eat much, but he does eat fancy. You won't be mooning over him, will you?"

"No, Mother. I shall be quite proper and self-contained." She downed her sherry in a gulp. "I'll see about dinner." She left the room in a hurry, and Helga knew she was angry. Well, they'll all be angry when they get wind of the subject matter of my new novel. Why didn't I think of it before? No one's ever thought of using the subject matter, certainly not since Robert Louis Stevenson did in *The Wrong Box*. And here it was right under Helga's nose all this time. The tontine.

* * *

"I've been thinking," Nicholas said at the dinner table, and Harvey almost choked on his drink. "I've been thinking, what do any of us know about our *real* parents?" Marjorie was busy attacking a chopped liver appetizer.

"Does it matter, at this stage of our lives?" Laura long ago had given up any interest in the identity of her own flesh and blood relations. If they didn't want her, she didn't want them. "And suppose you did find out who they are, met them, and were terribly disappointed? What then?"

"I know one thing about myself," said Nicholas somewhat smugly while wishing Marjorie would stop wolfing her food in public. She always ate as though in fear of the food being snatched away from her. "I know I was born on a Monday. You know, Monday's child is fair of face."

"And you are certainly beautiful," said Marjorie through a mouth full of food.

"How'd you know you were born on a Monday?" asked Harvey, not quite understanding why his interest was piqued.

"I remember as a kid hearing Helga tell that to some visitor. You know how she was always parading me around like some show horse with my little velvet suit and the pearl buttons..."

"And your Buster Brown haircut," remembered Laura. "He was so adorable," she said to Marjorie, who she wished didn't have such deplorable table manners. The idea of shoving chopped liver on a fork with thumb and index finger! She didn't ever remember reading that in Vanderbilt.

"Anyway," said Nicholas reclaiming center attention, "when someone commented how good-looking I was, Helga chanted, 'Monday's child is fair of face.' That's how I figured out I was born on a Monday." Laura hoped the effort hadn't been too painful, even though it had taken place over two decades ago.

Blissfully and, from the point of view of the others, thankfully, Marjorie completed demolishing her first course and, after sucking on a back tooth for a few seconds, asked Laura and Harvey, "Were you the only two in the bunch to become close? You know, like were any of the others attached to each other?"

Nicholas giggled as he said, "Martha's attached to Robert."

"Don't be mean, Nick," admonished Laura. "Robert never discouraged Martha, not when we were youngsters anyway. You have to remember they were the first two to be adopted, and until Helga found Victor, they only had each other to play with."

"By the time I came along," said Harvey, "I thought the three older ones were a cosy threesome. It wasn't until much later on I realized Robert wasn't all that fond of Victor."

"Is anybody?" asked Marjorie, who thought Victor was a pompous creep.

"Come to think of it," said Laura, "Victor seems to have lived most of his early life in neutral. I really never paid him much attention or gave him much thought. Did you, Harvey?"

"I didn't think about him until he married Greta. I was surprised anyone would marry Victor." Harvey was signaling for a fresh round of drinks.

"As a matter of fact," said Laura while watching the singles filling up the bar, "Victor never had a face until he reached adulthood. He didn't bother me one bit, but I could never figure out how he snared Greta. She was delicate, so waiflike, so vulnerable. With hindsight I can suggest she was probably doomed from birth."

"Wasn't she terribly rich?"

Laura thought the question had brought dollar signs to Marjorie's eyes. "I don't know how 'terribly rich' she was, but she did have money because her family had money, and I know she came to Victor with quite a dowry."

"How'd you know that?" asked Harvey. "I didn't know that."

"Greta told me. Didn't I tell you?"

"You did not."

"I was probably mad at you at the time."

Marjorie showed her surprise. "Do you two get mad at each other often?"

"There are times," said Laura huskily, "when I could kill him." Her knee connected gently with Harvey's under the table, and he wished the fresh round of drinks would arrive.

"I wonder why anybody would want to kill the twins?" Nicholas sounded as though he was playing "Twenty Questions." "What do you think, Harvey?"

"I've been letting the police do all my thinking." Nick didn't believe him. "I really mean it. I've had so many other things on my mind." So Nicholas sometimes thinks, thought Harvey. "What do *you* think, Nicholas? Obviously it's been preying on your mind."

"Sure it has. What with Manx being murdered, and he had met with the girls and then with me. . . ."

"He had a date to see Arnold the day he was murdered," contributed Laura.

"Manx did?" Nicholas's voice had gone up an octave. "Did Arnold see him?"

"Arnold saw him," said Laura as the waiter arrived with fresh drinks, "but Manx was already dead."

"Do the police know all about that?" Harvey told Nicholas about the earlier meeting with Wylie. When Harvey was finished, Nicholas reached for Marjorie's hand and pressed it. She returned the pressure reassuringly. "Does this mean we're all going to get the third degree?"

"Well, you might be questioned," suggested Harvey, "but I hardly think it'll be anything as ferocious as the third degree. They only do that when they suspect you're guilty."

"Oh, Nicholas, stop looking as though someone's stolen your candy," said Laura. "We know you don't have any killer instincts." Marjorie shrieked with laughter, and Harvey tried to look as though he'd just told a very funny joke inasmuch as several diners in their vicinity were staring at the table.

"Nicky can't swat a fly," said Marjorie, dabbing at her teary eyes with her napkin.

"Do you really think Greta really committed suicide?"

Laura wondered if Nicholas had memorized a list of items of dinner conversation in order to keep the evening moving. She knew she had and so far hadn't had the opportunity to use any of them.

"That's the way it looked," said Harvey. "I mean you know as much as we do. Greta was addicted to sleeping pills. Her medicine chest was jammed full with them. All sizes, shapes, and colors. Greta spent her short married life trying to blot out everything. It was pretty obvious she OD'd."

"Was there an autopsy?" interjected Marjorie.

"Why?" asked Harvey.

"In case there were bruises on her body." I wonder who she's been talking to, thought Laura; she's certainly not smart enough to conjure up these suppositions on her own. "I think Victor used to beat up Greta," Marjorie added.

"Where'd you ever get that idea?" asked Laura.

"Oh, well, one weekend out at the island, a couple of months before she died. It was terribly hot and everyone was wearing swim things except Greta. I remember taking a walk with her and asking her if she wasn't broiling in a skirt and blouse, and she said that to tell the truth, she had fallen in the shower and there were ugly bruises on her arms and she didn't want them to be seen. I once fell in the shower, remember Nicky?"

"I sure do. You screamed the place down."

"Right. I had a bruise on my thigh and one on my shoulder but there were no bruises on my arms."

"Well, now really, Marjorie," said Laura in exasperation, "not everybody sustains the same injuries when they fall."

"Listen, Laura," retorted Marjorie in a surprisingly authoritative tone of voice that seemed to command respect and attention, "there's bruises and there's bruises. Because Greta rolled up one sleeve to show me, and that wasn't just an ordinary bruise, that was a man-made injury. I know, because my father used to beat the hell out of my mother, and we didn't have any shower for her to use as an excuse. I wonder what they're doing in that kitchen. Trying to trap a cow for my steak?"

Laura was thinking, this girl is smarter than I thought. "What are you getting at?" she asked Marjorie.

"Well, it's just that anybody who could beat up his wife could also be a potential murderer, right, Nicholas?" Nicholas nodded in agreement. "Did Arnold have any special friend among you when you were kids?"

"Natalie," said Harvey.

"Natalie was my favorite too," added Laura.

"So you were kind of a foursome?" Marjorie was now ferociously buttering a piece of bread.

"Well, Natalie and I were closer in age," said Laura, "and a girl needs another girl to talk to, right?"

"I wouldn't know," said Marjorie sadly. "I never had much to talk about so I didn't look for anyone to tell it to." Laura still silently wondered how Marjorie and Nicholas had found each other. The manicurist and the salesperson.

"Where did you two meet?"

Harvey was astonished at the ferocity of Laura's question.

"Didn't you know?" asked Nicholas with a laugh. "We met at a disco in the Village. I was dancing with some girl from the store and out of the corner of my eye I saw this girl trip and start to fall, so I rushed over and caught her and, bless her heart, she said—"

Marjorie took over. "I said, I never fell for anyone like this before."

"And that's all it took?" asked Harvey incredulously.

"Here we are," said Nicholas as once again he clasped Marjorie's hand.

"Now why all the questions as to which of us liked each other when we were kids?" Laura leaned back while speaking to permit the rather ungraceful waiter to serve her rare roast beef.

"If I know who didn't like you, then I could figure out who might be trying to murder you." The roast beef almost landed in Laura's lap. "Careful, you!" snapped Marjorie at the waiter.

Harvey was thinking, for an imbecile, she's been making an awful lot of sense. Perhaps we have sadly underestimated our Marjorie. And likewise underestimated our Nicholas. He watched Marjorie as she attacked her steak as though it was more a victim than dinner. His eyes met Laura's, and she favored him with a subtle shrug. Marjorie was now ruminating with a look of passion just this side of the sexual. "Steak good?" asked Harvey.

"Super," said Marjorie, "which reminds me. Who was the old lady's favorite?"

"I keep telling you," whined Nicholas, "Robert's her favorite."

"I know, I know, but I just wanted to hear what the others had to say."

"It's Robert," corroborated Harvey.

"Well, so what about Martha?" persisted Marjorie. "She stayed on the island with the old lady. If she's so hot for Robert like Nicholas keeps telling me, why doesn't she move to New York and stake her claim? You can't win a guy by long distance. You've got to be there where he can notice you. You've got to fight for what you want and not give a damn about anything else."

"I think Martha found out a long time ago Robert's not the marrying kind." Laura was afraid she sounded like somebody's maiden aunt.

"Is he queer or something?"

Laura smiled at Marjorie. "I don't think he's queer or anything. You see Marjorie, Robert was perfectly fine until one day, thanks to our father, Robert found out about the meaning and importance of money. From that day forward, no woman had a chance with Robert."

"You so sure?" said Marjorie with a quizzical squint. "You can't do much in bed with a dollar bill." Nicholas chuckled, and Marjorie favored him with a wink.

"I wouldn't worry too much about Robert," said Harvey. "I have a suspicion he has a very healthy little black book filled with numbers."

"Ones you can dial, I hope," countered Marjorie.

Smarter than we think, thought Laura, much, much smarter than we think. And the way she's wielding that knife and fork, I wouldn't want to meet her on a field of battle. Her eyes collided with Harvey's and she wrinkled her nose.

"Is my darling having a good time?" asked Harvey.

"Oh, sweetheart," cooed Laura as she finally decided to pay some attention to her roast beef, "I'm having an even better time than I expected."

"Me too, sweetheart, me too."

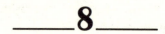

The exclusive Jitney Club on upper Fifth Avenue had been the creation of New York's immigrant parvenu families almost a century ago. It had been intended as a slap in the face and a thumbed nose at the establishments of the time who barred these newcomers from their hallowed halls. The Jitney and Robert Graymoor were made for each other, the Jitney having been patterned on the British club system. Here, Robert could wallow merrily in his "I say, old chap," "by Jove," and "the devil you say." Robert was so affected, there were those at the club who were astonished that he didn't insist on paying his bills with pound sterling. The Jitney Club made

Victor Graymoor uncomfortable. Victor's facade presented eternal youth (he hoped); the Jitney's facade suggested impending death. The dinner with Robert had been as lackluster as Victor had expected: tired mutton, damp brussels sprouts, weary boiled potatoes, followed by a sagging rum-soaked trifle that would soon plead for an antacid tablet. Hadn't the Jitney heard that the cuisine in Great Britain had vastly improved over the past decade and was now, in fact, in certain restaurants, quite brilliant? Victor stared glumly into his snifter of brandy as Robert cleared his throat and formed a cat's cradle with his fingers. Victor picked up the thread of conversation they had left unraveled at the dinner table.

"I don't think Helga's getting senile," said Victor. "She was always a bit fey."

"But Martha insists Helga is beginning to go overboard with her whispering walls."

Victor chuckled. "When I was a kid, I thought the whispering walls were enchanting. Didn't you? Those terrible stories she used to tell us at bedtime. Who dreamt then they'd lead to dozens of best-sellers? What's really on your mind, Bobby?"

Robert was warming his snifter between the palms of his hands. "This morning, in a conversation over the telephone with Harvey, he asked me if the tontine was breakable."

"It isn't, is it?"

"No."

"I suppose we've all thought at one time or another it would be nice to get our rightful share while still mortal. Haven't you?"

"I don't need the money," replied Robert sharply.

"I'm sure Harvey doesn't either. He and Laura are both doing well, I'm sure. If they weren't, sooner or later we'd have heard."

"Have you ever heard of a man named Nathan Manx?"

Victor screwed up his face while Manx's name did a few pirouettes in his mind. Then he remembered. "Wasn't there something about him in the newspapers recently?"

"Yes. He was a sleazy operator who was found murdered a few days ago. I wouldn't have paid much attention to the item, I rarely do to that sort of thing. So many people get murdered in this city, old chap, it's impossible to keep score. But then I recalled a phone conversation I'd had with Arnold, a few days ago." Victor leaned forward with interest. "He asked me for some advice."

"In lieu of a loan?"

"He asked for that too. But that came later. It seems this Manx had approached him and made him an offer for his potential interest in the tontine."

"I've heard of that sort of thing going on in Europe. I didn't know it had reached here." Victor sipped his brandy and then asked, "Isn't that one hell of a gamble since the tontine only goes to a single survivor?"

"It wouldn't be a gamble if they could buy up all of us."

Victor considered this for a moment. "Were you approached?"

"No. You?"

"No way. If I had, I'd have been in touch with you immediately." He paused for a few moments, and then asked, "Do you suppose that's why Harvey called? Because maybe Manx had approached him?"

"I think Harvey heard from one of the others whom Manx must have contacted. I would assume Nicholas or perhaps Natalie, the ones we know exist just short of poverty."

"How would Manx know which of us was hard up or not?"

"Privileged information."

"Who from?"

Robert shrugged. "Search me."

"What did you tell Arnold to do?"

"I told Arnold that if the price was right he should grab it. It's better than the odds on his outliving the rest of us. Money's my business; I deal in odds."

Victor was searching Robert's face. He was looking for a

clue, but as to what he wasn't sure. Something was troubling Robert, and he had a feeling it wasn't just this strange business of the tontine. Perhaps it was something to do with Helga after all. He had a direct line to Martha, and Martha was a Helga-watcher. He assumed she had little else to do in her isolation. And Robert rarely invited Victor to dinner of late. Perhaps an occasional drink and a very occasional luncheon, but dinner, especially at the Jitney, his sacred Jitney, breathed of matters more momentous. "Do you suspect Manx was in touch with the twins?"

"I have an idea that he was." Robert had placed his snifter on the table at his elbow and was massaging his temples. He looks terribly tired, thought Victor. I haven't seen him in over a month, and in that time he seems to have aged years. Does he have a girlfriend? What does he do with himself after office hours? Does he go to the theater or the opera or to the occasional movie? Does he frequent sex clubs or massage parlors? Does he read best-sellers not for entertainment but to hold up his end of banal chitchat at banal cocktail parties? Does he go to parties; does he do anything to relieve the tension of a day at the office? Whatever became of that mischievous youngster who scampered along the cliff top pulling his kite with little Esmaralda yapping at his heels?

Robert had caught the expression of amusement on Victor's face and asked, "What's so funny?"

Victor laughed. "I was thinking of you and Esmaralda."

Robert's eyes narrowed and his mouth tightened. "What about me and Esmaralda?"

"I just saw you flying your kite with Esmaralda yapping at your heels."

Robert said pointedly, "I think there might be some connection between the murders of the twins and Manx."

"I was afraid that was what you were thinking," Victor rejoined with a sigh. "I've been thinking it too and was hoping it could be avoided."

"You were never one to avoid anything."

"Murder I avoid. Because if there *is* a connection between Lydia, Annette, and Nathan Manx, then that means one of us is the murderer." Robert didn't blink an eye. His face was a mask. "And that's exactly what you've been thinking. Hell, I don't want to be a marked man. I'm having too good a time." He sipped his brandy. "I wonder if the walls have whispered the culprit's name to Helga."

"I hope not."

"Is that why you're going out to the island a little earlier?"

"I could use some rest."

"You look it."

"I'm very tired. You know what's been going on with the market and the economy. I feel like a juggler whose hands are becoming paralyzed."

"You need a steady shoulder to rest your head on. Why don't you marry Martha?"

"I think it's too late for that."

"Nonsense."

"It is. It's too late. But, as a matter of fact, Martha called me just before I left the office to meet you." He told Victor Martha's description of the stranger who had visited the island briefly that afternoon.

Victor was unfazed by the news. The island had always been plagued by unexpected drop-ins. It was mostly local fishermen or the occasional water skier who had lost his tow. "I don't think there's any danger."

"Helga does." Victor listened while Robert told him about Helga's insisting that Martha contact the East Gate police and demand surveillance.

"Helga always looks under the bed before she goes to sleep. She used to drive Andrew batty sending him out in the middle of the night to investigate noises."

"Another brandy?"

"No, thanks, Bobby. Let's get back to murder. What do you suppose we ought to do about it?"

"I don't think there's much we can do, old boy." Victor

squirmed. He was never comfortable with Robert's anglomania. "I'll have a word with Norman Wylie tomorrow."

"Who's that?"

"The detective assigned to the girls' murder."

"Is he any good?"

"He seems bright enough, as policemen go. I've never had much truck with that kind of mind. But Harvey's done business with him in the past and gives him full marks."

"Hasn't anybody considered the fact that Helga will also be leaving a lot of money?"

"Yes, I'm sure. But the contents of her will are a big question mark, while all of us are privy to the tontine. Damned old Andrew. Why do you suppose he hated us?"

"I've often wondered about that. I think it has something to do with Helga before she married him. Wasn't there some rumor about Helga and Andrew's partner while she was working as Andrew's stenographer?"

"Where did you hear that?"

"You know something, I don't remember. But I heard it. Maybe from Martha. Helga was always letting little odd items drop around the place."

"I always thought Helga was wildly in love with Andrew."

"I suppose she was. She would have had to have been to put up with him all those years." Victor scratched his head and then frowned at his fingernails. The hair dye was running slightly. Victor was perspiring. He mopped his brow with his handkerchief and wished he carried a nail file.

Robert stared at Victor, wondering if he dared pop his next question. "Victor?" His brother turned to him while putting the handkerchief back in his jacket pocket. "What about Helga's will?"

"What about it?" Victor had heard the question before and often. They all knew the will wasn't filed with him, but they all persisted in asking. They were like terminally ill patients waiting for the doctor to assure them there had been a wrong diagnosis. "You know it's filed with someone in East Gate. I haven't a clue as to its contents. I don't even think Martha knows. Bobby, I think you need some sleep. Why don't we call it a night?"

In a secluded booth at Dombey's, Norman Wylie sat across from Bella Wallace, holding her right hand and staring professionally at her upturned palm. "Hmmm," he murmured.

Bella's heart skipped a beat. It had been skipping beats all night since he arrived at her overdecorated and overexpensive cooperative apartment for drinks. It skipped beats all through dinner at an overpriced Upper East Side Italian restaurant where the food was as second-rate as the proprietor's origins. And now here they were, cozying up at this dingy little bar in Bella's neighborhood, a place as nondescript and impersonal as Bella's attitude to her fellow man. She must have passed Dombey's dozens of times in the past three years but she had never once noticed it. Tonight she hadn't even noticed the woman playing the piano except to give her a stern look of disapproval when she mangled a Gershwin ballad. And now Norman Wylie, creator of skipped heartbeats, was reading her palm. Bella giggled and asked coyly, "You don't really read palms, do you?"

"I have to have something to fall back on. I mean my sleuthing days will be numbered once my nose goes back on me. Hmmm." He drew the palm closer to his face.

Perhaps, hoped Bella, he'll kiss it. Sweetly, tenderly, with just a hint of passion but a plethora of promise. Perhaps he would bury his face in her palm, and then trace her heart line with his wicked, dangerous tongue until he came to her wrist, and then pioneer a trail to the crook of her elbow and then to her shoulder and at last bury his teeth in her neck with a passion as unbridled as a hungry man tearing into a steak. All this, of course, would require his leaning awkwardly over the table, thereby spilling their drinks, causing all sorts of commotion, and bringing a waiter with a cloth to sop up the damage. Bella scratched her thigh with her free hand and wondered if they'd end up in bed. (Your place or mine, darling. Mine's closer, isn't it?)

"Hmmmm," said Wylie.

Bella was growing impatient. She wanted either love or information. "Well, what do you see?"

"I see a dark stranger." Wylie was dark. Bella felt better. "He will mug you."

Bella pulled her hand away. "You're a fraud. And that woman at the piano is a disgrace."

Wylie folded his arms and rested them on the table. "She's a Graymoor."

"Oh, my God, of course. The one who thinks she can sing."

"Natalie."

"Do you know her?"

"Not to talk to. I've been in before just to case her and the place. She's awful old for one so young."

"Laura told me she wasn't thirty yet."

"Widowed three times and not yet thirty. That could age anybody."

"Three times unlucky. She should have consulted her stars."

"She should have consulted their doctors."

Bella tabled her passion and returned to business. "You've investigated their deaths."

Wylie nodded and then sipped his drink. "I've investigated everybody connected with the Graymoor family."

"Tell me about the husbands. Anything suspicious there?"

"She married husband number one when she was nineteen. She met him at a music school. He committed suicide just a few months into the marriage. Seems he couldn't perform."

"Musically or sexually?"

"I'd assume both."

"Husband number two?"

"He was the other extreme. Very macho. Motorcycles. Hang gliding. Gymnasiums."

"What did he do for a living?"

"He was a masseur."

"I suppose he rubbed someone the wrong way."

"He died of a heart attack at the corner of Sixth Avenue and Tenth Street. He lay there for two days before some good samaritan finally found the courage to see if he needed some help."

"Poor Natalie. No wonder she sings so poorly. All this tragedy's left her with shaky vocal chords. Who was husband number three?"

"He was a nerd she met at some music festival in Massachusetts."

"What was he doing there?"

"He had composed an opera based on Marie Antoinette. Not too untalented, from what I could gather. Natalie was up there singing one of the supporting roles."

"If she was as bad as we're told, I should have thought he'd murdered her rather than married her."

"The impression I get is that he got the impression she was an heiress and therefore loaded. Of course, the only time she's loaded is when she drinks, such as right now." Natalie was destroying Irving Berlin at the moment.

"She's looking very angry," commented Bella.

"I think she's just lonely and maybe a little afraid. You want to know how number three died?"

"I'm all ears."

You're more than that, thought Wylie. You're all sex and bursting at the seams. Your knee pressing mine is sending an electric charge and giving me a hunger that had better be fulfilled. And it'd better be your place. It's closer and besides, mine might be occupied by a surprise guest who just happens to have a set of keys, and neither one of us fancies three ways.

"Hey! Where are you?" Bella was feeling lonely. Wylie had suddenly gone quiet on her.

"Sorry, I was trying to figure out the song she's playing."

"'The Girl That I Marry.'" Bella fluttered her eyelashes provocatively.

"Oh, sure. Anyway, husband number three. That marriage lasted the longest, and according to Harvey, it looked like a good one. The guy showed lots of promise and had lots of hope. But then came a series of setbacks. Bang bang bang, one right after the other. So one sunny July morning, he picked up a beach towel and told Natalie he was going up on the roof to sun bathe. Ten minutes later, she was standing at the living room window putting mascara on her eyelids. A body came hurtling past her line of vision, and it took her about sixty seconds to realize she was a widow again."

Bella stared at Natalie and at last felt some compassion. "What a star-crossed life. The poor thing. But she's still young. There's still hope for a better future. Why does she have to work in a dump like this?"

"To eat."

Bella had submerged an index finger in her drink and was swishing the ice cubes around, causing a minor whirlpool. "She doesn't look like a murderer to me."

"Murderers never look like murderers. Did you ever hear of Albert Fish?" Bella shook her head. "He murdered children. Show you a picture of him. You'll see a sweet, nothing little old man. He could be your Uncle Irving. Then there's Madeline Smith, who supposedly poisoned her kid brother. You look at her and you see the girl next door."

"I think my girl next door is a hooker."

"Even hookers are deceptive, except the ones on the street, and they wouldn't take on any class if you put them indoors. You can't look at a face and recognize murder. Murder is anonymous. It's private. I'm talking about the premeditated kind, of course."

"Do you mind if I send Natalie a drink?"

"Feeling sorry for her?"

"What I'm feeling is the usual there-but-for-the-grace-of-God, etcetera."

Wylie signaled a waiter, who came to table, heard the detective's instruction, and went to the bar. Wylie then returned his attention to Bella, who was lost in thought.

"A penny for them," said Wylie.

"I was thinking about the Graymoors. What a disparate lot they are. How did Helga find them? Through what agencies? Who were their real parents? Is bad blood hereditary? If one of them is a murderer, it had to begin someplace."

"The bad seed theory?"

"I've talked to a doctor about this. He says there's no true genetic proof about inheriting traits of abnormal malfunction, but still. . ." She sank back into silence while staring at Natalie. The waiter brought her the drink ordered by Wylie, indicated with his head the identity of the donor, and Natalie lifted the drink in their direction by way of salute. The smile she had mustered was winsome and pathetic, a silent screen heroine crossing the ice pursued by wolves. "Smile at Miss Graymoor," Bella said to Wylie, "she's miming thanks for the drink." Wylie turned and waved at Natalie.

"Anything special?" shouted Natalie.

Bella felt like requesting her to stop singing but instead took a moment to think, making a bit of a performance of the effort, and then asked for "Laura." Surprisingly enough, Natalie played the lovely ballad with the delicacy and warmth it deserved. Wylie was looking past Bella at the entrance. Bella turned and saw a rather good-looking man in what was apparently his late thirties or early forties enter with a woman who was possibly a dwarf and positively drunk. "Do you know them?" Bella asked Wylie.

"I don't know the midget, but I've seen the boyfriend. It's another Graymoor."

"Which one?" Bella asked eagerly.

"It's Arnold."

"Oh, yes. The woman-eater." She felt her cheeks redden. "No pun intended. He looks a bit déclassé."

"Yes," agreed Wylie, "our Arnold looks as though he needs to be recycled."

They watched as Natalie recognized her brother and then looked bemused while she tried to understand the strange woman accompanying him.

Arnold was helping the buyer from Dallas divest herself of her mink coat, which he gave to the hatcheck girl along with his trenchcoat. Arnold then asked his date, "Olivia, would you like to sit at a booth or at the bar?"

"Arrumph," replied Olivia.

"There's a nice big empty booth next to the piano. Do you like piano music?" Olivia was teetering, and Arnold used both hands to steady her.

"Arrumph," said Olivia.

Arnold led her to the booth while the bartender stared at Olivia with undisguised fascination. After seating themselves, Olivia sitting somewhat uncomfortably as the table almost met her chin, Arnold asked affably, "Shall I order the same?"

"Arrumph."

Arnold signaled the waiter, ordering a Scotch on the rocks for himself and a double Sazerac for the lady. "None of my business," said the waiter as he eyed the unsteady Olivia, "but do you think the double Sazerac is a good idea for her?"

"It's a good idea for *me*," said Arnold coolly, underlining the last. The waiter got the message and retreated. "Natalie, darling," shouted Arnold over the din of the piano, "this is Olivia Cedarwood. She's from Dallas. She's a buyer for a chain of department stores. She's just given Laura a whopping big order today."

"Then we whopping big love her, don't we? She looks a little unsteady to me."

"She is. You sound a little unsteady to me."

"I am."

Bella smiled at Wylie. "You had planned to bring me here all along, hadn't you? That's sweet. It does help give me a perspective on my story."

"It's a case of one hand washing the other. I wanted a closer look for myself at as many of them as possible without causing any undue suspicion. I'm using you as my beard."

"I do love intrigue." She pressed her knee against his a bit harder. He signaled for a fresh round of drinks. "How'd you know Arnold would be here?"

"I didn't. He's a bonus."

"How'd you recognize him?"

"From pictures I found in Annette and Lydia's apartment. They had a photo album I studied and restudied. I know all the Graymoors by sight." Once again he was looking past her at the entrance. "Well kid, it looks like we've blown our cover. Here comes the rest of the jackpot." Bella turned and stared at the entrance.

Laura and Harvey were entering with Nicholas and Marjorie in their wake. Natalie let out a whoop of delight. Arnold waved and then with his head indicated Olivia Cedarwood, who seemed on the verge of disappearing out of sight under the table. Laura had been checking out the room. She looked from Arnold and Olivia to Natalie at the piano and then past her to the secluded booth harboring Bella Wallace and Norman Wylie. "Oh, Harvey darling," cried Laura gaily, "will you just look at who's all here." Harvey looked. So did Nicholas and Marjorie, who recognized Bella Wallace but hadn't the vaguest idea as to Wylie's identity.

"Why, Laura darling," said Harvey through a faint smile, "our cups runneth over."

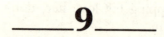

9

Had Lewis Carroll and his Alice come tripping arm in arm into Dombey's and seen the crowded booth next to the piano, they'd have shared a feeling of déjà vu. Somehow, Laura, Harvey, Marjorie, Nicholas, Norman Wylie, and Bella Wallace had shoehorned themselves into the booth with Arnold and Olivia Cedarwood. Natalie had wisely remained at the piano. It was indeed like the Mad Hatter's tea party, though there were no cries of "No more room! No more room!" The bartender thought he hadn't worked this hard since New Year's Eve. The waiter hoped the tip would be as large as the party.

And Natalie was uneasy. There's something wrong with all this, she was thinking, while tapering off on the booze. It's the sort of devil-may-care hysteria she envisioned on the *Titanic* when it was apparent there were no more lifeboats available. Even the usual reliables, Harvey and Laura, were behaving like tour guides in the Tower of Babel. Bella Wallace looked as though she was smelling bad fish while gulping double whatevers. Arnold had his arms around Nicholas and Marjorie and assumed it was Marjorie who was groping him under the table. Norman Wylie, seated on the other side of Marjorie, was entertaining the same puzzle as somehow Harvey had wedged himself in between Bella and Norman. Laura, who had been counting noses, yelled, "Where's Olivia Cedarwood?"

"I think she's under the table," said Nicholas. Norman and Arnold now knew what was going on under the table. With an effort, Arnold looked under the table and found Olivia about to favor Harvey.

"Why, Olivia Cedarwood! Whatever are you down to?" Arnold reached under the table and managed to get his hands under Olivia's arms and help her to surface. Laura hoped that when Olivia sobered up the next morning, she would suffer a severe lapse of memory and thereby not rescind the large order she had given Laura.

"Arrumph!" snorted Olivia with a saintly smile, now wedged securely between Nicholas and Arnold. With her chin on the table, Olivia stared hungrily at the variety of glasses filled with liquor.

"I think Olivia's thirsty," said Harvey.

"Another drink might kill her," suggested Laura.

"I'll get her another drink," offered Arnold with a whimsical look. Norman leaned past Harvey to whisper something to Bella. Bella heard him suggest they leave soon and countered with "Just a few more minutes." Harvey wondered what Bella was gaining from the bedlam. All it was giving him was a heavy headache, and catching a look at Natalie's sad face, he wondered what new crisis afflicted her. Laura looked around the room and realized they were the last party left.

"What time is it?" Laura shouted across to Harvey. He looked at his wristwatch and groaned. It was after two A.M., he told Laura, who responded by crossing her eyes.

Nicholas moaned and said, "I've got to go to work tomorrow."

"Tomorrow's Saturday, for crying out loud," cried Arnold.

"He's got the Saturday shift," said Marjorie.

"What do you do with yourself all day?" Bella asked Marjorie.

"I'm also working tomorrow," said Marjorie through a yawn. "I do manicuring."

"I know," said Bella.

"How do you know?"

"I think Laura told me."

Marjorie directed her mouth at Laura. "Did you tell her I was a manicurist?" Laura nodded yes and hoped Marjorie didn't know she had also told Bella she thought Marjorie was an imbecile, as she had since revised that opinion. After tonight's dinner with Marjorie and Nicholas, Laura decided they had both been vastly underrated. "When did you tell her I was a manicurist?"

Bella took charge immediately and told Marjorie she had interviewed Laura a few days ago with a possible program on Garment Center dress designers in mind. She didn't elaborate on her interest in the Graymoors, and Marjorie seemed satisfied. Marjorie's interest was now aimed at Norman Wylie, who had managed to keep a low profile since joining the chaos in the booth. "And what do you do?"

"He's my friend," said Bella, blowing a kiss at Norman, whose face reddened. "He's my new best friend."

"I didn't ask you," said Marjorie, "I asked Norman. Well, Norman, don't you do anything?"

"I'm a detective." Suddenly he was starring in the main ring.

"What kind of a detective?" persisted Marjorie.

"A very good one," said Harvey.

Marjorie cocked her head and looked like a lap dog. "You've met before?" Harvey explained that Norman had been very helpful on some of his claims cases. "Is he here to be helpful?"

Oh, yes, thought Laura, little Marjorie has been vastly underrated.

Nicholas was biting his lower lip. Olivia was trying to bite Nicholas. Arnold pulled her head back and wagged a reproving finger under her nose. Olivia tried to bite the finger. Arnold shoved the Sazerac under her chin and Olivia's abnormally long tongue began lapping greedily. Arnold was equally fascinated and repulsed by her. He had a feeling that a session in bed with Olivia would be nothing less than instructive, but he wasn't sure he was up to being her student. Arnold suddenly lost interest in Olivia and stared at Norman Wylie. He thought he heard him say something about the twins and asked Wylie what he had just said about Lydia and Annette.

"I said I was the detective investigating their murders."

Natalie ran her fingers across the keys, and Arnold shouted, "Oh cut that out, Nat!" Natalie left the piano and sat at a table next to their booth. The waiter brought her a drink. Harvey now understood why Wylie had acquiesced so readily to not interviewing all the Graymoors. He was employing his own system of studying them. Too bad Robert, Victor, and Martha were absent. Automatically, Harvey stared around the room to make sure they weren't there.

"What are you looking for?" Laura asked him, her words slightly slurred.

"Absent friends," replied Harvey.

Marjorie was jockeying back into position again. "Do you think somebody in the family murdered the twins?"

"I have lots of suspects," said Wylie affably. "In fact, I have too many suspects."

"Oh, you can never have too many suspects," offered Bella, sounding like Julia Child cajoling an unsuspecting audience into trying one of her sloppier recipes.

"I wish Manx had lived long enough for me to make a deal with him. Then I'd be safe." All eyes were on Nicholas. His eyes were wet, and his hair was tousled. Laura happened to gaze in Majorie's direction and briefly saw an expression on her face that she didn't like. Contempt might have described it, but that didn't seem quite right. She would have to discuss it with Harvey later. She hoped when she sobered up she'd remember. Wylie's eyes were craftily sweeping the table. He was looking for a reaction to Manx's name. He saw what he expected to see. Nobody was surprised or puzzled. Everybody knew Manx except Olivia Cedarwood, who seemed to be trying to crawl onto Arnold's lap. Arnold struggled valiantly to keep her in her place. "Don't you wish it too, Arnold?" pleaded Nicholas, "don't you?" Arnold stared daggers at Harvey, who was staring at Wylie, who was running an index finger around the rim of his glass.

"Harvey, darling," cooed Laura, "Arnold is giving you a filthy look."

"Thank you, Arnold," said Harvey softly, "but I have more than enough." Now Arnold was staring at Wylie, realizing the detective also knew he had been to Manx's office the day he was murdered. Later he would wonder why Wylie hadn't called him in for questioning and would remind himself that another detective from another precinct would probably be on the Manx case. Arnold was thinking about disliking Harvey until he reminded himself of the sizable check Laura had presented him with that afternoon.

"You haven't answered me, Arnold!" said Nicholas sharply.

"I haven't answered you," said Arnold suavely, "because Mr. Manx never mentioned numbers; he only requested an audience. In fact," he added bravely, "I saw Manx the day he was murdered." Somebody gasped. Laura thought it might have been Bella. "He was already dead, so I got the hell out of there as fast as I could."

Wylie said to Arnold, "You should have told that to the police."

"That isn't the first thing you think about when you come across a dead body. Ouch!" He slapped Olivia's hand under the table. "Fingers, Olivia." Olivia pouted.

"It might be a good idea to phone in the morning." Bella was pleased at how charming Wylie sounded. It was as though he was offering Arnold a second cup of tea. Wylie named a precinct and a detective, and Arnold said he would call in the morning.

"I'll get the tab," said Harvey, signaling the waiter.

"Let me," said Wylie, who had already settled his and Bella's bill before joining the others.

"Oh, no no no," said Harvey, reaching into his pocket for his wallet, "let me do it. I have a rich wife." Laura smiled sweetly, and Bella thought she looked like a sophisticated version of a *Good Housekeeping* cover.

"I wish I had a rich wife," said Nicholas wistfully.

"Maybe your next one," suggested Marjorie, without looking at her husband. She was looking at Laura and thinking to herself, you're damned right, lady, I'm as smart as the rest of you; I only act dumb.

"Guess what," said Natalie, holding her glass in the air. "I've been fired."

"Oh, Natalie," groaned Laura.

"I asked the mother for next weekend off, and he says you can take the rest of the year off, you're fired. How about that?" She flung the glass across the room, and it shattered on the floor just short of hitting the bar. "Don't I have all the luck? Don't I really have all the luck?"

Robert Graymoor's town house was one of the last remaining private residences in the Gramercy Square area. It stood four stories high and was wedged between a hotel and a reconverted brownstone. Robert's study was on the second floor, and it was here, shortly after two A.M., that he sat at his desk staring at a page in his diary. He had kept a diary since he was old enough to write, which was in his sixth year. He stared at the ceiling, searching for the name of the tutor Helga had hired to oversee his education along with that of Martha and Victor, then later Harvey and Laura. The name materialized. Cedric Longstreet. Dear Cedric Longstreet, newly arrived from Great Britain, so eager, so naïve, so pliant, so very British. "We shall take tea at four and then resume our lessons, children," Cedric would say somewhat prissily, clapping his hands for emphasis. It was Cedric who had infected Robert with his passion for anything British. It was Cedric who had protected Robert from Andrew's wrath whenever he was caught at some mischief. It was Cedric who had left the island under mysterious circumstances shortly before Arnold and Natalie joined the family.

"But *why* has he gone?" Robert shouted at Helga. "What has he done?"

"Your father will explain it to you. Starting next Monday, Winston will take you children in the boat to East Gate where you shall be registered in the public school. I think your father's right about that. It's time you children met with other children your age. You're much too isolated here."

"But I *love* Cedric."

"Yes, dear," said Helga, putting her arms around Robert in a futile attempt to console him, "but Cedric also wanted to improve his future."

"But he didn't even say good-bye." Robert's voice was a ghostly whisper.

Even now, thirty years later, seated at his desk, Robert could remember the hurt sound of himself when he realized he might never see Cedric Longstreet again. Robert sighed and reread what he had written, what he had been writing for the past two hours. He picked up his pen and added a few more sentences, then shut the book, replaced it in its drawer, and locked the drawer with the key he kept on a thin silver chain that hung about his neck. Only Helga knew about Robert's diaries. It was Helga who had found his diary shortly before the tutor's departure. Even now, with the event so many years in the past, he wondered if it was anything she had read that caused them to send the man packing. What could it have been? How could I have written anything incriminating about the man who was my idol? Perhaps that was it, Robert began to realize thirty years too late; perhaps I overemphasized my fondness for Cedric and it was misunderstood. But Helga knew better. Robert's eyes narrowed. Andrew. It was probably Andrew who chose to misunderstand. That terrible man. Yet he had been so tender with Helga. Nevertheless he had been a terrible man who had loved a terrible dog named Esmaralda and had left a fiendish legacy called a tontine.

Victor Graymoor's soundproofed penthouse topped a high-rise on Fifth Avenue overlooking Central Park. There were many reasons for the soundproofing, least of which were the exterior noises of the city. It was two A.M. and Victor lay face downward, spread-eagled on the floor of his gymnasium. His wrists and his ankles were tightly shackled to the floor. Sweat flooded his forehead, and there was a small brown puddle under his face. Towering over him was a six-foot-tall black woman wearing a leather ski mask, her upper body tightly sheathed in a sleeveless leather jacket, giving breathing space to her magnificently muscled arms. Over her skintight leather pants she wore knee-high, magnificently polished black boots. In her right hand she held a cat-o'-nine-tails. She looked down with contempt at Victor's nude body and at the number of red welts on his back. In a voice that sounded like the bass notes of a cathedral organ she boomed, "Slave, have you had enough?"

"More, more" whimpered Victor. "Beat the backs of my legs." She looked at her wristwatch, favored the ceiling with a heaven-help-me look, then raised the cat-o'-nine-tails high over her head, and brought it thundering down on the backs of Victor's legs. Victor screamed with a combination of agony and ecstasy, and the woman made a mental note to charge the perverted bastard at her feet an extra fifty dollars overtime.

"More, more. Make me scream. More, more!"

"Now listen," said the slave mistress in a reasonable voice, "it's after two in the morning and I have to be up early to get my kids off to their grandparents for the weekend. So a couple of more slashes and we're finished, right?"

"Make it another fifteen minutes and I'll give you an extra hundred, okay?"

"For an extra hundred I'd sell my mother to the Arabs." Smash, she brought the whip down, this time with a fresh ferociousness that caused Victor to scream with perverse ecstasy.

Shortly after three A.M., Laura gently closed the door to the guest room and tiptoed back to the living room. Natalie looked like a sleeping cherub, curled up in a fetal position, fist clenched and set against her mouth. Her cheeks were tear-stained, and she would undoubtedly look like hell in the morning.

"She asleep?" asked Harvey as Laura joined him at the bar for a nightcap.

"Out like a light. I'm glad you suggested bringing her home with us."

"Couldn't let little sister spend the night by herself after what she's just suffered."

"Why the hell was Natalie singled out for this succession of outrageous fortune?" She was perched precariously on a bar stool. Harvey was searching on a shelf behind the bar for a box of pretzels he'd remembered stashing there days ago.

"What Natalie needs now, I think, is a long, long rest, or else she's going to settle into a very nasty nervous breakdown." He found the box of pretzels and selected one. "I think I'll ask Helga to keep her on the island for a couple of weeks."

"Sound thinking. What are you eating?"

"Pretzel. Want one?"

"No, thanks."

"Smart. They're stale." He continued munching.

"Marjorie's no dummy."

"Where'd that come from?"

"From spending the evening with Marjorie. She's smarter than we think."

"I was wondering when you'd catch up."

"So you've been ahead of me."

"I think Majorie married Nicholas because she thought she was swan-diving into Graymoor millions. They meet in a disco, they're both attractive, it's sex at first sight. Nicholas fills her with stories of the Graymoor world he comes from, and this poor kid from an upstate slum thinks she's hit the jackpot."

"I caught a look on her face earlier when Nicholas was whining about not having had a chance to deal with Manx. It was absolute hatred."

"You sure?"

"I know absolute hatred when I see it. Like the look on your face when I've made dinner. I think Marjorie's beginning to set her sights elsewhere if they aren't already set."

"Too soon for me to prognosticate," said Harvey, now feeling nauseated by the pretzels. He dropped the box into a wastebasket behind the bar. "Do you sense any danger in the pairing of Norman Wylie and Bella Wallace?"

"Only for Norman Wylie. When she looks at him, Bella resembles a great white shark. Jaws Wallace."

"I'm just hoping he isn't telling her more about the Graymoor situation than he ought to." Harvey looked seriously concerned.

"I don't think you ought to worry yourself about that. Whatever Bella wants to find out, she will find out. The woman's tenacious. She should run for president. I'm sure she has a team of investigators probing into all of us right now."

"Robert will just love that." The irony didn't escape Laura. Sometimes she felt sorry for Robert and his abnormal passion for privacy. "And what was that tiny apparition with Arnold?"

"That was an invoice for one hundred thousand dollars worth of clothing designed by me. Olivia Cedarwood may be short in stature but she's tall in buying power. She's also very rich in her own right, very Texas oil-rich. Arnold wasn't liking you much tonight."

"I know. He'll get over it."

Laura had crossed the room to a window and stood staring out at the half-asleep city. "Could Arnold be a murderer?" Harvey gave no reply; he knew Laura didn't expect one. "Natalie or Nicholas, you or me, Robert or Victor."

"It's probably the least suspected person."

Laura turned and smiled. "Cedric Longstreet."

"Cedric *who?*"

"Cedric Longstreet, you dummy. How could you ever forget him?" She was crossing back to Harvey. "Old 'we'll-have-tea-at-four-children-and-then-back-to-our-lessons' Cedric Longstreet. You couldn't *stand* him!"

"Oh my God!" Harvey slapped his forehead with the palm of a hand. "How could I forget him indeed? Bobby's favorite. He ruined Bobby forever with his 'old boy's' and 'I say's' and 'old chap's.' I mean he was so British he made Noel Coward sound Jewish. From out of what dark recently unfathomed recess of your mind did you dredge up Cedric Longstreet?"

"How do I know? He just came to me the way I sometimes think of Wallace Beery or Amelia Earhart. I was at the dock that morning when Winston came hustling down to the boat carrying Cedric's luggage with Cedric following him carrying his umbrella and his toilet case and bristling like an angry porcupine. I remember Andrew stood at the top of the path watching the two coming toward me, standing there like some God-fearing patroon swearing retribution. But it was Cedric who was doing the swearing. 'How can you do this to an innocent chap! How dare you, sir! I'll see you in a court of law! This is slander of the very lowest! Why, that child Robert is mad, mad I tell you, mad!'" Harvey thought Laura looked delightful as she stood facing him, shaking her fist. "'My curse on you and all your stupid children! I hope the lot of you rot in hell.' Now them's appropriate words from a least-suspected person. That was thirty years ago. I was all of six or seven, and I remember every bit of it. It was my first taste of melodrama."

"What were you doing on the dock, for crying out loud?"

"Imitating you, you dummy. I was fishing. You loved to sit on the pier and fish, and I was already in love with you and wanting to do everything you did."

"Cedric Longstreet must be dead by now."

"Not necessarily. We probably thought he was long in the tooth, but I'll bet you he was barely thirty, if that. He could still be around."

"And just now getting around to avenging a three-decades-old slight? Naw. And besides, he doesn't benefit from the tontine. Maybe, on the other hand. . ." His voice drifted away as he retreated into thought, which annoyed Laura. She was equally annoyed that they were still awake at this late hour and knew now she'd never have a restful night's sleep.

"Maybe *what* on the other hand?"

"Maybe the murders have nothing at all to do with the tontine."

"Nathan Manx had something to do with the tontine."

"Right. That's what you get for bringing up a red herring like Cedric Longstreet. Say, you have any idea what brought him into disfavor?"

"Well, I remember Victor thinking Cedric was suspected of having designs on Robert."

"Oh, God," sighed Harvey. "Who could have designs on Robert?"

"Martha."

"Will you please stop nibbling on my ear?"

"I'm wide awake and I'm very horny."

"I'm sorry, Laura dear, but I've got a headache."

"We've got lots of aspirin."

Nicholas was talking in his sleep and, as usual, not making much sense. Marjorie stood in the doorway separating the bedroom from the living room, holding a cup of cocoa that was beginning to congeal. She stared at Nicholas's face, which was expressing the agony of a nightmare. This marriage is a nightmare, Marjorie was thinking as she crossed to the window that led to the fire escape. And I sure let them know tonight I'm not the dummy they thought I was. Those rich, smug bastards. Who the hell are they to patronize me? Maybe Laura's not so bad, though I sure caught her staring at me a lot tonight, especially in that dismal watering hole we ended up in. And there goes hard-luck Natalie again. If anybody needs death, she certainly does. Where's she got to go, anyway?

Bella Wallace. Big deal. Eating up that detective with her eyes. Shameless. And that lisp. So cute on the tube, so embarrassingly childish in person. Marjorie set the cup down on the window ledge and pressed her head against the pane. Arnold and the dwarf, another unappetizing twosome. How does he do it? How does he live that way? Is my way better than his way? Wylie the detective. Those eyes. They were like radar. Forever scanning the table, missing nothing. The way he nailed Arnold. The way he's probably nailed all of us.

She looked at her wristwatch. It's too late to phone now. He's probably fast asleep. And I might awaken Nicholas. She moved away from the window, arms interlaced, head down and staring at the floor, impatient, confused, unhappy.

Then Nicholas shrieked. It was a horrible cry of pain and fear. She hurried to him and sat on the bed, cradling him in her arms. "Ssssh," she whispered, "sssssh." He hadn't awakened. The scream had burrowed its way out of the recesses of his inner gut. Still asleep, he whimpered pathetically, and Marjorie gently laid his head back on the pillow. Quietly propping herself against the headboard, Marjorie examined the fingernails of her right hand.

Courage, girl, courage. There's next weekend to be gotten through and then . . . and then.

At four in the morning, Arnold Graymoor was applying peroxide to the scratches on his shoulders. At some point during the past hour, Olivia's dainty little fingers had metamorphosized into claws. As Arnold suspected, in bed Olivia became a tigress. For the first time in his life, Arnold hadn't been sure which way to turn. But Olivia knew. She grunted and groaned and mewled and puled and bit and scratched and in general made a great nuisance of herself. Arnold couldn't wait to be rid of her. Finally, when he assumed all her passions were spent, having fallen back on the pillow in what he hoped was a coma, Arnold went in search of his clothes, dressed rapidly, and hurried to his apartment to apply first aid.

I could kill Harvey. Big mouth. The cool way that detective told me to phone the other precinct in the morning. What's my opening gambit? "Oh, hi there, my name is Arnold Graymoor, and the other day I came across Nathan Manx's body with his throat slit. What was that? That's right. It just happened to slip my mind." Arnold stared at his shoulders and then at himself in the bathroom mirror. You know, Arnold, he said to his likeness, your adult life has been one long obscenity. Tonight, with Olivia Cedarwood, you plumbed the depths of degradation. What's worse, she might phone tomorrow looking for a rematch and how do you weasel out of that? You're up to your ears in poverty and murder and when she finds most of her bankroll missing and decides to yell for the cops, what do you say to that?

He winked at himself in the mirror and said, "Arrumph."

At five in the morning, Norman Wylie wearily trudged along Second Avenue despairing of ever finding a cab. First light was beginning to appear in the east but there was no hope appearing from the north. Where do taxis disappear to at five in the morning? It's a long walk to Greenwich Village, and there could be many muggers en route. Stay away, muggers, I've already been attacked tonight. I have scored with the celebrated, fascinating, never-to-be-forgotten queen of video, Bella Wallace, the kid herself. I have never been directed in sex this way before. "This way, dear." "Now this way, dear." "Let's try this, dear." "And now, dear. . ." I didn't get laid, Norman decided, I got interviewed.

And then at last when the smoke had settled and peace reigned again, it was business as before. "Do you think Arnold Graymoor murdered Nathan Manx? He certainly behaved like a murderer."

"He behaved like a suspect," Norman corrected her.

"I don't like Marjorie one bit. She's very deceptive." Bingo to that, thought Wylie. "And that poor pathetic, no talent. . ."

"Natalie."

"God, she's a character out of Tennessee Williams. I mean talk about being destiny's child. She is just ill-fated forever. I'm hungry." She leapt out of bed with an amazing agility for one who had eaten so much, drunk so much, and indulged in such heavy athletics. He knew she was in her forties, but she had the spring and agility of a woman half her age. While she disappeared to the kitchen, Wylie swiftly dressed and went looking for his overcoat. "You're not leaving me!" he heard her yelp from behind him as he had one arm in an overcoat sleeve.

"I've got early duty."

"But don't you want something to eat?"

"I couldn't eat another thing."

He promised he would call the next day. He kissed her and she tasted of salami, and he hurried out the door to the elevator. Now he was looking for a taxicab, and he spotted one parked in front of an all-night cafeteria. He hurried to the taxi and waited for the driver, his detective shield in his hand in case the driver gave him any lip. The Graymoors, he thought, while waiting. He played a game with himself. He guessed how many additional victims there would be before the Graymoor murderer was caught. He didn't enjoy the game one bit.

10

In a luncheonette across from the wharf at East Gate, Mickey Redfern sat at a window table eating breakfast. He was drinking his second cup of coffee and smoking a cigarette when he saw Martha Graymoor dock and tie up the Graymoor boat, and then with long, graceful strides cross the gangplank that led to the street. Not yet eight A.M., thought Mickey, and Martha Graymoor is already abroad on the mainland. Probably doing the weekly shopping. Mickey was almost right. Martha was preparing for the coming weekend. She and Helga and Rebecca, their cook-housekeeper, had spent most of the previous afternoon planning the necessary menus with the intensity and purpose of racetrack touts doping the horses. First Martha had phoned the butcher to prepare him for a council of war. He was her first appointment of the morning. Then there was the greengrocer and the baker and then something had to be done about flowers and table accessories. Fresh decks of cards were necessary as there were bound to be eruptions of bridge, poker, and canasta. The island's supply of candles needed replenishing, and there never could be enough emergency oil lamps, especially since the long-range weather forecast predicted storms for the end of the week. Mickey hoped Martha was planning to spend most of the day in East Gate. He paid his bill and then bought some sandwiches and a six-pack of beer to go. Twenty minutes later, he settled on renting a pretty sturdy outboard motorboat; most of the bigger boats had already been reserved by the steady Saturday fishing trade. Mickey stored the food, the drink, a big coil of rope, and a powerful flashlight and headed for Graymoor Island.

In Laura and Harvey's guest room, Natalie was awake, staring at the ceiling. Her wristwatch told her it was eight A.M., but her heart was telling her that time was running out. No job, no man, no money, no prospects. Where was left to go but up? Was there an up in her future? She sat up and stared out the window. New York was looking as bleak as her future. Her tongue felt as though it was covered with moss, her eyes were damp, and there was some unwanted tap dancer occupying her head. She couldn't remember where she was, let alone why she was, until she recognized a Modigliani print on the wall. She'd seen that print before and remembered it belonged in Laura and Harvey's guest room. At the foot of the bed, Natalie saw a negligee. Pretty. How thoughtful of Laura. With her kind of money, Laura could afford to be thoughtful. Natalie groaned and chided herself. Don't be a bitch, you bitch; Laura's always been the kind and thoughtful one. It's always been Laura to the rescue. Fifty dollars the other night knowing full well there was little chance she'd ever get it back. But now what? And how? And where? She needed aspirin. She got out of bed and unsteadily made it to the bathroom and the medicine chest. She saw a face in the mirror and almost cried out with fear until she realized it was her own. She found the aspirin. Would that they were sleeping pills.

As Laura had predicted, it had been a sleepless night for her and therefore a sleepless night for Harvey. Now he sat up in bed watching Tom and Jerry cartoons on the television screen, sipping a mug of very strong black coffee thoughtfully provided by Laura. In the living room, Laura sat at the desk waiting for someone to answer the phone at Graymoor mansion. It was Helga who replied, and there were three minutes of questions and answers before Laura was able to get to the nitty-gritty.

"Of course Natalie can stay with us," said Helga gravely. "But are you sure she'll want to? She's such a restless creature."

"I'll have a long talk with her as soon as she gets up. I think she'll welcome this chance to get away for a while and catch up on herself. As big as this city is, it can get very claustrophobic."

Their conversation then veered to other matters. There was the coming weekend to be discussed and the fact that at this very moment Martha was in East Gate doing the ordering and the shopping and would probably be away most of the day as there was so much for Helga to do on her newest novel. She told Laura the title.

Laura winced. "Oh, I think *Love's Lascivious Lips* is just what your reading public is waiting for." She hoped a bolt of lightning wouldn't strike her dead in the chair. She waited patiently while Helga hesitated. There was something the older woman wanted to talk about, but she was having difficulty finding the words. She wants to talk about murder, Laura thought, but to Helga, murder is so impolite. And then Helga was speaking. She was telling Laura this novel would be her first attempt at a murder thriller. So, thought Laura, murder may be impolite, but it can also be profitable. Laura made the right noises of excitement, which pleased Helga, and then Laura said the words she wished she had strangled at birth.

"Are you writing from experience, Mother?"

Helga made a noise that was probably a gasp. "I'll explain it when I see you. I don't want to talk about it now."

"Oh, damn me, now I've distressed you."

"Not you. Never you, Laura darling. I've been distressed for a very long time about a lot of things. The twins . . . there's so much."

"Mother, you sound frightened. Have there been any strange occurrences on the island?" Harvey had come into the room wondering if Laura had swallowed the telephone.

"The usual strangers chancing by. There was one yesterday, or so Martha tells me. She saw someone sailing into your favorite place, the hidden cove. Now don't you worry about us, Laura. We're just fine. It'll be good having Natalie here with us. She'll be safer here." Laura didn't ask what she meant by "safer." "You know what I mean. Safer someplace where she can rest and think. I love you, darling. And I love Harvey. And I can't wait till the weekend."

Laura repeated the conversation to Harvey, who said, "The stranger at the cove was probably Mickey Redfern. Good man. He doesn't waste any time. As to Natalie being safer on Graymoor. . ."

"Why would I be safer on Graymoor?" asked Natalie, sweeping in like one of Laura's models. The negligee became her, and she looked less haggard and timeworn after showering and making up her face.

"I've been talking to Helga."

"I'll get us fresh coffee," said Harvey and disappeared to the kitchen.

"You've been talking to Helga about me." Natalie sat in an easy chair opposite Laura and crossed her legs.

"Nat, we think you ought to spend a couple of weeks on the island and have a good rest. I mean you've been serving time at Dombey's, which is hardly a health spa, and really, sweetie, I think your nerves are shot."

"They are." She uncrossed her legs. "Maybe you're right. Maybe a couple of weeks of fresh air, good food, and boredom are what I need. Maybe I would be safer there. Maybe that's what I need. Some kind words, somebody who cares. I was never Helga's favorite. I was never anybody's favorite."

When Harvey returned with a tray holding three mugs of coffee and a plate heaped with buttered toast, he found Laura on her knees with her arms around their weeping sister. Laura's eyes signaled more sympathy for Natalie, and Harvey trumpeted in a Santa Claus voice, "Here's hot coffee and hot buttered toast and just what the doctor ordered. Cheer up, Nat, we love you and that's more than anybody needs."

Natalie dried her eyes while telling them she felt so foolish, and accepted a mug of coffee and a slice of toast. Then they fell to rehashing the previous evening's comedy of errors and wondering about the outcome of l'affaire Olivia and Arnold.

Being such a small woman, Olivia Cedarwood had a very small headache. Her bags were packed, and she was waiting for the bellboy to come for them. She had phoned the desk and told them to have her bill ready. While waiting, she worked on her fingernails, cleaning them of Arnold's skin. After checking her purse, she was not too surprised to find most of her cash missing. She wondered if Laura Graymoor knew her brother was a thief and a whore. Oh, well. What difference did it make? Olivia had had a perfectly lovely time, and she was sure she could cash a check at the desk. Then she thought about Dallas and what lay ahead of her. Years ago she had dreamt of being a big fish in a big pond. But her money couldn't buy that, so she had learned a profession and contented herself instead with being a small joke in a big town. Olivia sighed. It was better than total obscurity.

Norman Wylie was on the phone with Ike Tabor, the detective assigned to the Manx case. Ike thanked him for the information about Arnold Graymoor and said he hadn't phoned yet, but it was still a bit early for playboys. They exchanged some additional information that might be pertinent to the three murders and promised to keep in touch. Then Dan Wright, Norman's superior, came into the office, chuckling sardonically. "Guess who wants to do a television show about detectives?" Norman's face betrayed nothing. Only his stomach acted up. "Bella Wallace. She just had me on the phone for a good fifteen minutes. It took five minutes to convince me she was really Bella Wallace. I didn't think her type got up this early on a Saturday. Come to think of it, I didn't know her type worked weekends."

"Her type never stops working." Norman had a vision of Bella sitting up all night and staring at the telephone until she thought it was the right time to make the call. "So what happens? Did you agree to cooperate with her?"

"I gave her the usual. It has to go through channels. Red tape and paperwork. She assured me there'd be no problem." Norman envisioned Bella clearing the decks like a Conestoga wagon cutting a swath across a prairie. "What the hell? The publicity might do us good. It won't get us a raise in pay, but it might win us some friends." Leaning against the wall and studying Norman, who was making a grand opera production of going through some official forms, Dan Wright suddenly remembered something. "Didn't you have an appointment with the Wallace broad yesterday?" Norman nodded. Dan flashed his solid white ivory smile. "And you scored?" Dan hadn't risen to his position in the police force on ambition alone.

"I scored," responded Norman.

"Norman." Dan spoke his name solemnly and Norman looked up. "Whatever it is you've got, you ought to patent it and market it at a favorable price."

"Take it from me, Dan, she belongs in the *Book of Records.*"

"Hot damn! I shall give her my personal cooperation."

After Dan returned to his own office, Norman chewed over the thought of an ongoing relationship with Bella. She'd already made the next move. He decided to wait on further developments from her. He had more important things to think about, such as the Graymoors.

After dropping Natalie off at her apartment house, Laura and Harvey decided to go shopping for Helga's birthday gift. They directed the taxi to Bloomingdale's, figuring on killing two birds with one stone, maybe find a gift for Helga and see what condition Nicholas was in.

Nicholas's condition was somewhere between crisis and death. He stood behind the men's dress shirts counter, staring at a customer through stained-glass eyes. From the vantage point of ties and socks, Harvey and Laura thought he was bending over the counter at a precarious angle and feared his weight would send him crashing into the showcase. But Nicholas was only pointing at a pile of brand name shirts. The customer, hands on hips, stood back, and Harvey wasn't sure if he was coming to a decision about the shirts or Nicholas. Finally, they saw the customer mouth, "Thank you, but no," and move away. They zeroed in on their brother.

"You look as though you need a blood transfusion," said Laura cheerfully.

"What a horrible night," groaned Nicholas. Then under his breath he said, "The supervisor's watching me. Go through the motions of thinking of buying something." Harvey fingered a shirt on display on top of the counter and lavishly grimaced with distaste. Nicholas hastily showed him something else.

"Lace fringe is not me," muttered Harvey. "Will you survive the day?"

"Barely."

"And how's Marjorie?"

"I don't know. She was gone when I woke up." Laura and Harvey exchanged glances. "Did you two drop by just to check up on me?"

"No, sweetheart," said Laura with a smile she hoped would impress the supervisor that she was being brilliantly ministered to by Nicholas, "we're looking for a gift for Helga. Any suggestions?"

"I got her some imported soap. I get a discount. There are some lovely Swiss music boxes on display on the fifth floor. They've only just arrived."

"Probably cost a fortune," said Harvey grimly.

"How's Natalie?"

"Not in very good shape. We took her home with us," Laura told him, "and arranged for her to spend a couple of weeks resting on the island with Helga and Martha."

"I wish I could join her." His voice betrayed unhappiness.

After raising an eyebrow for Laura's benefit, Harvey asked, "What's wrong besides the boredom of the daily grind?"

"I'm not sure," said Nicholas, looking past them and seeing with relief that the supervisor was now spying on another employee. "Something happened last night that changed her."

"We sometimes have a strange effect on people," said Laura.

"It wasn't just the conversation at dinner, it was the madness that followed. Did I make a damn fool of myself?"

"You were perfectly fine," Harvey assured him.

"Marjorie didn't seem to think so. I had terrible nightmares. One was so bad, Marjorie had to wake me up. She seemed sympathetic enough, but I thought it was taking a big effort on her part. Remember last night when I said 'I wish I had a rich wife?'"

"Oh, were you the one who said that?" asked Laura brightly.

"Marjorie replied 'Maybe your next one.'" Nicholas kept his hands busy refolding shirts, but it didn't escape either Harvey or Laura's notice that his hands were trembling. "She didn't mean it as a joke. Marjorie doesn't make jokes. Marjorie says what she means. 'Maybe your next one.' It made me think at the back of her mind she's thinking of leaving me. I don't want her to leave me. I love her. I was only kidding when I said I wished I had a rich wife. And this is the first time she's ever left the house without leaving me a note. You know, something cute like 'I love you. See you later alligator.' Something cute like that."

Laura shuddered. She was thinking if Harvey ever left her a note like that she'd fracture his fingers at the first opportunity. "Well, if you're this upset, why don't you call her at work?" she suggested.

"I did." Nicholas spoke the two words with an effort. "She wasn't there. She wasn't expected. Didn't we all hear her say she had to work today?"

"I heard her," said Harvey, wishing he had Marjorie's neck between his fingers.

"I think she's two-timing me."

Laura jumped in. "Now, Nicky, stop jumping to melodramatic conclusions. There may be a perfectly reasonable explanation as to why she lied about having to work today." Laura could remember times when she had sounded more convincing. "Maybe she's planning some kind of surprise for you."

"I hate surprises. I think what's happened is that all this business involving the three murders has unsettled her. You know, like maybe she thinks she'll soon be a widow since it's pretty obvious I'm on the killer's list. I think she's out looking for someone else."

I think she may have already found him, thought Harvey. What he said was, "I think you're overreacting, Nick. Last night's booze and excitement. You need some food. Do you want to have lunch?"

"No, thanks. I have things to do here on the floor. The other salesman called in sick. I'll be all right. You'd better not hang around much longer if you're not going to buy anything. The supervisor's a fussbudget. He's looking this way again. I'll phone you later."

"We'll be home," said Laura as she put her arm through Harvey's and steered him toward the escalator. As they passed the supervisor, Laura smiled at him and said enthusiastically, "What a charming young salesman. I wish there were others in this store like him." They breezed past him and melted into a throng of shoppers. The supervisor thought Laura was insane. Nicholas Graymoor was a nerd with one of the store's lowest sales records. He's lucky he's so good-looking, the supervisor reflected; he only stays on the payroll because he's so decorative.

When they reached the escalator, Harvey took Laura by the hand and pulled her in the opposite direction. "I can't stand these crowds. Let's get out of here." A few minutes later, walking along Lexington Avenue toward Fifty-seventh Street and a boutique Laura wanted to investigate, Harvey said, "I think Helga should entertain the idea of turning Graymoor into a retreat. With Natalie on the verge of a nervous breakdown, can Nicholas be far behind? And I agree with Nicky. I think Marjorie's playing around."

"Oh? Do you recognize the symptoms?"

"To be perfectly frank, yes."

"Well, if she is playing around, I wonder if it's anyone Nicholas knows."

Harvey didn't reply. His mind was on murder, and Laura respected his silence. She knew there was some heavy thinking going on when he knitted his brows this way and his lips moved nervously without uttering a sound. She had first noticed that look when she came down the aisle of the chapel on the island on their wedding day with her fingers crossed because she feared that at any moment her beloved might bolt. But he hadn't, she thought with satisfaction, and she prayed he never would. Trial that he was on occasion and would undoubtedly continue to be, Laura couldn't imagine a permanent separation from Harvey caused by anything but death. Yet there had been many a morning when she had awakened and Harvey was already out of the apartment, leaving no note behind him, only the strong scent of shaving lotion. It never occurred to Laura there might be something final about such ordinary behavior. She rarely called him at his office unless there was something pressing, such as, were they dining out or in and if in what did he fancy for dinner besides her? "Nicholas is such a child," she said aloud. "If he's feeling so insecure in his marriage, he should have it out with Marjorie. There's the boutique up ahead. Are you up to it?"

He tightened his grip on her hand, and Laura smiled. She was feeling very, very secure.

Mickey Redfern tied one end of the big coil of rope tightly around the post to which his rented boat was tied. Then he played the coil out, and it seemed to run for miles. When he got to the other end, he tied it securely around his waist. A compact, snub-nosed automatic rested in his left trouser pocket. In his right hand, he held a flashlight that sent a powerful beam. Now he was prepared to investigate the interior of the cave. He had memorized all the information given him by Harvey, who had admitted during that dinner they'd shared that Laura probably knew more about the interior of the cave than he did. He was prepared for the maze of underground passages, most of them leading into each other, causing a dangerous confusion for the uninitiated. He knew there was one direct passage that led to Graymoor Mansion and the wine cellars, but it was difficult to find without previous experience of it. He remembered to watch out for the underground stream that in some areas widened into a small river with an unfathomable depth. Half a mile in he knew he would find the old slave cells. Mickey wondered if *National Geographic* magazine had ever explored here. He wondered how many innocent wayfarers might have found their way into the cave and gotten lost and never been heard from again. It was a possibility. Harvey had told him there were several cases of missing persons from the mainland suspected of having gotten lost in the caves and perishing there. But there was no evidence, and search parties had traversed the underground maze on various occasions, especially in his own childhood when Robert Graymoor had been lost there for three days.

Mickey ventured slowly into the cave. It was dank and damp and slippery and would harbor any number of distasteful little creatures in its stygian depths. Although he walked slowly and with great care, Mickey could hear an echo of his footsteps. He had never been afraid of the dark or backed away from danger, but a first experience with the unknown always left him with a longing for company. He'd never been on his own in Vietnam or Angola or San Salvador or in the Sahara where he'd almost been drawn and quartered by a maniacal Berber until they had found they shared a mutual passion for Doris Day. He moved the flashlight from side to side and overhead and began to understand how Tom and Huck felt when they were lost in the caves trying to elude the murderous Indian Joe. Mickey patted his left trouser pocket for assurance. In addition to the gun it held a reserve flashlight battery, though Mickey didn't plan to spend more than half an hour in the cave during this first investigation of it. He tested the rope, and it held secure. At the first feeling of tautness, he would immediately begin backtracking. He heard a sound overhead in front of him and stopped in his tracks. He worked the flashlight slowly until he found a rat on a ledge blinking its eyes like a semaphore gone mad. Then it turned and scurried away. He moved the flashlight upward and found another ledge smothered with bats. Harvey had assured him whatever bats he came across would not be of the rabid species usually found in the caves of the Southwest. He hoped Harvey knew what he was talking about. He checked his wristwatch. He decided another five minutes of exploring and then he would turn back. He had still not come upon the underground stream or found any divergence from the passage he was following. He was perspiring and drew a handkerchief from his back pocket and wiped his face and brow. After replacing the handkerchief, he started forward slowly, the flashlight piercing the blackness directly ahead of him.

He came to a cell. The bars were solid iron interlaced with huge white cobwebs. The door was ajar. Mickey tested it; he swung it back and forth and then rattled the bars with his free hand. It was solid iron. Mickey was glad he wasn't locked inside. He had spent a lot of time behind bars and had maneuvered escapes from a number of such incarcerations, but this cell was solidly constructed, a tribute to the genius of the artisan who had built it centuries ago. There was still a wooden cot in the cell and a stool and a hole in the floor to receive waste. To his surprise, there was also a bundle of clothes on the cot, or at least it looked like a bundle of clothes. Mickey recognized a frayed and worn jacket that looked as if it had once been tweed. The trousers had been either black or dark gray and there was a cap, and then, to Mickey's horror, as he looked closer he realized the cap was covering a skull. Further investigation proved the jacket and trousers contained a human skeleton. The bones had been picked clean. Mickey was whistling under his breath. He was not repelled by his find; he was excited by it. He moved the flashlight around the cell in search of further evidence and found it. At the base of the wall opposite the cot was a man's umbrella and a leather case. Mickey knelt and with some effort forced the case open. It contained toilet articles. He closed the case and tucked it under an arm. He took another examination of the obscene pile on the cot.

"Whoever you were, you poor son of a bitch, I hope you went fast."

He directed the beam back to the skull and then to its base. Mickey grunted. He'd gone fast. His neck had been broken.

Proceed with caution, Mickey Redfern kept muttering under his breath, just proceed with caution. With the toilet case firmly clasped under his left arm, Mickey steadied the flashlight in his right hand while using the rope tied around his waist to make his way back to the mouth of the cave. Somehow the return seemed to be taking longer. Was it possible that someone, possibly Martha returning earlier than planned to the island, would find the rope tied to the post and cut it, and then set the outboard motorboat adrift? Could Martha have had the strength to murder a man by breaking his neck and then leaving the corpse in the cell to rot without so much as a by-your-leave? From the look of it, from the condition of the skeleton and the clothes, from the amount of rust and decay collected on the toilet case, Mickey's guess was that the poor man had met his fate a good many years ago. And then he thought, might the remains have been a woman? In his mind he reexamined what was left of the tweed jacket and the dark trousers and decided only a man would have favored such dress. Mickey kept sloshing forward through the mire and the murk, blessing the manufacturer who had created the solid leather boots he was wearing, wishing he'd feel that first caress of sea air that would assure him he was out of this fearful hole. *Harvey and Laura played in here when they were kids.* Robert spent *three whole days* lost in this underground maze and survived. Well, Mickey reminded himself, kids are made of sterner stuff. Hadn't he shot the rapids of a treacherous river in a canoe at the age of ten, succeeding in making a run that had proven fatal to at least half a dozen adults? "Old Mick goes where angels fear to tread," Nolan Whitehouse had said that time in Angola. "You'd better do something about that death wish, Mick, or you ain't never gonna taste the fruits of civilization again." He could still hear Nolan's harsh, cynical chuckle just before the bomb exploded and Nolan lost his head.

The sea air. Mickey could smell the sea air. He took a firmer grasp of the rope and accelerated himself forward. He almost lost his grip on the toilet case and while steadying it almost dropped the flashlight. Take it easy. He stopped walking. He did a deep breathing exercise and took the time to let his brain settle down. The blood vessels of his temples were throbbing. He was back staving off suffocation that time when he had been trapped in a cave in Afghanistan, when what seemed like an eternity was actually fewer than fifteen minutes before his confederates dug him out. The next day, he had gone back into another cave and sat there for an hour to overcome the phobia the previous day's horror had given him. It was this determination and fortitude that kept Mickey Redfern a maverick, an unbranded animal, and still alive. He didn't worry about a lonely old age because, in his line of work, the odds were against it. Yes, that's sea air. I'm almost out. I'm almost there. He started moving again, slowly, still with caution, *there's many a slip.* He saw daylight and the mouth of the cave and beyond that his boat was tied to the pole. Everything was fine. Redfern had triumphed again. Now all that remained for him to do was to return to the motel in East Gate, examine the toilet case more thoroughly, then phone New York to tell Harvey of his gruesome discovery. He was sure Harvey would agree with him about saying nothing to the local police. Not yet. That thing in there had gone undiscovered for a long long time; what was another week or so?

In New York City, Robert Graymoor sat in the study of his Gramercy Square town house holding the phone lightly to his ear while reassuring Helga on the other end that she was doing the right thing about Natalie.

"She always had such a delicate little mind," Helga was saying by way of reassuring herself that if Natalie did suffer a breakdown, it was the result of the pressures of being an adult and not of any flaw in her upbringing. "That's why she was musical. Robert, are you there?"

"Of course I'm here. I'm digesting everything you're saying. Yes, Natalie has always had a delicate mind. Would you like her to come up right away rather than wait for the weekend?"

"That would be fine."

"You're sure it wouldn't be inconvenient?"

"Not to me, it wouldn't. The staff can look after her. I mean I'm busy with my new novel and you know how I am when I'm working. I still keep very strict office hours and mustn't be disturbed. Robert?"

"Yes, Mother, yes?"

Helga was getting irritated. "I get the feeling that you may be listening to me but you're absorbing nothing. It's one of your worst traits. You always did it as a child. I remember that terrible tutor we hired briefly was the first to bring it to my attention."

"Cedric Longstreet." Robert was resting his chin on the palm of his free hand and wishing there was some way to terminate this tiresome conversation.

"Yes! How clever of you to remember his name!" Helga almost bit her lip. Of course he remembered his name. How could he forget it? If what she had read by chance in Robert's diary was true, then the man might have scarred Robert for life. She sighed softly. So many other things had scarred Robert. There was Andrew, there was . . .

"Mother!"

"What? What? Oh, I *am* sorry! Now it's my turn to apologize. I just slipped into a brown study without realizing it. Well, anyway, I'm so glad Harvey and Laura have taken the trouble to look after Natalie. I mean, I've never really known them to be concerned about anything except each other. They've always been so sophisticated. Well, darling, let me know what Natalie decides to do. And, if she's coming up today or tomorrow, let us know which train so Martha can meet her." Her voice softened into a rare motherly tenderness. "I love you, darling."

"I love you too, Mother." They said their good-byes and hung up their phones, and Robert leaned back with a groan. *It's one of your worst traits.* Robert leaned forward, folded his arms on the desk and rested his head.

In the privacy of his motel room in East Gate, Mickey sat on the bed and examined the toilet case. It contained a safety razor, a bottle of shaving lotion, a comb and a hair brush, a package of razor blades, and, in an oilskin pouch, a hundred-dollar bill, four twenty-dollar bills, and four tens. Mickey studied the serial numbers and decided they deserved a bank trace, but from his previous experience, he guessed the issues dated anywhere from twenty to thirty years back. The shaving lotion had evaporated. The razor blades were rusty. The hairbrush looked as faded and decayed as an aging Southern belle. Mickey carried the case to the window and held it up against the strong northern light. He could discern two initials etched into the lid. They were badly faded, but after a struggle and some guesswork, Mickey decided the initials were a *C* and an *L*. He hoped they might mean something to Harvey Graymoor. Then out on the street he saw Martha Graymoor, arms laden with packages, making her way back to the pier.

She stopped for a moment to chat with a woman who had waylaid her, and Mickey was able to get a better look at her. Attractive, he decided, even if the mouth was a little too tight and the hair sticking out from under the knitted cap she was wearing seemed a bit woebegone from neglect. He couldn't judge the legs because they were encased in blue jeans, and there was no decision on the shape of her body because it was camouflaged by a loose-fitting windbreaker. As he watched her shake the woman's hand and resume walking toward the pier, Mickey came to a decision about Martha. She had thrown in the towel a long time ago where feminine allure was concerned. Maybe she didn't give a damn about Robert Graymoor any longer. From what he had heard about Robert from Harvey, he sounded more like a wimp than a potential murderer, but then, that's how a policeman buddy of his in Massachusetts had once described the Boston Strangler.

Finished with the shopping and back in their apartment, Laura was in the bedroom modeling the suede coat she had bought in the boutique on East Fifty-seventh Street. "Why, my dear," she could hear the manager saying, "it's a steal at eight hundred." "It's highway robbery," Harvey had whispered loud enough for the manager, a dowager distinguished only by a beehive of slate blue hair and a wart at the end of her chin, to hear and favor him with a frown. Laura had agreed with the manager. It was a steal and she appropriated it. Now, studying herself in the floor length mirror, she wondered if the eight hundred dollars might have been better served by psychiatric treatment.

"Harvey," she wailed to her husband, who was in the living room talking to someone on the telephone, "you were absolutely right! The coat's all wrong! We've got to exchange it! I'll plead insanity!" There was no response from Harvey. With a look of curiosity, she crossed into the living room. Harvey was holding the phone somewhat gingerly, as though it might be the carrier of some dread disease. "Who are you talking to?" Harvey waved her to be quiet. She waited for about a minute with fists clenched and pressed against her hips, then she heard him make some reassuring noises as he promised to be there at six o'clock. He hung up the phone. Now he found time for her.

"Say, that doesn't look too bad." He stood up and composed his hands into an imaginary viewfinder, thumbs outstretched and connecting, fingers rigidly upright, forming a square through which he squinted knowledgeably at Laura and the suede coat. "Very pretty. I'm sorry I shot my mouth off in the store."

"Well, I don't like it."

"Hang it in the closet and don't look at it for a week and then you'll love it."

"Who were you talking to?"

"Robert. He's invited us for drinks tonight at six. Helga phoned him about Natalie, and he's decided we all had better have a talk about it. Then we can tell him to start worrying about Nicholas and Marjorie."

"And I'll tell him about my troubles with this coat. I thought we promised ourselves a quiet evening at home."

"We can do that afterward." The phone rang, and Harvey picked it up. He recognized Mickey Redfern's voice and sat down at the desk. Laura removed the coat and laid it across the back of a straight-back chair. Then she sat in an easy chair facing Harvey, her legs curled up under her. Harvey glanced at her every so often and remembered pleasantly Laura's sitting this way as a child, especially when engrossed in somebody else's conversation. "What?" cried Harvey in astonishment.

Laura leaned forward. She mouthed at Harvey, "Who is it?" without actually speaking, but he waved at her impatiently. She settled back, equally impatient.

"No, no, absolutely nothing to the police. That's right, it's been there all these years, it can wait a little longer." Laura was consumed with curiosity and anxiety. "What were those initials again? Wait a minute. I'll double-check with my wife." At last he paid attention to Laura. "What do the initials *C* and *L* mean to you?"

Laura thought for a moment and then her face brightened. "Charles Laughton!"

"Try a name closer to home."

"I can't think." Laura shook her head in frustration.

"Maybe Cedric Longstreet?"

"Oh, right. Cedric Longstreet!" Now Laura leaned forward, her interest piqued.

Harvey returned to his phone conversation. "I warned you against exploring the cave, but now I'm glad you did. Please, Mickey, promise me you'll stay out of there. Had you gone a few feet further, you might have misguessed your bearings and walked into one of the passageways that just goes around in circles leading nowhere." Laura listened while Harvey explained about Cedric Longstreet. At the other end, Mickey's head was beginning to hurt from the overload of information he was receiving, digesting, and filing away. Harvey listened while Mickey described the toilet case and its contents. "Over one hundred bucks? Still in good shape? Wait a minute." Harvey opened the top drawer of the desk and found a pencil. He began making notes on the desk pad. "Are those all the serial numbers? I'll have a tracer put on them first thing Monday morning. Now, listen, do you want to stay out there or come back to town for a few days?" He told Mickey about the possibility of Natalie arriving in a day or so and Robert's plan to come to the island either late Wednesday or early Thursday. Mickey decided to remain in East Gate. "You're a good man, Redfern. *Ciao.*" Harvey replaced the phone in its cradle and gave Laura all of Mickey's information, including the gruesome discovery that they both agreed could very well have once been their English tutor, Cedric Longstreet.

Laura suppressed a shudder. "To think of the number of times we passed that cell when playing at spelunking." She thought for a moment and then her eyes widened as she asked, "You don't suppose that was one of *our* cells!"

"No, sweetheart," Harvey reassured her; "we explored each other in the cells closer to the wine cellars."

Laura thought to herself, 'explored each other'—why, you dear, sweet, prudish, old-fashioned darling—and then said, "Why would anyone want to murder Cedric Longstreet?"

"Andrew wanted to murder him."

Laura shifted in her seat, freeing her legs. "But I saw Cedric leave. I was on the dock fishing when Andrew and Winston were marching him to the boat. You don't suppose Winston sailed him around to our inlet and then disposed of him?"

"Do you remember if Longstreet was carrying an umbrella?"

Laura thought deeply. "He was, though he rarely used it on the Island. Don't you remember how he used to love to go tramping about in rainstorms wearing his sou'wester and that grungy oilskin thing on his head. He always reminded me of some stalwart character out of Thomas Hardy."

"Tess of the D'Urbervilles."

"Don't be cruel. It's not nice to make disparaging remarks about the dead." She sank back in the chair. "So murder's really not all that new in our lives."

Harvey knew exactly what she meant. The deaths of the twins and Nathan Manx were recent. The possibility of Andrew's being pushed to his death from the clifftop onto the rocks below would have occurred five years ago. But the murder of Cedric Longstreet would have been committed almost thirty years ago.

"Now what made him come back to the island with an umbrella and a toilet case?"

"Maybe he'd been invited back," said Laura solemnly. "Makes sense if he was carrying his toilet case. He made a lot of noise about suing Andrew for smearing his reputation. I mean, I assume Helga found something in Robert's diary that led her and Andrew to believe that Cedric had either made a pass at Robert or had scored."

"Not our Robert. I always want to think of him as simon-pure."

"And Mickey thinks Cedric's neck was broken?" Harvey nodded. "He might have suffered a fall."

"He might have."

"But you prefer to think the murder was premeditated?"

"I do."

"Okay, so who's next?"

"That's what I love about you, Laura. Heavy, heavy hangs over our heads but you remain practical."

"The thing is, Harvey, if we're about to be murdered, I for one would like to set my house in order. Such as the disposition of my business, etcetera, etcetera."

Harvey went to her, knelt at her side, took her in his arms and kissed her.

Laura said, "I hope that means whither I goeth you goeth. Unless of course you precede me and I'm not so sure I'm ready to commit suttee or whatever they call it in India when the wives hurl themselves on their husband's funeral pyre like any good, faithful wife, who just also happens to be out of her mind, should. I can see you're not paying attention to anything I've said. What *are* you thinking about?"

Harvey got to his feet and began pacing the room as he spoke. "I'm wondering if I should pass this information on to Norman Wylie."

"It's out of his jurisdiction."

"It belongs to the case."

Laura snapped her fingers. "Wait a minute. A thought just struck me." Now she was also on her feet and pacing. "Just because Helga found something in Robert's diary causing her distress about old Cedric doesn't necessarily mean it had anything to do with Robert." Harvey stopped pacing and stared at her. "Well, Robert may have seen something or sensed something or suspected something that caused him to finger Cedric in his diary. Maybe it was something involving Victor or Arnold or one of the girls." She also stopped pacing and returned Harvey's look. "Or you or me."

Harvey smiled. "You're sometimes terribly bright. Now how do we bring this up without tipping our mitt and having to explain Mickey Redfern's presence in the area?"

"That's easy. At drinks tonight, I shall suddenly start wallowing in the memory of our childhood. I'll just look at Robert and say, 'Robert, dear, exactly what was the scandal involving dear Cedric Longstreet?'"

Three hours later, Robert heard her question and stared at her somewhat stupidly. "*Cedric Longstreet?* Where the hell did you conjure *him* up from?" The three were seated in what Robert called the Music Room. The Music Room was in the rear of the house on the first floor just behind the kitchen and was glass-enclosed. It contained a grand piano, a console stereo, shelves of recordings, a bar, and a number of comfortable, oversized easy chairs. Laura had always thought it was the most charming room in the town house and suspected that Robert didn't use it too often. There was little music in Robert; there never had been.

Laura was explaining the reemergence of Cedric Longstreet. "I think I told you I was being interviewed by Bella Wallace."

"I seem to remember your mentioning that," said Robert as he served them each a perfect dry vodka martini, rye on the rocks for himself.

"Well, when she started digging into my childhood, from out of nowhere I conjured up Cedric Longstreet." She reminded Robert she'd been present on the dock when Longstreet was taking his enforced departure. "Did you ever hear from him again?"

Robert was looking decidedly uncomfortable as he leaned against the bar staring at Laura. "I didn't. But I have a suspicion Andrew did."

Harvey picked up the conversation here. "Wasn't there some talk about defamation of character?"

Robert pursed his lips and then shrugged. "Andrew never liked him. He was always looking for an excuse to be rid of him. I remember hearing him tell Mother that Cedric made him uncomfortable."

Laura intrepidly ploughed onward. "Wasn't there something about his being too fond of you?"

"Oh, no no no, nothing like that," said Robert, a bit too hastily, Harvey thought. "Andrew thought he was too eccentric. You remember, the wild way he had of walking in those awful rainstorms, and those spartan midwinter dips he'd take, making everybody else's teeth chatter. Besides, he wasn't a very good teacher."

"I thought he was all right," said Laura. "I mean he got me to understand parsing a sentence at a very delicate age. He was a hell of a lot more fun then that lousy school in East Gate." They heard the doorbell. "Were you expecting someone else?"

"Yes, Victor." He hurried from the room to answer the door, a short journey that took him through the kitchen into a narrow corridor past the dining room and into the foyer.

In the Music Room, Harvey and Laura conferred hastily in whispers. "Did I blow it?" asked Laura.

"Not at all, you were terrific. You just took him by surprise, that's all."

"I thought for a moment there he looked faint, didn't you? I mean all that junk about Longstreet's not being a very good teacher. Why, I remember Robert *doted* on him. I mean, wasn't Longstreet such a comfort after we found Esmaralda strangled...?"

"Careful," warned Harvey, "here they come."

"And here's Victor," announced Robert as he entered followed by Victor who seemed to be walking with a painful effort.

"Hello, Laura. Hello, Harvey. Robert, could I have a strong brandy?"

"Coming right up," said Robert as Victor eased himself onto a chair with a grimace.

"Why, poor Victor, you look as though you're in agony," commented Laura.

"I'm just a bit sore," said Victor. "I've been working out in the gym."

"Better go easy on that stuff, old chap," said Robert, who had seen a barbell just once in his life, and that was in a magazine illustration. He gave Victor a healthy snifter of brandy.

Laura was examining Victor as though he were a specimen under a microscope. She disapproved of his dyed brown hair and strongly suspected he was wearing an athletic girdle. His trousers, she decided, were a little too snug for someone his age, and the sports jacket he was wearing belonged on a young athlete, not on an aging lawyer. Victor took a healthy draught of brandy, ran it around his mouth and then swallowed it, punctuating the action with a contented and long, drawn out "Ahhhhh!" Then he settled back for a better look at the three and spoke to Laura. "We don't see enough of each other."

"There's the weekend coming up," said Laura. Victor had never been one of her favorites.

"Now what's all this jazz about Natalie?" Natalie had never been one of Victor's favorites. Laura wondered if Natalie had ever been anybody's favorite. Harvey took over and explained their sister's predicament, which Victor punctuated with an "I see" or "oh, yes" or "that's too bad" and then finally, "Sounds like she needs a good doctor."

"She needs some loving attention," said Laura.

"Is she broke?" asked Victor.

"Very," said Laura, "and tonight's her last night at

Dombey's. I told her not to go in, but she has to, to collect her money."

"I'll help her out," said Victor. "But she'll have to start working to get herself back on her feet."

Laura said pointedly, "Natalie doesn't enjoy charity. She's had a very bad time of it. Have you ever been to this Dombey's?" Victor said he hadn't. "Well, it's dismal. No one should have to make a living doing that sort of thing. I mean playing piano for a minimal salary and waiting for tips that are rarely forthcoming. It's degrading."

"Well, after tonight she'll be out of it," countered Robert. He then said to Victor, "Helga's willing to have Natalie stay indefinitely."

"How does Martha feel about that?" asked Victor. "They were never the best of friends."

"Whatever Helga wants, Martha agrees to. You know that." Robert poured himself a stiffer drink.

"There's also a problem with Nicholas," said Harvey. Victor groaned. Laura waved her glass at Robert for a refill. Robert took the glass and asked Harvey if he was ready for another. Harvey was ready for another. Harvey was ready for anything, but what he wanted was to go home to that quiet evening with Laura they had promised themselves. He didn't want to be burdened with Graymoor problems or Graymoor murders or speculation as to who would be the next victim, if there was to be a next victim, which, in his heart he suspected there would be . . . and probably more than one, probably an epidemic.

Laura was explaining the Nicholas and Marjorie situation. Robert was stirring the martinis in the pitcher with a bland expression on his face. Victor was contemplating the tips of his shoes. Harvey studied his adoptive brothers and wondered how it was possible for two people to be so selfishly unconcerned about the well-being of others. He listened while Victor said there was nothing he could do to help Nicholas in this predicament as Nicholas had been an idiot to marry Marjorie in the first place. Robert suddenly said Marjorie wasn't all that bad, and that personally he thought she had been a good influence on Nicholas and he was sorry the marriage was suddenly turning sour. All agreed there was little to do for Nicholas at the moment except to wait and hear what he had to say after his confrontation with Marjorie, which was planned for sometime this evening, assuming she came home. Laura was sure she'd come home, since Nicholas hadn't mentioned any of her clothes were missing; she had just departed that morning without leaving a note of explanation.

And then in the middle of a lengthening silence, Laura turned to Victor and asked, "Hey, Victor, do you remember Cedric Longstreet?"

"Cedric Longstreet!" Victor seemed to spit the name venomously. "Sure I remember Cedric Longstreet. How could I forget him? I hated the son of a bitch's guts."

12

"Why, Victor!" cried Laura with mock astonishment, "such passion!"

Victor said matter-of-factly, "I passionately hated his guts."

"Perhaps you were too young to remember," said Robert to Laura and Harvey, "but Cedric chose Victor as his whipping boy."

"And he does mean whipping boy. Cedric Longstreet was a true exponent of the British school of punishment. He found any excuse to cane me." Victor crossed one leg over the other with a painful effort. This morning he had come to the conclusion that perhaps a cat-o'-nine-tails was going too far. "I'll never forget those beatings. I can still feel them."

"You look as though you do," commiserated Laura.

Now it was Victor's turn to ask a question. "Has either of you two ever heard of a man named Nathan Manx?" Harvey told him they'd read about his murder. "Did you know he'd met the twins?"

"And Nicholas and he spoke to Arnold and me," said Harvey with what he hoped was an air of nonchalance. "In fact, I had an appointment to meet him the day he was murdered." Laura studied Victor's face and then Robert's, but she read nothing of importance. If they were poker enthusiasts, she suspected they were both remarkably good players.

"You weren't interested in the deal he was offering?" asked Victor.

"I was just interested in meeting him. Marjorie told Laura he'd met the twins and put a feeler out to Nicholas so I decided to look into Mr. Manx."

"What was he like?" asked Robert.

"Oh, he was already dead when I got there," said Harvey. Robert's mouth formed an O, and Victor was now perched at the edge of his seat, not because of the suspense but because it was less painful. With great relish, Harvey described the corpse, the slit throat, the quantity of blood, the shabby office, and then concluded with the suspicion he might have missed the murderer by just a few minutes.

"Lucky that you did," said Robert. "The man must be a maniac."

Victor beamed and said, "But Laura would have been such a pretty widow."

"Gee, thanks a lot, Victor." Laura drained her martini and motioned for another one. Robert moved to her glass with alacrity. He took great pride in his prowess at mixing the perfect dry martini, but then he remembered this would be Laura's third and he couldn't remember if she could or couldn't hold her liquor. This time Laura could read his face. "Not to worry. I have a hollow leg."

While Robert stirred a fresh batch of martinis, Victor asked Laura and Harvey if they thought the murders of the twins and Manx were related. "Of course they're related," insisted Laura, "and stop pussyfooting, the two of you. We're not here because of Natalie or Nicholas or how we're going to spend next weekend. You two have undoubtedly chewed this situation over in private and then decided four heads are better then two. Well, Robert, you may as well know we've had talks with Norman Wylie—you remember, Victor, he's the detective assigned to the murder of the twins—and he agrees with us that someone in this family is out to eliminate the rest of us and claim the tontine for his own."

"Or her own," said Robert as he refilled their glasses.

Laura thanked Robert for the refill and then said, "Frankly, I'm glad we're all going to be together on the island. There's supposed to be safety in numbers."

Victor cleared his throat and got the attention he wanted. "The four of us don't need money."

"Right off the bat that's a suspicious sounding statement," said Laura, winning a dirty look from Victor. "I mean, that's just copping a plea for the four of us. Who knows how well off we are? That's just a supposition. Maybe my fall season looks like a flop and I can't meet the payroll. Maybe Harvey's business has been in a slump we haven't discussed with anyone else. Maybe Robert's been caught by the recession and the sliding economy and the erratic market, and for all we know the tontine isn't worth a fraction of what we think it's worth. I mean it was established when? Twenty years ago?"

"When I went into business," said Robert with a smile. "Andrew was my first client."

"And what about *you,* Victor?" Victor didn't enjoy being a target and asked for his glass to be refilled. "You live as though money's going out of style. A lavish penthouse, charge accounts at the most expensive restaurants, a wardrobe that even royalty couldn't match." Laura restrained herself from asking the price of hair dye and girdles.

Redfaced, Victor stormed, "How do you know all that?"

"Greta told me." Victor's face sagged, and Laura regretted

mentioning the suicide. "I'm sorry, Victor."

Harvey intervened swiftly. "I can tell you this too, if Norman Wylie had better evidence, he'd make it tough for all of us to leave town."

"I'd like to see him try," boomed Victor. "I mean Helga's birthday is a tradition. How many birthdays do you suppose she has left?"

"I don't know," said Laura in a small voice. "Perhaps the murderer can tell us."

"Where the hell have you been all day?" Marjorie had never seen Nicholas in such a rage. The voice didn't belong to him either. It was harsh and guttural, and his eyes were bloodshot and narrowed with menace. She would have thought it funny except his grip on her wrist was painful and made her wonder later why that surprise show of strength couldn't be channeled into the energy for bettering his future.

"Let go of my wrist! You're hurting me!"

"Where have you been?"

"At work!"

"You're lying! I called you there! They said you weren't expected!"

Marjorie thought fast. "I worked at another place today! Didn't I tell you I was moonlighting?"

"You didn't tell me anything! You didn't even leave me a note!"

"I couldn't find a pencil! Now let go of my wrist, damn you!" He pushed her onto a chair and stood staring down at her with menace. Marjorie let out a howl as she rubbed her backside. "That hurt! What the hell's gotten into you?"

"You've got someone else." Ominous.

"There's nobody." Plaintive.

"You can't fool me." Dramatic.

"I'm not trying to fool you." Coquettish.

"I ought to kill you." Rasping.

Marjorie whimpered. "Nicky, what's got into you?"

"Where's this place you said you worked today?"
"It's . . . it's . . . it's in Brooklyn Heights."
"You never mentioned it before."
"I never worked there before."
"What's the name?"
"Oh, Nicky!" howled Marjorie.
"The name, Marjorie, the name!"

She sank back into the chair, wondering if he was really capable of murder. She knew she wasn't capable of telling him the truth. She didn't dare. "Nicky, I wanted to be alone. I wanted to be by myself and to think. About us and about where we're heading."

"There's another man."

She leaned forward in a crouch like a tigress about to spring. "There's going to be another man if you don't start deciding what you want to be when you grow up."

He slapped her so hard, she fell off the chair. She sat on the floor staring at his shoes, absolutely astonished. Nicholas stepped backward, both surprised and dismayed by the violence.

"I'm sorry," he finally said.

"Sure."

"I mean it. I'm sorry, Marjorie. I didn't mean to do that." He moved to help her to her feet, but she pushed him away. "Don't think of leaving me, Marjorie.'" He was a little boy again. "I mean, don't embarrass me until after the weekend."

She was on her feet and rummaging in her handbag for her makeup kit. She knew her lipstick was smeared and her mouth needed redoing. "Just don't lay another finger on me. Just don't you try that again or you'll be minus a hand."

Nicholas went into the kitchen and sat at the table in the dark. He hadn't the vaguest idea what to do next. He had rehearsed the previous scene with Marjorie while walking home from work. But slapping her face had been totally unexpected, an improvisation. He knew there was violence in him, lurking somewhere waiting to be unleashed, the way he had screamed and kicked and scratched his way through childhood. He had heard Andrew angrily say to Helga, "That child's a time bomb. One of these days he's going to explode and detonate the lot of us!"

"Stop picking on him, Andrew. All you ever do is pick on him, just because he's the smallest!" What she had really meant to say was, "Just because he's the weakest."

Marjorie came to the door of the kitchen and said sympathetically, "Now Nicky, stop crying. Please, Nicky, you sound just awful." She went to him and put her hands on his shaking shoulders. "Now stop it, Nicky. Okay, I forgive you. Let's go out and eat a pizza or something."

Or something, thought Nicholas. That about sums us up. *Or something.*

"Some quiet evening at home," said Laura with a pout as she unpacked the containers of food they had picked up at a delicatessen on their way home. Harvey had located Norman Wylie at his precinct and invited him up for a drink. The invitation included dinner if Norman was available, but Norman wasn't. Laura and Harvey had hashed and rehashed their hour or so with Robert and Victor and come to the conclusion that both men were behaving amazingly coolly and calmly in the face of the threat of murder. Harvey joined Laura in the kitchen carrying two freshly concocted martinis and was awarded with a look of gratitude. As Laura dumped potato salad into a deep dish, she asked, "Which one of them's a killer?"

"They're both killers," said Harvey as he dug into the potato salad with his fingers. Laura slapped his hand away. "I'm referring, of course, to their business dealings. We know from experience that Victor is ruthless, and from hearsay I gather the same is true of Robert."

"They were monstrous kids. At least to me they were." Laura was slicing a tomato to perk up the sorry-looking coleslaw. "You know, I never realized it was Andrew who set Robert up in business."

"I heard it from Helga, but I don't remember when or why. Probably one of those storm-tossed nights on the island when the electricity had failed and we were boozing by candlelight, she nipping at the port and me nipping at her memory and Helga all warm and cozy and gossipy." He sipped his drink and then began poking into the other packages. "I'd like to get her into that kind of mood again and then bring up Cedric Longstreet and the strangulation of Esmaralda and why Robert remained lost in the underground maze for three days."

"How many search parties did it take to find him?"

"Five. Andrew led one of them."

"In circles, I bet. Robert was positively not one of his favorites." The doorbell rang, and Harvey went to greet Norman Wylie. After settling in the living room with drinks and nibbles for all, Harvey told Wylie about Mickey Redfern's adventure that morning and the discovery of the remains they had decided had once been Cedric Longstreet. "And don't tell Bella Wallace," concluded Harvey.

At this moment Bella was the least of Wylie's problems. What had begun as the simple murder of two naïve twin sisters was now broadening into a case that was beginning to boggle Wylie's mind. "So we go from this Longstreet to the possibility that your father was pushed off a cliff to the twins and Nathan Manx." He exhaled loudly and then clasped his hands behind his head with an impish expression. "I think you're going to need more protection than your buddy Redfern this coming weekend."

"You think the murderer would dare strike while we're all together on the island?" Laura was looking surprisingly ingenuous.

"Lady, to say the least, we are dealing here with a most unusual criminal. I mean the first murder takes place some twenty-five or thirty years ago depending when and why this Longstreet came back to the island after his banishment. Also it's not going to be that easy proving murder from a cot full of bones, regardless of the broken neck. That could have taken place from a fall in that cave, which I gather I'd sooner avoid.

Then some twenty or twenty-five years later the old man takes a dive and even there we can't prove murder because as far as we know there were no witnesses or. . ."

"Or there was a witness who for some reason or another has chosen to remain silent." Harvey was wondering if he could handle another martini.

"Right," said Wylie. "Now five years later we get the twins and Nathan Manx, and the catalyst for these crimes appears to be the tontine. And if I could, I'd keep the lot of you from leaving town."

Harvey said to Laura, "What did I tell you?"

"Nothing's keeping me from leaving town," said Laura. "The way I'm beginning to feel, and I mean terribly frightened, I don't know whether to go to pieces or to Paris."

"We're going to Graymoor," said Harvey, his decision being to risk another martini. "And we're going to trap a murderer. You see Norman, the killer knows we're on to him. He's going to have to do something very foolish. I know it sounds corny. . ."

"Hell, no. Most logical thinking is corn and six feet tall." Wylie scratched a knee and wished he could spend the rest of the evening with Harvey and Laura. They were his kind of people. But just a few blocks north of here waited a panther in her overdecorated living room whose invitation was a subterfuge for discussing a future program about the activities of a police precinct. But this panther was really more interested in getting her claws into him, and Wylie had not yet fully recovered from the previous night's encounter.

"I think Helga could break this case for us without realizing it." Harvey had Wylie's attention again. Laura sat with her arms folded around herself, thinking about turning up the heat. "My older brothers are all for closing ranks and protecting her, but I think she's the only one who doesn't need protecting."

"She's part of the tontine." Wylie sounded as though he were pronouncing sentence.

"Helga's safe." Harvey smiled at Laura. "Cold, sweetheart?"

"Freezing. I may succumb to a natural death." Harvey crossed to the automatic switch and turned up the heat.

"Why do you think Helga could break this case?" Wylie desperately wanted to meet Helga Graymoor.

"I think she knows who the murderer is. And when I get her alone on the island, I intend to ask her."

Wylie sat up straight. "Why don't you phone her now and ask her?"

"When you want to know something from Helga, it's got to be a one-on-one confrontation. You see, she won't answer a question until she's sure of the answer. I said I *think* she knows who the murderer is, but maybe she's not sure yet. That's what this coming weekend is all about. It's not so much a celebration as the opportunity for Helga to come to a decision. Another drink?"

"No, thanks, I'd better be on my way," said Wylie with a weary sigh.

Laura's eyes twinkled. "You sound like you're in for a rematch with a famous network personality."

"I never met a woman before who didn't understand the meaning of a one-night stand." Wylie shook his head sadly from side to side and then told them of Bella's latest ploy, the program about the police precinct.

"If her energy were properly channeled," commented Laura, "she could rule the world."

"That's the trouble. She thinks she does. And my superior insists I play ball with her. Little does he know. Thanks for the drink and the information. I'll call you tomorrow."

After Wylie left, Harvey followed Laura into the kitchen where she set the table and they finally sat down to dine. Neither one had much appetite, and finally Laura said, "I could kill our father."

"He's already dead."

"I know. But not soon enough."

* * *

It was almost time to leave for Dombey's, and Natalie Graymoor was working hard to camouflage her tired face. She had spent the day alone in the studio apartment, dialing the weather, Dial-a-Joke, and her horoscope just to hear another voice. She had eaten very little, but drunk a great deal. She brooded and brooded and then, like a healthy hen, eventually hatched an idea that might rescue her from her bleak future. She didn't want to spend any more time than necessary on Graymoor Island. She wanted to get out of New York and into a fresh beginning. And she finally decided how to get her hands on the sum of money she needed. Under her breath she hummed "California, Here I Come" and then snarled at her reflection in the mirror. "You're not yet thirty, how dare you look like a hag of sixty?" Then with a brazen smile at the prospect of a better future, she blew her reflection a kiss and gathered up her coat and handbag, prepared to sally forth and endure her closing night at Dombey's.

A heavy wind attacked Graymoor Island, and the howling outside the windows of the mansion caused Helga to comment to Martha that it sounded like the dead were arisen and abroad. Martha had been busy checking all the rooms to make sure doors and windows were secured, hesitating for a while in the room Natalie would occupy. It had been little changed since Natalie's childhood. None of the rooms had been changed since their childhood. It was the way Helga wanted it, ten shrines at which there was no one to worship.

Now, in the writing room, Martha sat near the fireplace knitting, watching Helga at the desk rereading some copy. Then Helga put down the red pencil that she used for editing and spoke to Martha. "I think Natalie is unbalanced."

"What do you mean?"

"The strange things she said to me on the phone. First she said she's looking forward to the weekend and I told her how glad I was she'll be remaining after the others leave and then she said she's planning to go to California!"

"What's she using for money?"

"I asked her, and she said not to worry, it was in hand. I wonder if I should call Robert and ask him what he knows about this."

"Why bother? Natalie was always the strange one. Always a bit fey. Father was always saying she needed to be chased with a butterfly net."

Helga stared at Martha, whose head was bowed to her knitting, the clicking needles a weak counterpoint to the angry winds outside. "Natalie sounded manic."

Martha stopped knitting and returned Helga's look. "Mother, you're well aware that Natalie's a pill popper. She takes pills to be happy and pills to be sad. Pills to put her to sleep and pills to awaken her. This is Saturday night, her last night on the job. I'm sure she's on happy pills. Next weekend, she'll arrive sad and depressed as she usually does."

"She's had such bad luck."

"She has such bad taste. Look at the men she married."

"I tried to discourage her, but you could never tell Natalie anything. She was always the headstrong one. It's a good thing she's not here tonight. You know what the howling wind does to her. She'd be out there flying about caroling some Wagner." Martha winced at the thought. Martha winced at the thought of an additional two weeks of Natalie. Maybe it's not a pipe dream. Maybe she fell into a windfall. Maybe she's really going to California after all. Away from us. Away from danger. "You're frowning," Helga said.

"I wasn't aware I was frowning. Would you like some hot cocoa?"

"Oh, yes, what a good idea. And how's for a game of Scrabble? We haven't played in days."

Martha acquiesced and then left Helga to go to the kitchen. Hot cocoa. Scrabble. How much longer, oh Lord, how much longer?

* * *

So it's money you want, you little bitch. It's money, is it? You know what I did, do you? Okay, you little bitch, you want what's coming to you?

That's just what you're going to get.

13

The man who was assumed to be one of the owners of Dombey's was named Nick Hobart, but the bartender referred to him as the Cheshire Cat. He materialized twice a week, always on Saturday night, because it was the busiest night of the week, and on one other night, which he seemed to select at random so as to keep his staff guessing. Nick was short and squat and reminded Natalie of the otiose toad that used to inhabit the lily pond behind Graymoor Mansion. Natalie had once caught the toad and kissed it, but it hadn't turned into a prince. It took her days to shake the scaly taste. Tonight she couldn't shake Hobart. He stood behind the bar at the cash register watching her perform at the piano through hooded lids, and Natalie wondered if he was considering rescinding her dismissal. She was cold sober and playing better than ever, now that she could tell the white keys from the black. The bar was jammed with singles mostly performing the eloquent body language reserved for Saturday nights and the desperately lonely. There were some dollar tips in the glass Natalie kept atop the piano. Even the diners were eating without complaint. After her first visit to the kitchen, Natalie had never set foot in it again. She wondered how much Hobart was bribing the inspector from the Department of Health. Tonight Natalie was feeling gloriously alive and independent, and her mood was infectious. At the bar, several drinkers sang along with her, and even the bartender was impressed. Thought Natalie, I'll bet he too is wondering if Hobart is changing his mind about me. Little toad. Ugly little toad. Change your mind if you like. Come crawling to me if it suits you. It won't do you a damned bit of good. Not one damned bit of good. Her fingers caressed the keyboards with "I Guess I'll Have To Change My Plans."

"What's that you're playing?" asked a pretty little thing.

"Why, this is just a private joke," said Natalie and then softly crooned the words. "Change my plans?" Fat chance.

Laura was on the phone, hating this Saturday night worse than she hated Labor Day Weekend. Harvey was at the stereo looking for his favorite Brahms. He heard Laura say, "He didn't!" Harvey stepped down from the chair on which he was balanced and stared at Laura.

Her hand over the mouthpiece, she stage-whispered, "Nicky took a sock at Marjorie!"

"Goodness," murmured Harvey.

Marjorie was curled up on the couch sobbing into the phone. "I mean the things he's accused me of. I've tried to call Robert and tell *him,* but all I get the past hour is a busy signal."

"Maybe his phone's out of order," suggested Laura.

"It's Nicholas who's out of order! How dare he accuse me of having a lover!"

"Do you?" Laura had always been practical.

"Oh, not you too! Where'd your parents find you orphans? In some nuthouse?" Marjorie rolled a tissue into a ball and dabbed at her eyes.

"Where's Nicholas now?"

"How should I know? After he hit me he went into the kitchen and started crying!"

"Well, Nicky was always a softie." Imagine Nicholas hitting Marjorie, thought Laura. She covered the mouthpiece again and repeated the thought to Harvey. Harvey shrugged. He was reminded of Noel Coward's line, "Women should be struck regularly, like gongs," and his shoulders heaved as he started chuckling. Laura covered the mouthpiece again and asked, "What's so funny?"

"Noel Coward."

"What's he got to do with this?" Harvey ignored the question and chose to resume his search for the Brahms. He wondered if their cleaning woman had borrowed it again.

Marjorie now had the dry heaves and spoke with difficulty. "You . . . you should have heard . . . you . . . should . . ."

"Marjorie, you've got the dry heaves," advised Laura. "Take five deep breaths and it'll go away." She wished Marjorie would go away, but she'd learned a long time ago wishing won't make it so.

Marjorie was back in command and in full voice. "When I tried to console him, he shoved my hand aside *brutally*. Then he got up and went for his coat and opened the front door and then he yelled at me in this horrible voice, 'One of these days you're gonna get what's coming to you' or something like that and then he slammed the door behind him and that was more than two hours ago."

"And I thought you two were so happy," said Laura in what she hoped was her best Dear Abby voice. "What's gone wrong?"

"I'll tell you what's gone wrong. I have matured. I have outgrown him. I've gotten wise to what's going on in this world." You sure have, thought Laura, and I'll bet one day you write a best-seller. "Now I know there's something better out there than what I've got, and I want mine." And I'll bet you get it, sweetie, my money's on you.

Laura's hand was back on the mouthpiece as she called for Harvey's attention. "Boy, what you are missing." Harvey said nothing, knowing he'd soon get the replay. The Brahms was missing, and he was annoyed. Curse Laura for hiring an intellectual daily. Why couldn't she find one of those stereotyped slatterns who inspired situation comedies? Laura was speaking into the phone. "Marjorie, I respect everything you tell me. You absolutely know your own mind, but I get the feeling you don't know Nicky's."

"I've been trying," she wailed, "but ever since that Nathan Manx whetted his appetite for ready cash, there's been no living with him. I mean the past two days have been hell except for last night when I had more fun than I've had since the first time I ran away from home." Laura dreaded ever having to listen to what took place during that misbegotten adventure. "First he's running scared like a mouse afraid he's going to be knocked off and then all of a sudden he becomes the menace. I tell you he's Jekyll and Hyde!"

"Now look, Marjorie, you called me for advice so I'm going to give it to you." She exchanged a worried look with Harvey, who was now sitting behind the bar munching on a stale pretzel from a cannister on a shelf. Nothing behind this bar but stale pretzels. Why don't we have some stale potato chips? He concentrated on Laura, who seemed to mean business. "When he gets back tonight, be friendly and affectionate. Nicky needs a lot of affection." She suddenly wondered if he had ever had any friends.

"Supposing he doesn't come home tonight? Well, he'd better, damn it, I don't want to sleep alone in this place."

"He'll come home. I know Nicky. Then in the morning, tell him you want bygones to be bygones and you've got to do this for the sake of the weekend. I mean we can't dump any more aggravation on Helga. She's an old lady, and she's very frail."

"Ha!" bellowed Harvey, and Laura shushed him.

To Marjorie's query Laura said, "That was only Harvey. We're supposed to be spending a quiet evening at home. The next time we'll try it in a hotel suite. Now has what I have said sunk in?"

"Yes. I don't want to screw up the weekend. I want to wear that gorgeous thing you gave me." Laura cringed. *Thing.* "I'm sorry I interrupted your quiet evening at home, but I had to talk to somebody."

"Of course, darling, that's what family is for. Why don't you take a pill and go to sleep?"

"I'm all out of them."

Laura mentioned other remedies for inducing sleep but stopped short of suggesting a hammer blow to the skull, and then hung up. She leaned back in the chair, hands hanging limply at her side, and said hoarsely, "What a night."

"Isn't this blow up between them rather sudden?" Harvey was spraying seltzer into a mug of Campari.

"Not on Marjorie's side. She's obviously been festering for months."

"Did he only hit her once?"

"How many times does he have to hit her? Mix me one of those."

"Drink this one. I'm going out for the newspapers. Then we can snuggle into bed and do the crossword puzzle together."

Laura crossed to him to claim the drink and murmured, "Some girls have all the luck." Then she shivered.

"What's wrong?"

"I think somebody just walked across my grave."

Nicholas sat in the last row of the cinema, eyes glued to the screen but absorbing nothing. He didn't even know the name of the movie. It had been the only cinema on Third Avenue that didn't have a line of customers snaking around the block, so he had gone in. He slouched in his seat, his right leg sprawled out into the aisle as though waiting to catch and trip some unsuspecting patron. His brain was a maelstrom of emotions. There was anger and self-pity and hatred, a witch's brew, a poisonous concoction. Methinks the lady doth protest too much. There's another man, he thought. There has to be. Who could it be? When did it begin? She's done nothing to make me suspicious until today. Why was she so dumb about it? Why'd she say she was working today and then leave without writing me a note?

Because she wanted me to know.

Nicholas groaned, and a woman seated in front of him hurriedly moved to another row. She wanted me to know. She's going to leave me and I can't stand it. She was so animated at dinner last night with Laura and Harvey. I was so proud of her. And she certainly held her own later at Dombey's. He sighed. She's not the Marjorie I married. Not the sweet, simple, uncomplicated kid I picked up in a disco.

"Picked her up in a disco?" Helga had piped. "I don't believe it. Romances don't begin that way." Not in the books Helga wrote. Her protagonists met on yachts, on the ski slopes of Gstaad, during intermission at the opera, and just once on a jetliner that seemed on the verge of crashing. But a disco? "Who is she? What do you know about her? What about her family?"

"Who am I?" asked Nicholas. "What do I know about me? Who was my family?"

"You were especially selected," Helga had said grandly, as though conferring a knighthood on him. And in a way, thought Nicholas, she had. We were all especially selected. But that was the only luck we had in common. When the fates got to me and the twins, they ran out of special favors. Now the twins are dead and Marjorie is probably planning to leave me.

Or maybe I'll help Marjorie leave me.

He heard a horrendous shriek and sat up sharply, eyes blinking rapidly. On the screen, a hideous monster was pursuing a young girl through a nightmare forest. The monster was threatening her with a hatchet. She tripped over something. The monster leapt on her and brought the hatchet crashing down on her neck. Crrrrrunch. Off with her head. Someone in the audience laughed. It was Nicholas.

The oldie proclaimed Saturday night as the loneliest night of the week, and this Saturday night Arnold Graymoor was inclined to agree. It was after midnight, and he was at the bar of a celebrity haunt on the Upper East Side. Janie's was famous for familiar faces and lonely middle-aged ladies, but tonight Arnold didn't recognize anybody and the smattering of middle-aged ladies in the room were accompanied by middle-aged men. The bar was too crowded to be comfortable, and as always, the drinks were undernourished and overpriced. He was trying to decide on his next port of call while visiting the men's room in the rear of the restaurant. At a secluded table under a Murillo print he saw Norman Wylie and Bella Wallace. Wylie was stifling a yawn, and Bella was stifling her libido.

"Well, hello there!" Bella and Wylie looked up. "So we meet again!"

Bella didn't recognize Arnold. Wylie did. "It's Arnold Graymoor," he reminded Bella. "You two met last night."

"Oh, of course," said Bella with an artificial smile. "I thought you were but I wasn't sure. I was a bit hazy last night, wasn't I?"

"Weren't we all," said Arnold, waiting to be invited to join them.

"I'd ask you to join us," said Wylie, who knew exactly what Arnold was waiting for, "but we've just paid the tab. I've got an early morning call."

"Oh, that's okay. I've got a late date. Just killing time and stopped in here for a quick one."

"How'd you make out with Dallas, what was her name?" Wylie was snapping his fingers, trying to remember Olivia Cedarwood's name.

"Olivia Cedarwood," prompted Arnold.

"Oh, the midget thing," Bella suddenly remembered. "Wasn't she spending an awful lot of time under the table?"

"She was a bundle of eccentricities," said Arnold with a smile. He gave Wylie a knowing wink that Bella didn't miss. "Well, it was nice seeing you again." He continued to the men's room, feeling foolish for even thinking they'd ask him to join them. Bella Wallace was a middle-aged lady, and middle-aged ladies usually melted at the sight of him, yet Bella Wallace didn't get his message. He must be losing it, that must be what was happening, he was losing it, and he had to decide on the alternative. A profitable alternative.

Wylie hailed a cab. He helped Bella in, got in beside her, slammed the door shut and gave the driver Bella's address.

"Coming up for a nightcap?" she asked coyly.

"Sorry, Bella, I really do have an early morning tomorrow and," he emphasized with good humor, "I had absolutely no sleep last night."

"All right, darling," she reached over and took his hand, "I'll give you a raincheck." She squeezed his hand. He managed half-heartedly to respond in kind. "I think we're beginning to shape up the precinct story. I should come down and spend some time there to get the feel of the place."

"The boys will love that." Wylie suppressed a grimace.

"Do you suppose I ought to watch an autopsy?"

"Autopsies take place at the morgue."

"Oh. Then can I watch you grill someone?"

"That kind of questioning mostly takes place in the movies."

"Well, then what do you really do all day?"

"We work very hard, Bella, we work very, very hard." They rode for a while in silence, Bella wondering if her pursuit of Wylie was just another Bella mistake. Wylie stared out the window and wondered why people thought police work was glamorous. It was tedious and tiresome and cursed with repetition and dreary trips down blind alleys. It was rewarded with contempt and suspicion and hatred, and nice, hard-working guys were labeled pigs or targeted for murder. "Hero Cop Shot in Bar." Cops should stay out of bars when they're off duty, thought Wylie, or at least carry their service revolvers with them. Sometimes the job had its rewards, like this Graymoor case. It gave him two new friends, Laura and Harvey. He hoped they'd remain friends once the case was wrapped up.

The wrap-up. How far away was he from the wrap-up? Cedric Longstreet. Andrew Graymoor. Lydia Graymoor. Annette Graymoor. Who was next? What was the pecking order? Who was conducting this vicious orchestration of murder? What about Mickey Redfern? Where did Harvey touch base with him first time out? Was it an ad in one of the two popular mercenary journals, *Soldiers of Fortune* or *Gung Ho?*

"Arnold's the playboy of the family, isn't he?"

"Yes, for want of a better description," replied Wylie.

"He's rather attractive, I suppose. I hadn't noticed last night." She cozied up to him. "That's because I only had eyes for you."

"Now see what you've been missing?"

"Well, Arnold is sort of a cutie."

"He might also be a murderer."

The cab driver almost sideswiped a bus.

Marjorie drained a glass of wine and then drank a cup of warm milk, but neither induced slumber. She glanced at her wristwatch. It was after two in the morning. Where the hell was Nicholas? What was the damn fool up to? She wondered if he was with Laura and Harvey but didn't dare phone now, in case he was not there and they were asleep. She dialed Robert's number again. It was still busy. Earlier she had reported the number as being out of order. That wasn't all that was out of order. Nicholas was out of order. She was out of order. The whole damned family was out of order.

She heard a noise on the fire escape.

Marjorie froze. She heard the noise again. She wondered if she should scream or just open the blinds and have a look. The window was tightly secured, she had seen to that. She opened a drawer and selected a carving knife. Then cautiously she tiptoed to the window. Even more cautiously she opened the blind. She came face to face with a pigeon. It was as startled as she was and flew off. She shut the blind and had another glass of wine.

She thought she heard a noise at the door. "Nicholas?" She hurried to the door. "Nick?" There was no reply. She backed away from the door and sat down, still holding the knife. Had the twins been this frightened that awful night when they were murdered, she wondered. There were two of them, but they were still no match for the killer. And Marjorie was alone. Just Marjorie and a carving knife. And if I have to, she decided, I'll use it.

Victor wasn't enjoying skulking in the doorway. It was almost three in the morning, and there was still no sign of the bitch. He worried that a prowl car might come by and discover him. How would he explain himself? Sorry officers, but I'm waiting for a nasty bitch to come home. I plan to ambush her and really let her have it. She wouldn't come to my place. Oh no, not her, not to my place anymore. I'm going to really let her have it. She's going to get what's coming to her.

The house was quiet. The phone was off the hook. He made his way from the Music Room to the kitchen with stealth and determination. Then he went up the stairs to the bedroom. Cautiously, he opened the bedroom door and went in. The drapes weren't drawn, and the room was flooded with moonlight. Should he have replaced the phone on the hook? The hell with it. He went to the bed and sat down. He needed sleep so badly but there was so much to do, so little time in which to do it. So little time.

"I'm dying for a pizza," said Laura.

"At this hour of the night? It's after three!" Harvey's eyes widened with apprehension. "My God, you're not pregnant, are you?"

"No, I'm not pregnant; I'm just dying for a pizza. Come on, darling, go down to the all-night place and get one with all the trimmings. Pretty please?"

* * *

It was almost four in the morning when Natalie reached the entrance to her apartment house. There was no doorman. It was a prewar building with a new owner who was planning to convert it into a cooperative. Natalie fumbled in her purse for her keys. Imagine that toad finally making a pass at her. Imagine him daring to suggest he just might change his mind about firing her if she went to bed with him. The toad. The revolting little toad. She hummed "California, Here I Come" under her breath.

Where the hell were those keys? Dear God, had she forgotten them? Had she left them on the table? Her fingers found the keys. She sighed with relief.

Then she gasped. The purse slipped from her fingers. Her left hand grabbed the doorknob. Her mouth opened to cry out in anguish, but nothing came out. Her vocal chords were paralyzed with fear and agony.

The knife had plunged in from behind, swiftly and accurately. It cut through her coat and her dress and her underslip into her heart. Just as swiftly it was withdrawn and plunged again. The next two wounds were unnecessary. The second had done its job.

Natalie lay face down on the sidewalk, arms outstretched as though trying desperately to reach a goal she would never attain.

14

At five o'clock in the morning, Helga's eyes flew open. She fluttered her eyelids to keep herself awake. "Yes? Yes, who is it?" Someone had called to her. She was sure someone had called out her name. Was it something she heard in a dream, or was someone calling to her above the wind, which was creating a cacophony of weird and eerie howling outside, the miserable wailing of a thousand hornpipes that caused Helga's imagination to dance a jig of fear? "Who is it? Who's there?" Her voice softened into maternal tenderness. "What's wrong, my dear, what's wrong?" Still half-awake, Helga struggled to sit up. She managed to prop herself up on her right elbow and with her other hand groped for the bedside lamp and finally found the switch. She was positive she had heard a woman's voice. It had sounded like such a heart-rending plea, a cry for help, a cry for love. She struggled into a sitting position and then flung aside the counterpane. Her feet found her bedroom slippers, and she put on the negligee that lay across the foot of the bed. She went to a window and pulled back the drapes. The moon was full and seductive, but it did little to assuage Helga's fear. Who had called? Was it the walls whispering again? Helga hurried to the light switch next to the door, and the room was soon bathed in comforting illumination. The wind was growing shriller and rattling the windows. Helga drew the negligee tightly around herself and then went looking for Martha.

Martha will think me mad, thought Helga, as she groped along the wall of the hallway to Martha's room. After the others had moved away, Martha had rejected Helga's suggestion that she vacate her own quarters at the other end of the mansion in a wing that afforded a beautiful view of the mainland. Martha treasured the independence of the separation. There was little enough for her to treasure in her life. "Please, Mother, it's your imagination. The walls don't whisper. It's just the wind penetrating the passages underneath the house." But someone had cried for help, Helga insisted to herself. I swear it. It was a voice I thought I recognized.

Helga knocked lightly and entered Martha's room. The drapes on the windows were still open. The moonlight shafted in, and Helga could see Martha's bed had not been slept in. Helga felt befuddled. Martha's bed not slept in? Perhaps this was still the dream. Perhaps she hadn't awakened at all. She made her way back to her own room. This was no dream. There was her bed, and there was the window with the drapes she had flung aside, and the wind was worrying the windows as though trying desperately to enter and claim her. She dressed quickly and went downstairs, turning on every light switch in her path.

"Martha? Martha, where are you?"

She went from the great entrance hall to the reception room to the conservatory and from there to the dining hall and the music room, looking even into rooms that she knew were long unoccupied, the furniture covered with dust protectors. At last she came to the kitchen, and still not a sign of Martha. Now she was angry. How dare her daughter go off in the middle of the night and leave her alone and unprotected? Where could she have gone to? She couldn't have been daft enough to take the boat out. They'd heard the small craft warnings on the radio during their game of Scrabble. Martha had said before turning in she'd go down to the dock and make sure their boat was secure. Martha was a marvelous sailor. She had a strong back and strong hands. She could wield an axe like a lumberjack and didn't need to wait on Winston or a handyman from the mainland to provide their fireplaces with logs and kindling.

Helga heard the noise behind her. Someone was in the hall about to enter the kitchen. Helga sat perfectly still and waited. Martha entered and emitted a startled gasp. "Mother! What in heaven's name are you doing up this early?"

Helga looked into Martha's eyes and then at her clothes. She was dressed for the outdoors, heavily protected against the bitter winds. "Where have you been all night?"

"I haven't been out all night."

"I've been to your room. The bed's not been slept in."

Martha busied herself making coffee. "Oh, after I went upstairs I read for awhile and then found I wasn't the least bit sleepy. I know you're going to think this awfully insane of me, but I suddenly got this strange compulsion to visit the cabin."

"Yes, that was awfully insane of you, especially in the dead of night and in the face of this dreadful windstorm."

Martha laughed lightly as she squeezed fresh orange juice. "Well, it served me right. The wind was so awful once I got to the cabin, I lay down on the cot waiting for it to subside. The next thing you know, I must have fallen fast asleep. It gave me quite a start when I woke up. Here. Drink your juice. Why did you go to my room?"

Helga took the glass of juice and placed it on the table. This was no time to mention voices or whispering walls. Martha's strange behavior and nervous demeanor took precedence. There was something unnatural going on around here, and it was affecting Helga and her family. There were facts that could no longer lie unexamined and forgotten in her subconscious. Martha had been acting strangely for months, probably longer, though Helga hadn't recognized and examined it until shortly before the murder of the twins. Now murder had to be faced, and she was beginning to dread the coming weekend. Things would come to a head then, and she would probably suffer a tragedy even greater than the death of Andrew.

"Mother," said Martha softly, "why are you crying?"

"I am crying for so many things," replied Helga. She left the kitchen in search of privacy, leaving her juice untasted and Martha unnerved.

"Damn it," said Martha. "God damn it."

Natalie's murder occurred too late for the Sunday papers, but it provided juicy reading for Monday morning's commuters. The front page of the *Daily News* had a grotesque picture of Natalie's body sprawled face downward on the pavement. The centerfold featured photographs of Natalie as she had looked ten years earlier on the first of her three wedding days. There was a photograph of Harvey, Laura, and Robert leaving the morgue after they identified her body. There was a photograph of Ike Tabor, the detective assigned to Natalie's case, at Norman Wylie's insistence, once the news of Natalie's murder had arrived at his precinct. His superior listened respectfully to Norman's theory about Natalie's death and got in touch with Ike Tabor's superior, who thought Nathan Manx's murder would soon open up into something sensational that would give him the notoriety he needed to shore up his political ambitions. There was no reason he couldn't be mayor of New York, especially since he thought the incumbent looked as though he belonged behind a delicatessen counter slicing smoked salmon. He cooperated greedily with Norman's superior, and Ike Tabor announced to the reporters that Natalie had obviously been the victim of an incredibly brutal mugging. Her purse had been rifled of her final week's salary from Dombey's. Wylie had put Tabor in touch with Harvey, Laura, and Robert. It was Harvey who advised Tabor to begin his investigation at Dombey's, and Tabor lost no time in tracking down Nick Hobart and the bartender. Both men agreed that when Natalie had left the bar around half past three in the morning, she was sober and in good spirits. She had left the bar unaccompanied. Nick Hobart said he had offered to walk her home because of the dangers awaiting anyone, let alone a fragile, unaccompanied woman, on the streets of New York, especially at that deadly hour of the morning, but Natalie had refused his generous offer. After studying Hobart carefully and listening to the frog croak that passed for his voice, Tabor, an excellent judge of character, decided poor Natalie would have met with a different form of deadly fate had she accepted Hobart's offer. Hobart said he had given her three hundred and fifty dollars in cash, her final salary, but he also saw her stuffing a wad of dollar bills representing her tips into her purse. The bartender added very little that was helpful other than to say that Natalie had been one hell of a good gal and that if crime in the streets continued to escalate, he for one was all for forming vigilante committees. Tabor recognized a racist when he heard one. Later, Tabor and Wylie agreed to keep to their story of Natalie as the victim of a mugging and to soft pedal her relation to the murdered twins and her connection to Nathan Manx. Unfortunately, in the heat of the excitement of this fresh crime, Wylie forgot about Bella Wallace. On Monday, Bella arranged to make a special appearance on the six o'clock news and blabbed all. Later, when Wylie finally reached her and excoriated her, Bella feigned a mock contrition and said she could bite her tongue in two. Wylie said even if she did bite her tongue in two, she'd have plenty left. Bella permitted his crack to die an unmourned death and plunged into her projected program on the Graymoors with the relish of a hyena tearing into the carcass of a slaughtered eland.

Natalie's body had been discovered about fifteen minutes after her murder by two call girls who lived in the ground floor rear of her apartment building. They recognized her immediately, as they also frequented Dombey's. After alerting the police and identifying Natalie, they set their answering machine in operation and wondered if they were up to the nocturnal assignments offered. They were saving their money to buy an inn somewhere in Maine, which they hoped to operate after they retired. They had been lovers since meeting as schoolgirls in a convent outside Chicago. Later, they gaily posed for the newspaper photographers who were swarming around the building and then, refreshed by the activity, went off to their assignations.

When Wylie arrived at his precinct shortly after six that morning, news of Natalie's murder preceded him, and he set his plans into motion immediately. After apprising Tabor of the Graymoor background, Wylie called Harvey and Laura. A shocked Harvey broke the tragic news to Laura, who stared dumbly at him before giving in to hysterics. Before hanging up on Wylie, Harvey assured him he'd break the news to the rest of the family. Harvey held Laura, kissing the top of her head, her brow, and then each cheek, both tasting damp and salty. Laura managed to pull herself together and asked for the details, which Harvey supplied, albeit reluctantly.

"Four stab wounds," repeated Laura. "The son of a bitch, four of them."

"Now listen, baby. Just remember Wylie's warned us not to jump to conclusions. Natalie was robbed, so it could very well have been a mugging."

"My foot," snapped Laura. "She was robbed to make it look like a mugging. Hell! What time did it happen?"

"Sometime between half past three when she left Dombey's and a quarter after four when two hookers who live in her building found her dead." Laura let out a wail. "Will you please take hold of yourself?"

"Harvey. That was about the time you went out to buy the pizza."

"Oh, for crying out loud, Laura." He was dialing Robert. There was no busy signal now. It rang several times before a sleepy voiced Robert answered. Harvey told him the bad news. Robert was immediately alert, although shocked. Harvey advised him he'd be hearing from Ike Tabor and then said after he did, to please call Harvey back and then they'd meet and go to the morgue to identify Natalie and afterward go someplace nice for breakfast. They hung up simultaneously. Harvey wished Ike Tabor would get a move on. He wanted to contact the others. Then he groaned.

"What now?" asked Laura.

"Who'll tell Helga?"

Laura thought for a moment. "That had better be Robert. He has a special way of breaking bad news to her."

"Where were you all night?" Marjorie demanded when Nicholas finally came home shortly before six that Sunday morning.

"None of your damn business," snapped Nicholas as he went to the bathroom and slammed the door shut behind him. Marjorie went to the kitchen to prepare juice, coffee, and toast. She was determined to set things right with Nicholas as she had promised Laura. While sitting up all night waiting for Nicholas to reappear or at least show some sign that he still existed, sleep having eluded her regardless of the administrations of wine and warm milk, she had made up her mind to put up a warm, friendly, understanding false front until the party weekend was history. She went about her domestic chores as though being photographed for a commercial. She heard Nicholas in the shower and knew the morning boded ill because he wasn't singing.

None of your damn business.

This wasn't Dr. Jekyll, this was Mr. Hyde. This wasn't Nicholas Graymoor, the happy-go-lucky noodleheaded scion of the Graymoor establishment; this was Nicholas Graymoor in a new and vastly unpleasant incarnation. And she was the cause of it. Grimly determined, Marjorie was prepared to accept the consequences. She hoped his heart contained only bitterness and not the threat of murder. She was lavish with the butter on the toast.

At last the phone rang. It was Ike Tabor. Tabor had just been on the phone with Robert. Harvey made all the right sounds. Shock, horror, then anger. He told Laura that was Tabor. She said she could tell by the way Harvey was overacting. The phone rang again, and this time it was Robert. Such a busy Sunday morning, thought Laura sadly. The plan was for Harvey and Laura to pick Robert up and proceed together to the morgue. Robert said he'd phone Helga, hoping Martha would be the one to answer the phone so he could have her prime Helga for what was to come. Harvey offered to tell Nicholas and Victor. "What about Arnold?" interjected Laura from her dressing table where she was doing her best to camouflage the dark circles under her eyes. Harvey added Arnold to his assignment. When he was finally rid of Robert, he dialed Victor's number.

By the sixth ring, Victor answered the phone with a hacking

cough. Harvey told him the grisly news. Victor sounded genuinely shocked and horrified and then growled, "Are they sure it was a mugger?"

"If it wasn't, I hope you have an alibi," suggested Harvey pleasantly. Victor rewarded him with an expletive, then got a promise from Harvey to call again after he and the others identified the body. Victor hung up and repeated the word "alibi" over and over. Alibi. I'd better have an alibi. He muttered another expletive and then staggered out of bed in search of a cigarette.

Arnold was strangely unresponsive to Harvey's news, or so Harvey thought. "Damn it," said Arnold, "I thought of going over to Dombey's last night and picking her up. Maybe if I had, she'd be alive today." She might be, thought Harvey, but sooner or later, he had a feeling, fate would have caught up with Natalie. "Will there be an autopsy?"

"There usually is."

"Don't you have to give permission?"

"It's up to Robert as the head of the family. But I'm sure he'll give his permission. The British dote on autopsies."

"Shouldn't we all meet later or something? And what about Helga?" Harvey told him Robert was taking care of Helga. As an afterthought, Arnold told him he had run into Wylie and Bella Wallace the previous evening. The mention of Bella Wallace's name made Harvey's face turn gray. Then he figured, oh, what the hell, it'll be in the newspapers anyway so there's no avoiding Bella. He hoped Tabor would bear down on the theory that Natalie was the victim of a mugger. The robbery certainly helped to make it look like that. Harvey promised Arnold he'd call him later and arrange some sort of get-together, maybe something like a wake, and then hung up.

"A wake is just what we need," said Laura grimly as she entered from the bedroom while checking the contents of her alligator handbag. "What we need are bodyguards."

"We've got each other."

"And I want you at my side constantly." She sighed. "I'll never get through this week. Never." Harvey was dialing Nicholas.

It seemed to Marjorie as though the shower had washed some of the bitterness and hatred out of Nicholas. He even permitted her to scramble him some eggs with bacon. It was his favorite Sunday breakfast. When he had returned that morning, he brought a newspaper with him and, over breakfast, tried to lose himself in the theater section.

"Nicholas." Marjorie spoke his name in a small voice, and he didn't look up. "For the sake of the weekend and your mother's birthday, let's try to be friends again."

Friends, thought Nicholas, not husband and wife. He looked at her and cleared his throat. "You're right. I suppose you've discussed our fight with Laura?"

"I had to talk to somebody." She was pouring herself a third cup of coffee. "I was afraid being left alone here all night."

"Did you tell her I was out all night?"

"No. I didn't know you were going to be out all night when I talked to her."

"I'd prefer you didn't tell anyone. It's nobody's business but ours."

He's probably ashamed of himself, thought Marjorie and the idea made her feel better. The phone rang in the living room. "I'll get it," said Marjorie, sounding like a dutiful wife. Nicholas watched her leave the kitchen and then sadly shook his head. The weekend. Helga. Last night. Wouldn't it all be simpler, he thought, if I just went raving mad? Marjorie was calling to him, to tell him it was Harvey and it was urgent. Nicholas hurried to the phone.

"Hi, Harvey, what's up?" What was up was unpleasant to listen to, and Nicholas shut his eyes tightly. Marjorie felt a sinking feeling in the pit of her stomach, a premonition of disaster that Nicholas would soon confirm. Then she heard

Nicholas say, "They're sure she was killed by a mugger?" and her hand flew to her mouth. Nicholas agreed to stay home until he heard from Harvey later. He hung up the phone and told Marjorie the news. She burst into tears and sat down on the couch. Nicholas found her a tissue and pressed it into her hands. Marjorie dabbed at her eyes, but the flood continued unabated. She had liked Natalie. She liked most of the family. She still liked Nicholas, and she hoped Natalie had truly been the victim of the mugger or else she'd have to tell somebody he'd been out all night. "I'll get you your coffee," said Nicholas and went to the kitchen.

The tears abated. Marjorie blew her nose. Then she stared at the floor. Where were you last night, Nicholas?

Robert's luck held. Martha answered the telephone and as always when she heard Robert's voice, her face took on a special glow rarely seen by others. Her eyes brightened perceptibly, and her voice was girlishly eager. Then her mood was shattered by the news of Natalie's death. "Are you all right?" asked Robert.

"Well, not too good under the circumstances. Shall I tell Helga or will you?"

"Just prepare her for the bad news, and I'll handle it from there."

Certainly Robert, certainly. You above all of us know how to handle Helga. She found her mother in the writing room and told her Robert was on the phone and that it was bad news. Helga had already cried this morning; she was prepared to cry again. Helga picked up the extension and greeted her favorite son with all the warmth he expected. Martha hurried back to the other phone to replace the receiver. By the time she returned to Helga, the old lady was sobbing softly. Martha went to the small bar near the window and poured them each a glass of port. Helga sounded in control again as she said into the phone, "Are the police positive it was an unknown assailant?" She couldn't bring herself ever to say "mugger." It was such an ugly word, appropriately ugly for the filthy deed it implied. "Are they sure, Robert, are they sure?" Robert repeated the details of Natalie's death in an accurate reproduction of the information as given to him by Ike Tabor. Next he told Helga he was about to be joined by Harvey and Laura for the grim visit to the morgue to identify Natalie's body officially. "How awful," said Helga and then, assuming full control of herself as matriarch of the family, told him she would make plans for the funeral and burial in the family cemetery behind the chapel. "It won't be a very festive reunion after all," said Helga sadly.

"At least we'll all be together," countered Robert.

"But for the wrong reason, darling."

Five minutes later, after each had had a healthy belt of the port, Martha sat with Helga and listened to her brisk, businesslike outline of the upcoming funeral. There was the minister to be contacted and the flowers to be ordered, and oh, yes, the transportation of the body must be arranged as soon as it was released by the police following the autopsy. "The services are to be private. Very, very private," added Helga solemnly. "Just the family, a few chosen friends."

"Of course, Mother. Why are you staring at me like that?"

"Was I staring? I'm sorry. My mind was on Natalie." I'm sure she's bought the lie, Helga thought. My mind wasn't on Natalie, though it will be at times for the rest of my life. What I was really thinking, darling, when I was staring at you, was where were you all of last night? Were you really asleep in the cabin? *Were you?*

15

The identification of Natalie's body was so bizarrely theatrical, Laura couldn't resist referring to it later as Natalie's farewell performance. Laura, Harvey, and Robert viewed the body from behind a pane of glass that separated them from the viewing room. The body had been wheeled in by two morgue attendants who, at a prearranged signal, partially removed the sheet baring Natalie's head. Laura stifled a sob and clung to Harvey's hand. Robert said to Ike Tabor, "Yes, that's Natalie Graymoor, our sister," and saw for the first time that Norman Wylie had joined the group. Ike signaled the attendants, who replaced the sheet over Natalie's head and wheeled the body out. Harvey resisted a perverse urge to applaud. They left the room in silence.

"I know it's a bit early, even for a Sunday," said Harvey, "but I could use a drink." Then he said to Wylie, "To what do we owe the honor?"

"I'm dodging Bella Wallace," said Norman wryly. "I figured the morgue would be a safe house."

"I invited him to join us," said Ike Tabor in what Laura assumed was his official tone of voice. "We're cooperating with each other."

"We have to do something about Natalie's apartment. Her belongings. Do you suppose she left a will?" Laura directed this to Robert.

"What for?" asked Robert.

"As a token gesture," suggested Harvey.

"Her apartment's sealed," said Tabor. "It's going to be fine-tooth combed. When we're satisfied, we'll let you know when you can go in."

"I had no idea a mugging would generate so much police activity." Robert sounded properly bewildered. Tabor said nothing, and Wylie suggested they repair to a nearby restaurant. Laura couldn't believe anybody had an appetite and Robert agreed with her.

"I just want a drink," said Harvey.

Wylie led the way to the restaurant. Once they were seated and a waitress had taken their orders, Robert said to Tabor, "What do you find so suspicious about Natalie's death? Don't you believe she was killed by a mugger?"

"I believe she was killed by a mugger because that's the

way it looks right now. But it could have been something else, right, Norman?" Wylie nodded solemnly. Tabor resumed his explanation for Robert. "After all, Mr. Graymoor, your twin sisters were murdered. And they had met Nathan Manx, who was also murdered. And Nathan Manx contacted Natalie, who has also been murdered. And Wylie, who's assigned to the twins, and I, having inherited Manx and Natalie, are swapping information because we need to help each other."

The waitress was back almost immediately with five Bloody Marys. Laura assumed she knew Tabor and Wylie from past experience. She thought she saw Tabor gently pinch the waitress's thigh as she deposited the fifth drink in front of him. The girl's face flushed as she hurried away.

Robert turned to Tabor. "I suppose you know about this tontine, which only one of us stands to inherit."

"I do."

"With three of the heirs dead under mysterious circumstances, I assume you think the rest of us are potential victims."

"It's a strong consideration."

"Well, then," said Robert, "I think I had a visitor last night."

Harvey leaned forward. "What do you mean you *think* you had a visitor?"

"Well, around two in the morning I woke up with a terrible stomachache. I couldn't find any medication in the bathroom, so I decided to phone an all-night drugstore on Third Avenue to have them send something over. They've accommodated me before."

"Your phone was out of order," said Laura.

Robert was wide-eyed. "Are you psychic?"

"No, Marjorie was trying to get hold of you last night. That private matter we discussed in the taxi coming down here." Wylie and Tabor were both determined to become privy to the private matter. Harvey thought he saw their noses twitching. "Your line, she decided after a couple of hours of busy signals, must be out of order, so she reported it to the telephone company."

"The pain was so bad," said Robert, resuming his narrative, "that after the delivery boy left I got dressed and went out. I must have been gone about half an hour or so, and when I got back, I went into the conservatory to listen to some music while I waited for the medicine to take effect. Well, the extension there was off the hook." Tabor and Wylie exchanged glances. "That was why I couldn't phone out. . ."

"Or Marjorie couldn't phone in." Laura thought her Bloody Mary was too citrusy, but the jolt of vodka was comforting.

"Well that made me feel very uneasy, so I decided to investigate further. I found one of the basement windows unlatched, and they are always kept locked."

"Did you find anything missing?" asked Tabor.

"There's really nothing small worth stealing. The cash I had left on my dressing room table was untouched, and I checked my jewel box and the cuff links were all there. Anyway, I spent a very uneasy night."

"Why didn't you call the police?" asked Laura.

"Well, there was nothing missing. And maybe one of the hired help had left the window unlocked by mistake. I have a couple who come in to clean every Saturday."

Wylie sounded ominous when he said to Robert, "Did it occur to you your intruder might still have been in the house?"

Robert gave a nervous little laugh. "Actually, old boy, it didn't. And apparently, he wasn't, because here I am."

"Here you are," agreed Wylie, exchanging another quick look with Tabor. "Does Natalie's murder change the weekend excursion?"

"No," said Harvey, "it only puts a damper on it. Natalie will be buried on the island. We have a private cemetery there."

Robert interrupted, addressing Tabor. "It would help to

know when Natalie's body will be released. I mean, there's the funeral arrangements to be made and well, you know."

"I know," said Tabor, having buried a few of his own, "and I think you can plan to pick her up on Tuesday."

"What do you mean 'pick her up,'" demanded a very ruffled Laura. "'Pick her up,' indeed. I mean she was a human being, our sister."

"Sorry," said Tabor and meaning it, "but we get so much of this every week, one stiff is like any other." Laura slumped in her chair as she rifled her handbag for a handkerchief. Harvey patted her gently on the back and handed her his handkerchief. Laura dried her eyes, blew her nose, and morosely polished off the Bloody Mary.

"What was that private matter you were discussing in the taxi?" asked Wylie as he lazily stirred his drink.

"That private matter was private," said Laura in a voice dripping with icicles.

Harvey knew there was little privacy in a murder investigation. He told Wylie and Tabor about the Nicholas and Marjorie problem.

When he finished, Tabor asked, "Did she report what time he finally got in last night?"

"We were too concerned with Natalie's tragedy to consider anything else," replied Harvey. "Now I'm hungry." They ordered food.

Laura asked Wylie, "How come Bella got wind of the murder so soon?"

"She's got a direct line to the station house. And as soon as I uncover the mole feeding her. . ." He made a whacking motion with his right hand that the waitress, watching from her station near the kitchen door, found sexually exciting.

"I suppose the story will be plastered over tomorrow's papers," asked Robert.

"Of course," said Tabor. "Sordid murders are more popular than wars."

Robert turned to Harvey and Laura. "That means the reporters will be after all of us. There must be some way to protect Helga and Martha. We can't have newspapermen swarming over the island."

"We could send them shotguns," suggested Laura.

"There'll be no avoiding the press at the funeral," said Harvey.

"We could keep the services secret," Robert suggested. Laura felt like belting him in the arm with a hearty "stout fellow."

"We could try, but it won't work," said Harvey. "They'll keep an around the clock vigil until they strike pay dirt."

"Damn it," muttered Robert.

"You should have seen them flocking around her body this morning," said Wylie as he buttered a toasted bagel. "I mean they were on the scene of the crime before Tabor was." He took a wolf's size bite of the bagel and then turned to Robert. "Mr. Graymoor, a word of well-intentioned advice. When you're in a spotlight, don't spend too much energy trying to dodge it. Just stand patiently and wait for your audience to get bored with you. In a day or so, there'll be another scandal taking precedence. You forgot so soon you had the same butterflies when the twins were murdered? In less than two days, they went from banner headlines on the front page to a four-line item in the back of the paper."

"Bella's going to make a meal out of this," warned Laura.

"Well, there's no stopping Bella," said Wylie who certainly knew whereof he spoke, "short of a silver bullet."

"I won't have her at Natalie's funeral," said Robert with a strange and unbecoming harshness. "I won't have a spectacle made of her funeral."

"Then we'll have to hire some private guards and place them strategically around the island to prevent anyone from landing." Once having made the suggestion, Harvey regretted it; he had forgotten there was Mickey Redfern to consider. He reminded himself that the man was a past master at slipping past obstacles undetected.

"If that's what we have to do, then we'll do it." Harvey asked Tabor and Wylie for some recommendations, and Wylie explained that Graymoor Island was out of their jurisdiction; they'd have to seek the advice of the Connecticut police. Tabor had contacts in Connecticut and told them he'd take care of everything. Laura was surprised at how friendly and cooperative the police were. She was even impressed by Tabor's somewhat dainty table manners. He didn't pick up his bacon with his fingers. He very delicately bisected it, and bisection made her think of autopsy and autopsy caused her to set her plate aside and renew her acquaintance with a second Bloody Mary.

Harvey asked her, "Are you okay?"

"I'm just not hungry. We have to change all our plans now, don't we? This means all of us will have to be on the island earlier than Friday."

"That depends on the day we schedule the funeral," said Robert.

"It'll certainly be on Wednesday or Thursday, won't it?" persisted Laura. "I mean if her body can be collected on Tuesday, we can arrange to have her on the island by the following day and. . ." She was rummaging for her handkerchief again. Harvey again patted her gently on the back. "I don't know why," said Laura in a husky voice, "but I somehow feel it'll be safer on the island. Safer for all of us. We'll be safer together, right, Harvey?"

"You don't really believe Natalie was killed by a mugger," said Robert, "do you?"

"Not really," said Tabor, "and I'd really like to know where all of you were between three and four this morning."

"It's the strangest thing," Arnold was saying to Nicholas over the telephone that same morning, "but I've been invited to lunch by Bella Wallace of all people."

"Lucky you," responded Nicholas sullenly.

"Well, I'm not calling to tell you I've made a lucky strike," he said as he examined his face in a wall mirror and decided he was still an alluring charmer. "It's just that I promised Harvey I'd stay home until I heard from him. I suppose you know we're all going to get together at their place this evening?" Nicholas said of course he knew. "Well, anyway, just in case Harvey calls before I get back from lunch, will you advise him I've been kidnapped by the inimitable Miss Wallace and I'll check in with him later? Is that okay with you, Nicholas?"

"Of course," said Nicholas.

"You don't sound like yourself. Is something wrong?"

"I'm just dandy." Marjorie looked up from the skirt hem she was darning. Nicholas wasn't sounding like Nicholas. She wished he'd get off the phone and that Harvey would come through. She wanted to get out of the apartment. Take a walk. Breathe some fresh air. Find a pay phone and try to contact Robert to see if he could advise her on her problem with Nicholas. She wondered if the dress Laura had given her on Friday would be too frivolous to wear at the funeral. Nicholas had gone to the bedroom, and she heard the bedsprings groan as he sank down atop the bed. They had nothing to say to each other. It was amazing to her how short a time it had taken for their relationship to disintegrate.

After dropping Robert off at his town house, with a cautionary suggestion from Laura that he call the police immediately at the first sign of a fresh invasion, Laura waited for the taxi to pull away before asking Harvey, "Do you really believe his story?"

"Don't you?"

"Well, he told it so matter of factly. I mean intrepid Robert, and fearless he isn't, suddenly thumbing his nose at possible danger."

"I'm sure Tabor will send a man over to the all-night drugstore to check Robert's story."

"I hope they remember you at the pizza parlor."

Harvey took Laura's hand. "I want you to promise me something." Laura waited. "Whenever we're not together between now and the time we leave for the island, I want you to make sure there's always somebody with you."

"What about when I go to the john?"

He kissed the tip of her nose. "Then too."

"What do we do about tonight? Just drinks and nibbles? And how do we explain Norman Wylie and Ike Tabor to the others?" The detectives had invited themselves to the family gathering, and Laura, for one, was glad. If there was a murderer among them, she wanted the culprit to know the police were on the job and meant business. She shared the thought with Harvey.

"The police were on the job and meant business when the twins were murdered," replied Harvey. "That didn't stop Natalie's tragedy."

Laura felt deflated. "Thanks for your vote of confidence."

"Sorry darling, I'm being realistic, and I'm damned glad I've got Mickey Redfern on the job. I wonder if he's heard about Natalie yet?"

"It must have been on the news programs by now. If he has a radio, he's heard." She leaned forward and asked the cabdriver, "Have you heard the news yet today?" The cabdriver told her he had. "Was there anything about the murder of Natalie Graymoor."

"Oh, yeah," he replied merrily, "that one's getting a lot of coverage."

Laura leaned back, muttering under breath, "I'm sorry I asked."

"Just drinks and nibbles," said Harvey, sounding somewhat distrait.

"Well, thank God that's one decision I don't have to make. Now I can give some time to thinking about Nicholas and Marjorie. I hope she's not planning on wearing that dress I gave her to the funeral."

* * *

Bella Wallace was pleased. Arnold was indeed sexy and marvelously talkative. From the moment he joined her at the Third Avenue restaurant, owned by three male models, she found him warm, charming, and intimate. He certainly knew how to handle women. Practice certainly makes perfect.

"How sweet of you to join me," said Bella. She hadn't brought her tape recorder with her because this was supposed to be a social luncheon. "I mean what with your poor sister being so brutally murdered last night."

"It was pretty depressing sitting around the house. I was glad for the chance to get out." He hoped she recognized the meal was on her. He had very little cash on him, and he had been warned two months ago by American Express to stop using his credit card. His knee gently contacted hers. "And who could resist the chance to get to know you better?"

"Aren't you nice? When's the funeral?"

"What?"

"Your sister's funeral. When's it take place?"

"I really don't know. If it's been decided, I haven't been told. Robert, Harvey, and Laura went to the morgue this morning to identify her body."

"Which means there'll be an autopsy, probably tomorrow," said Bella with the efficiency one usually expected to hear from someone giving dictation, "and that means they can send a mortician to claim the body on Tuesday. Then another twenty-four hours to pretty her up. Where will the funeral services be held?" Arnold told her. "So by the time they get the body shipped to the island, and I suppose that'll be followed by twenty-four hours of meditation and letting friends sail over to pay their last respects, that probably means she'll be interred sometime on Thursday."

"That's a pretty good timetable. I'm very impressed." Arnold wasn't lying. He wondered if she was planning to attend the funeral, but didn't ask. Without being told, he knew Helga would want the services to be very simple and very private. It had been that way with the twins and with Andrew before them. Helga did not look kindly on intruders at any private occasion, and he hoped Bella wasn't planning on giving them trouble.

"I'd certainly like to come to that funeral." Bella was toying with the fruit in her old-fashioned. She felt her low blood sugar beginning to act up and thought of asking the waiter to bring a plate of the miniature Danish pastries the restaurant specialized in.

"My mother is very strict about strangers at private occasions."

"I'm not such a stranger. I met Natalie. She was nice. I liked her." She almost added, and she wasn't very talented and she drank too much, and she was too depressing, but she decided to keep that in reserve for the television program.

"You learn to respect Helga's wishes. She's abnormally firm about that."

"She must be quite a lady."

"Very much something special. What else do you want to know?"

Bella smiled. "I haven't been too subtle, have I?" Subtlety had never been her strong point.

"I suddenly realized today I was the most accessible, so here I am. I can't tell you very much because I don't know very much. Harvey phoned me early to tell me the awful news and then said stick around and 'I'll get back to you.' I've listened to the radio and they reported little more than I know. Are you still buying me lunch?" He was glad he'd decided to make it clear the lunch was on her.

"Of course," said Bella. "Do you know what you want?"

"Of course I know what I want? Don't you?"

Her knee gently contacted his. She knew what she wanted.

Mickey Redfern had heard the news on the radio in the luncheonette on the wharf. He thought about trying to reach Harvey for any sudden change of instructions, but then decided it might be wiser to wait until later in the day, when the smoke had settled and Harvey would have more information for him. He planned to return to the island to continue his investigation of the cave. His previous adventure there had whetted his appetite. Now more than ever he wanted to meet the challenge of the underground danger. He wanted to move past that cell where the remains rested and try to locate the passage that led to the mansion. He was pretty positive Natalie's tragedy would keep Martha close to the house and the old lady. He felt free to move about and relished the thought of the freedom. He was taking a small pick axe with him to the island. This time he would eschew the rope; he'd just make markings on the cave walls and use them to find his way back. And to be on the safe side, he would bring along his fishing gear and a can of fresh bait. Miss Martha just might be unpredictable. She just might catch sight of his boat entering the secret cove and come to investigate. Mickey hoped he was prepared for everything.

"It was so strange," Helga was saying to Martha as they sat in the conservatory having tea. The wind had settled down and the island was once more at peace. "But now I realize it was Natalie's voice that awakened me." She saw the strange look on Martha's face and returned it with one of self-confidence. "No, I'm not mad, Martha."

"No one thinks you're mad, Mother."

"You had a very dubious expression on your face."

"I was thinking that perhaps you're really psychic."

"Oh, I know I am. Believe me, darling, it was a voice crying for help. It wasn't the wind either, it was our poor Natalie crying for help. Or perhaps her soul touching my heart in passing. Oh, poor, poor Natalie. So soon to die. Too soon to die. She had no life at all."

"She had three husbands." Martha almost added, that's three more than I'll ever know, but thought better of it. One must restrain envy when one is in mourning.

"*Those* miserable creatures. When did Robert say he thought we could hold the funeral?"

It was the fifth time she had asked the question, but Martha was patient. "Thursday."

"The minister is definitely free on Thursday?"

"Absolutely. The way his voice fluttered and gurgled over the telephone, I strongly suspected he favored Graymoor funerals."

"That sounds so awful!" Helga slammed her cup and saucer down on the table. Then she settled back with a sigh. "I must explain to the mortician to use a gentle hand with the cosmetics. She mustn't look garish."

"You know the lighting in the chapel."

"Then we must do something about the lighting." The chapel was at the northern edge of the cemetery. Helga had designed it many years before. When she came to Graymoor as a bride, although not particularly religious, her first alteration was to insist on the construction of a chapel. She found chapels romantic. Andrew gave it to her as a first anniversary present. She went there frequently to meditate. But later, when she started writing novels, she seemed to draw greater inner strength from her writing room. "What do we do about the press?" Helga was on her feet, pacing the room with a stride that belied her years. "I won't have a repetition of the circus when the twins were buried. The media were disgraceful with their cameras clicking like a mad orgy of castanets."

"Robert is making arrangements for private guards. What do we do about those on the mainland who want to come and pay their respects? Natalie had friends in East Gate, the people she went to school with."

"We must place a notice in the *East Gate Press* asking those who wish to come over on Wednesday to phone us at once so that they can be processed. Isn't that a good idea?"

"It's absolutely dandy except the *Press* only publishes once a week, and that's on Friday, which of course is too late for us."

"So what do we do?" Helga was seated again with her hands resting in her lap.

"I'll take the boat over tomorrow and put up a notice in the post office. I'll also spread the word among the tradespeople. That ought to cover it. The staff will be here to look after you, so you'll be all right."

"Martha? You sound as though you think my life is in danger."

"I just don't think you should be alone at this time."

"You're always thoughtful."

Martha was staring at her fingernails. She couldn't remember the last time she'd had a manicure. She'd get one tomorrow. She wanted to look nice for Helga's birthday. Oh, and of course, for Natalie's funeral.

"But, Victor," said Mona Norris, his secretary, "you're asking me to lie." He had phoned her at home that morning and told her it was urgent she come to the penthouse after lunch. She hoped it didn't mean his chasing her around the apartment for fifteen minutes and then repairing to the gym for one of his "workouts." It was nothing like that at all.

"I'm telling you you have to help me. I can't explain why, but just in case the police ask, you're to swear that I spent last night with you at your apartment." He pinched her cheek gently. "I'll make it worth your while."

"Well, all right," said Mona somewhat reluctantly. Then after some thought she asked, "Why would the police ask where you were last night? Does it have something to do with your sister's murder?"

Victor stood up and towered over Mona, who sank back in the easy chair. "Mona, stop asking so many questions. Just do as I tell you. Okay?"

"Sure," said Mona, not liking this one bit, "sure, it's okay."

16

Norman Wylie had given up trying to remember the last time he had spent a Sunday relaxing with the newspapers. It was tougher on Ike Tabor. Ike had a wife and three children and a mortgaged split-level house in Brooklyn with a basketball hoop in the backyard. His sons had long ago learned to stop asking their father for a timetable and accepted practicing baskets on their own. His daughter, age ten and the youngest, occasionally waxed nostalgic over the one time her father had taken her and her brothers on an excursion to the zoo. Ike's wife accepted his erratic hours when he won his promotion. She had only one ambition in life—never to be a hero's widow. As Wylie and Tabor sat in the back of the patrol car that was chauffeuring them to Laura and Harvey's apartment, newspapers and families were the furthest things from their minds.

"This case beats hell," grumbled Tabor. "What kind of a murderer are we dealing with? Is this a maniac who's decided he was born into the wrong family or a cool, calculating killer who knows what he's after? What do you think, Norman?"

"In the first place, Ike, he or she was adopted into the family. So he's not killing his own flesh and blood."

"This makes him likable?"

Norman smiled. "And yes, the murderer is cool and calculating and knows what he's after. As far as I can determine, the tontine is the prize. If the tontine's just a beard for another motive, then I haven't spotted it yet."

"Likewise."

"So let's start at the top with what Harvey Graymoor's told us. First we got Cedric Longstreet, former tutor to the kids, who may or may not have been murdered around thirty years or so ago. Since there's a toilet case with his initials on it as evidence, although we have yet to see it, we accept that the remains are Longstreet. By the way, Ike, we ought to do a back check with missing persons."

"I've already got somebody on it." Ike shifted in his seat. Norman should know better by now then to question his efficiency.

"I thought you might." Ike felt better. Wylie continued, "Now we come to the adoptive father, Andrew Wylie. Was he or was he not shoved off a cliff? It was during one of the birthday celebrations when the whole clan was gathered on the island."

"Must have made the funeral more convenient." They were caught in a congested snarl-up on Madison Avenue, and Tabor told the driver to use his siren.

"It might confuse them," said the driver.

"Go on and use it! We're taxpayers too." The siren wailed as though in mourning for a lost love, and Wylie returned to his theories.

"As far as Harvey knows, there were no witnesses to the old man's swan dive. Now we come to last month and the murders of the twins, Lydia and Annette, who we know were approached by Nathan Manx, who was murdered a couple of days ago."

"You think Manx might have killed the twins?" Tabor always enjoyed suggesting unnecessary complications.

"No way. Not the killer type. No, Manx was go-betweening, hired to make the offers to buy out the heirs to the tontine. What I think may have happened is one of the twins was smart enough to work out which of her siblings was behind the offer, she made the mistake of confiding in her sister and then confronting the perpetrator in their own apartment. So they were duly dispatched. It's easy for Manx to figure out who did them in and the dummy turns the screws on with blackmail. Hence, his throat gets cut."

"Not bad, Norman, not bad at all," commended Tabor. "Sounds like it has the makings of a good television movie. And now for this morning's stiff."

"Poor Natalie." Norman had told Tabor about the Friday night spree at Dombey's. "I suppose getting bounced made her that much more desperate. I mean, along with her brothers, Nicholas and Arnold, they're the hardest up. She probably lived from paycheck to paycheck with little or nothing stored away. Let's say she knows something from the time they were all kids living together on the island—or about Andrew's death. She wants money and she wants it badly. So she hits the killer up for a loan. He gives her a hard time about it, so she drops the clanger, something like, 'You give me the money or I'll tell what I know about such and such all those years ago.' They made a date to meet this morning or some such thing, which gives him plenty of time to sharpen a knife and set up an alibi."

"I think he waited for her outside the club and followed her home. I mean if he wants to cloud the scent by setting up this mugger gambit, makes more sense to do it on her own turf, right?"

"Six of one, half a dozen of another. Murder shouldn't be too meticulous." Someday Wylie planned to write a book. "You know what I mean?" Tabor grunted. "Now our boy, or maybe girl, has a very meticulous mind. Everything has got to be just so. Who in this family fits the bill? Certainly Harvey and Laura Graymoor because we know how their minds work. Like clockwork."

"How about brother Robert this morning, with the 'old boy' and 'old chap' until I thought I might maybe puke? How about him?" Tabor enjoyed this kind of give and take guesswork. It stepped up the flow of his adrenaline and sometimes, without his realizing it, led to a useful deduction.

"I've got one problem with Robert," said Wylie, somewhat mysteriously.

"Don't tell me you like him?" Tabor felt Robert had been

too patronizing that morning at breakfast.

"I couldn't care less about him one way or another. My problem with Robert is he doesn't need the tontine."

"He's that rich?"

"I don't know what 'that rich' means because nobody knows the value of the tontine, except Robert because his company looks after it and does the investing. But I've done a solid investigation of Robert's financial background, and he checks out A-okay."

"And he owns a town house," added Tabor begrudgingly. It reminded him of his own mortgaged house in Brooklyn, which reminded him to phone his wife at the first opportunity. Maybe he might make it home for dinner and even a movie. He doubted it, but he liked to think about it. Much as he enjoyed being a detective, and ambitious as he was, he missed spending time with his family.

"Laura and Harvey also seem not to need the money."

"What about the sister on the island?"

"Martha?"

"Yeah, Martha."

"It doesn't matter. She couldn't have killed the twins or Manx or Natalie. Too far away on the island."

"She could have pushed the old man off the cliff."

"She could have, but from what I've learned about her, she had no motive."

"Maybe she did the old lady a favor."

"From what I've heard about Helga Graymoor, I have an idea she can do her own dirty work once she sets her mind to it."

"Okay," said Tabor, sounding very weary. "Who's next?"

"Next is Victor, who is also very well off financially. Smart lawyer. I'm not mad about smart lawyers myself, but there are them what dotes on them. Victor seems to have operated in the past just a hair this side of the law. He's known to have close connections with syndicates involved in Nevada and New Jersey gambling and recently won a big case for a suspected porn kingpin. His wife committed suicide, though there are some who hint she might have been coaxed. Harvey and Laura were told by Nicholas's wife, Marjorie, that she suspected Victor used to beat up on her every so often."

"So Victor is a sadist." Tabor didn't like violence or those who begot violence, including himself.

"You can't prove it by me. So again we have to figure Victor doesn't need the rewards of the tontine. Now who would really benefit if they outlived the others?"

"Nicholas and Arnold."

"Right on. You're forgetting a third party."

"If you mean Mrs. Nicholas, whatsername again—"

"Marjorie."

"—I haven't forgotten her, it's just that she wasn't in the picture when Longstreet and the old man got theirs."

"And I still question if the tontine is the real motive behind the murders."

"What have you got on Arnold?"

"Nothing tasteful." He delivered a brief litany on the loves and lives of an aging rake, and Tabor listened with disgust. Then Wylie continued with a briefing on Nicholas that was very brief.

Tabor commented, "Nicholas sounds like a latent nut. How the hell did the old lady choose this bunch for adoption?"

"Well, Ike," replied Wylie, stretching his arms and legs as they approached Harvey and Laura's apartment house, "I assume when they were little babies, they must all have been cuter than buttons."

Harvey heard the sound of the siren in the distance and said to Laura, "Here comes the rest of them." Robert and Victor had been the first to arrive, having met at Victor's penthouse for a quick drink and discussion of the funeral plans that Robert had gotten from Helga during the afternoon. Nicholas and Marjorie arrived about ten minutes later, Marjorie gray and looking uncomfortable, Nicholas pale and, Laura thought, looking badly in need of a good night's sleep. Laura took the orders and Harvey poured the drinks, and by the time Arnold had arrived looking like the cat who had swallowed the canary, Laura was serving snacks. They chatted about the funeral and heard about the grisly morning Laura, Harvey, and Robert had spent at the morgue. They discussed the probable nuisance of reporters and television cameras. Robert assured them that Helga was in control of herself and bearing up nobly, and Marjorie asked what would become of Natalie's effects. Laura told them that Tabor had said the apartment was to be sealed indefinitely, and this made them all very uncomfortable.

"I don't enjoy being a murder suspect," said Laura, and she had not yet had her first drink of the evening. "It makes me feel so vulnerable."

"I think you look fine under the circumstance," said Harvey graciously.

"Are the police so sure that it's one of us?" growled Victor while he moved to a bar stool.

"It's an important theory, old boy, but I didn't hear them say 'positively.'" Robert wasn't happy with his brandy. It had too much bite.

Laura suddenly realized everybody was looking at everybody else with different eyes. They were each trying to find a murderer or trying not to look like one. She found it quaintly bizarre. Harvey wondered aloud if the murderer might not stand up and say, "Okay, gang, I did it," and let them go about the rest of their lives in peace. Robert scolded him for being frivolous. Norman Wylie and Ike Tabor finally arrived. When Harvey went to the door and greeted them, Laura noticed the others exchanging anxious glances.

Laura addressed the family warmly and, she hoped, reassuringly. "They're just here to confirm that there'll be no let-up in the investigation."

"I thought you said this was going to be just for the family." Tabor decided that the speaker was Victor. Wylie's description was perfect. Dyed hair. Corseted midriff. The kind that dropped dead of a heart attack on the tennis court. This time Harvey took care of the introductions while Laura served the drinks. After the small talk and chitchat faded away, Tabor took center stage and advised them Natalie's autopsy was scheduled for the next morning and the body would be released to the mortician on Tuesday. Nicholas felt nauseated and asked Laura for a glass of water. Robert then said the funeral would definitely be planned for Thursday morning, which meant the family would convene on the island Wednesday evening. All said they would make their own arrangements. They discussed the problems of unwanted spectators, and Tabor assured them he'd been in touch with the Connecticut police, who had set in motion the hiring of some trusted private guards. Marjorie was fascinated by the plotting and subplotting; it was the sort of thing she had read about in magazines at beauty parlors but never expected she'd be participating in.

Arnold said, too matter-of-factly, "I have a suspicion Bella Wallace is plotting to be at the funeral." Now that he had their full attention, he told them he had lunched with her. Wylie speculated as to what had passed for dessert. He almost hoped Arnold had proved satisfying enough for Bella to drop her pursuit of him.

"How'd Bella come to latch onto you?" asked Harvey.

"She probably had to latch on to one of us," said Laura, "once she heard the news about Natalie. Did you spill all, Arnold?"

"I knew about as much as she did. But let me tell you, that's a very powerful lady."

About as powerful as a devalued peso, thought Wylie, and then realized he was being spiteful. Laura wondered why Wylie was blushing, and couldn't believe he could possibly be jealous of the Arnold and Bella tryst. Men could be so complicated.

Tabor said, "I'll have a talk with my superior about Miss Wallace."

"Or maybe Norman Wylie can handle it." Harvey was being cute and winked at Norman.

"Tabor's superior is a better idea. He's got more will power."

Ike Tabor now reclaimed the spotlight. "We're not too happy about what's going on with you people. So far, all roads in our investigation lead right back to the family. I hope we're wrong. I've never been up against a situation like this before. I mean in England when they want to get rid of a family, they usually poison the lot of them at dinner and that's that." There'll be a lot of dining on the island, Laura reminded herself and made a mental note to make sure that dear old Rebecca and only dear old Rebecca did all the cooking. Or else bring along a food taster. "I hate to admit it, but I've got nothing on any of you. Like, for instance, if out of the clear blue I turned to you, Mr. Graymoor," he was speaking to Victor, "and asked you where were you between three and four o'clock this morning, what would you tell me?"

"I'd tell you I'd like to talk to my lawyer." Victor laughed at his own little joke, but the laugh evaporated when he realized no one else had joined in. He looked into Tabor's steel gray eyes. "You really want to know?"

"I do."

"It's a little embarrassing, but oh, well, I spent last night with Mona Norris. She's my secretary."

"Okay, and should I call your office in the morning, your secretary would confirm, right?" Tabor was smiling, the smile Wylie recognized as the one usually camouflaging an explosion.

"Well, if you're impatient, I can give you her home phone number. I think she's at home now." Victor was overplaying his hand but didn't realize it. He thought he was winning points for being cooperative.

But Tabor seemed to have lost interest in Victor. Arnold was his new target. "And you, Mr. Graymoor?"

"Well, actually," said Arnold with an air of innocence, "I was on my way home from a singles bar on First Avenue." He mentioned the name. It meant nothing to Tabor, but Wylie made a mental note of it. "As a matter of fact, I told Harvey and Laura I had thought of dropping by Dombey's and picking up Natalie. Now I wish I had."

"Are you sure you didn't?" Tabor's tone was conversational. He wasn't pressing. He was a good detective doing a good job. Harvey was impressed by how suavely he had made the transposition from small talk to inquiry.

"Very sure," replied Arnold. Tabor wondered aloud where he had left his drink. Harvey got him a fresh one. Nicholas was looking as though he had been caught with his hand in the cookie jar. Marjorie's heart was beating so loudly, she was positive everyone in the room could hear it. Tabor now directed his attention to them.

"I suppose you two were together at home all night?"

Marjorie looked at Nicholas. Nicholas stared into the detective's face defiantly. Laura was staring at Marjorie, then she turned subtly to Harvey, who was looking at a bottle of Scotch he was about to open. "Well. . ." began Marjorie. Tabor waited for the lie.

"I spent the night in a seedy hotel on Eighth Avenue." It was Nicholas speaking in a voice no one recognized. "I spent it with a prostitute. She told me her name was Alice. I suppose she has a name for every score and every occasion. I think I'd recognize her again if I saw her, but I'm sure she doesn't live at that hotel. She just uses it." Then his eyes locked with Marjorie's, and he didn't see hatred, he saw pity, and that was worse. There was an embarrassed silence. Even Wylie wished he was someplace else.

"My wife demanded a pizza at three in the morning and fearing for my life if I didn't get her one, I went to the all-night joint near Fiftieth Street and bought one." Harvey had poured himself a large Scotch and was already looking forward to the next one.

"Which meant I was home alone and unaccounted for," said Laura.

Tabor said to Marjorie, "You never left your apartment last night?"

"I was home all night," said Marjorie hoarsely. "I was waiting for Nicholas." She didn't believe what Nicholas had told Tabor, not because she was jealous—she knew no man could ever be completely faithful (her mother had taught her that)—but because she could never conceive of Nicholas with a whore. She felt like screaming at Tabor, you shouldn't believe my husband. He wouldn't know how to pick up a hooker. He doesn't know how to pick up anything. The first night we met I had to do all the work. I instigated the flirtation. I set my sights on him and went after him, and I got him. One of the girls I was with knew Nicholas and told me he was one of the Graymoor heirs. Real rich and in line to inherit a lot more. And what's more, his fingernails were clean. I went after him and I got him and now the joke's on me.

"You see what I mean?" Tabor stood like a comedian in a night club who couldn't understand why he was getting so few laughs. "I've got nothing on nobody. Absolutely nothing." He turned to Robert. "You're still sure your burglar took nothing?"

"When were you burgled?" asked Victor, who couldn't understand Robert's not mentioning it when they had met earlier. "Why didn't you tell me?"

"It slipped my mind." Robert then answered Tabor, "There's nothing missing. Or let's just say there's nothing I'm missing."

"I'm missing an awful lot," Tabor muttered, mostly to himself. Wylie heard the comment. You're missing nothing, thought Wylie, and I'd love to pat you on the back, but it'll have to wait until we're alone later.

Laura looked at her siblings and then couldn't resist asking in a chirpy, hostessy voice, "Now wasn't that fun?"

* * *

Mickey Redfern thought he had covered over a mile in the cavern. He had long since left behind the cell with the remains of Cecil Longstreet and had reached the stream that Harvey had warned him contained unfathomable depths. He knelt and played the flashlight along the stream until he found the huge rock beneath which it apparently originated. He wondered if there was another passageway or cave behind the rock. He had studied up on the history of the many small islands dotting the Eastern seaboard and knew that most of them were of volcanic origin. He had traced Graymoor Island's history back hundreds of years, back beyond the slave trade and pirates to the evidence supplied by artifacts that the island must have existed ages before being inhabited and cultivated by the Shinnecock tribes.

He looked at his wristwatch. It was getting late, time to get back. Heavy winds were forecast for tonight, and Redfern didn't relish the thought of being buffeted about in a small boat. When he reached the cell containing Longstreet's remains, he flashed the light onto the cot. They were there all right. He ran the flash around the cell and froze.

The umbrella was gone.

"I thought they'd never go." Laura was sprawled across the sofa with her shoes off. She had managed a moment alone with Marjorie and found out she didn't have an appropriate outfit for the funeral. Laura said she'd provide one. Then she cautioned Marjorie against any further verbal sparring with Nicholas. Marjorie told her she didn't believe his alibi. Neither did Laura. Harvey had chatted with the others about whether he and Laura would take a train to East Gate or hire a car and drive. "Let's hire a car and drive," said Laura, "then we can ask Nicholas and Marjorie. It'll save them the fare."

"If we get one big enough, we can also accommodate Arnold," suggested Harvey.

"Maybe he'll be driving up with Bella." Laura snorted and

then burst into laughter. "Can you imagine? Arnold and Bella Wallace? My God, but she's predatory." She paused and then had a thought, which she was quick to share. "I hope Arnold marries Bella and takes her for all she's got and then he won't have any need for an inheritance."

Harvey had settled on the floor next to the sofa and lay his head on Laura's lap. She cradled his head and stroked his chin. "That was Mickey Redfern I was talking to." He knew Laura had been about to ask him. The phone had rung just a few seconds after the last guests, Nicholas and Marjorie, had left. "He was very brave and did an even fuller exploration of the cave."

"The dummy."

"He found the stream."

"He's lucky he didn't fall in."

"That might happen to him tomorrow. He's going back. He wants to know as much about that underground maze as possible. He seems to think there might be some action there when we all convene on the island. I might as well tell you, so do Wylie and Tabor."

"Continue. Frighten me further."

"On his way out of the cave, he decided to do a quick reexamination of the cell containing Cedric's remains. This time, Cedric's umbrella was gone."

"Was it raining out?"

"Don't be facetious. Someone was in the cave the same time Mickey was in the cave. Someone who obviously knows the caves better than he does."

Laura sat up, knocking his head to one side. He thought of hitting her back, but didn't. "That can only be Martha."

"Exactly. So Martha knows Cedric was murdered. She also knows there's someone on the island who doesn't belong there and is up to nothing kosher, because she couldn't help but see Mickey's boat at its mooring. Now I'm wondering if she's told anyone else. Because if she does, and Mickey's cover is blown, then we might be minus a very important man looking after us."

"What does Mickey think?"

"Oh, he thinks he has to be that much more cautious tomorrow. He's not worried about running into Martha. He's supplied himself with any number of cover stories to explain his presence in the cave. But what's got him wondering is what's got me wondering. If she removed the umbrella, she certainly knows the toilet case is missing. And if the toilet case is missing, she's got something to worry about. But what's really worrying me is, if Martha's known all this time Cedric Longstreet was murdered, why hasn't she reported it to anyone?"

"Maybe she's afraid."

"Or maybe she's just covering up for someone. I know where to call Wylie. I want to tell him about this. And then how about going out for a sandwich and a movie?"

"Movie's a good idea. I'll look in the papers. Maybe there's a juicy murder mystery on someplace."

"That was Laura," Marjorie said to Nicholas an hour later. "They're hiring a car to drive out to East Gate. They've invited us to join them. Arnold's coming too. I said it was okay."

"Sure, it's okay. It'll save us some money." He was standing at a window in the living room staring out.

"What should we do about dinner? Should I go out and get some Chinese?"

"We'll go out together. Didn't that detective advise us to stick together as much as possible?"

"Don't remind me."

"You haven't said a thing to me about what I did last night. Aren't you angry? Weren't you embarrassed?"

"I'm not angry and I'm not embarrassed because I don't believe a word of it. I'll get my coat." She went to the bedroom. He turned to watch her go. What a trim figure. What a beautiful body. He wondered if he had ever really loved her.

Later that night, Bella said to Arnold, as he came out of the bathroom and got back into bed with her, "Watch the six o'clock news tomorrow night. I'm doing a five-minute special on the Graymoor murders." Arnold groaned. "What's the matter?"

"The 'Graymoor murders.' It sounds so penny dreadful."

"Well, it's plenty dreadful and it's worth more than a penny. And so, baby doll, are you. God, but you're wonderful."

"I dare you explain that on the news."

Bella shrieked with laughter and pulled him down on top of her.

Martha listened outside Helga's room. She could detect nothing but silence on the opposite side of the door. Carefully, she opened the door and looked in. Helga's night light was on, but in the dimness, Martha could see that Helga was asleep. She closed the door gently and then hurried to Helga's writing room. She switched on the desk lamp and began opening drawers, looking for Helga's notes for the new book. Helga was being too secretive about this one. When questioned, she looked sly and then noncommital. But Martha found nothing. Where is Helga hiding the material, Martha wondered. What is she up to? What was all that Robert told her on the phone earlier about the detectives at Laura and Harvey's? Who is the man in the cave? Is he the one who took the toilet case? Why did I take the umbrella? Why did I put it in the cabin? Why did Helga say at dinner, seemingly from out of the clear blue sky, "Martha, dear, sometimes it is dangerous to know too much."

17

Anton Coen, who was performing the autopsy on Natalie Graymoor, had studied to be a surgeon. The inspiration for this ambition was a seed sown in early childhood when he mastered the fine art of trapping flies in a mason jar and then pulled off their wings. From this he graduated to trapping grasshoppers and locusts and mutilating them with an artistry that won him fresh respect from his father, who was an alcoholic. As a teenager he was at the head of his science class, thanks to the deftness with which he dissected frogs and mice. A wealthy aunt subsidized his medical training, and he planned on a wealthy wife with which to furnish an expensive office in a desirable area of New York's East Side. Unfortunately, his childhood proclivities as a vivisectionist never matured into the genius he and his doting aunt thought would materialize, and when an offer came his way to join the coroner's office, he snapped at it. As an autopsyist (a word Coen claimed to have coined), he stood head and shoulders above his peers. He usually performed the operation with an audience of medical students, some of whom referred to him as the Laurence Olivier of coroners. Coen had a lush, fruity theatrical voice and used it to its fullest effect as he described each probe and investigation. Such as, "And now we shall enter the realm of the liver to explore the possibility of damage brought on by either an excess of alcoholic intake or a rude shove." The delicate movements of his wrists as he wielded the appropriate instruments were a hymn to choreographic genius. Had he been born a Japanese, he might have made his mark with the Grand Kabuki. All this artistry he accomplished without musical accompaniment. An educational channel on television was thinking of devoting an hour to him. Natalie was Coen's four hundred and thirty-sixth autopsy. He was a vegetarian.

Later, when Ike Tabor read Coen's report to Norman Wylie over the telephone, he commented, "It's a wonder Anton doesn't decorate his reports with pretty little drawings of flowers and butterflies. I mean it's practically greeting card poetry. I hope Hallmark doesn't get wind of him, he's too good a coroner. Get this line." At his office, Wylie cozied up to the telephone. "I am quoting verbatim," said Tabor. "'There is a nimiety of stab wounds.' I looked up 'nimiety.' It means excess. He must have found that in a crossword puzzle. Further, 'There are four knife wounds arching through the rib cage and penetrating the heart from the rear, I fear.' Now we could do without the 'I fear.'"

"I think it's sweet," said Wylie. "Get to the point. Did he find anything unusual, like three kidneys?"

"The second knife wound was the fatal one. It had to be something like a stiletto because the heart isn't that easily reached from the rear. But on the other hand, Natalie was so skinny she barely cast a shadow. He suspects she was anorexic, which means she didn't eat much. She also drank a lot but not the night she was murdered. He wants to release the body to the relatives, and I see no reason to hold him up. You got any questions?"

"None at all. You got any fresh leads?"

"None at all. You want to play a game?"

"Go ahead."

"It's called, 'Who's Next?'"

They each chose a potential Graymoor victim and pledged a ten-dollar bet. Then in their respective precincts, they went in search of a television set to check the reception. Neither man was about to miss Bella's appearance on the six o'clock news.

* * *

On the island, Mickey Redfern was in the cabin sitting on the cot and staring at Cedric Longstreet's umbrella, which lay across a chair. He smiled. He liked Martha's style, for he assumed it was Martha who had retrieved the piece of evidence from the cell and brought it to the cabin—one way of letting him know she knew about his presence on the island. On the other hand, he considered the possibility she was undertaking the task of removing everything from the cell. Where did she get the stomach to deal with the remains, he wondered. From what he had seen of Martha, he knew he wasn't dealing with someone delicate or fragile. Either word could describe her facial features, but not her physical attributes. Martha was of medium height, but carried herself as though possessed of great strength. Her hands were large and powerful, and Mickey thought she walked like a lumberjack. He didn't doubt for one moment that she was anything but completely feminine, but life on the island had undoubtedly forced her into a dichotomous position as both a daughter and a son substitute. She undoubtedly was strong enough to strangle a man or push one over a cliff, and, as Mickey had explained to Harvey on the telephone earlier that day, he wasn't sure they were dealing with more than one murderer but he didn't want to dismiss the possibility that the killings were the result of an unholy partnership. He wondered why Martha didn't make a move to confront him directly. It couldn't be for fear of him because she had followed him into the cave to get the umbrella. On the other hand, she most certainly knew the underground passages much better than he did and could move about without fear of detection. What other mysteries does that damned place conceal, wondered Mickey. Is it haunted by the ghosts of ancient slaves who must have died there? Did any Graymoors of yore perish there? He got up from the cot, looked at his wristwatch, and decided it was time to get moving if he wanted to make the mainland before sunset.

He wished the umbrella was in less of a state of decay. For

one quixotic moment he had entertained the foolish notion of strolling to his boat with the umbrella open and poised over his head, in case Martha had caught up with him with her binoculars. But then, he reminded himself, that sort of horseplay could get him killed. And he wasn't interested in dying just yet.

In the mansion, Helga was considering a confrontation with Martha. She knew her desk had been investigated because the prowler had been too hasty and disturbed some things in the drawers that Helga had left precisely in place. Helga had a magnificent eye for detail, as any reader of her books would recognize. To pad her novels to a reasonable length and convince her readers they were getting a bargain for the price, Helga dwelt long and lovingly on descriptions of tapestries, exotic oriental rugs, the patterns on chinaware, and the designs of wallpaper. Her female readers found this astonishing and awarded her full marks for such diligent research. Her critics, until they took to ignoring her completely because they realized they in no way influenced her popularity or her sales, took to skipping these pages and found they could accomplish the job of reading a Helga Graymoor in two hours. At this particular moment, Helga wasn't interested in what her audience thought of her talent. She was wondering what Martha had been after. There was another drawer in the desk that neither Martha nor anyone else in the family knew existed. It was reached from the back of the desk and required the use of a certain hidden spring to release it. Helga crossed to the back of the desk, released the spring and pulled the drawer open. Her notes and manuscript pages were untouched. Helga's secret was secure. I'll bet this is what Martha was after, thought Helga. Why, of course, it has to be. It's the first time I've ever been secretive about the plot of a novel, and so she's suspicious. Is she clever enough to suspect I'm writing about the tontine, Andrew's devilish legal instrument to revenge himself on the children he despised? "My poor Andrew," whispered Helga, "why couldn't you learn to forgive me? Was it my fault the poor child was possessed by demons? Was it the child who sent you to your death? Or am I responsible for these crimes?" She slammed the drawer shut and walked to the bar to pour herself a glass of port, wondering where Martha was. She stared at her face in the mirror that hung over the bar. She wondered how much time was left for her.

From the window seat in her room that afforded a magnificent view of the mainland, Martha was studying Mickey as he piloted his boat to the mainland. The binoculars had belonged to her father and had been especially built for him. They provided a superb long-range power, and Martha wondered if the man in the boat suspected this. He never turned his face to the right or to the left. He kept the boat on a straight course to East Gate. The waters were choppy and the skies were heavy with clouds, but never once did the man lose control of the boat. His hands were shielded by gloves, but she imagined they would be strong and sinewy. His shoulders were broad and impressive, and she guessed the back was strong enough to manage a heavy load. She lowered the binoculars and moved away from the windows. She might be wrong. He might not be the one who had removed the toilet case from the cell. Perhaps she was confused. Perhaps he really was just a fisherman who wandered into the cave out of curiosity and with some sort of luck managed not to get lost. But it had been the same outboard motor for the past three days and, from what she could detect through the binoculars, the same fishing gear she had seen when she went into the cave and removed the umbrella. Then a disturbing thought came to her that made her lightheaded with worry. Martha sat down on a chair and folded her hands together. Supposing he was with the police. Supposing he was an investigator. But he'd seen the remains. Why had there been no hue and cry? Why hadn't the police come here to question them about that foul thing in the cell? The knock at her door was so faint, she almost didn't hear it.

"Miss Martha?" It was Juanita, the cleaning woman.

"Come in," said Martha.

Juanita entered with her usual affable smile on her face. "Your mother would like you to join her in the writing room. She's drinking port and she doesn't like to drink alone."

"I'm on my way," said Martha. "Port is just what the doctor ordered."

It was shortly before six o'clock, and Ike Tabor was very tired. He had visited the all-night drugstore on Third Avenue, and the proprietor certainly did know Robert Graymoor, whom he described as an excellent customer with fine manners. He couldn't say if Robert had received a delivery Saturday morning around three or so because he'd been at home, asleep; he'd have to ask the night manager. Prodded by Tabor, he phoned the night manager, who remembered Robert had some medicine delivered but wasn't sure what time. Tabor seemed satisfied with that information and then went to Victor's office for a chat with Mona Norris. When the receptionist informed Mona there was a detective in the outer office who wanted to talk to her, Mona said she'd be right out. Then she went into Victor's office without knocking to tell him she was about to corroborate his alibi and to remind him he had promised to make the coercion profitable. He hissed something nasty, and she repaired to the reception room, first stopping at a mirror to make sure her grooming was still impeccable. Tabor saw her swivel-hipping her way toward him and decided that in this area Victor Graymoor had good taste. Mona introduced herself, and Tabor responded by showing her his badge and his identification. Mona suggested the privacy of the conference room, which was just fine by Tabor, and as she led the way from the outer office, the receptionist got on the phone and blabbed heatedly to her girlfriend, who was a file clerk, that there was a detective grilling that rotten Mona Norris in the conference room, and I'll bet you she's been up to no good like we always expected. In the conference room, seated next to each other on a leather couch, Tabor fought the overpowering urge to fondle Mona's impressive breasts. It wasn't that Mona was all that beautiful; it was just that she was sexually provocative (and always had been, even at the age of six, when she accomplished her first seduction, her cousin Herbert, who was then an elderly nine years of age).

Tabor began by saying he wasn't trying to embarrass her but that she certainly must be aware of Natalie Graymoor's murder, to which Mona clucked her magnificent tongue and said, oh, yes, and wasn't it awful, and Tabor informed her they were checking on the movements of everyone who knew Natalie Graymoor, not just her immediate family. Mona told him that was fine by her and coyly admitted that Victor had been with her from about one A.M. in the morning until about seven when he finally went back to his penthouse. From the pat manner in which she recited her information, Tabor recognized a resourceful liar and lost all interest in her breasts. He didn't spend much time with her because it was apparent she had no intention of varying her details with even a modicum of what might pass for the truth. Tabor reported the results of these inquiries to Wylie at the same time he read him the autopsy report, and Wylie after a pregnant pause, wistfully asked Tabor to once more describe Mona Norris's mammarial magnificence. It was foolish to have asked because Tabor complied with alacrity and gave Wylie a hunger he knew there was no way of satisfying. Wylie asked Tabor if he was sure Mona had been lying and Tabor reminded him that they usually heard the truth in nervous fits and starts, not a well-rehearsed recitation.

"Shall you or I tell one of the Graymoors they can pick up the body tomorrow?" asked Wylie, fighting a feeling of depression brought on by the news that the spectacularly endowed Mona was a liar. Now he was wondering to himself if the endowment was also spurious.

"I'll try to reach Robert," said Tabor while glancing at his wristwatch. "He might still be at the office."

Wylie had also checked his watch. "He's probably on his way home to catch Bella's act on the tube."

"Probably. I'll give it another fifteen minutes and try him at home. You doing anything special tonight?"

"No, I'm planning to go home and put my feet up and think. Why, you on the loose?"

"No," said Tabor, "I promised the wife I'd be home. But I'd sure like to know what Victor Graymoor really was up to Saturday night and why he was so quick to con his secretary into lying for him. I'd also like to know more about Robert and his burglar, but I can't figure a way to get started on it without getting his back up."

"What about Nicholas?"

"What about him?" asked Tabor while scratching his chin.

"Well, Ike, there are whore types and there are whore types. Nicholas doesn't strike me as a whore type. He's chicken. A babe in the woods. He's acting strange because his marriage has gone sour overnight, but Nicholas isn't the type to fly into the arms of a prostitute at the first sign of marital discord. I see him flying into the arms of his mother, which will be in a couple of days. And the wife bugs me too."

"She's awful cute," said Tabor, and Wylie decided he most definitely needed to go home to his wife.

"She's awful deceptive," said Wylie, who always took a measurement and examined it meticulously. "There's a strong probability there's a new man in her life."

"Sure, but do you think that has anything to do with our case?"

"It could if she's playing around with a Graymoor."

"Maybe Arnold?"

Wylie wasn't buying Arnold. "He's as poor as Nicholas and

probably poorer. At least Nicholas draws a weekly salary. Arnold's life with women is another form of Russian roulette."

"Maybe Harvey Graymoor? I've looked into his past, and let me tell you, it's plenty checkered."

"I don't know. I hate to think so. I really like him and the wife." He felt like adding, "I like the wife even more." If Harvey cheats on the side that often, maybe I can offer a sympathetic shoulder for Laura to rest her head on.

He heard Tabor saying, "It's bad to get emotional about suspects, Norman. It could color your judgment."

"Don't worry about me, Ike. I wish there was some way of settling this case before we lose them all to the island."

"Well, we might hit something lucky, but I doubt it. You know, Norman, there's something nagging me. Like I heard something that is very close to the answer we're looking for, but I didn't recognize it when I heard it. You know what I mean? You ever get that feeling when you're dealing with a suspect?"

"All the time, Ike. All it does is give me insomnia." He took another glance at his wristwatch. "I'm signing off. It's almost Bella Wallace time."

"Okay, kid. Keep in touch."

The edacious Bella Wallace was on the verge of racking up one of the highest Nielsen ratings her network's six o'clock news ever garnered. Her appearance had been advertised between programs every half hour for the previous twenty-four hours promising tantalizing tidbits about the Graymoor murders. The ads promised everything except Bella's private number and the identity of the murderer. Bella's personal makeup man had spent an hour softening her look. Her hairdresser reshaped her coiffure to deemphasize her high forehead. Her costumer had convinced her to dress in the simplicity of a blue skirt and jacket with a pale yellow blouse and a simple pin placed over her left breast. The lighting expert promised she would look at least ten years younger, and she remembered to wear contact lenses instead of her usual oversized spectacles because on the news program she'd be looking directly into the camera, and spectacles would cause a glare. At approximately twenty minutes after six, Bella got her cue from the floor manager and sailed into the Graymoor story like a wolf set loose in a sheep cote. She had been alloted five minutes, which was a lavish amount of air time for a news program usually pressed for time, and made the most of it. Her voice skipped from murder to murder with the agility of a mountain goat, saving Nathan Manx's connection for the third minute. The majority of her viewers were indeed titillated, although there were those out there who kept wondering what all the fuss was about. Bella went on to mention the forthcoming reunion with Helga and then informed her audience that the unfortunate Natalie would be buried on Thursday. Then she inquired darkly, "Who will be next?"

Marjorie stared at Nicholas in their living room because she thought she had heard him whimper.

Bella was now concluding her piece as the camera moved in for a tight close-up. In a voice that belonged in a graveyard after midnight, Bella demanded of her viewers, "What do you think? Is this a case of 'am I my brother's keeper'. . .," now pausing for a dramatic effect, ". . . or am I my brother's *killer?*"

Harvey snapped off the set and turned to look at Laura, who had one leg crossed over another and was swinging it ominously. Laura looked up at him and said, "Well, she hasn't told us anything we didn't already know. All she's done is turn a big fat spotlight on all of us and shall we be grateful she didn't illustrate with snapshots of the family? I just love what some of my clients might be thinking."

Harvey said consolingly, "She was only on local. The six o'clock news isn't nationwide."

"So what? People phone each other, don't they? And to think she's having a thing with Arnold."

"Off with his head. Martini?"

"Very. You're sure Helga couldn't have seen this?"

"No way. Don't you think that was a cute touch, Mickey finding the umbrella in the cabin?" He had spoken to Mickey shortly before Bella had taken center stage.

"I don't know if Martha was being brave or brazen, supposing it was Martha."

"It certainly couldn't have been Helga."

"Why not?" asked Laura. "She knows the cave. In fact, I've always thought she's known more than we thought she knew. There's a vein of dark secrets in our mother waiting to be mined. I've long suspected that and so have you."

"Helga's too placid to be a murderer."

"Still waters run deep," Laura reminded him while hating herself for resorting to a cliché. "And we've all seen her temper. You haven't forgotten how nasty it can get."

Harvey brought the martinis and sat next to Laura. "Neither Helga nor Martha could have made it into town to murder Natalie."

"Why not?" Laura met Harvey's bemused look with troubled assurance. "It's less than half an hour to take the boat to the mainland, then get into one of the cars and drive into town. The drive takes only a little over an hour. It could have been managed."

Harvey was very pleased with Laura. "You've really been giving this a lot of thought! Aren't you the clever little girl?"

"Harvey, darling, since I've become a marked woman, I am clinging to all available straws. Like what about everybody else's alibis for Natalie's murder?" She began to enumerate. "Nicholas with a prostitute, an Eighth Avenue prostitute yet, which is the lowest to which a man can sink. And Nicholas is rarely given to fits of degradation. Fits, yes, because we've seen them, but degradation, never. Nicholas is a ninny, but he is also a thoroughbred. In my books Nicky is lying."

"Maybe behind this marital discord bit, Nicholas and Marjorie are really covering for each other?" Harvey was munching an olive and spoke with difficulty, but Laura easily interpreted and didn't like it.

"Save that can of peas for another time," said Laura forcefully. "That marriage is definitely on the rocks. Not even a sudden windfall could save it. But you've got a glimmer of an idea there. Marjorie was alone all night."

Harvey squashed her theory at birth. "She wasn't around to kill Cedric or Father."

"Maybe there are two murderers."

"My head is spinning," said Harvey with a heaven-help-me look at the ceiling.

"Sip slowly," cautioned Laura. "Now Victor and his secretary. That's shaky."

"I wouldn't say that too quickly. I've seen her. She's solid."

Laura nibbled at a cuticle and then said, "Although I've always figured they shack up every now and then. And then there's Robert and his burglar."

"I find that one rather endearing. The thought of an invasion of Robert's domain rather fascinates me. I've always considered Robert so impenetrable, so impervious to the world about him. How did he ever get to be that good with money?"

"Andrew. He learned it all from Andrew." Laura's brows were furrowed. "Now what about Arnold?"

"I know. Bedding Bella Wallace. Disgusting."

"That was yesterday afternoon. But the previous night is unaccounted for."

"'Tis a puzzlement."

"You're not the murderer, are you, darling?"

"Well, if I was, I certainly wouldn't tell you. You'd blab it to everybody." He kissed her lightly on the lips, but Laura was unresponsive. There was a faraway look in her eye, and Harvey wondered what secret planet she was visiting. What fresh deduction was she entertaining? How close was she possibly getting to the truth?

* * *

Several hours later in an unprepossessing Italian restaurant in Greenwich Village that she cherished for its occasionally desired anonymity, Bella Wallace asked Arnold Graymoor, "Well, what do you think? How was I?"

"I could have lived without the 'or am I my brother's *killer*.'" Arnold looked as though he meant it. He had little appetite this night.

"I thought that was a wonderfully dramatic touch. If you're not going to finish your gnocchi, do you mind if I pick?"

"Help yourself." Arnold pushed the plate toward her and then watched her spear the food greedily.

Through a mouth full of food she asked, "You speak to any of the others?"

"No, there's been nothing but silence. I wasn't at home anyway. I saw the program at my local bar."

"Oh, yes? How'd I go over?"

"To tell you the truth, Bella, in my bar they come there to drink, not to watch television. The set was only on to accommodate me. I'm just glad the program didn't reach Connecticut. I'm glad Helga couldn't have seen it."

"And what if she had?"

"I hate to think."

Bella was now hungrier than ever, but her hunger had to do with Helga. She wanted to meet Helga. She *had* to meet Helga.

Ike Tabor phoned Robert at home, and Robert was grateful for being informed Natalie's body was awaiting the mortuary's hearse. Tabor was tempted to ask him what his reaction had been to Bella Wallace's broadcast, positive that all the Graymoors had tuned in to her, but he managed to rein in his curiosity and left Robert to make arrangements with the funeral parlor. This Robert did the moment Tabor freed the phone, and then he dialed Victor to tell him he had arranged for a car and chauffeur to drive the two of them to East Gate.

"Are we carting anybody else?" asked Victor, and Robert

reminded him Harvey and Laura were accommodating the others. "Did you watch the Wallace pig?" Robert told him he found her very unimpressive. "Unimpressive! 'Am I my brother's *killer*' you find unimpressive? It's practically slander!"

"Victor," said Robert calmly, "don't make waves."

Nicholas was enraged. Bella had offended him. Marjorie was trying on the black dress she had picked up at Laura's showroom after work. It was a perfect fit. It wasn't her best color, but it would suit the occasion. From the bedroom she could hear Nicholas slamming things around in the living room. She crossed to the doorway in time to hear him shout into the telephone, "I could murder Bella Wallace!" His voice chilled Marjorie.

Laura, at the other end of the phone asked Nicholas in a pleasant, sisterly voice, "Now really, Nicky, could you really murder anyone?"

18

A pair of wooden horses bore the weight of Natalie's coffin. In the simple pine box, wearing a simple gray dress, plain and unadorned, Natalie looked like a wax doll in a furniture display case. Outside the chapel, the wind whistled, howled, and frequently shrieked, and Helga prayed the children would arrive before the threatening storm broke. She also wished Natalie's coiffure was less frivolous, but the gentleman who created it had required three stiff drinks before he could touch the body, and after a fourth drink, threw caution to the winds and let his fingers run wild. In the chapel with Helga were the three members of the household staff who had agreed to spend the night, since the reunion was a special occasion. The funeral, thought Juanita, the cleaning woman, was a ghoulish touch, and she was glad she was occupying a bedroom that didn't face the chapel. Since the service was to be nondenominational, Juanita was reserving her Hail Mary's for the privacy of her bedroom. Winston, the handyman, and Rebecca, the cook and housekeeper, had earlier, over cups of coffee in the kitchen, reminisced about Natalie as a child, and that conversation was their memorial. Now the wind seemed determined to topple the foundation. Helga shivered and drew her mink coat tightly around her. She asked Winston, "Are you sure the storm's not due to break until late tomorrow night?"

"I'm not sure about anything where the weather's concerned, Miss Helga. But the forecast is for strong winds through tomorrow night and then rain, lots of rain. Small craft warnings too."

"Martha's a good sailor. She can pilot that boat through any kind of weather." Helga waited for someone to second her comment reassuringly, but no one did. Juanita crossed herself three times, and Helga felt like asking her to add one more for luck.

"The floral arrangements are so pretty," said Rebecca.

"Oh, thank you, dear," said Helga, rewarding Rebecca with a lavish smile. "Martha was hours getting them done. She does have a good eye for color, doesn't she? Winston, do you think the candles will last through tomorrow night?"

"Oh, sure, they did the last time, didn't they?" Winston restrained the urge to shudder. The last time, when the twins were buried, the coffins had been closed. Having read in various newspaper accounts that when their bodies were discovered, they were unrecognizable, Winston's usually dormant imagination had begun acting up, and he had suffered over a week of nightmares. "Miss Natalie looks real pretty."

"Too much rouge," said Helga peevishly. "I told them to go easy on the cosmetics, but oh, no, they must have their own way about this sort of thing." She stood up abruptly and announced, "It's time we returned to the house. I'd like to rest a bit before the family arrives."

In the privacy of her suite, Helga reclined on a divan, fingering her pearls, which she thought needed restringing, wondering what to make of Martha's odd behavior for the past three days. On Monday night after dinner, when Helga finally asked her if she had been searching Helga's desk, Martha had apologized and said she'd been looking for a flashlight she had misplaced. Helga did not aggravate the situation by telling Martha her desk would hardly be the place to find a lost flashlight, but she hated both the lie and the authority with which it was spoken. Yesterday and today, Martha had spent hours away from the house. The boat was still tied at the dock, so she hadn't gone sailing. Helga assumed she had been prowling about the maze beneath the island, but in search of what? And Martha seemed to be making abnormally frequent use of Andrew's powerful binoculars. What was she looking for? Or *who* was she looking for? And as for the floral arrangements that Rebecca found so pretty, Helga thought they were a disgrace and had every intention of telling Martha so. They looked hastily patched together, as though there were more urgent tasks awaiting Martha elsewhere. And the night Martha said she had slept in the cabin was the night Natalie had been murdered in New York. I must think no further along those lines, Helga warned herself. I must be very careful. I must sit back and watch and then decide and then judge. With an effort, she raised herself to a sitting position, alert and listening. Was it the awful wind, or was it the walls?

"What is it?" she whispered, "What, what?"

"It's me," cried Juanita from the other side of the door. "It's Juanita! Do you need anything?"

I need a great many things, Helga wanted to shout back, a great many things. I need an answer, although I'm afraid to hear it. Helga arose, went to the door and opened it. "What is it, Juanita?"

"I was passing your room, and I thought I heard you calling."

"No. It wasn't me. It was probably the wind."

The wind buffeted East Gate mercilessly. Shutters banged and store signs creaked, and Mickey Redfern sat at the bar of Ernie's waterfront café nursing a beer. He had watched Robert's chauffeur-driven car pull up, depositing Robert, Victor and their luggage, and then watched as Robert gave the chauffeur some instructions. After the car and chauffeur left, Mickey saw the brothers bend their heads together in a hasty conference.

"There's no sign of the others yet," shouted Victor above the wind. "Let's have a drink."

Robert shouted back, "No sign of Martha either. The boat's not tied to the dock. I hope she's all right. I suppose it's safe to leave the luggage here." But Victor was already making his way toward Ernie's. Robert hurried after him. They took a table against the window and both ordered brandies. Mickey chewed a potato chip while studying the brothers. Harvey had provided him with snapshots of all the surviving members of the family, and Victor's now proved to be more than flattering. Victor in the snapshot looked like an old-time matinee idol. In the flesh he was a tired, middle-aged man who used too much hair dye. Robert was exactly what Mickey expected, sitting erect with the hauteur of royalty, a valet posing as a prince. After serving their brandies, the waiter, who was also the bartender, who was really Ernie the proprietor, put a head on Mickey's beer. Then in a stage aside he identified Robert and Victor.

"Brothers of them murdered girls," said Ernie in his strong New England accent.

"How about that," said Mickey.

"Natalie's funeral is tomorrow. She's the one what got knifed over the weekend."

"Yeah, I read about that."

"Natalie was a real nice kid. Used to come in and play at my upright every so often. Sang too. Awful. But she was a nice kid. The wife and daughter are planning on going to the funeral tomorrow, but if this wind keeps up, I don't know. They got private guards hired to keep any snoopers away. You know, news people, that sort of thing. Martha, that's another daughter, she was in town today making a list of who could come to the funeral. There won't be too many. The Graymoors mostly kept to themselves. The old man was a tyrant."

"I think the brothers want a refill." Mickey saw Victor wigwagging a finger at Ernie, who had his back to them. Ernie turned to their table, and Victor requested repeats.

"That one's Victor," whispered Ernie as he poured the brandies. "Uses hair dye." Ernie voiced the information as though condemning Victor for witchcraft. Mickey's attention was now on Martha, who appeared on the wharf in a state of disarray. She saw her brothers at the window table and hurried into the cafe. The brothers got up and took turns embracing her. Victor called for a third brandy while Robert appropriated a chair for Martha from an adjoining table. Martha hadn't seemed to notice Mickey. If she had, she made no sign of recognition, subtle or otherwise. He doubted if she had ever had a look at his face, although he had sensed the force of her eyes boring into his back through the binoculars. Ernie arrived at their table, and Martha was friendly. Mickey heard her soft hello and inquiry as to the state of health of his wife and daughter, and Ernie's expression of sympathy over Natalie's tragedy. After Ernie returned to the bar, Mickey strained to hear the conversation at the Graymoor table, but it was impossible, what with the wind howling and Ernie holding forth on Martha and what a comfort she was to the old lady. Mickey saw Harvey pull up and park the car.

Martha said, "Oh, thank God, here's the rest of them, now

we can get moving." Laura got out of the car first and hurried into Ernie's.

"Hi, Ernie," she greeted the proprietor warmly. "Five very large brandies, please." Martha was on her feet, crossing to meet Laura, and they embraced. "That's one hell of a wind out there," said Laura. "Do you think it's safe to chance it?" Before Martha could reply, Harvey, Marjorie, Nicholas, and Arnold came trooping in, and Martha was soon swimming in a sea of outstretched arms. Then Ernie was greeted while he lined up their brandies on the bar. Harvey took a bill from his wallet and saw Mickey. Mickey was staring into his beer, the family reunion having made him feel rather left out and melancholy.

Nicholas was saying, "I don't like the sound of that wind out there, Martha." Marjorie was holding her brandy glass with both hands and wishing it were next Monday. Laura was sneaking a glance at the man at the end of the bar who looked unhappy; she wondered if he was Mickey Redfern.

Arnold chose the moment to ask Martha, "Did Natalie arrive safely?" Ernie winced.

"How's Helga?" Robert asked Martha.

"The Rock of Gibraltar." She held up her glass. "To Helga." The others joined in the toast.

Mickey downed his beer and placed some cash on the bar. He took his windbreaker from a hook on the wall behind him and struggled into it. As he went by Harvey, he tripped, fell against him and apologized. Harvey felt him slipping the note into his coat pocket. Now Laura was positive this was Mickey Redfern. After Mickey left, Laura edged next to Harvey and, looking as though she was bestowing a kiss on his cheek, whispered her question. Harvey winked, and Laura was satisfied.

"Come on, gang," said Martha, "drink up."

"Let's get the show on the road," cried Harvey. "We'll drop in on the way back, Ernie!"

I hope we do, thought Laura; I really hope we all do.

While the others piled themselves and their luggage into the Graymoor boat, Harvey drove the car to the parking lot behind Ernie's. He read Mickey's note. "Martha spends too much time underground. Moving to the island tomorrow after funeral." Harvey tore up the note and flung the pieces of paper into the wind after he locked the car.

"Fine way to treat my handiwork," said Mickey who had come up silently behind him.

"You almost gave me a heart attack. I didn't hear you coming."

"You weren't supposed to. Jungle training. If I'd known you were going to pull in here, I wouldn't have bothered with the note and that bum act in Ernie's."

"My wife figured it was you. What do you think Martha's up to?"

"Not sure. I thought at first she was getting rid of the bones, but they were still there today. Now listen, I don't think the cabin's all that safe. Martha keeps dropping in on it like she's looking for somebody. Probably me. So I'll be using my sleeping bag. We can still use the cabin as a drop. Leave notes under the stove. There's a hell of a storm predicted for tomorrow night, a mini-hurricane by the sound of it. What happens if the island gets cut off?"

"It has its own resources. We've been isolated there before. It doesn't last long. Somebody always comes over from the mainland to investigate."

"But what if they can't get there?"

"Then we take our chances."

"No problem for me. I've gotten to know that cave pretty well now. I don't like any of it. Anything new on Natalie's murder?"

"Only that the police think my family's a bunch of liars. Watch yourself. When Martha's suspicious, that's dangerous. I'd better get back to the others. Now you be careful." He hurried to the boat, and Mickey went off in the opposite direction.

"What the hell kept you!" shouted Martha as Harvey leapt aboard the boat.

"The car stalled for a minute. It's okay now. Cast off, sweetheart!"

The engine purred until Martha increased the gas pressure and they moved away from the wharf. The wind was showing them no mercy, rocking the boat like a toy in a bathtub. Marjorie held on to Nicholas, giving the illusion of having effected a reconciliation. She was absolutely terrified, and Nicholas was the port in the storm. Laura glanced her way and thought her face was turning a most unflattering shade of green. The men of the family clung to the railings as Martha, her layers of oilskins protecting her from the wind and spray, directed the craft to Graymoor Island.

Laura was hanging on to Harvey, who was humming a sea chantey. With her arms around her husband, her eyes were on Martha. If she wants to, thought Laura, if she really wants to, one sudden swerve could send one or more of us into the angry brink. Just one sudden swerve.

Marjorie got sick.

Helga spotted the boat with the binoculars. She was in the conservatory, where drinks and appetizers were to be served, with Winston and Rebecca. "I see them!" cried Helga, "I see them! They're almost at the dock! Oh, dear! Marjorie is hanging over the rail. Oh, good, Nicky seems to have a tight hold on her. Oh and good, Laura has a tight hold on Harvey. My poor boys look so windblown."

"Shall I go down to the pier and give them a hand with the luggage?" inquired Winston.

"You stay right here. They can look after the luggage themselves. I don't want you getting wet and catching cold." She lowered her binoculars. They were here. The drama was about to commence.

In New York, Norman Wylie was with Ike Tabor at Tabor's precinct. They were putting together a Graymoor family tree for their own investigative purposes. It was crudely drawn on a blackboard in Tabor's office, but it sufficed. Tabor had ordered sandwiches and coffee, and while they ate, he asked Wylie, "Say, Norman, what's the penalty for breaking and entering?"

"This is a joke, right?"

"Wrong. I was just thinking, while the family's away, we could play. I'd kind of like to have a look around Victor's penthouse and then drop in on Robert's town house. You interested?"

"Very."

"How's about tomorrow night?"

"You got a date."

"Neither one of them has live-in servants, do they?"

"Not that I know of."

"You don't suppose that secretary might be using Victor's place while he was away."

"That would be fun." Wylie was leering, and Tabor nodded in agreement. "We'll phone Robert's place before trying it in case he decided to hire a house sitter, what with that maybe-burglary scare."

"Yeah. 'Maybe-burglary scare.' This corned beef is awful."

"That's because it's tongue," said Wylie.

Bella was working late in her office, and Arabella Keats, her secretary, wished she'd get off the phone and finish the dictation and let Arabella get home at a reasonable hour. Bella held her producer trapped at the other end of the phone in the study of his Westchester split-level. "Use your head, Irv, a helicopter would be too obvious."

"Not if you crash land," said Irv, who had once produced a prime time adventure series.

"Not funny, Irv. Don't you know some ex-commando who might sneak me onto the island under cover of night, or something?"

"As a matter of fact," said Irv, "I used to know a professional mercenary a couple of years ago. We used him as an advisor on one of the episodes of *The Boomerangs*. Now let me think, what the hell was his name?" Irv's wife poked her head into the study and asked if he was ever going to get off the phone because the roast beef was beginning to look leatherish. He waved her away. "Got it. His name is Mickey Redfern. He does private protection and investigation now."

"See if you can find him," said Bella eagerly. "I've got to get on Graymoor Island!"

"Well, I can't do anything until the morning, so you might as well call it a day. See you tomorrow."

Bella slammed the phone down and asked Arabella, "Where was I?"

Arabella looked at her pad and read back in a deadly monotone, "Of all the family members, Arnold Graymoor seems to have the potential for an interesting future."

"Oh, yes," said Bella, smiling dreamily, "I was doing Arnold. Well, to continue. . ."

"I thought Helga was clinging to all of us as though she knew our days were numbered." Laura had changed into slacks and a blouse and was putting on a sweet little jacket of her own design. Harvey was waiting patiently at the door with his hand on the knob, anxious to join the others in the conservatory, not for the pleasure of their company but for the bounty promised by the well-stocked bar. "She was even more than affectionate to Marjorie, and we know how she feels about Marjorie. And I wonder how Marjorie's feeling."

"Inadequate, I should think. Come on, get a move on."

"There's no rush, Harvey. I know what you want and I wish you'd stop behaving like an alcoholic. Do we have to go to the chapel for prayers after dinner?"

"We must humor Helga."

Laura groaned. "We'll probably be too sloshed to pray."

"We can admire the floral arrangements." Harvey leaned against the door while Laura repaired her makeup.

"What did Mickey Redfern tell you in the car lot?"

"You're too smart."

"Well, you took so damned long, I figured Mickey saw you driving in and decided to add to the note he slipped you."

"I hope you're the only one who saw that."

"I think I was. The others were all too absorbed in each other. What did he tell you?"

Harvey moved away from the door and crossed over to Laura. He told her what Mickey had told him about Martha's behavior the past few days, and after Laura digested the information, she rewarded Harvey with a Gallic shrug. Then she asked Harvey, "Did you pack your gun?"

"Yes, but I hope I don't have to use it."

"I hope so too, sweetheart, I hope so too. Well, let's get moving. On with the show."

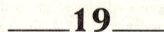

19

The small talk was volleying back and forth in the conservatory. It was all so artificial and unreal, Harvey felt as though he had stumbled onto the stage of some obscure repertory company performing one of those mild little British comedies Broadway used to import back in the twenties and thirties. Murder and danger had taken a back seat to the stock market and next season's fashions. Helga moderated the drinking party like an empress of a mythical kingdom, for the first time in Harvey's memory not admonishing him or anyone else about drinking too much. From the dining room he could hear the clatter of Rebecca and Juanita setting up the buffet dinner. Winston as bartender was proving to be more than adequate, whipping around the room filling orders like someone half his age. Harvey wondered what the servants thought about the sword of Damocles hanging over the family, or didn't they give a damn? They had to feel something. Certainly Rebecca and Winston, who were with the Graymoors even before Harvey had been adopted almost forty years ago, had to feel some sort of sympathetic emotion. Rebecca, who was a spinster, had been almost a surrogate mother to the youngest adoptees. Nicholas had often turned to her for solace, not Helga. Winston, who had been a widower for almost ten years, had taught them to fish and boat and was the person who had introduced them to the mysteries of the underground passageways. Juanita was a late arrival to the family. Harvey assumed she was a poor swimmer and so had had a tougher time making it across a Mexican border river into Texas. He wasn't even sure if her status as an illegal immigrant had ever been rectified. Helga had found her in a halfway house for unwed mothers in Hartford, one of Helga's infrequent excursions into the land of good deeds (Helga was there researching one of her most successful novels, *Love's Languishing Lies*). Juanita now resided in East Gate with a man she claimed to be her husband, somewhat dissimilar in looks to the last three men she had claimed as husbands. Her child had been put out for adoption, and to Harvey's knowledge, Juanita chose to remain infertile after that. Juanita worshipped Helga, who somehow learned to tolerate what Helga referred to as "Juanita's passionate Catholicism."

Helga had at one time dabbled in Christian Science but soon found she could not subscribe to any formal religion, which was just as well, as the children were from disparate denominations. She personally read to them from the Bible every Sunday, which she found quite agreeable as the stories were so well constructed, and eventually lifted some ideas to incorporate into her own work.

Rebecca announced dinner but the family was slow to leave the conservatory. Harvey had his eye on Laura, who was deep in conversation with Marjorie. Martha sat with Nicholas on the piano bench patting his hand while Helga continued to appropriate the attention of Robert and Victor. Only Arnold made a beeline for the groaning board in the dining room, whispering to Harvey as he passed him, "I'm starving to death." Harvey refrained from replying, "That's one way to go, but not in this family."

Loudly, Harvey cried, "Come on, gang, let's eat," and Laura gave him a funny look.

Marjorie got up and said to Laura, "I guess we should eat something. Smells good." She left Laura, who was trying to get Martha's attention away from Nicholas. Happily, Nicholas stood up and left Martha, and Laura claimed her at once.

Laura asked Martha, "Would it be too awkward to prepare a separate room for Marjorie?"

"Not at all," said Martha, "especially since Nicholas has asked for a room for himself. Too bad about those two, I thought it was a marriage made in heaven."

"No, dear," said Laura, taking Martha's arm and escorting her to the dining room, "it was a marriage made in cloud cuckoo land. How have you been? It's been ages. You look tired. Been keeping late hours?"

"Been worried to death."

"I know, dear. Aren't we all?" Laura couldn't wait to repeat Martha's fear to Harvey. A short while ago, before choosing to stand to one side while considering the strangeness of the evening, Harvey had asked her if she didn't think the family was behaving with an abnormal display of cool.

Robert took Helga into dinner with Victor trailing in their wake. Victor paused for a moment to talk to Winston and to inquire politely as to his well-being. Winston responded with a dignified declaration of sympathy for Natalie, and Victor sighed and continued on into the dining room.

Rebecca seemed to have outdone herself, and Harvey was impressed as he browsed about the buffet. He wasn't particularly hungry, but at least this sort of smorgasbord was more appetizing than the one presented by his family. A very heavy sensation had come over Harvey from the moment he set foot on the island, an oppressive, almost smothering sensation brought about by the realization that here they were all confined in this small, suffocating world, anticipating tragedy. In New York there was space and taxis and doormen and sometimes policemen, even though none of that had been of any avail for Natalie and the twins. Here it was something different, even with the knowledge that tomorrow there would be Mickey Redfern to back up Harvey and Laura and, if there were no flaws in their plan, trap the killer. He realized Nicholas was standing next to him and staring at him with a peculiar expression. "Is something the matter?" asked Harvey.

"Your lips were moving. Are you talking to yourself?"

"I always talk to myself," replied Harvey, arching his eyebrows. "It's the only time I can enjoy an intelligent conversation."

Laura joined them. "Don't the deviled eggs look enticing?"

"They're loaded with cholestorol," warned Harvey. Nicholas helped himself to two. Harvey wondered if he was supposed to be impressed by this sudden display of bravery.

Laura waited until Nicholas went zeroing in on a tray of sliced ham and said to Harvey, "Marjorie is moving into a room of her own."

Harvey groaned. "That's bad."

"They find the idea of sleeping together somewhat awkward. At home, Nicholas has been banished to the couch in the living room."

"Separating them makes them each an easier target."

Laura wondered if Harvey noticed her appetite slipping away. "I hadn't thought of that. Who would want to kill Marjorie?"

"It's not Marjorie I'm worried about."

"Oh."

"The tomato aspic is a poem!" trumpeted Helga, and Rebecca, positioned behind the chafing dishes, looked like a pouter pigeon who had made her first triumphant solo flight.

"What's this?" asked Victor, poking about a plate that contained something resembling a steaming pie.

"Why, that's my potato and onion pie," explained Rebecca, sounding as though she had just discovered fire. "It was Miss Natalie's favorite."

The sudden silence that blanketed the room was thick enough to be cut with a sharp tongue, and Helga provided it. "We can't spend the weekend sidestepping the inevitable. Three of us have been murdered."

Not four, thought Harvey, not Andrew too? And you don't know about Cedric Longstreet, or do you?

"Must you, Mother, while we're eating?" Robert had heaped his plate greedily.

"Stop acting the fool, Robert. And the same goes for the rest of you. There's every likelihood there's a murderer in this room. I hope with all my heart that there isn't. I hope the murders that have already been committed were sheer coincidence. But I'm an author. I don't buy that kind of slipshod plotting. I think one of you is out to eliminate the rest of us in order to claim the tontine. At least that's the only motive I can find that makes any sense."

"It doesn't make much sense to me," bellowed Victor. "Say the killer succeeds in eliminating the competition, the survivor would stand out as the guilty party."

"Victor," said Helga in a voice heavy enough to hammer nails, "I've always realized you operate in mysterious ways, but that doesn't mean you're terribly clever when confronted by a mystery. The solution to your observation is quite simple. There's more than one of you involved. Rebecca, darling, more aspic, but don't let me make a pig of myself."

Laura was sitting next to Harvey in a window seat, impervious to the wind rattling against the panes behind her, seemingly deaf to the roar of the ocean beyond the cliffs. "Full marks for Helga. Called her shot like a pro."

"It was a nice performance," said Harvey while chewing a mouthful of turkey, "but the tontine isn't all of it." Now he had Laura's undivided attention. "It goes back a long time ago, back to when Esmaralda was strangled. After the dog's body was found, Andrew and Helga had a real dustup because Andrew wanted one of us sent away, back to the home from which we'd been adopted." Laura was ignoring her food. "But Helga prevailed and there was no banishment."

"Too bad," said Laura.

"That's right," agreed Harvey, "because I think that's the murderer. Note that Helga has avoided any mention of Cedric Longstreet."

"Maybe she's saving that for dessert."

"Maybe she doesn't know he's dead," said Harvey. "She didn't mention Andrew, either."

"There's no proof he was murdered, that's probably why."

"Helga doesn't need proof." Harvey put his plate aside on a convenient table. "She gave herself away when she made that crack about not buying slipshod plotting. Whatever you say about those books of hers, you have to admire their solid construction."

Laura nodded in agreement. "Brick upon banal brick."

"I've got a theory about why Andrew was murdered." Laura's lips were suddenly dry. "I remember that weekend vividly. There was a lot of tenseness and strain between Andrew and Helga. There was something he wanted to do that she was against. You heard them arguing in the writing room, you told me about it."

"Correction. I heard the noise of an argument. It went on for a long time. At one point or another, there were others who heard. I remember going outside and finding Winston working in the shrubbery under the writing room windows, which were open. He looked very uncomfortable, as though I thought he was eavesdropping."

"I think after the argument, when most of us were off on our own—"

"Didn't we go spooking about in the cave?"

"Whatever we did, we did it together. We've got an alibi."

"Everybody's got an alibi, like the night Natalie was murdered. This family's big on alibis."

"Let me finish. After the argument with Helga, Andrew had a confrontation and made an accusation."

"You're sure?"

"I'm guessing, but it makes sense. So he was pushed off the cliff."

Laura looked at Harvey with affectionate admiration. "You're running hot."

"Things have been starting to fall into place in my mind. Returning to the island has triggered a fresh line of thinking. It's as though it's all been laid out in front of me, if I only knew where to look. Now the other thing I'm sure of is someone saw Andrew killed."

"Natalie?"

"Very possibly. If it was the twins, then they had to share the secret because they were inseparable. But the twins would have blabbed. They could never keep a secret."

"Then if it was Natalie, she might have been blackmailing—"

Harvey interrupted her. "If she'd been blackmailing, she'd have been dead a long time ago. I think she was waiting. She waited for five years, holding that secret like a nest egg. When she was fired from Dombey's, it was the straw that broke her ambition. I think then she went after the money she wanted and that's that."

"And somewhere in all this there's Nathan Manx."

"A small supporting role. Mind you, important enough to

warrant billing, but small. He was unlucky. Which brings us here to the island, and stop looking so solemn, because here comes Martha, and bless my soul, she looks a bit unsteady on her feet."

Martha settled herself on an ottoman she pulled directly in front of them. "Well, my dears," she said in a voice shrill and sharp enough to cut steel, "isn't this the perfect setting for murder?" Her voice had carried across the room, and Rebecca hoped it hadn't reached Juanita in the kitchen. Juanita had overheard Helga's ominous prediction of murder earlier and had recited the stations of the cross half a dozen times in hopes of warding off any evil spirits. Winston had come from the kitchen bearing a beautiful cut glass bowl of mixed fruits. Martha was holding a glass of white wine, freshly filled before joining Harvey and Laura, and managed not to spill a drop while punctuating each word of her statement with dramatic flourishes of the hand. "I mean, isn't it absolutely perfect? Isolated island, mysterious old mansion, the wind howling like a chorus of banshees, a dead body in the chapel, secret passageways and hidden panels, and all the other accoutrements needed for a horror show, and Mother letting us know she just might be wise to one of us."

"Well, sweetheart, Mother knows best," said Harvey lightly. He looked at Helga, whose face had frozen into a scowl.

"You've had too much to drink, Martha," scolded Helga. "You've never drunk like this before, what's wrong with you?"

"What's *wrong* with me? Need you ask? I'm frightened. If I'm about to be polished off, I don't want to know about it. Take me, whoever you are, but take me in a state of alcohol-induced lethe!"

"Rather flowery, don't you think?" Laura asked Harvey in a stage whisper.

"I kind of like it. It's impressive. It's the most vocal she's been since Robert appropriated her bicycle."

"I think you should go to your room, Martha." Helga was speaking in her celebrated "deal with naughty child" voice and it brought Laura a feeling of *déjà vu*. Laura was remembering Helga speaking to one of the others in that same tone of voice at least thirty years ago, but to whom, when, and why? And hadn't that banishment been imposed by something graver than an overindulgence of liquor?

"I am *not* going to my room, Mother, and I wish all of you would stop eavesdropping. It's very rude. I'm talking to Harvey and Laura. They're the only sensible people in this room."

"Oh, dear," murmured Laura, "that's the kiss of death," and too late wished she hadn't said it.

Robert studiously engaged Marjorie in conversation. Victor joined Arnold at the bowl of mixed fruit, and Helga begrudgingly accepted a chance for a talk with Nicholas.

Martha looked at all of them and then redirected her attention to Harvey and Laura. "I'm the biggest fool of all, aren't I?"

"Don't be so hard on yourself," advised Laura.

"Hard on myself? I should have taken myself to task years ago, when I was younger and there was still hope. I should have left this bloody island long before Andrew died and found another life for myself." Laura was amazed by this sudden outburst of bitterness. Harvey wanted Martha to continue talking. He wanted them all to do a lot of talking, because now he was prepared to listen very carefully. To listen very carefully to what was said and not said, because he knew it was between the lines that he stood the greatest chance of isolating a murderer. "When was it you told me to get away from here, Laura?"

"It was a long time ago."

"I should have listened. I shouldn't have hypnotized myself into believing Robert would one day rescue me from this oblivion." She sipped the wine and showed distaste. "It's warm. Oh, well, they tell me warm works quicker." She smiled at Harvey. "I'll bet you've got some idea about what's really going on around here. I'll bet you do, Harvey."

"I'm as confused as you are."

"I'm not confused. I'm just mad at myself." She stared into her drink disconsolately.

Laura could guess what was wrong. Martha had seen Robert alone and probably found out there was little hope of his finally proposing marriage. Unless she made a positive move to rescue the rest of her life, she was condemned to remain here with Helga, until either Helga was dead or both were murdered.

"It's too gruesome, it's just too gruesome," said Martha in a ghostly whisper. "In the morning we bury Natalie, in the evening we watch Helga opening her birthday presents. In the morning we weep, in the evening we listen to her coo with joy over her loot. I never much liked Natalie, but tomorrow I think I'll cry for her."

You'll be crying for yourself, thought Laura.

"Help me up, Harvey." Martha held out a hand to him, and he steadied her on her feet. "I think I'll have some coffee. You see, Helga expects us all to go trooping down to the chapel before bedtime for one last meeting with Natalie before the outside chosen few descend on us for the funeral." She faced the window and said, "Blow, winds, blow! Blow us up a real Shakespearian tempest. Let's keep the real world out of Helga's never-never land."

"Let me escort you to the coffee." Harvey offered Martha his arm, and she accepted with alacrity. As they walked away, over her shoulder Martha quipped to Laura, "Bet you never expected to see me walking off with your husband." Laura almost replied, "Bet you didn't either," but then thought better of it as Marjorie was now approaching her.

"Thanks for arranging for the bedroom," she said to Laura.

"It was no problem. Nicholas was of the same mind."

"Helga's been very sweet and understanding." They could both see Helga and Nicholas deep in conversation. "I think she's actually glad we're finished. She never approved of me, did she?"

"What does it matter?"

"You're right. What does it matter? Listen, I want your advice. Now that Helga knows the score, is there any reason why I have to stick around for the rest of the weekend?"

"Well, you can't leave the island tonight. It's late and the wind out there sounds just terrible."

"I was thinking of going sometime after the funeral."

"Is there really no hope of you two working this out?"

"Nicky hates me. Try to catch his face when he happens to be looking at me. I've seen it. It's awful. Laura, this place frightens the hell out of me. I want to get away."

"Let's wait until tomorrow. Don't bring it up tonight to anyone else. I'll talk it over with Harvey as soon as I can."

In the kitchen, Juanita was clutching the crucifix that always hung around her neck, speaking to Rebecca and Winston in a teardrenched voice. "I don't want to go to the chapel tonight."

"Nobody says you have to," said Rebecca.

"Miss Helga said she wanted everybody there. I've already prayed for Miss Natalie."

"You can't pray too often for a departed soul," offered Winston, who was a great fan of Oral Roberts.

"Santa Maria, why did I agree to spend the night here? I'll never sleep, and if I do I'll have nightmares. And after what Miss Helga said about murder, I don't want to be alone."

"If you don't want to be alone," said Rebecca testily, "you'd better come along with us to the chapel, because the rest of us are all going and that means you'll be alone in the house."

Juanita recognized defeat when she was confronted with it. When the sheriff's deputy had collared her as she climbed out of the river in Texas, she had accepted the bargain he offered in return for her freedom, which eventually led her to the home for unmarried mothers. Here she couldn't fight them, so she had to join them. Tomorrow, if she survived the night, she'd be home safe. But Rebecca had mentioned something about remaining to serve for Helga's birthday dinner. There had to be a way to get out of that.

Robert had come into the kitchen. "What's the menu for tomorrow night, Rebecca darling? I want to know what wines to select from the cellar." Juanita was sniveling. "What's wrong with you?"

"She's frightened," said Rebecca.

"Now Juanita, old girl, there's no need for you to be frightened." Juanita wasn't buying any of it. "You're in no danger." He winked at Rebecca, and Rebecca started reciting the birthday dinner menu.

Bundled in coats, heads covered with either hats or scarves, the family and the servants battled against the ferocious wind, making their way to the chapel. Martha held on to Robert while playing her flashlight in front of her. Harvey, Nicholas, and Winston carried lanterns. Harvey, who brought up the rear of the procession, was reminded of a scene from Poe. And when we get to the chapel, he wondered, will we find that Natalie is, after all, not dead? That she is arisen, that there has been a miracle?

He felt the hair at the back of his neck stiffening.

Mercifully, the pilgrimage to the chapel returned to the house within fifteen minutes. Juanita fled to her room and bolted the door. Rebecca accompanied Martha to her room, providing Martha with comfort as she became ill just after crossing the threshhold. Helga, informed by Robert that Marjorie wanted to leave the island after the funeral, was having none of it.

"The newspaper people will be polluting East Gate, especially since they've been banned from the island. You'll be recognized, and you know how newspaper people are. They get suspicious and will ask questions that could embarrass us, and I will not be embarrassed. I am suffering enough with these infernal murders. It is dreadful living under a cloud of fear, and the least you can do, Marjorie Graymoor, is stay on this island until this ridiculous charade is played out. What have you got to be afraid about? You're not an entrant in the tontine steeplechase." The tirade, which was spewed forth in the conservatory, seemed to leave Marjorie unmoved. She was standing behind the piano, framed in a window against black drapes, with what looked to Laura like a very set and determined expression. "You were certainly anxious enough to become a member of this family and until this weekend is concluded, I insist that you continue to act like one." Laura's eyes never left Marjorie. Marjorie was staring at Robert, who was at the bar with Arnold, both drinking brandies. Or was she staring at Arnold? Winston arrived from the kitchen carrying a bucket of ice, and Rebecca returned to announce that Martha wasn't feeling too well and had asked to be excused. Laura made a mental note to look in on Martha before breakfast and provide her with a hangover remedy.

"Of course, I'll stay," said Marjorie, "if you insist." Harvey cheerfully offered to play waiter to Winston's bartender, and Victor tried to recruit three players for a game of bridge. Helga and Nicholas volunteered, and when a third pledge was not forthcoming, Helga commandeered Winston. "He's a very good player," Helga said to Victor. "His bidding is erratic but he's a whiz at false carding." Rebecca went to the library to set up the bridge table and chairs. Arnold had moved to the piano, apparently making sympathetic noises for Marjorie's benefit. Laura hoped he wasn't stupid enough to seduce Marjorie under Helga's roof. She smiled warmly at

Harvey who had put his arm around her.

"Why do corpses have to look so waxen?" asked Harvey.

"What a charming gambit," said Laura. "You must try it sometime when you're trying to score a pickup in a bar."

"I already have. Arnold and Marjorie are getting awfully cozy. Shall we join them? It's too damned early to go to bed."

"It is if you only intend to sleep. I don't think they want company."

"Marjorie's afraid of something," said Harvey.

"Correction," amended Laura, "she's afraid of some*one*. And it's not Nicholas. I caught her looking at Robert during Helga's peroration, and if looks could kill, my dear . . . On the other hand, Arnold was standing next to Robert, so he might have been the object of her disfavor, except they look so lovey-dovey at the moment, I think I'll have to scrub him as one of the candidates. Why don't I have a drink?"

"Situation to be remedied at once. What'll it be?"

"How's for some bourbon on the rocks?"

"You loathe bourbon."

"Exactly. This way I'll drink less."

Arnold led Marjorie to the bar. "Marjorie needs a drink," he announced. She asked for a tall Scotch and water, and Harvey poured. Arnold was paying the kind of attention to Marjorie he usually reserved for his wealthier prey. Laura wondered if he possessed some information about Marjorie's hoarding some secret cache of wealth.

Marjorie asked, "Shouldn't someone look in on Martha?"

"Rebecca will," advised Laura. "Sorry about Helga's tirade. Are you staying?"

"Arnold's convinced me I should." Marjorie was looking at Arnold with the anxious appeal of an unpurchased puppy in a pet shop.

"Arnold is such a good convincer," said Laura, and Arnold shot her a dirty look.

"Where's Robert?" They looked at Harvey. No one had seen Robert leave the room.

"Where indeed *is* Robert?" wondered Laura. "Certainly not wandering about outdoors. 'T'ain't a fit night out there for man nor dog."

Robert was visiting Martha, who was looking particularly unappealing in her man-sized bathrobe, worn bedroom slippers, and pearl gray face. "Are you sure there's nothing I can get you?"

"You can get me off this island."

"You can't leave Helga."

"I don't like that tone of voice, Robert. I'm free to make my own choices."

"Where would you go? You have no money."

"I've got enough."

Robert laughed. "You're such an innocent. That's a nasty world out there. You'd be gobbled up."

"Don't be too sure of that. I'm not all that innocent."

"Get some sleep. You'll feel better in the morning."

"I'll feel no different than I feel right now." There was a light knock on the door. "Come in." Rebecca entered.

"Oh! I thought you were alone." Rebecca had intruded on too many of their private scenes in the past and was familiar with the mixed look of frustration and despair on Martha's face.

"Robert was just leaving," said Martha.

"Good night," said Robert amiably, and left.

"Oh, Rebecca!" wailed Martha. The older woman took the younger woman in her arms, rocking her gently back and forth and evoking all the soothing noises in her repertoire.

In the conservatory, Harvey was the first to see Robert enter and cried out, "Why, there's old reliable Robert! We were just wondering where you'd disappeared to."

"I looked in on Martha," said Robert as he helped himself to a brandy.

"And how is she?" asked Laura.

"She'll survive," said Robert.

"I hope so," said Laura, and the others looked at her with varying degrees of reaction. Laura feigned surprise. "Was it something I said?"

"Who's for a game of poker?" suggested Arnold.

"I can't afford it," said Marjorie glumly.

"We only play for pennies," said Arnold. Laura had an idea poor Marjorie wasn't even in that financial league.

"I'm not too good at it," insisted Marjorie.

"Now don't be a spoilsport," said Robert. The way Marjorie looked at him, she was being anything but a spoilsport. Laura thought she was Medea casing Jason's children for their impending dispatch. "I'll underwrite your losses."

"Take him up on that offer," said Arnold. "It's a rare occasion when Robert displays any generosity." Laura and Harvey didn't miss the undertone of irony. How often, wondered Harvey, has Arnold sought out Robert for financial assistance and been rejected?

"We could play on the dining room table," said Harvey as he headed for the dining room, expecting the others to follow.

"Isn't the dining room a long way from the bar?" asked Arnold as he took Marjorie by the arm to escort her to the game. Laura wished Marjorie didn't look as though she was being led down the last mile.

In his motel room, Mickey Redfern was worrying about the weather. The radio was playing softly, Mickey waiting for the next forecast. Meanwhile, he checked the haldric he would wear around his waist the next day. There was his gun holster with weapon and his sheathed hunting knife, all securely in place. He checked again his powerful flashlight and his provisions. He had left his fishing gear safely stashed in the island behind the cabin, camouflaged by some undergrowth. He tapped the compass that had seen duty with him for almost twenty years in some parts of the world even mercenaries had never heard of. Then he opened a can of beer and lay back on the bed. He wondered what was going on at Graymoor Mansion. Certainly there were tensions, and he wondered how they were being dealt with. He had seen the boat transporting Natalie's coffin to the island and wished the beer-swilling gravediggers had shown a bit more respect for their cargo. He had been to Dombey's to reconnoiter Natalie the night before he departed for East Gate. He couldn't believe the haggard creature was not yet thirty years old. He recalled what he had thought then; she's already lived her life and doesn't know it. She's burnt out and doesn't accept it. He wondered if he would know when he was finished. Probably not. Probably too dead to know. On the radio, the weather forecaster, after predicting an overcast morning, breezily added the afternoon would bring gloom and doom with heavy rains and winds of hurricane force that had been traveling up from the Bahamas. Mickey had never liked the Bahamas. He had once gotten knifed there by a Portuguese whore. He switched off the radio, got off the bed, and went to the window. He pulled back the curtains and looked out. It was indeed a lousy night. He thought of Harvey and Laura, and then the projectors in his mind switched to some footage featuring Martha. Someday I'd like to get to know Martha, he thought, if Martha survives. He drew the curtains together and went to the television set. He inserted coins into the slot, selected the X-rated channel, and then lay back on the bed to experience a few hours of frustration.

"Nicholas," said Helga at the bridge table, "it's your bid."

Nicholas swam out of his reverie. "May we review the bidding?" He wished he were anywhere but at this bridge table. The playing was protracted and tedious. Winston selected cards like a blind dentist pulling teeth. Helga continually lost the count and behaved as if she were in her dotage. Victor was out for blood and succeeded in drawing it. Nicholas had never been a good player and was perpetually apologizing. By this time, their final rubber, Helga was beginning to sympathize with Marjorie.

"Nicholas," said Helga with forced patience, "the bidding has already been reviewed. One club, pass, one diamond, double, two hearts, pass, three hearts, pass, and now it's up to you, dear. It's your turn. What do you bid?"

"Four spades."

"You're mad!" shouted Helga, "you're absolutely mad! How dare you introduce a new suit at the four level?"

Nicholas banged a fist on the table, astonishing the three players. "I God damn well bid four spades, and I God damn well mean it! Four God damn spades!"

He's mad, Helga was thinking; he's absolutely mad. I think I shall bid five hearts and watch him go berserk. I'm fully prepared for that. I've seen him run amok before.

"Five hearts!" trumpeted Helga.

"Six spades," countered Nicholas.

"Double," said Victor with sadistic relish.

Winston, whose lead it was, took an eternity to select a card, and by the time he chose one, cooler heads prevailed. Helga carefully laid her cards on the table, and, as dummy, sat back to watch Nicholas be destroyed.

"I don't know why I'm winning," said Marjorie weakly, embarrassed by the heap of pennies in front of her, "I really don't play all that well."

"You're doing just dandy," said Arnold through clenched teeth. The winds were continuing their onslaught. Laura's eyes pleaded with Harvey to bring the tiresome game to an end. Robert yawned, and Harvey suggested they call it a night. Marjorie collected her final pot of the evening, and Arnold was wondering if it would be too outrageous to try and collect Marjorie. Marjorie was hoping he'd make his move because she didn't want to spend the night alone. From the doorway, Helga rasped, "Good night, children," and Laura guessed that bridge hadn't gone at all well. "Breakfast will be at eight sharp, the service at ten." She was gone, followed by Victor, Nicholas, Winston, and their Greek chorus of good nights. Marjorie hoped Nicholas had noticed she was the big winner, but if he did, he made no comment. He just drifted away like a wraith. Victor didn't even suggest a nightcap, though he looked slightly the worse for wear. Winston asked if there was anything he could do for anybody and was grateful not to be needed. Robert was the next to depart, and Laura decided she'd better get Harvey out of there so that Marjorie and Arnold would be free to make an arrangement, if an arrangement was to be made.

"Sleep tight, don't let the bedbugs bite," chirped Laura as she led Harvey out of the room. Once out of sight of the others, Harvey took the upper hand and steered Laura to the bar in the conservatory. "But I don't want a nightcap," insisted Laura.

"I do, and I'm not leaving you out of my sight for one minute."

"My hero," replied Laura in a tired voice. In the conservatory, she changed her mind, as Harvey had known she would, and he poured two generous drinks.

"What about all the innuendo at the table?" asked Harvey.

"What innuendo?" Laura was suddenly awake and thinking of killing her husband for piquing her interest when she'd prefer to be in bed, safe in his arms.

"Those snide remarks between Arnold and Robert."

"There are always snide remarks between Arnold and Robert when they're together. Robert disapproves of Arnold and is very outspoken about it."

"I think Robert's afraid of Arnold," said Harvey.

"You can't tell by me," countered Laura, "not tonight, when I know the whole family's afraid of each other. Oh, God."

"What's wrong?"

"The whole family's afraid of each other. Tonight. Our first night on the island since last year."

"Since Labor Day weekend," corrected Harvey.

"The twins weren't here."

"The twins aren't here now." Harvey's voice was calm and steady. "I'm not being mean, I'm just trying to remind you there's no avoiding the possibility that something terrible will probably happen before this weekend's over. That's why I don't want you out of my sight ever."

"Then take me upstairs. Let's go to bed. Let's make love."

They went upstairs, they went to bed, and they made love, but it wasn't one of their memorable performances.

At eight the next morning in New York, Irv Lewis, Bella's producer, tried Mickey Redfern's private number, before driving into the city to his office. Mickey's answering machine and Mickey's macho baritone informed him that Mickey was out of town and expected to return some time Monday morning. Lewis spat an expletive and then dialed Bella at home. He was surprised to find her wide awake. When he told her the disappointing news about Mickey, Bella spat an expletive, and then said she'd call him later at the office. With a cup of steaming decaffeinated coffee in her hand, Bella paced her living room until a scheme took shape. She crossed to the telephone, dialed information, and then called Grand Central Station. A pleasant voice told her the next train for East Gate would depart in two hours. Bella hurried to catch the train.

In the cozy apartment above Ernie's bar, Ernie was cautioning his wife and daughter. The forecast was ominous, and he wanted them to head back from the island the moment the services were concluded. The minister had been in the bar the previous evening for his usual three double whiskies and had confided to Ernie that he planned to keep the service short and sweet. There wasn't all that much material anyway for a fitting eulogy for Natalie. She had accomplished so little, except for three marriages, and that, said the minister, was hardly a fit theme for a eulogy. Ernie's daughter wondered if Nicholas Graymoor was still handsome and admitted to once having had a crush on him. Ernie was grateful the crush had not developed into anything serious. He would have dreaded seeing his precious only daughter enter into a marriage with one of those crazy Graymoors. He walked with them to the boat that was waiting to transport some of the invitees to the island. There were newspaper and television people all over the place trying to make deals for boats to take them across, but the conspiracy to deny them transportation masterminded by the chief of police held firm. Several television reporters used their ingenuity and interviewed the minister and some of the mourners, figuring that even this feeble material was better than no material at all. Ernie's wife didn't like the way their boat was rocking, but the pilot assured them it was a trustworthy craft; Mrs. Ernie tartly admitted that she wished they were on the minister's boat because God would be looking after him.

"Kippers," said Laura with disgust. Rebecca and Juanita had laid out a buffet breakfast. They were conserving their energies for Helga's birthday dinner, which Rebecca was orchestrating in the kitchen with the genius one would expect of the debut of a major new symphony. Harvey poked Laura with his elbow because Helga was within hearing distance.
"I thought you liked kippers, dear," said Helga. She'd had a bad night and didn't care who knew it. Helga had never been one for disguising her emotions.
"A little too heavy for the morning," said Laura, who decided to settle for toast and tea.
By accident, Marjorie and Nicholas met on the upper landing, Arnold having discreetly made tracks for his own room shortly before sunrise. Marjorie was tired of the silence between Nicholas and herself and told him so. "For your mother's sake, let's at least try to act civil to each other."
"All right," said Nicholas, "I'll play the game." This reminded Marjorie she'd been the big winner at poker the night before and she told Nicholas. "How nice," he said. "I

screwed up the bridge game. I couldn't concentrate."

"I'm sorry," said Marjorie. She made an involuntary gesture to take his hand, but then thought better of it. They descended the stairs together. Helga saw them enter the breakfast room and felt better. Perhaps they'd made it up. Perhaps they'd talked last night or this morning and realized how foolishly they were behaving. Maybe they did belong together, they were both such innocents.

Harvey was counting noses. Helga and Laura were sharing a table. Here came Nicholas and Marjorie. From the window, he had seen Victor strolling in the garden; he would probably come in soon ravenously looking for his breakfast. Harvey was right. Victor entered bellowing, "What's for breakfast?" Arnold came downstairs soberly dressed in dark gray suit and black tie. Harvey could tell he'd been up most of the night. He stared at Marjorie. She was piling her plate with eggs, bacon, home fries, and toast. Sex made Harvey hungry too. He was eating kippers, but at a table away from Laura, who had banished him. It didn't occur to him to be annoyed that Laura had such a meager appetite this morning.

"Good morning all," said Robert as he entered rubbing his hands together like a usurer who had just concluded a favorable deal. He kissed Helga's cheek and then went in search of food. He sat down with Harvey and asked, "Why the troubled look?"

Harvey looked at his wristwatch. "Has anyone seen Martha this morning?" There were various exchanges of glances, and then Rebecca said, "I'll go see where she is." Rebecca hurried out.

"Probably overslept," said Victor with a knowing wink at Harvey.

"Martha never oversleeps." As she spoke, Helga didn't realize her hands had begun to tremble.

Laura reached for Helga's hand while remembering aloud she had meant to pop in on Martha first thing this morning to see if she had any need of Laura's hangover remedy. Helga rewarded Laura with a look of gratitude but withdrew her hand to resume eating.

Rebecca entered Martha's room after receiving no response to her persistent knocking on the door. One window was wide open. The room was frigid. Rebecca ran to the window and looked out. Behind her, Martha gasped as she entered from the bathroom. "You frightened the hell out of me!"

"You frightened the hell out of me," said Rebecca as she closed the window.

Martha walked slowly to her dressing table in search of comb and brush. "Ah, of course. I'm late for breakfast. The others were concerned. How nice. Tell them I'll be down in a few minutes and that I'm still among the living."

"How do you feel?"

"Alive." Martha picked up the comb and attacked her hair with unusual vigor.

21

Bella made the ten o'clock train for East Gate with minutes to spare. She was disguised in a black wig and oversized dark glasses. She wore boots, and her ski suit was enveloped by a sensible winter coat she had purchased in London several years ago. She was very pleased with the disguise. No one had recognized her; even her trademark lisp had gone undetected when she bought her ticket. She was traveling light. Her shoulder bag, in addition to the usual female necessities, contained a flashlight and an automatic revolver. Somewhere in East Gate there had to be a mariner with larceny in his soul.

Someone in East Gate just had to be waiting for someone to bribe him to make a trip to Graymoor Island undetected. She hoped the other newshawks hadn't beaten her to him.

By ten o'clock, Ike Tabor had already been in contact with East Gate's chief of police, who assured him there were six of his worthiest men on the island guarding the Graymoors from interlopers. He also advised Tabor that the island and village were in the direct path of the hurricane storming up from the Bahamas, and he hoped to hell his men wouldn't end up stranded. Ike hoped to hell they wouldn't either. He also feared that if the island were cut off by the storm, with no phone, no electricity, and no means of access by air or sea, then the murderer could have himself a field day. He told this to Norman Wylie, the object of his next phone call. Wylie reminded him that Harvey Graymoor had hired his own private protection, but Tabor compared that pessimistically to a drop in the bucket. Wylie told him not to underestimate Mickey Redfern. "He's a one-man army. He's got a hell of a reputation."

"He won the reputation when he was younger," grumbled Tabor. "But oh, well, let's discuss our own situation. Whose place do we break into first? Robert Graymoor's? Victor Graymoor's?"

"Arnold Graymoor's," replied Wylie. "It's the smallest of the three. I like to start at the bottom and work my way to the top." They set a time to meet. A few minutes later, Wylie poured himself a cup of hot coffee. He was looking to drown the uncomfortable sensation of uneasiness in the pit of his stomach, a feeling that had been growing like a cancer since he had awakened this morning. But there was only one way to trap a murderer like the Graymoor killer, on his own turf, on the island. Wylie was positive he'd make a move there. It was an explosive situation destined to detonate and supply the police with their solution. He hoped to God that Tabor was wrong. He hoped Mickey Redfern, competent though he was, was equipped to deal with the situation.

Shortly after ten o'clock, Mickey Redfern set out in his outboard motorboat. He had changed his timetable, deciding to wait until after the three boats from East Gate had departed. One contained the crew that would dig the grave and carry the coffin to its resting place. A second boat contained the minister, his wife, the church organist, and three choir boys who had been photographed by some of the television cameramen. One of the boys was harboring an ambition to conquer show business. Another boy planned to go to sea and wished he didn't feel like throwing up. The third boy was not impressed by either show business or the sea. He planned to rob banks. The last boat to depart contained the select list of mourners from East Gate. Most of them had preened and primped as though they were this century's candidates for God's Chosen People. In addition to Ernie's wife and daughter, there were three tradespeople and their wives, the high school principal and his wife, and a man and woman who had befriended Natalie in school when they were all teen-agers. A motley assortment, decided Mickey, while looking at the threatening sky with apprehension as he took off. He decided he'd have to beach the boat or stand the risk of having it washed away in the hurricane. Even now, it was bobbing about like a cork in a whirlpool, and he was having trouble keeping on course. For several harrowing moments, he was attacked by a crosscurrent of wind that threatened to capsize him. He wished he had checked his horoscope in the morning newspaper.

From Graymoor Mansion, Robert and Martha were at the window in the great hall downstairs watching the boats arrive. "That's a very choppy sea out there," said Robert. "I hope they'll be able to make it back."

"They had better," said Martha. "Helga will have none of

it if they're stranded here. I'll urge the minister to speed up the service."

Ten minutes later, all were assembled in the chapel. The organist was playing a medley of Natalie's favorite songs, and Laura thought it was a mistake, regardless of the fact that the request had been found in the papers Natalie had left with Victor. "I mean but really," she whispered to Harvey, "'Getting To Know You' is hardly the sort of thing for a funeral." Harvey shushed her and wondered whose false teeth were loose. He turned around subtly and saw it was Juanita saying her beads. Marjorie fidgeted through the next selection, which was "I'll Be Seeing You." On this occasion the song put her in mind of ghosts and an afterlife. And if there was an afterlife, she hoped she'd make a better marriage there. Victor kept groaning, and Robert asked if he was feeling ill. Victor wasn't ill; he was anxious to get the service over with. Martha was massaging her temples with her fingers, explaining to a concerned Helga that she had a splitting headache and how much more of this nonsense did she have to endure? Arnold had his eye on Ernie's daughter. What was such a luscious creature doing in a God-forsaken hole like East Gate? Nicholas's head was bowed. His eyes were red-rimmed with tearstains. "Hello Young Lovers" always affected him this way. Rebecca twisted and untwisted her handkerchief and worried about the funeral guests and the possibility of their being stranded. There simply was not enough food in the freezer to handle this crowd. Dear God, let's finish this recital and get on to the minister and the burial and send them on their way. In his mind, Winston had absented himself from the service. He had traveled back to the time over four decades ago when he first came to Graymoor and agreed to sign on as handyman. Other men had been interviewed, but it was Helga who had insisted on hiring Winston, and in most matters at Graymoor, Helga's will prevailed. Then the children began arriving, and Winston knew he was destined to remain on the island for as long as he was wanted. Even though he finally married a local woman, there had been no children. The Graymoor brood were all he needed. As to his wife, she couldn't have cared less. She had married for security, which she got, and from a man who was away most of the time, which suited her just fine. Even when she died, it seemed as though few had noticed her departure, so nondescript had she been in her lifetime. Winston was startled out of his reverie by the sound of someone choking in front of him. It was Laura, trying to suppress a guffaw. The organist was into a blaring rendition of "Bewitched, Bothered and Bewildered."

Mickey arrived at the secret cove and immediately separated the motor from the boat. He found a haven for the components near the mouth of the cave, which he figured would provide adequate protection from the hurricane. He almost gave himself a hernia carrying the motor and briefly worried that age was catching up with him. This damned weather. He might have to chance the cabin after all. The sleeping bag would be useless once the storm broke, unless he decided to shack up in one of the underground cells. It might prove to be an interesting experience at that.

The minister was blessedly brief, and his wife managed to sing the closing hymn on key. Natalie's brothers then carried the coffin to the gravesite, followed by mourners in lines of two, looking as though they were boarding Noah's Ark. While the coffin was lowered into the grave, the minister said some additional words, which were carried away by the wind. Helga threw the first dirt on the coffin; then stared at her fingers with distaste.

Farewell, Natalie, thought Laura, farewell to your afflicted life, a life that refused to become airborne. Harvey had his arm around her and felt her body trembling. Was it from the winds, he wondered, or was it from fear? Now the mourners were wandering among the family paying their respects. Martha prayed Helga wouldn't invite them back to the mansion for refreshments. Helga had absolutely no intention of doing anything of the sort. She wanted to be rid of them and to be rid of this day and to be back comfortably seated at her desk and working. Later she planned to have a long talk with Martha about last night's rebellious display. There was another long talk she was planning, but she didn't quite know how to go about that one. She needed advice, and she rarely sought advice. In this particular matter she needed to proceed with caution. Her eyes were on Winston as he escorted Rebecca and Juanita back to the mansion. She felt a hand support her elbow, and she turned and looked into Robert's eyes. She accepted his assistance, and together they fought the wind back to the house, the others behind them.

The funeral crew was quick to cover the coffin with earth. Only Nicholas remained behind to keep Natalie company, hands folded in front of him. When the others arrived at the house, Rebecca busied herself heating up a clear broth, which would have to hold them until lunch. Victor announced from the window in the library, where he had helped himself to a brandy, "The boats have taken off. I don't envy them the trip. I hope they make it back safely."

Harvey was astonished. He had never heard Victor express concern about anyone or anything at any time, and it was a rather refreshing experience. So Victor had a bit of a heart after all. Martha had brought her petit point from her bedroom, and Laura thought "God Bless Our Happy Home" was a bit of a redundancy under the circumstances. Marjorie found a deck of cards and set up the card table and engaged herself in a game of solitaire. Arnold was cross-examining Martha about Ernie's daughter, but Martha knew very little about the young woman and resumed looking sullen. Robert, Helga, and Rebecca had a brief discussion about the selection of wines for dinner, and then Robert decided he'd go choose the wines before lunch to give them time to breathe. Helga excused herself to return to her writing room.

"Where's Nicholas?" asked Harvey.

"Didn't he come back with us?" asked Victor. "Marjorie? Wasn't he with you?"

"I came back with Arnold," said Marjorie, who was reshuffling the cards.

"Maybe he's gone for a walk," suggested Arnold.

"In this weather?" Robert looked genuinely concerned. "He has to be mad."

"Perhaps he is." Having said it, Marjorie regretted it. She didn't bother looking for reactions. She concerned herself with dealing out the new hand.

Victor was back looking out the window. "Here he comes. I guess he stayed behind in the cemetery for a while. Nicky is such a sentimentalist."

"He adored Natalie," said Laura, and was sorry she hadn't remained behind with Nicholas. Harvey looked relieved. There was really nothing to worry about, he now realized, what with all the family gathered in this room. But still, whenever one went off alone, he would worry. He turned to Laura, who went to help Rebecca with a tray of cups filled with steaming broth. Juanita came behind, carrying a plate of biscuits. Laura cleared a table for Rebecca, and Harvey, watching her, wondered why he ever cheated on his wife. She was so lovely and so loving. So generous and understanding. His first love and his only love. Then he reminded himself she could also be a mean snarling bitch under fire and it was better never to cross her. His thoughts were sidetracked when Robert announced he was going to the wine cellar.

"Certainly not by yourself," said Harvey.

"I'll help," volunteered Arnold, which was startling news to Harvey. Arnold never volunteered to do anything unless there was a woman or cash attached to the deal. "I haven't been down to the catacombs in years. I'll get some flashlights."

Laura brought a cup of broth to Harvey as Arnold and Robert went to the kitchen for flashlights. "What's come over

Arnold? At this late date offering to be helpful."

"Maybe he's trying to buy his way into heaven," said Harvey, taking the cup and sipping some broth.

"I wish you wouldn't say things like that," said Laura testily. "I'm on edge as it is. Why didn't Andrew ever have the cellars wired for electricity, I wonder."

"Andrew was never big on improvements. This broth's good. Why aren't you having some?"

"In a while. Nicky?" She caught her brother's attention as he entered the room. "Are you all right, Nicky?"

"I'm chilled to the bone, that's what I am." He went eagerly to take the cup of broth Rebecca was holding out to him.

"Any last words from Natalie?" asked Victor.

"That's in very bad taste," chided Martha, looking up from her sewing.

"No offense taken," said Nicholas. Then to Victor he said, "If you had tried offering her some generosity, she might still be alive today."

"What do you mean by that!" Victor's entire visage had reddened, making his dyed hair appear more garish than usual.

"You know exactly what I mean by that. Her hand-to-mouth existence was pitiful."

"Oh, let her rest in peace!" snapped Martha, knowing there'd be little peace for the living this weekend.

"Tempers, tempers," cautioned Harvey.

"It's raining," said Marjorie, her major contribution to the conversation.

"Raining!" exclaimed Laura. "That's an understatement. It's a deluge!"She and Harvey joined Victor at the window. Laura put her arm through Harvey's. He switched the cup of broth to his other hand. "I remember one storm as bad as this when we were kids. Remember, Harvey? We couldn't get off the island for days!"

"Oh, no!" whimpered Juanita.

"And there was no electricity," reminisced Nicholas. "We had to use kerosene lamps. Remember, Laura? You took me exploring under the house, and I almost fell into the stream."

"You were never too surefooted," remembered Laura ungraciously.

"Where was I all that time?" asked Harvey.

"Oh, you finally came looking for us," said Laura. "And then Helga sent Andrew out to find the three of us and when he did, he gave us all hell for scaring Helga."

"You mean we cannot leave here?" Juanita whispered to Rebecca.

"Now, now, dear," said Rebecca sympathetically, "I'll look after you."

"And who will look after you?" asked Juanita with her native practicality.

Winston entered carrying kerosene lamps. "An ounce of prevention," he announced. "I'm setting them up in all the rooms, just in case."

Bella sat at a table in Ernie's bar, looking out at the fury of the storm. She was cursing herself for being an impetuous fool. As a reverse prototype of Diogenes, seeking a dishonest man, Bella had been unsuccessful. There wasn't a sailor in East Gate brave or foolish enough to set out for the island in this treacherous weather. She went to the bar for another drink and sat on a stool.

"Any hope this might let up?" she asked Ernie.

"This is good for the weekend." He placed a bowl of pretzels in front of her. She was having a good look at herself in the bar mirror. She was a mess.

"What a mistake."

"Ma'am?"

"What a mistake. My coming here. A mistake." She attacked the pretzels.

"Oh, East Gate's lovely in good weather."

"I didn't come to visit East Gate. I was trying to get out to Graymoor." She looked like a dessicated owl with the large dark glasses and the cloche that kept the wig tight around her head.

"Well, if you're expected for the funeral, you're late. That was a couple of hours ago. Everybody's already back from the service, and they made it by the skin of their teeth. My wife and daughter were on one of the boats and were caught in that downpour, and let me tell you, my Effie said she never did so much sincere praying before in her life."

"Is there a decent motel in this town?"

"Real nice one just behind me. I can lend you an umbrella."

"Oh, no kind words, please, no kind words. I might cry."

The deluge nailed Mickey Redfern's decision. He decided to chance the cabin and was drenched by the time he made it there with his gear and provisions. He wondered if he dared light a fire in the stove and, remembering Harvey's injunction, decided against it. He got undressed and hoped his outer garments wouldn't take too long to dry. He wrapped himself in a blanket and sat down to lunch on a sandwich and a beer. In a few hours, dry clothes or not, he intended to enter the cave. On his last exploration, he had found the stream and stumbled across one of the wine cellars. The passage to the mansion had to be located somewhere in that area, and he was determined to pinpoint it today. He stared at the ceiling. The rain pounding on the roof sounded as though he were under a landslide. He had seen some lanterns and a container of kerosene in the storeroom. As soon as he finished his sandwich, he would put them to use. His flashlight batteries were precious, and he worried he wouldn't have enough of a supply for the weekend.

It was just a little after noon and pitch black outside. Blacker than midnight. Blacker than a murderer's heart. And it looked as if there was a long, black midnight in store for the Graymoors.

Getting into Arnold Graymoor's apartment had been a piece of cake for Ike Tabor and Norman Wylie. As in Natalie's apartment, there was no security, just a locked front door, and a clever lady with a hairpin could have opened that. The elevator agonized its way to the tenth floor. Arnold's apartment was just opposite the elevator. It had a Yale lock. Real easy. Once inside, Norman Wylie sniffed with distaste. The air was polluted with a variety of scents that bespoke a mixture of shaving lotions, expensive perfumes, talcum powder, hair spray, and bacon grease. As to the furnishings, Tabor commented, "Looks like a sultan's palace."

"Well, Arnold had quite a harem. What's behind that door?"

Tabor opened the door. It led to a small bedroom, the unmade bed evidence of Arnold's hasty departure yesterday. The living room, the bedroom, the kitchenette, and bath, and that was it. They methodically inventoried the closets and drawers and came to the amused conclusion that Arnold must have bought out a sex shop. There was nothing lacking that might titillate milady's moods or whims, and that wasn't what they were after. They were looking for a daily diary or a private diary. Letters or notes that would give some indication that Arnold had murder on his mind. They found nothing. No weapons other than the usual kitchen cutlery. No knife that resembled a stiletto, which was the sort of weapon the coroner told them had probably polished off Natalie. The detectives, when they left, were no converts to Arnold's taste in decor or choice of habitat. Wylie decided Arnold was either very innocent or very smart and said so to Tabor.

"Didn't you notice something else?" asked Tabor as they were descending in the elevator.

"What?" asked Wylie, annoyed that something pertinent might have escaped his attention.

"No books."

"You know something, you're absolutely right. But then, when would a man like Arnold Graymoor have time to read?"

In the motel in East Gate, Bella Wallace didn't know it, but she'd been assigned the room directly across from Mickey Redfern's. Once settled, which meant removing glasses, cloche, and wig, she tried to reach her producer, Irv Lewis, in New York. He wasn't to be found. Then she tried her secretary. Arabella was frantic.

"Oh, thank God! We thought you had disappeared!"

"Didn't Irv tell you I was planning to get to Graymoor?"

"Irv's in the hospital." Bella shrieked. "He was in a car crash. The car's totaled, but Irv's all right. Broken arm and contusions. Where are you?"

"I'm in East Gate, and there's no train out until tomorrow, damn it. There's also a hurricane going on here."

"I can hear it."

"I've checked into a motel." Bella gave Arabella the name and telephone number. Arabella gave her the number of the hospital and Irv Lewis's extension.

"Are you fixed okay for cash? I mean tomorrow's Saturday, so if you need any money, I'll wire it to you now."

"No, I'm fine, but you'd better be where I can find you tomorrow in case of an emergency."

Arabella groaned inwardly. "I'll be at home with Mother."

"Fine. I'll phone you later just to check in." She rang off and next tried to reach Irv Lewis. She was told he was being X-rayed and would not be available until after lunch. Bella hung up. Lunch. That's what was bothering her. She was hungry. She pulled herself together and went in search of food.

Laura and Harvey were trying to look interested in one of the old family albums. They kept coming across snapshots of Natalie and the twins as children, and it made Laura uncomfortable. She hadn't cried for Natalie, nor had she cried for the twins. Would she ever cry for anyone? "Why am I so unemotional?" she asked Harvey.

"About what?" He was studying an old snapshot of Andrew and Cedric Longstreet. They certainly looked friendly enough here.

"About the family."

"I don't know. Maybe it has something to do with not being blood related. Come to think of it, you don't cry much at anything. You ought to take it up with your doctor." He flipped a page and found himself and Laura, who was holding a baby Nicholas's hand.

"Weren't we adorable?" gushed Laura, who was not usually given to gushing. She looked across the library at Nicholas, who was slumped in an easy chair acting as though he was absorbed in a copy of *National Geographic,* and not looking particularly adorable.

Harvey was glancing at his wristwatch. "Isn't it almost time for lunch?"

"Yes, come to think of it," agreed Laura, "and I'm finally hungry." She called to Martha, who was threading a needle with difficulty, "Isn't it about time for lunch?"

Martha gave up on the needle and thread and set her petit point on a table. "I'll see what's holding it up."

As she left for the kitchen, Victor arrived from the conservatory. "It's freezing in the conservatory. Do you suppose the heat's off?"

The heat's not off us, thought Laura.

"Winston! Winston?" It was Helga shouting from the head of the stairs and Winston came hurrying in from the storeroom. He entered the great hall as Helga descended the staircase. "The telephone's dead. I've been trying to phone the village newspaper to dictate Natalie's obituary."

Winston tried the extension in the hall. "It's dead all right. The lines must be down. Guess the electricity's next. I'd better get those lamps lit."

"Where are the others?"

"Mostly in the library when I last saw them," Winston said over his shoulder as he returned to the storeroom.

Helga swept into the library and did a quick head count. Of Nicholas she inquired, "Where's your wife?"

"I haven't the vaguest idea," said Nicholas. "Maybe up in her room resting."

"And Robert? And where's Arnold? And Martha? Where's Martha?"

Martha returned from the kitchen. "I'm here. Lunch will be ready in about fifteen minutes."

Helga's voice rose an octave. "Where's Robert?"

Victor told her, "He went down to the cellars for some wine. Arnold went with him."

Harvey was on his feet. "That was over an hour ago." Laura closed the album and set it aside. Was it really over an hour since Robert and Arnold had descended to the wine cellar?

"Maybe they're back and we didn't see them," suggested Laura, wishing her voice didn't sound so frail.

Martha hurried back to the kitchen. No, Rebecca hadn't seen either missing brother. They would have brought the wine directly to her. Martha then went to the dining room. There were no fresh bottles of wine on the sideboard where they were usually placed for dusting. She almost ran back to the library.

"Harvey!" she shouted. "Harvey!"

Harvey hurried to her. "What's wrong?"

"They're not back. There's no sign of the wine. Harvey, they're both still down there!"

22

It was a storm as bad as any storm the area had experienced. So ferocious was the combined force of hurricane winds and torrential rains that boats were torn from their moorings, trees were uprooted and fell across roads, making them impassable, roofs were blown away and, in at least seven cases, houses collapsed. The blackouts of the telephone and electricity systems gave the majority of frightened residents of East Gate the eerie feeling that they were isolated in a ghost town. The waters were rising and waves were crashing against the piers, threatening to bring about their collapse. Ernie, huddled in the kitchen of his apartment above the café with his wife and daughter, the room faintly illuminated by a kerosene lamp, hoped the shutters protecting his café were adequate. In the motel, Bella had joined the few other guests and minimum staff huddled in the lobby, wondering if there was any hot line to the Almighty available for an atheist. The chief of police had opened the station house as a refuge for the homeless and was grateful the men he had assigned as guards for Natalie's funeral had made it back to the mainland without any mishap. His battery-operated radio told him the entire Eastern seaboard, stretching from Maine to southern New Jersey, was taking a severe pounding. He hoped the water supply wouldn't be affected.

At the motel, Bella extracted a promise from the manager to keep the bar open indefinitely. If East Gate was to be her Samarra and her appointment with death, then she wanted to be taken in a state of oblivion. After her third double Scotch on the rocks, she felt generous enough to consider the situation of the Graymoors and their horrible isolation. She wondered if Arnold was thinking of her, and then cursed herself for the rashness that brought her to this miserable little village without giving the move sufficient thought.

In New York City, wind and rain rattled the windows of Victor's penthouse, and Norman Wylie expected them to collapse momentarily. He and Tabor had breezed past the doorman and the man at the desk as though they belonged in the building. "So much for security," commented Ike Tabor after arriving and deftly making child's play of the police lock on the penthouse's door. Wylie whistled with amazement at the decor Victor favored, cream walls and thick purple carpeting with provocative oil paintings of nymphs and satyrs by an artist unfamiliar to Wylie. If his subject matter was any indication, the man most probably was in residence at some baroque country sanitarium.

"Hey, Norman," said Tabor from the doorway of the gymnasium, "come feast your eyes in here."

Wylie went to the gymnasium. There was a full display of Victor's instruments for torture. "Who'd have suspected?" asked Wylie, flicking a bull whip with a beautifully hand-carved handle.

"Didn't I read somewhere Victor was thinking of going into politics?" asked Tabor.

"Better he should go into intensive care," replied Wylie. They left the gymnasium to prowl in the other rooms.

"This damn storm," muttered Tabor.

"It's supposed to clear up after the weekend," said Wylie, suddenly feeling melancholy. The weekend reminded him of the Graymoors and especially Harvey and Laura, and he wondered how they were faring.

"You've got an awful look on your face," said Tabor. "Is it those hot dogs we wolfed down?"

"I was thinking about the Graymoors and their island. In a storm like this, it must be hell." A window crashed in the living room.

"It's not much better here," said Tabor. They went to the den and started in on the desk.

Mickey Redfern could hear neither wind nor rain. He was deep in the bowels of the underground caverns, and experiencing a wonderful feeling of exhilaration. He was back in his element with danger and the unknown. He had been following the stream for about ten minutes, moving slowly and with caution, using the pick axe carefully to mark his progress on the wet, dank walls. The air was foul with the smell of the past. The flashlight occasionally spotlighted objects that brought him up sharply. It wasn't the rats and mice that astonished him so much as the occasional snake and lizard. What did they feed on, he wondered. There were probably hundreds of tiny burrows all over the place leading above ground. Rodents were notorious busybodies; they snooped and explored at random when foraging for food. Mickey kept playing the flashlight along the stream, suspecting he might have to ford it soon and search for a passageway on the opposite side. The stream had seemed, for the most part, to be amazingly fresh and clear except for the occasional patches of bracken and algae or the remains of a small animal. But now he spotted something different, something ugly. It looked like blood. Mickey hunkered down for a closer examination. Yes, it was blood in the water. He stood up and played the light upstream. Slowly, he followed the flashlight's path. He wasn't looking forward to what he was sure he would find.

In the library of the mansion, Laura sat opposite Helga and Marjorie. Nicholas had gone to the kitchen to be with Rebecca and Juanita. Victor was at a library window seemingly looking out at the angry elements. "She's mad. She's absolutely mad."

Helga sat up and looked at Victor with alarm. "Who are you talking about?"

"Martha! Martha's out there!"

"She said something about the boat," said Marjorie.

"I didn't see her go!" Helga's voice was just a shade short of sounding hysterical. Laura hoped she wasn't heading for a breakdown. "Did anyone see her go?"

No one had seen Martha leave the house. She had slipped out just as she had slipped out shortly after Robert and Arnold had gone down to the wine cellar. At the time Laura had thought she was still huddled in the oversized wing chair working at her petit point and had been surprised when Martha came in from the hallway announcing she'd been down to the landing to make sure the boat was secure. Now, presumably, she'd gone out again. "Are you sure you saw her?" Laura asked Victor.

"I saw someone hurrying down the path to the landing. It had to be Martha. She was wearing those filthy oilskins of hers."

"She must be mad, absolutely mad." Helga had joined Victor at the window. "Go after her, Victor."

"He can't leave us alone in here," squeaked Marjorie. "Harvey said Victor was to stay with us."

Laura was now pacing. Harvey and Winston had gone searching for Robert and Arnold. Harvey had first gone upstairs to change into a heavy sweater, and when he came back, she hoped the bulge in his right trouser pocket was his gun. Harvey had been quick to select Winston as his companion in the search. Laura could guess why he didn't want either of his brothers for company. Winston he could trust, and Winston knew the catacombs better than any of them. It was while Harvey was changing that the electricity failed, and Winston had hurried off to light all the kerosene lamps in the first floor rooms before going below. This had given Laura a chance for a quick huddle with Harvey out of earshot of the others.

"Don't you dare get separated from Winston! None of that 'I'll take this passage, you take that one.' You two stay together!" Laura was almost of a mind to join them and said so.

"You stay right here. We'll be safe. I have a suspicion Mickey's prowling around down there. Maybe we'll meet up with him."

"If someone else hasn't met up with him," said Laura darkly.

"You're a bundle of joy."

"There's nothing joyful about the occasion," said Laura sharply. "I didn't think anything ugly would happen this soon."

"Maybe it hasn't happened. Maybe they're lost."

"I hope you do meet up with Mickey. It's time for him to surface. Let the family know he's been hired to protect us and to find a murderer. Let's all stop being so polite about the situation."

Helga had heard her and left Winston with whom she had been conferring. "You're right. It's time to stop this pussyfooting. We're all in danger. We're in terrible danger. And there's no hope of securing help from the mainland now. Harvey, do you have a gun?" Harvey patted his right trouser pocket assuringly. "Well, if you have to, use it. But don't. . ." Her voice began to waver. Laura put her arm around her and led her to a chair. Harvey signaled Winston and they left. Winston led the way to the cellar door, which was in the hallway that led to the kitchen. It was then that Nicholas assigned himself to the kitchen and Victor chose to remain in the library with Laura, Martha, Marjorie, and Helga.

And now there was Martha to worry about. Marjorie was whimpering. "You can't leave us alone, Victor. You mustn't."

"Laura!" Laura stopped pacing and turned to Helga. "Come with me. Marjorie will be perfectly safe with Victor." Laura hurried after Helga, who led her upstairs to her writing room where she began foraging in a desk drawer. "Damn!" She looked in another drawer. She opened drawer after drawer, apparently searching in vain. "It's gone. Martha must have taken it."

"What are you looking for?"

"My gun. Andrew gave it to me years ago. A lovely little thing with a pearl handle. Now Martha's got it." She told Laura that Martha had been prowling about the other night, searching Helga's desk.

"I hope she's got it with her right now," said Laura.

"I don't like the way you're looking at me," said Helga suddenly. "You don't believe the gun exists? Do you think I've gone dotty from the excitement?"

"No. I think you know how to end this monstrous affair."

"I wish I could." Helga had slumped into the chair behind the desk.

"Who is it? Who's behind this?" Laura was leaning across the desk. "You know, don't you?"

"I don't *know.*" She started to say more but then hesitated. "I have suspicions. I have lots of suspicions, and they frighten me."

"Do you want to see us all killed?"

"No, no, of course not."

"I tell you this, Mother. Harvey had better return safely. If anything happens to him down there, I shall go berserk. If I have to, I'll wring the truth out of you." Helga was weeping softly. Laura couldn't believe she had spoken so sharply to Helga, but she had long suspected her mother was harboring clues and possible answers. She was terribly afraid for Harvey. The fact that she herself might soon be a victim was of minor consequence. Her whole life was wrapped up in Harvey, and without Harvey, she'd just as soon be dead. Of course if Harvey survived her, she knew he'd manage just fine. Helga was dabbing at her eyes, and Laura suggested they return to the library.

Harvey and Winston reached the wine cellars without incident. They consisted of a series of rooms carved out of rock, four rooms in all. What their original purpose had been was anybody's guess, but Andrew's father had converted them into storage rooms for the fine wines and liqueurs he had imported. They approached the first room with caution. There was no one there. Harvey could feel the beads of perspiration forming on his forehead and stole a quick look at Winston, who was already heading for the second room. Winston almost slipped and fell into the stream, but Harvey caught him from behind. There was nothing in the second room or in the third. But in the fourth room they found a shambles, permeated with the strong odor of wine. There were broken bottles on the floor, and in a pool of wine, Harvey saw Robert's list. Winston looked dazed.

"Are you all right?" Harvey asked the older man.

"I was just wondering, why in this room? Why did Robert come to this cellar?"

"Probably the wines he wanted were in this cellar."

Winston picked up the soggy list and studied Robert's notations. "No. All this stuff's in the first room. I did an inventory down here with Miss Helga and Rebecca only last month. There was no need for them to come this far. What have you found?"

Harvey was kneeling for a closer look at a puddle that Winston thought was wine. "This isn't wine, it's blood." Winston squatted and took a better look for himself.

"Jesus," whispered Winston. They stood up, and Harvey led the way out of the room. With his flashlight he methodically beamed up and down the stream and then across. He worked the tool slowly and then aimed it at the path on which they stood. They both saw the blood leading straight ahead, beyond the wine cellars.

"I'm going on," said Harvey. "I want to see what's ahead."

"I'll be right behind you," responded Winston.

As Laura and Helga descended the stairs to the great hall, Martha entered from outside. Laura ran to help her shut the door, the wind and rain behaving like monstrous marauders intent on overwhelming the domain. Breathless, Martha leaned against the door, unbuckling her oilskin. "Are you out of your mind?" rasped Helga. "You might have been killed out there."

"I had this." Martha drew Helga's pearl-handled revolver from her coat pocket.

"I knew it," Helga said to Laura, "I knew she took it."

"Stop aiming that damn thing at Helga," snapped Laura. Martha lowered her hand. Helga went to her and snatched the gun away.

"The boat's gone," said Martha. "And the dock's about to join it. Dear God, it's like an apocalypse out there." She was hanging her soaked outer garments in a closet. "Have they found Robert and Arnold?"

"None of them are back. At least, we didn't hear anything. I was upstairs with Helga in the writing room."

"I was looking for this." Helga was waving the gun. "I don't like you stealing my things, Martha."

"I didn't steal it; I borrowed it for protection."

"You should have asked me."

"Ask for a gun in front of the others? Are you insane?"

"No, but I think you are." Martha and Laura followed Helga to the library. None of the men had returned.

"I feel so damned useless!" cried Victor. He was standing near a lamp and looked Mephistophelian in the weird reflections created by the uneven flame. Laura wondered if Marjorie would ever leave the chair in which she was cowering.

"There's nothing to do until the men come back," said Martha.

"And what if they don't come back?" asked Victor, crossing the room with purposeful strides. "Do you expect me to go after them? And then Nicholas? And then who?"

"I don't think anyone expects anything of you, Victor," said Laura, "except an occasional look of reassurance. Has he been reassuring you, Marjorie?"

"He hasn't said a damn word. I don't know about anybody else, but I need a drink."

Martha said, "I need something to eat." To Helga she said,

"Do you think we need the gun to go to the kitchen?"

"I'll go with you," said Laura to Martha and they left.

When they were alone in the hallway, Martha grabbed Laura's wrist. "The rope was cut," she hissed. "The rope that hitched the boat, it was cut." She relaxed her grip, and Laura withdrew her hand.

"Don't tell the others." Laura's voice was strangely calm. "There's no need to alarm them unnecessarily." She thought for a moment and then remembered something. "The signal flares. Are they still stored in the cabin?"

"You can't expect to use them in this weather, for crying out loud," reasoned Martha. "I thought of them immediately, but it's no use until the storm dies down."

The door to the kitchen opened, and Rebecca appeared. "I thought I heard voices out here. Are the men still down there?"

"Yes," said Laura. Rebecca stood to one side as Laura and Martha entered the kitchen. Juanita sat at a table clutching her rosary. Nicholas was peeling potatoes and wondered aloud if he and Victor should form a second search party.

"You'll do no such thing," said Laura firmly.

"I don't suppose anyone has much appetite," said Rebecca.

"Marjorie does," said Martha, and inexplicably, Nicholas threw back his head, roaring with laughter.

Mickey Redfern found the body lying half submerged in the underground stream. The head was face down in the water, and the rear of the skull had been crushed. It was a revolting wound. The body was submerged up to the waist, the legs sprawled as though they had crumpled like a puppet's. Mickey was about to turn the corpse over when he heard voices shouting names. They were calling for Robert and Arnold. One voice belonged to an old man, the other voice Mickey recognized as Harvey's and was thankful. Having come across the corpse, he knew he would have to surface and make his identity known to the household. Harvey's presence would make the task easier.

"Harvey! Harvey!" Mickey flashed his light up and down. Harvey responded by flicking his light up and down in recognition.

"Who the hell's that?" asked Winston. "That's not Robert or Arnold." Harvey quickly explained about Mickey Redfern. Winston thought Harvey's providing them with a Mickey Redfern was good thinking and even better action.

Mickey stood patiently waiting for the two men to join him. It was only a matter of seconds. Harvey saw the corpse and said, "Hell."

"It's not Robert, is it?" Winston's voice was unsteady.

Harvey didn't have to see the face. He recognized the size of the body and the elegant cut of the jacket. Still, he knelt and with Mickey's help, turned the body over. Arnold's eyes were half shut. There were traces of blood about his nose and mouth. Mickey explained he must have hemorrhaged for several minutes before expiring.

"But how did he get this far?" wondered Harvey. He played his flashlight on the path he and Winston had followed. "Doesn't look as though the body was dragged here." He told Mickey about the broken wine bottles in the fourth cellar.

"Maybe Arnold's arms were loaded with bottles when the assailant struck him from behind, probably with a bottle."

"There's blood in the cell," said Harvey.

"Okay, so Arnold gets hit, drops the bottles, starts to crumple, but then manages to find some strength and stumbles out of the cell. He's dying but he doesn't know it. His skull's crushed and he's hemorrhaging badly. He's disoriented; he makes it this far not knowing he's going in the wrong direction and then collapses and dies."

Harvey shouted, "Robert!"

Mickey moved his flashlight to the opposite side of the stream. "Look at that."

Harvey and Winston saw a broken flashlight and a shoe. Harvey waded across the stream and examined the shoe. "It's one of Robert's!" He waded back with the shoe and the flash-

light. "Beats hell." He shouted Robert's name again.
"Where's the other flashlight?" wondered Winston. "They each had one." He had taken Robert's shoe, examined it, and then shook his head sadly.
"Robert!" shouted Harvey. The name echoed and re-echoed and bounced off the wall and the ceiling, but there was no sign of Robert.
"Robert must have been in one of the other cellars when Arnold was attacked," said Winston, "then when he heard the bottles crash, he came out to see what was up and saw the murderer and tried to run away."
"He would have run back to the stairs," said Harvey.
"There's other ways of getting into the house from here," said Winston. "There are passages that lead to hidden panels in some of the rooms. There's a passage right over across the stream just a little ways down from where you found the shoe and the flashlight." Harvey and Mickey exchanged looks.
"Let's have a look," said Harvey.
"Fine by me," replied Mickey.
"What about Arnold? We can't leave him laying here like this," said Winston. Harvey restrained from correcting Winston's grammar. Lying, Winston, not laying. "At least we can pull him out of the water." Harvey and Mickey each took a shoulder in a firm grip and moved the body out of the water.
"Okay, Winston," said Harvey, "lead the way."

In New York, Norman Wylie and Ike Tabor were completing their search of Robert's town house. They had started on the top floor and had worked their way down. Tabor was jimmying open a locked drawer in Robert's desk. "I always find locked drawers very suspicious, don't you, Norman?"
"I find them a challenge. Why would a man lock a drawer in a house in which he is the sole occupant?"
"An eccentricity. Why do nice ladies with college educations and families end up in the streets as bag women? Ahhh, there it comes. Nice and easy." He opened the drawer and

looked in. "Looks like a diary." He held it up for Wylie to see.

"It's also locked," said Wylie. "A cinch to open."

This was a new one on Harvey. He couldn't recall ever having explored this passage as a child, yet Winston led the way as easily as though he were heading an Indian file down East Gate's main street. Mickey, behind Harvey, kept looking back over his shoulder and flashing his light to reassure himself they weren't being followed. He had the uneasy feeling they were not alone. He saw nothing and heard nothing other than himself and the others, and yet he stayed uneasy. The passageway seemed endless. It twisted and turned, and at times he was grateful none of them was obese; it was that narrow a squeeze.

"This is an old slave tunnel," Winston explained. "There's a book in the library in East Gate that explains how Graymoor was used as part of the Underground Railway before the Civil War. That's what got me to exploring, after I came to work here. Came in handy that time Robert disappeared those three days."

Robert, thought Harvey, where the hell are you, Robert?

"I have to use the bathroom," said Marjorie in the study. Victor shrugged, and Helga sighed. The others were still in the kitchen. "Come use the one off the conservatory. It's in the kitchen vestibule." Marjorie had noticed it the night before. The two women left Victor alone. He went to the bar and poured himself a drink. There was no ice in the bucket, and Victor whispered an expletive. He took the bucket and went to the kitchen. In the kitchen he found only Rebecca, Juanita, and Nicholas.

"Where are Laura and Martha?" he asked.

Nicholas stood up slowly. "They said they were going back to the library."

"There's nobody in the library and I didn't run into them

on my way here. Helga took Marjorie to the john in the conservatory vestibule."

Nicholas didn't wait for any further explanation. He ran out of the kitchen. "Wait!" shouted Rebecca, and Juanita almost dropped the rosary. Victor left the ice bucket and hurried after Nicholas.

"Don't you leave us alone!" cried Juanita, but it was too late; she and Rebecca had been abandoned.

Victor could hear Nicholas shouting Laura and Martha's names, but he was not in the library. He had run somewhere to the back of the house toward the den. Victor cursed Nicholas and Laura and Martha and then himself for not getting the ice. He went back to the kitchen.

Marjorie came out of the bathroom, and there was no sign of Helga. "Mrs. Graymoor? Helga?" She looked to the right and thought she saw someone hurrying from the dining room. Marjorie was frightened. She ran into the dining room, her heels clicking on the highly polished floor. She ran into the library, but there was no one there. "Helga!" she cried again. "Victor!" and then as a last resort, "Nicky!"

She heard something behind her. She turned, and her face contorted with fear. A panel in the wall was creaking open. Marjorie's hands flew to her face, and then she screamed.

Winston stepped out of the wall followed by Harvey and Mickey Redfern.

23

There was something beautifully old-fashioned in the way Marjorie sank to the floor in a faint. Winston put aside his flashlight and Robert's shoe and knelt beside Marjorie, gently chafing her wrists. There was another unnerving shriek from the doorway. This time it came from Juanita, who had come rushing from the kitchen with Rebecca and Victor when they heard Marjorie.

"What the hell have you done to Marjorie?" demanded Victor in a booming voice, "and who's that!" He was pointing at Mickey. Harvey introduced and explained Mickey, realizing he looked like a one man arsenal with the haldric around his waist boasting a hunting knife, a pick axe, a flashlight, and a handgun.

"And Marjorie fainted when she saw us coming out of the wall." Harvey realized he must sound crazed, the wall panel having slid back into place after the three had emerged into the room. "There's a hidden panel that leads here from one of the underground passages. Winston's discovery." Rebecca had joined Winston and was holding smelling salts under Marjorie's nose. Juanita had the sense to pour a brandy and now was trying to force some of it into Marjorie's mouth. Mickey, while unbuckling his haldric, thought the three looked like a mini-witches' coven dispatching a sacrificial victim. "Where are the others?" Harvey asked Victor.

"I don't know where Helga is. She'd been with Marjorie, but now I don't know. Then Laura and Martha left the kitchen together, presumably to come back to this room, and they didn't. And this panicked Nicholas, who went flying all over the house shouting their names and God knows where he's gotten to. What about Robert and Arnold? Didn't you find them?"

"You tell them, Mickey, I've got to find Laura." Harvey left the room on the double, shouting Laura's name.

Mickey got right to the point. He told them Arnold had been brutally assaulted and was dead. Juanita crossed herself, and Marjorie groaned, fluttered her eyelashes, and with Winston's help sat up. Victor had paled and felt faint himself when Mickey picked up Robert's shoe and said, "This is all we found of Robert. That and a smashed flashlight. Mind if I help myself to a drink?" He didn't wait for an answer and went to the bar where he poured himself a stiff Scotch. Marjorie had been helped to a chair and sat trembling. Mickey had handed Robert's shoe to Victor who let it drop to the floor.

"Then Robert's still down there?" asked Victor in a hoarse voice.

Mickey shrugged. "Looks like that, unless he made his way back to the house through some other passage. And if he did, I'm sure you'd know it."

"What about Helga?" Winston asked anxiously. "We have to find her."

"She left me alone," cried Marjorie. "She shouldn't have left me alone like that." When prompted again she told Winston where she had last seen Helga, and Winston hurried to the conservatory.

Harvey was on the second floor shouting Laura's name. The door to Helga's writing room opened, and Laura came running out. "Darling! You're back! You're safe!" She flung herself into his outstretched arms, and he held her tightly, his face nuzzling her hair.

"Why the hell'd you go off on your own?" Harvey demanded.

"I didn't go off alone." Harvey followed Laura back into the writing room, where he saw Martha poking about Helga's desk. "I was with Martha."

Martha looked up. "Where are Robert and Arnold?" Harvey told them the bad news. Martha sank into Helga's chair. Laura leaned against the desk for support. Her knees felt weak. She heard Martha say in an unfamiliar voice, "Robert's still missing. He knows his way around down there, better than all of us. That time he was lost for three days when he was a kid, he explored and memorized everything. When they found him, it didn't seem to matter to him that he was hungry and thirsty; he just resented being interrupted."

Harvey's mind was working. Martha had said it. The thing he'd been waiting to hear. That unprepared statement that could unblock a stalemate in his deductive thinking. *It didn't seem to matter to him that he was hungry and thirsty; he just resented being interrupted.*

"Poor Arnold," whispered Laura, "poor elegant Arnold. What an insult to kill him in such a ratty setting." Now she was angry. "That's really a dirty trick. Arnold should have died in an expensive hotel suite on the Riviera attended by four servants and six mistresses. Oh, hell. Now it's getting funny and it shouldn't. How did Helga react?"

"I don't know. She wandered off." Martha and Laura looked at Martha. "You don't seem to be terribly concerned about her."

"Helga's in no danger. He wouldn't dare kill Helga."

"Who?" asked Harvey.

"You know damn well *who*. Robert."

Mickey and Victor went looking for Nicholas, leaving Marjorie with Rebecca and Juanita in the library. When Winston arrived at the conservatory, he found it in total darkness. The sound of the rain and the wind besieging the building reminded him of an air raid attack during the war. Winston groped in his pocket for matches. He had left two lamps in the room, both brightly lit. There was enough oil in each of them to last for hours. Someone had deliberately extinguished them. Winston found the matches and struck one. The kerosene lamps were where he had left them, one on the piano, one on the sideboard. The one on the sideboard was closer, and once that was lighted, he held it high above his head.

Helga was lying face up, her head looking as though it had hit a corner of the fireplace. There was blood on the floor. Winston hurried to her, placed the lamp on the floor, then lifted Helga and carried her to a couch. He held his handkerchief to the wound at the base of her skull. "Help!" he shouted, "Help!"

Mickey and Victor, who had been on their way to investigate the conservatory, rushed in to assist Winston.

"Helga!" cried Victor. "She's not dead?"

"No, no," said Winston, "I found her laying by the fireplace. It looks like she fell and hit her head."

"I didn't fall, I was pushed." Helga spoke in a weak voice. They hadn't realized she had revived. Victor was holding her hand while Mickey attended to her wound.

"Helga." Winston's hand caressed her cheek, and Helga smiled.

"He pushed me. I heard a noise in here while I was waiting for Marjorie. The room was well lit and I wasn't afraid." She struggled to sit up. Winston and Victor helped her.

"The cut's superficial, but it needs to be cleaned."

Helga glared at Mickey. "And *who* are *you?*"

"Mickey Redfern. Harvey hired me for protection."

"Aha! Some protection. So you're the one who's been snooping around the island."

"That's right."

"Who pushed you?" asked Winston, although he knew the answer to the question.

"Robert. Robert pushed me." Mickey heard a gurgle behind him and knew it was Victor. "He's gone completely mad. He's murdered Arnold. He told me he murdered him. Is this so?" Mickey told her how he had found Arnold's body. "He intends to murder all of us. Why am I still alive? I thought surely he was going to kill me when he pushed me away. The wall panel was open and he was going back in." Now her voice was very cold. "He must be stopped. But how? He can come and go like a phantom. He's done it before." She was clutching Winston's hand. "We could have stopped it then. We should have stopped it then, but we didn't. We were fools." She didn't notice that Harvey and Laura had entered the room with Martha. Martha was holding Helga's notes and preliminary draft for the new novel. Helga was saying: "He should have been strangled at birth. That's what Andrew wanted to do. I should have let him. Then I wouldn't have loved him so ferociously, so possessively." Mickey had gone to the vestibule bathroom and returned with peroxide and

some towels. He gently attended to Helga's wound while Martha stared at him. She recognized his back. She had seen it often enough through the binoculars. Helga was glaring at Martha. "You found the drawer. You've broken into my desk again! How dare you invade my privacy! How dare you!"
"Why didn't you strangle Robert at birth?" replied Martha harshly. "Why didn't you, instead of letting me waste half my life waiting for him?" She held up the pages she was holding for the others to see. "It's all here in the new novel. It's about us. The tontine. Robert, the bad seed." Helga sobbed and put her arms around Winston. Laura was touched. She wondered if they had ever had an affair. "The bad seed," whispered Martha. "Did you know his parents? Did you know who they were? Were they evil too?"
"In a way, I suppose," said Winston. "He's our son. Helga's and mine."

In the library, Rebecca and Juanita sat close to each other, watching Marjorie examine the wall panel from which the three men had materialized. Marjorie was angry. She was angry mostly at herself and then at Nicholas for having disappeared and then at the entire Graymoor family in no particular order. Marrying into them had been her own decision, but being forced to remain on the island was theirs, and she hated herself for so meekly subscribing to the pressure. She was going to find out how this panel worked if it was the last thing she did. She wasn't sure what she was going to do once she found the secret, but she suspected that Nicholas was now prowling about the underground foolishly attempting to be brave. She wanted to confront him as soon as possible. Not in an attempt to salvage their marriage, but to offer him a deep, heartfelt apology. She owed him that, and Marjorie always paid her debts.

In New York, Norman Wylie and Ike Tabor were at Tabor's precinct, feeling frustrated and impotent. They had read Robert's diary. They knew he was the murderer. But there was no way of getting through to East Gate. The phone lines were down. The road leading into it, they were told by the state police, was impassable. They would have to wait for the weather to let up and then commandeer a police helicopter. But by then it might be too late. Wylie told Tabor, "They could all be dead by the time we get there."

Tabor sighed and shrugged and said, "Well, Norman, that's life."

Winston sat next to Helga, holding her hand. Mickey had applied a very professional-looking bandage to Helga's wound and now stood near the fireplace watching the fragmented family gathering. Laura sat on a sofa with Harvey and Martha, while Victor stood near a window rocking back and forth on his heels, at times astonished, at times saddened, but mostly appalled by Helga's narration.

"Andrew and I were never lovers. But he needed a wife. He needed a wife for appearances. I was a greedy young woman with dreams of a life of luxury, and when Andrew proposed, I accepted. I didn't know I was sentencing myself to a very lonely existence on this island. But once we were married, Andrew was satisfied. It stayed the suspicious gossip about his sexual preferences, and he was now a respected pillar of the financial world. He went to New York every day, and I tried to do something with myself here. Then Winston came to be interviewed, and I was greedy again. I wanted him at once."

"I didn't put up any resistance," admitted Winston, and Laura flashed him a warm smile. She wasn't too sophisticated to appreciate a sweet love story.

"I became pregnant. By the time I showed, it was too late to do away with it. . ." she lowered her head and Laura could guess what she was thinking, ". . . and of course Andrew was furious. By this time I didn't give a damn how he felt. I had the upper hand. I made him accept our child as his own by threatening to tell the world the true story. He couldn't cope with that, so he grudgingly adopted Robert."

"He didn't know I was the father," interrupted Winston. "For some reason it never occurred to him. He thought it was his partner whom Helga had been seeing occasionally before she married Andrew."

"And then I decided that was what I needed on the island. More children! Lots and lots of children! Andrew didn't dare go against my wishes. He got his revenge later with the tontine. But then I was a bit of a fool too. One day Andrew suggested that the children needed schooling, and that he knew a superior tutor, an Englishman. I'm such a snob about the English, you know, so I agreed without interviewing the man. Enter Cedric Longstreet. Dear God!" She was clutching at her breast, and Laura worried there was a heart attack stirring. "Cedric Longstreet was Andrew's lover, and I never suspected."

Martha stole another look at Mickey. He was mesmerized.

"Esmaralda was actually Cedric's dog. When she adopted me, I didn't object to her. The children loved her. That is, all except Robert. Remember, he never knew that Winston and I were his natural parents. Robert, you see, adored Andrew, and Andrew rejected him. The more Robert was rejected, the more determined Robert became to win him over. But then he came across Cedric and Andrew one day in the cabin, and of course what he saw sent him into shock. He strangled Esmaralda, and that's when Andrew wanted Robert sent away. Away from the island. So Robert disappeared. For three days he disappeared. Search parties were organized out of East Gate, but they were no match for my diabolical son. He knew every square inch of the underground passages. Hungry? He was never hungry. He raided the kitchen nightly! That's how he survived. But he was plotting then to get rid of Cedric. And get rid of him he did."

Harvey wondered if she knew Cedric was dead, and if she did, how she could have lived with that grim knowledge all these years.

"Oh, my dears." She was addressing Harvey and Laura. "You know about his diaries. Well, he left his diary where he was positive Andrew would find it. He wrote there that Cedric was paying court to him! To Robert! What an explosion followed! The poor Englishman tried to plead his case, but Andrew, being the pigheaded martinet I should have recognized when I was his secretary, ordered him off the island. I haven't the vaguest idea what's become of him."

Harvey couldn't resist. "He's still on the island."

Helga snapped, "This is no time for any of your warped humor, Harvey."

Harvey turned the floor over to Mickey, who told them about Cedric's remains. "I think the lady over there," he indicated Martha, to whom he had not yet been properly introduced, "can corroborate my story."

Helga fixed Martha with a stern eye. "Martha, you couldn't possibly be Robert's accomplice."

"It wasn't me who found Cedric's remains. It was Natalie," said Martha. "By then the body was badly decomposed and unrecognizable, but she found Cedric's umbrella and toilet case and came to tell me about it. We both thought Andrew had killed him. We decided to keep our hideous discovery to ourselves—to protect Andrew. We assumed Cedric had come back to the island on his own to have it out with Andrew and was murdered. But it wasn't Andrew he was after. It was Robert. Natalie worked that out years later. I think she confronted Robert with it. He denied it, but if she ever talked, the implication could be dangerous to him."

"I think Natalie tried to blackmail Robert," interrupted Harvey. "Probably a day or so before he murdered her. Why did he murder Andrew?" This took Victor and Martha by surprise.

"He *murdered* Andrew?" Victor was genuinely aghast.

"I think he did," said Helga. "You see, when you were adults and off on your own, except for my dear Martha, and I shall make it all up to you, darling, Andrew mellowed. He realized what an awful thing the tontine was. He told me he was going to cancel it and make a proper will, leaving all the children an equitable share. When Robert was told this that awful weekend, he went berserk. Don't you understand? Don't *you*, Harvey? Robert's lifestyle. The way he lived. the Britishisms he adopted from Cedric. The town house. His club. *Robert had looted the tontine.* He had defalcated and was in terror of being apprehended. If Andrew hadn't made this surprise announcement, Robert might still have found a way of replacing the money. He came to me and begged me for the money, but I don't have anything close to that sum. I mean Robert stole millions! The amount staggers the mind!"

Mickey's mind wasn't staggering, it was boggling. He wished there wasn't such a sad expression on Martha's face. Martha was thinking, *'and I shall make it all up to you, darling,'* and knew Helga's words would haunt her for the rest of her life. I must get away from here. I must survive and get away from here. I have the right to a new life, a fresh start. She realized Mickey was staring at her. She stared back. Then she smiled. He smiled in return. Is this it, she hoped, is this what flirting is all about?

Harvey was talking. "So he invented a mysterious buyer for our possible interest in the tontine. Those who sold would have survived. Those who didn't were to be killed. Nathan Manx was his go-between." He explained Manx to Helga, who just kept shaking her head back and forth in disbelief. "The twins proved troublesome, so he murdered them, which must have made Manx suspicious and he asked for more money. So Robert murdered him too."

Helga wailed to Winston, "Our boy!"

Victor was dwelling on the halcyon days of his childhood,

when he and Robert had been pals. There had been so many opportunities then for Robert to kill him. Victor shuddered. "Can we move out of this room?"

"Yes, let's," agreed Martha as she got up. "Marjorie's with Rebecca and Juanita in the library. I think it's time we looked in on them." Winston and Victor assisted Helga, and Martha went straight to Mickey with her hand extended. "You know who I am and I know who you are, but this makes it official." They shook hands and walked to the library together.

In the library, they found Marjorie holding a glass of whisky and staring at the wall panel. "What ever are you up to?" asked Laura.

"I've been looking for the switch to open that panel." She looked at the group and then asked, "Nicky's not with you? But where is he?"

Laura groaned. Harvey explained to Marjorie how he and Mickey had examined every room in the house, but there was no sign of Nicholas. Helga emitted a dry, rasping sob, and Rebecca brought her a glass of port.

Marjorie pointed at the wall. Helga strained her ears but heard nothing. She hadn't heard the walls whisper for several days. Perhaps it was because they no longer had to chide and berate her. Not from the moment she had made up her mind to reveal the truth about Robert. She wondered if she would ever finish writing the book. Probably not, it would be too painful. She knew that unconsciously she had written the notes about the family and the tontine in the hope that Martha would find them and do what she couldn't bring herself to do: unmask Robert.

"Do you think he's down there?" she heard Marjorie ask. "Do you think Nicky's down there with Robert? He'd better not be. Somebody's better go after him." Her eyes were imploring Mickey to action. "You see, I think Nicky's guessed the truth."

Marjorie hadn't been privy to Helga's revelation, Laura realized. Had she guessed Robert was the murderer? How had

Nicky guessed? Nicky wasn't smart enough to guess at anything.

Marjorie drained her glass and then said, "I think Nicky's guessed Robert and I have been having an affair."

24

When Nicholas arrived at the den, the lone kerosene lamp cast a spectral glow. "Laura? Martha?" Neither woman was in the room, but there was still Andrew's portrait hanging over the fireplace, still dominating the room, still dominating their lives even after death. For a few unreal moments, Nicholas was transported back to his childhood, a little prince whose presence was sternly demanded by the tyrannical emperor. It was in this room that Andrew made decisions and handed out punishments and held audiences the prospect of which frightened a seven-year-old boy. It was no wonder the room was seldom used after Andrew's death; it still harbored too many ugly reminders of a man with an ugly disposition. "I don't care if he is delicate," he could hear Andrew raging at Helga, "he's got to behave like a man. He has to learn to swim and to fight and to protect himself when the other boys pick on him. Shape up, you little sissy, shape up!" And Helga had shouted, "That's the pot calling the kettle black!" A terrified Nicholas had not understood one word.

"*Nicky!*"

Nicholas spun around. "Who's there?"

"*Nicky!*"

He looked at the wall beyond the fireplace. The voice was coming from inside the wall! Helga's walls *do* whisper, they do, they do.

"*Sissy Nicky! Dumb Nicky! Baby Nicky! I stole your toys*

and I stole your sweets . . ." Nicholas was transfixed. *"And now I've stolen your wife!"*

Nicholas flung himself at the wall, pounding at the panel with his meager fists. "You son of a bitch! I know it's you! I know what you've done! I'll kill you, Robert, I'll kill you!" Slowly, the panel began to move inward. Nicholas's anger translated to hatred and revenge and without a thought of the danger that awaited him, he picked up the kerosene lamp and entered the hidden passageway. "Robert!" he shouted, unaware the panel had swung shut behind him. He held the lamp high. The passage ahead of him was long and narrow and fetid. Cobwebs decorated the ceiling, and Nicholas propelled himself forward, no longer afraid of the unknown, no longer afraid of the dark, no longer afraid of himself. "I'm going to kill you!" Had the others heard the magnificent new timbre of his voice they would have been impressed.

Robert was laughing. It was that silly moronic braying of his childhood, the one that used to tease and mock and send the twins scurrying for cover.

"He stole my yo-yo!" little Nicholas had whimpered.

"Well, go get it back from him!" shouted Andrew.

"He's bigger than me!" wailed little Nicholas.

Not any longer, thought Nicholas. He's no longer bigger, he's just older, and I'm going to kill him.

The bombshell Marjorie thought she had dropped proved to be little more effective than a firecracker. "At least you've kept it in the family," commented Laura.

Harvey said to Mickey, "The damn fool's probably down there with Robert. He's no match for Robert." Is anyone, wondered Laura. He's got the lot of us huddling here with fear and apprehension. How do we smoke him out? How do we force him to surface and reveal himself?

"We've got to smoke Robert out. We've got to kill him." Laura's voice was steady and forceful. "Well, we do. We've got to go after him and if we have to, we kill him." Mickey was buckling the haldric around his waist.

"That's very admirable, darling," said Harvey, "but Robert's got an edge on us. He knows his way around down there."

"So do you!" Laura faced Harvey with her hands on her hips. "And so do I and so does Winston!"

"I'm going in after him," said Mickey.

"Not alone, you're not." Harvey patted Laura's cheek. "And I thought you were too old to be a cheerleader."

"Winston's not going with you." Helga's voice was firm, her chin stubborn. "And you're both damn fools to try chasing after Robert. You can catch him right here. He'll come to us. He'll get hungry. He has to eat. He'll have to come to the kitchen, the way he came to the kitchen that time we thought he was lost." Now there was pride in Helga's voice. "Robert's clever. But there are some who have the edge on him."

"But poor Nicky, what about him?" And having said it, Martha knew what Helga was thinking about Nicholas. He is expendable. It is stupid to jeopardize the group to rescue one foolish young man. Poor Nicholas, Marjorie thought; there had never been anyone to rescue him.

Helga watched Marjorie, crying at last. But was she crying for Nicholas? Or for Robert? Or had the poor goose suddenly realized her lover was the murderer threatening the well-being of the rest of them? "Is that why you're crying, Marjorie? Has it finally penetrated that Robert is the murderer?"

"Oh, my God," wailed Marjorie, "what have I gotten myself into!"

"Now she asks," muttered Laura.

"What do you think?" Harvey asked Mickey, who was clenching and unclenching his fists while weighing heroics against common sense.

"I'm game. This is what you hired me for."

Laura folded her arms and faced Mickey. "That's a different kind of jungle down there. You know that by now. You'll think you're on top of him, but he'll be right behind you. It happened to us all the time when we were kids. Look, forget my outburst. Helga's right. When he pulled his disappearing act down there years ago, it took a dozen men three days before they nailed him. He wants to kill us. He'll have to come get us. And I'm hungry."

"But Nicholas!" cried Martha. "What about Nicholas?"

"I shall pray for him," said Juanita, and Laura hoped she had an in with God.

Harvey and Mickey were huddling with Winston. Victor and Martha accompanied Rebecca and Juanita to the kitchen where dinner was to be prepared. Victor was also anxious to arm himself with a forbidding and effective piece of cutlery. There was also something preying on his mind. The phony alibi he had whipped up for the police to explain his whereabouts the night of Natalie's murder. Would he ever have to admit he'd been staking out the residence of a tall black lady whose specialty was servicing middle-aged masochists? "Such a sigh," said Martha to Victor.

"Well, listen, sweetie, you've got to admit, there's an awful lot on my mind."

In answer to a question from Harvey, Winston was telling him which rooms had secret panels. "Besides this room, there's one in the den, and the conservatory—"

"And the kitchen," added Helga.

"What about the bedrooms?" asked Harvey.

"There was a panel in Andrew's suite," said Winston, "but after he died Helga had it removed and now the wall's solid."

"I always thought there might be one in my room," said Helga, "but we never found it. All that whispering, you know; it had to come from someplace."

"It came from the wind and from your imagination." Laura was rewarded with a Mona Lisa smile from Helga.

Harvey formulated a plan with which Mickey agreed. They

were nine imperiled people, and until Robert was brought to bay, there was never to be fewer than four of them in a group. "I'd like to get down to the cabin," said Mickey.

"What for?" asked Harvey.

"There's the stuff I brought over. Provisions and ammunition. Supposing Robert comes across them?"

"The ammunition'll do him no good because even if he's got a gun, the bullets you've brought, Mickey, are probably the wrong caliber."

"He's probably got a gun," said Mickey. "He's undoubtedly got a private store of his own cached away somewhere down there. What's going on around here isn't off the top of his head. He's been working this out for months."

"He's insane," said Helga, and Marjorie was on the verge of wringing her hands like a silent screen heroine in distress. "He's absolutely gone round the bend. There's no way out for him, you see. Like all homicidal maniacs, he fantasizes that he will emerge with a clean bill for having been a survivor. He's like those madmen who snipe at the innocent from bell towers. The only provision he's made to protect himself is her." She was pointing at Marjorie. "That one. She's to be his alibi."

"You're too damned smart, lady." Marjorie was leaning forward with a very unpleasant look. Harvey was fascinated by the change that had come over her.

Helga was smiling, triumphantly confident. "Robert needed an ally who was as greedy for wealth as he is. Marjorie was perfect. They'd be the two survivors who would alibi each other. What was to happen, Marjorie? The two of you return to the mainland to report the horrible murders and then blame someone who will never be found, the remains carefully hidden by Robert somewhere below? Well, dear? Was it to be Victor? I'll bet it was. He's really the likeliest candidate." Mickey was fascinated by the old lady's deductions. Helga continued, "But the best laid plans, and all that. Robert didn't plan on this awful storm forcing the help to share our isolation. Now it would mean killing them too. It also upset his timetable. I don't think he planned to take any action until after my birthday dinner. Oh, dear. It's going to be my birthday soon. What a bizarre celebration." She returned to Marjorie. "Did you ever love Nicholas?"

"Does it matter? And what's love anyway? It's nothing. It's just a word." She went to the bar and poured herself a drink.

Laura was on the verge of bristling. Just a *word* ? Why, the poor bitch. It's too late for her. She'll never know. She saw Mickey walking toward the hall. "Where's he going?" asked Laura, her voice suddenly shrill. In the hall, Mickey found the closet where the oilskins were kept and managed to find one that fit. He pulled a hat around his ears and, with his gun in his hand, set out for the cabin.

At the motel in East Gate, Bella Wallace was wondering what was happening at Graymoor. The storm just might send her into hysterics if it continued much longer. The battery-operated radio she was listening to at the bar remained pessimistic about the weather. Bella knew she was getting drunk and that she ought to have some dinner, but she didn't relish eating alone, or sleeping alone. I'll never forgive myself for this. Never!

He's playing with me. The son of a bitch is playing with me. Nicholas was tired. It seemed he'd been walking around in circles for hours. The kerosene lamp was still serviceable, but for how much longer, he couldn't be sure. Then what would he do? If he's going to kill me, Nicholas thought desperately, why doesn't he do it and get it over with? I've got no weapon, just this rock I picked up somewhere back there, or wherever I was. I don't know this place at all. I never knew it too well. I want to kill Robert, but I won't get the chance. He's outsmarted me. He got me angry and tricked me into chasing after him, just the way he used to do it when we were kids. Once he came up behind me and pushed me into the stream, and thank God Natalie was nearby and came to my rescue. Where am I? Where the hell am I? Dear God, be good to me. Get me out of here. He held the lamp over his head. He was standing outside a cell. There was something on the cot. Nicholas moved closer. Jesus! Bones! Human bones! Nicholas backed away with a look of revulsion. He left the cell and stood gasping for breath, trying to orient himself. Should he go back, retrace his steps, or go forward? What should he do?

"*Nicky.*"

He's behind me, Nicholas realized; he's coming closer. Nicholas's fist tightened on the rock. He moved back into the cell. There was no point in running. There was no place to run to. Robert means to kill me, and I'm no match for him down here. I'll just wait right here. Maybe I can get one in with the rock, just maybe. Just once before I die, I might luck out.

In the dining room, they were seated at dinner, but no one was paying much attention to the food. The place set for Mickey Redfern was unoccupied. He had been gone over an hour. Laura could guess what Harvey was thinking. Mickey's gone underground. He's going to earn his money, or die in the attempt. Only Marjorie was actually eating. She had already worked out her defense in case she was charged as an accomplice. Temporary insanity. That's why she was forcing herself to eat. You had to be crazy to eat this way with a jail sentence facing you.

"You're not going," said Laura to Harvey.

"What are you talking about?"

"You're not going after Mickey."

Helga looked from Laura to Harvey and realized what was going on. "He's gone after Robert?"

"Looks like it," said Harvey. "He's been gone now for over

an hour. He was only going to the cabin. He should have been back by now."

"The fool," murmured Martha, seeing another opportunity slipping away from her.

In the cell, Nicholas had set the lamp near the cot. He waited at the opposite side of the room, apprehensive, on the uneven floor perspiring. Footsteps were approaching. Slowly. Cautiously. They sounded as though they were coming from the right of the cell. Nicholas saw the reflection of a flashlight creeping insidiously along the ground, like a white serpent making its way ominously toward its prey. Nicholas raised the hand holding the rock.

The flashlight was turned off. The footsteps continued to approach.

"*Nicky!*"

"Answer him."

Nicholas froze.

"I said *answer* him." Mickey hissed each word.

Nicholas almost wept with joy. He wasn't alone any longer. There was hope, a chance. "Come and get me, you son of a bitch!"

Mickey was now in the cell. He extinguished the kerosene lamp and waited near the cot.

"Have you seen the bones, Nicky?" Robert's voice was lilting, unnatural. "That's Cedric! Remember Cedric? I say, old boy! I say, old top! Old bean!" Robert's flashlight was now caressing the path. Mickey waited, his gun ready. He'd played this scene before a hundred times in other settings. He knew his part well. He knew what had to happen. He just hoped Robert wouldn't suddenly ad lib something unexpected. "Dumb Nicky! Sissy Nicky! Someday, if they ever find you, you'll be just like Cedric. Bones and rags, bones and rags. And then I'll take care of the others." And then he made his mistake. He leapt into the cell, and Mickey fired. He should have played the flash around the cell before entering, but how was he to suspect Nicholas was not aione? He knew Nicholas was unarmed and therefore a pushover. Robert had played cat and mouse long enough and was now tired of the game. He wanted to get on with the nasty business ahead, get off the island, claim Helga's money and then rid himself of Marjorie. It had all been so beautifully planned. And now it was bungled. He fired two shots into the cell, but Mickey's second bullet sent Robert's revolver flying out of his hand. Mickey turned on his flashlight. Robert knelt as though in supplication; his right hand and his right arm were bleeding profusely. Robert looked up in a combination of pain and outrage. He didn't recognize his adversary.

"Hello. I'm Mickey Redfern. I'm a friend of your brother Harvey."

Nicholas giggled.

The family and the servants were in the library when Martha screamed. The secret panel was moving. Harvey had his gun out of his pocket. Victor, wielding a carving knife, had it raised over his head in a trembling hand, and Laura thought he looked terribly foolish. She could also detect some telltale gray roots in his hair and wondered if fear had made him forget to attend to his brown dye. Marjorie stood cowering behind Winston, who had a protective arm around Helga.

Mickey Redfern stood framed in the panel with Robert slung around his shoulders like a slaughtered stag. Robert struggled, but to little avail. "Redfern," said Harvey with admiration, "you're positively beautiful." Mickey smiled, and Martha's heart leapt. Then Nicholas appeared behind captor and captive.

"Nicky! Nicky! Silly Nicky!" cried Laura as she rushed to him and threw her arms around him. "Silly brave Nicky!"

The room erupted into a babble of voices. Winston went for some rope with which to truss up Robert. Mickey sent

Juanita for a first aid kit so that he could attend to Robert. Helga said things to Robert she would have never dared put into her manuscript. Nicholas said things to Marjorie that left her pale and staggered. Harvey poured drinks for everyone, and then Martha asked, "Where do we keep Robert, until we can signal for help?"

There was no safe place to keep Robert. He would have to remain tied up. He knew too many means of escape of which the others were not aware. Winston stared at his son and was sad. Robert sat there smiling. It was a strange, enigmatic smile. It chilled Laura. She had the feeling he was trying to tell them something, trying to tell them the melodrama was not yet over, trying to tell them that he just might have another string to his bow.

The next morning, although it was still raining, Norman Wylie and Ike Tabor found a pilot who was willing to take up a police helicopter. Graymoor was out of their territory, but if they got there first to claim Robert Graymoor, they'd worry about any repercussions from the Connecticut police when the situation would arise. They had his diary, which contained his confessions. How he had murdered the twins and Nathan Manx and Natalie. They had little trouble locating the cane which, when the head was unscrewed, revealed a long, thin stiletto. It was in Robert's closet along with several other expensive examples of British craftsmanship. Later, they would get the answers to the earlier murders; they were sure of that.

When they were airborne, Wylie wondered why he hadn't heard from Bella Wallace. Had she completely soured on the police story? On him? Well, there was one hell of a climax awaiting her with the Graymoor story. He wondered if Arnold Graymoor was just another of her one-night stands.

"Christ, but you've got a dumb look on your face," Ike Tabor said to Wylie.

"I was thinking of Bella Wallace."

"Well, that explains it."

* * *

The police in East Gate had seen the flares. The storm had abated sufficiently for the police to send a boat to Graymoor Island. In the library, Helga was discussing an offer she had to sell the island to a property developer. Victor said he'd look into it for her. Robert, who had spent an uncomfortable night tied to the chair, suddenly came alive and shouted, "The island's worth millions! Hold out for top price, do you hear me?"

"Yes, dear," said Helga, "we hear you."

Protected by oilskins, Harvey and Laura went to the dock to meet the boat from the mainland. Overhead, they heard a helicopter.

"It's landing!" cried Laura.

The aircraft touched down on the lawn in front of the house. Wylie and Tabor emerged. Laura and Harvey went to meet them. The pilot stayed aboard keeping the motor going. Harvey and Laura led the two detectives into the house, exchanging explanations. About three minutes later the police boat pulled in at the dock. Two deputies disembarked and then they helped Bella Wallace ashore. Bella, without thanking them, ran up the path to the mansion just as Norman Wylie and Ike Tabor came out of the house with Robert between them, now handcuffed. They were half-dragging him to the helicopter; Laura and Harvey were walking behind them.

"Wait! Wait!" screeched Bella, "Wait! Who's that you've got? Wait!"

The Connecticut police were still wondering what was going on as the helicopter took off. The family were at the windows watching the action outside. Helga was scribbling notes on a pad. Winston and Nicholas had earlier retrieved Arnold's body and put it in his bedroom. Martha was making preparations for Arnold's funeral. Mickey was at the secret cove carrying the outboard motor back to his hired boat. If the weather continued steady, he had promised to pilot Martha to the mainland where Martha could deal with the mortician, after which they would have lunch at Ernie's.

"Oh Harvey, it's Bella Wallace! The ubiquitous Bella Wallace!" Laura had an arm through one of Harvey's. He wondered how Bella would react to the news of Arnold's death.

"Who was it?" screeched Bella. "Who was that they shanghaied?"

"Robert," said Harvey, "our brother Robert."

"Come into the house," said Laura. "You look awful."

"Well, I've been having an awful time! But that's unimportant; what's been going on? How'd it all happen? Where's Arnold?"

Harvey stayed behind to greet the East Gate police and explain Wylie and Tabor's actions. Through a window he saw Laura introducing Bella to Helga and Martha. Helga was examining Bella as though she was a smear on a slide under a microscope. Martha was offering her a sherry. Laura came out of the house to see how Harvey was faring with the police. They weren't sure what Harvey was talking about. They had come to rescue the stranded Graymoors. Murder, it appeared, was something else.

Despite the continuing rain, Laura walked away from them. Hands plunged into the sou'wester's pockets, she walked around the house in the direction of the cliff. There were so many things troubling her, about herself, herself and Harvey, the surviving family. But mostly, she was troubled by her last look at Robert as the detectives led him out of the house. As he passed her, Robert mouthed two words that would haunt her forever.

"*You're next!*"

Epilogue

Helga raised her glass of champagne to respond to the number of birthday toasts she'd received. Dinner had been sumptuous, and her gifts had been opened and received with appropriate noises of surprise and appreciation. A stranger coming upon the celebration would have been hard put to guess the tragedies the family had recently suffered. It was as though Puccini, as an afterthought, had decided to append a showstopping geisha number to follow Cio-Cio-San's suicide in *Madama Butterfly*.

"To absent friends," said Helga succinctly. Laura blanched while the others sipped their champagne. Then she comforted herself with the memory of Harvey's holding her tightly when she told him of Robert's eerie cry, *"You're next!"* Winston put his arm around Helga's shoulders as Juanita refilled their glasses. Martha and Mickey Redfern were at the opposite side of the library deep in a warm and private conversation. They'd had a lovely afternoon in the village after Martha had arranged Arnold's funeral for the following day.

"Isn't that hurrying things a bit?" Helga had remonstrated.

"What's to hang around for?" asked Laura with her usual practicality. She wanted to get away from the island. She wanted to be back in the safety of her home and her office. She wanted to spend more time with Harvey. She wanted to prepare herself for the slime that would inevitably surface when Robert was brought to trial. She had watched the launch taking Marjorie to the mainland with envy. She hoped the police would leave Marjorie alone. Let her disappear. Out of everybody's lives, especially Nicky's. Laura watched Nicky, slumped on the couch next to Victor staring moodily into his empty glass.

"Nicky's glass is empty!" Victor shouted to no one in particular, and Juanita hurried over to Nicky with a freshly opened bottle of champagne. Harvey had done the honors while being interrogated by Bella Wallace, who had opted to remain on the island to complete the story of the Graymoors, which her producer now planned to squeeze into the schedule early the following week. The Graymoors were news. Hot news. Scandal. Murder. Laura suppressed a shudder as Harvey caught her eye and blew her a silent kiss.

"That's sweet," said Bella, enjoying her job of reportage but not looking forward to another night of sleeping alone. She made a mental note to contact Wylie when she returned to the city the following day.

"A penny for them." Helga's voice startled Laura. She hadn't heard Helga approach. "I'd be hard put to describe the look on your face. Not afraid of Bella's stealing Harvey away from you?"

"Fat chance." Laura took Helga by the arm and led her out of the earshot of the others. "I was thinking about the tontine. That bloody, infernal tontine."

I loathe funerals. There's Arnold's tomorrow and let's hope it's kept short and sweet. I've got to get back to New York and make plans. The tontine. I've got to make plans for the tontine. I'll have to be very careful. I have to wait. Wait and see what happens to Robert. I'll have to be very careful and very clever. And then I shall have the tontine. They'll soon find out I'm not so stupid anymore. Oh, yes, I'll be clever. By process of elimination.